P9-DWI-887

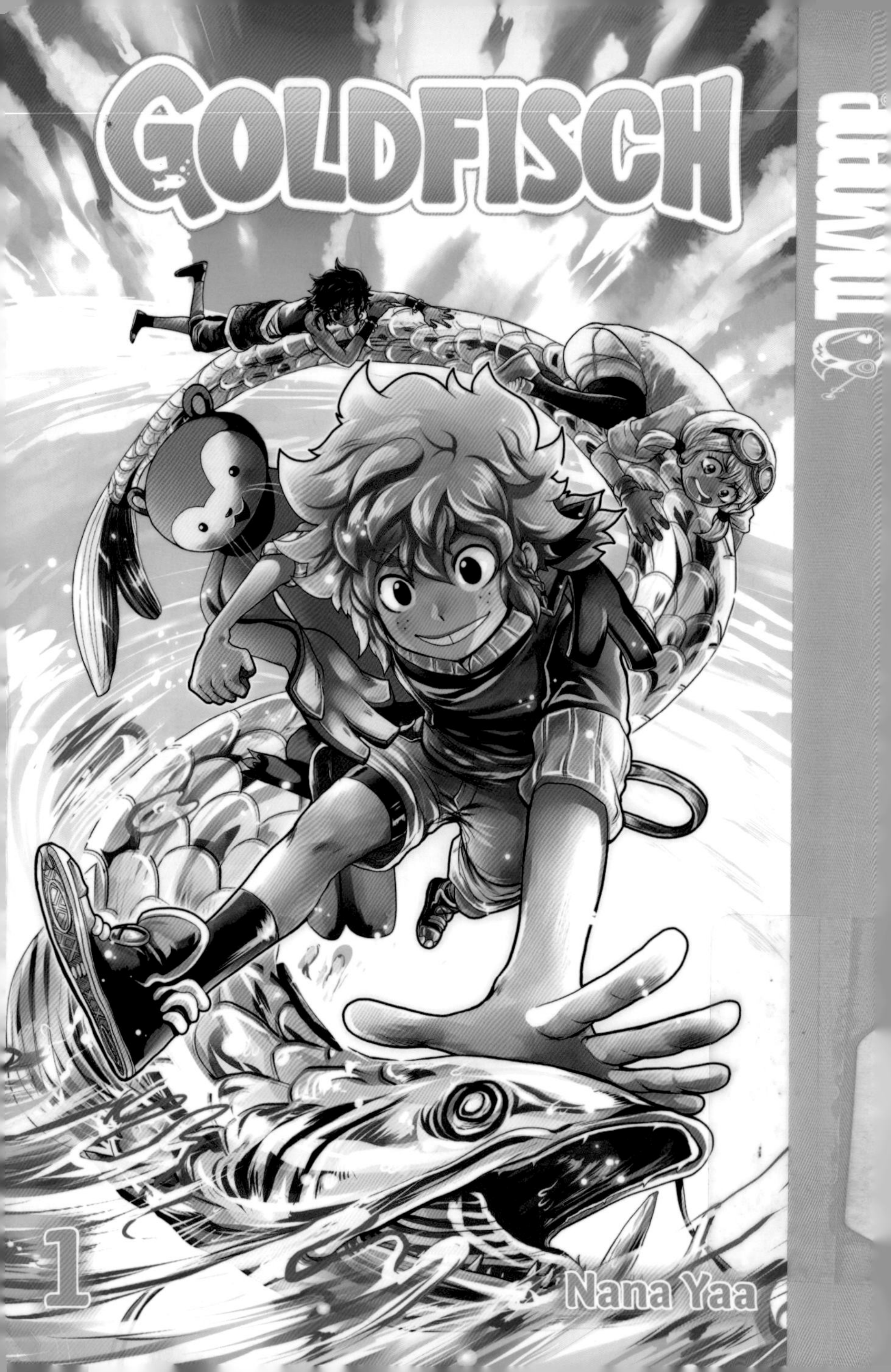
GOLDFISCH
TOKYOPOP
1
Nana Yaa

GOLDFISCH

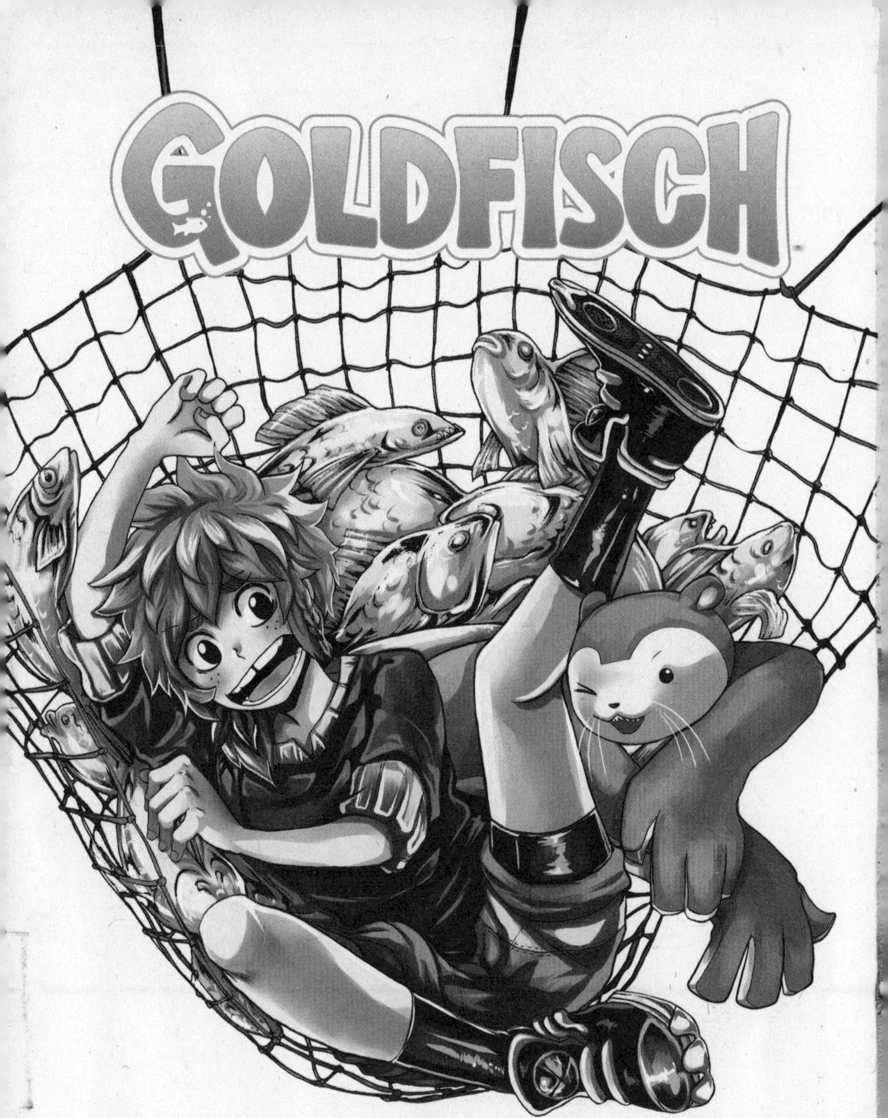

1

Nana Yaa

TOKYOPOP

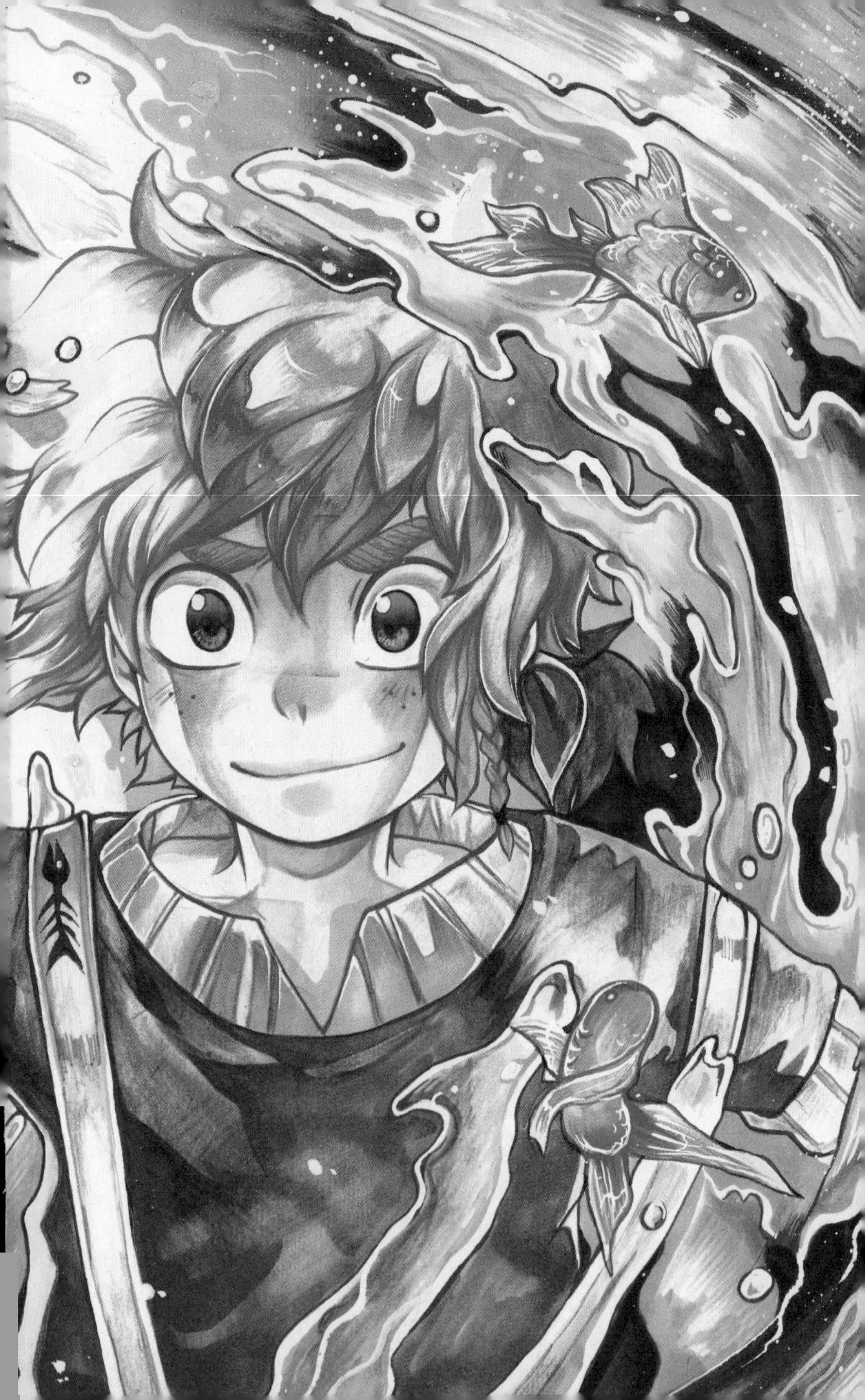

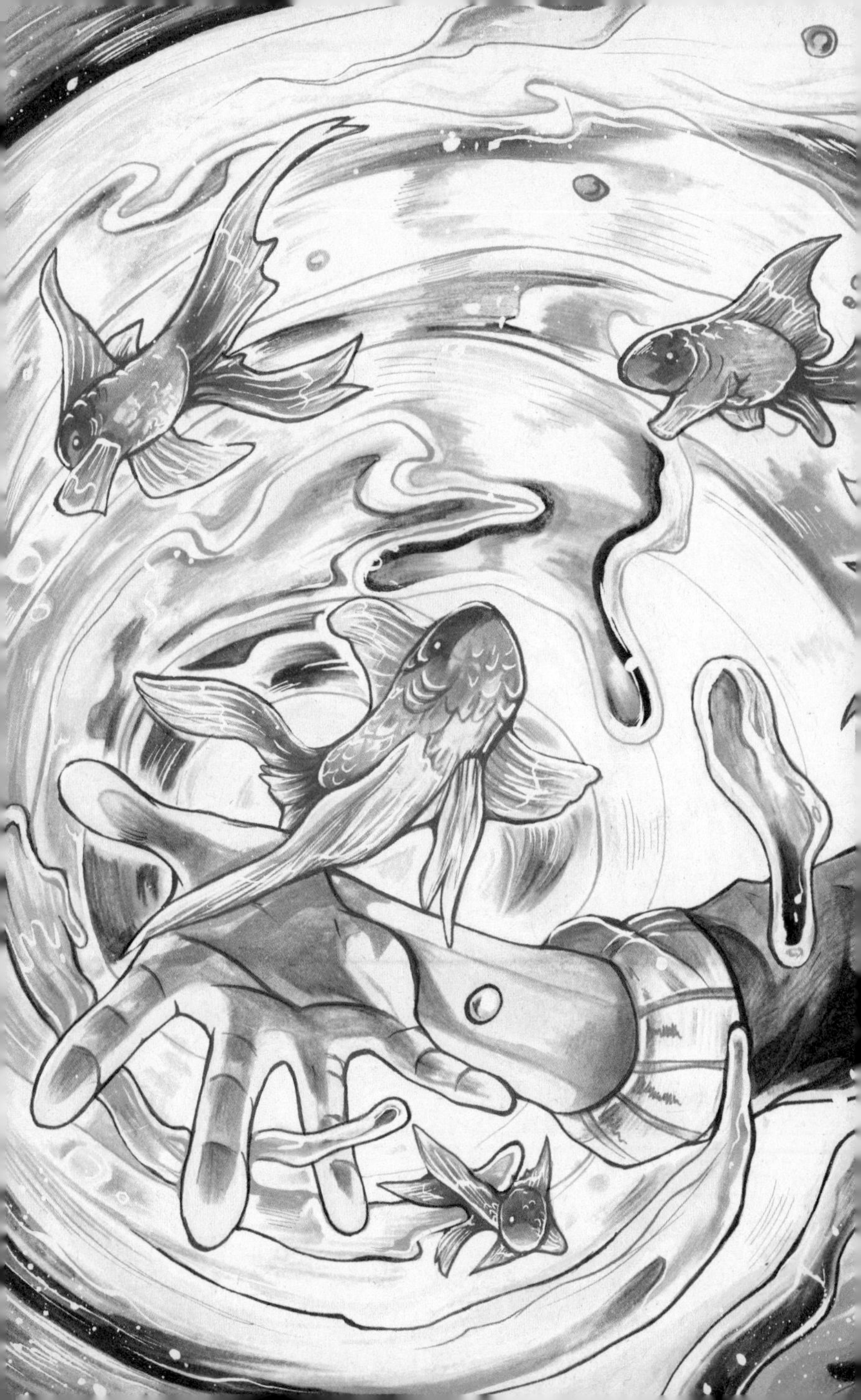

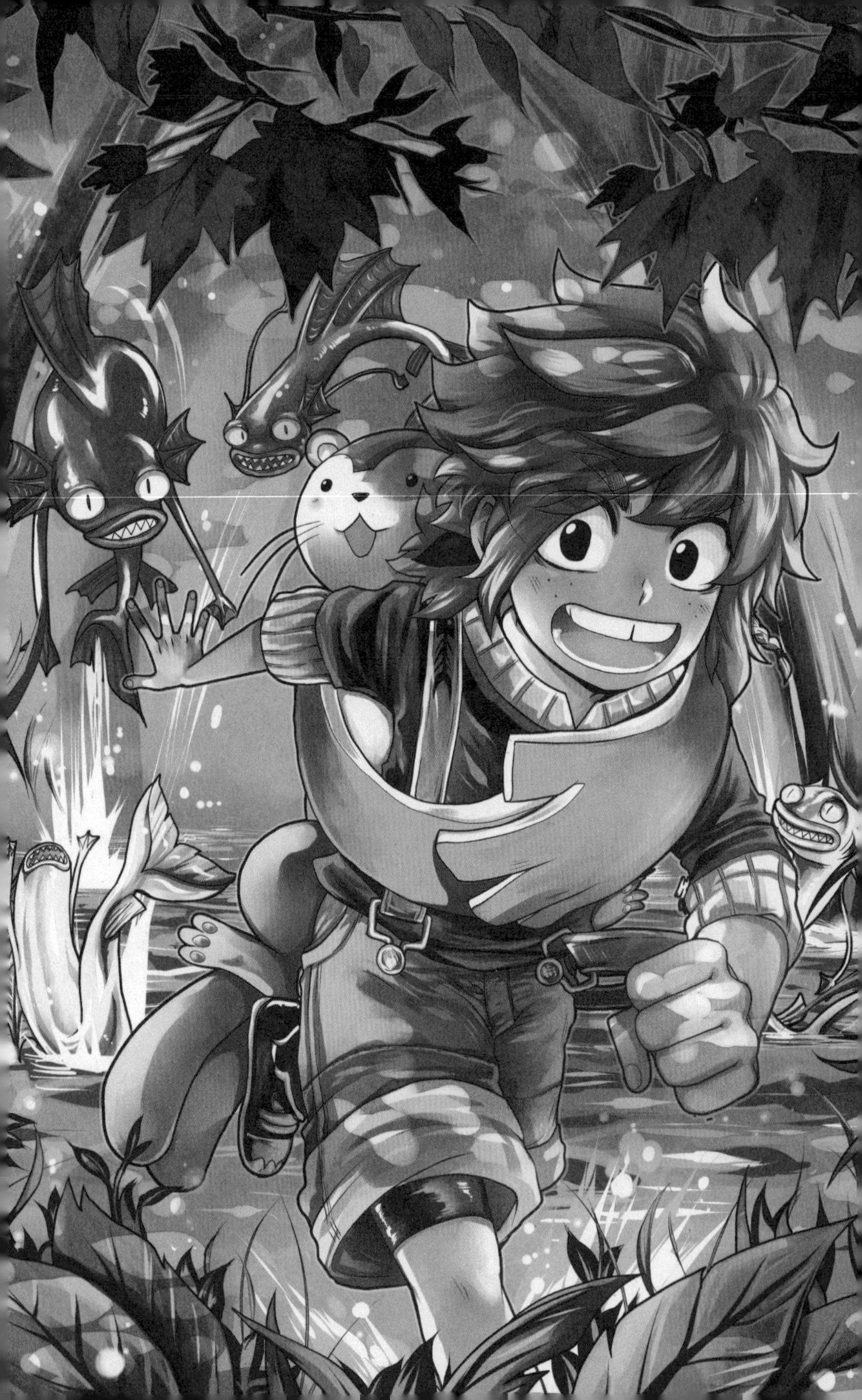

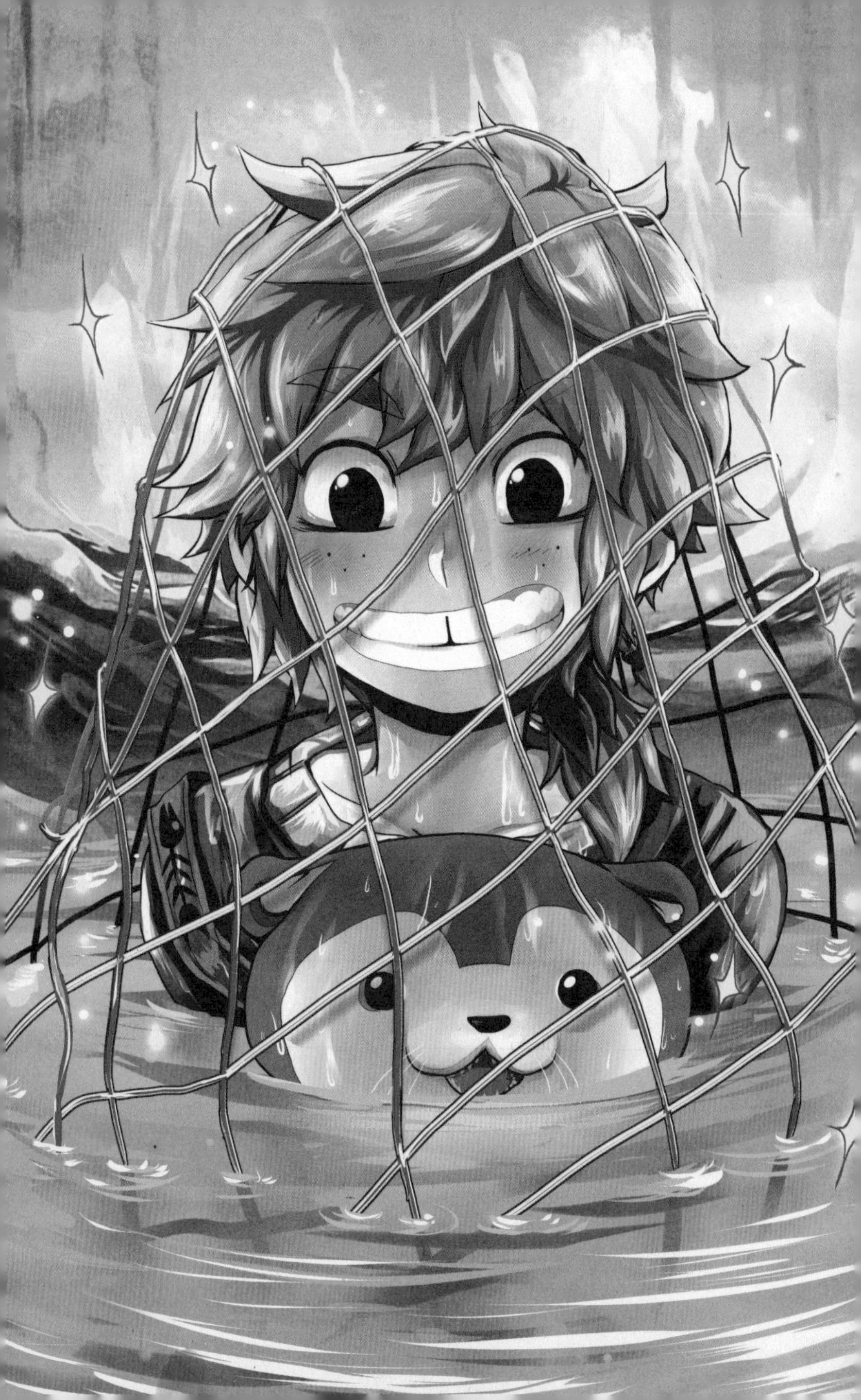

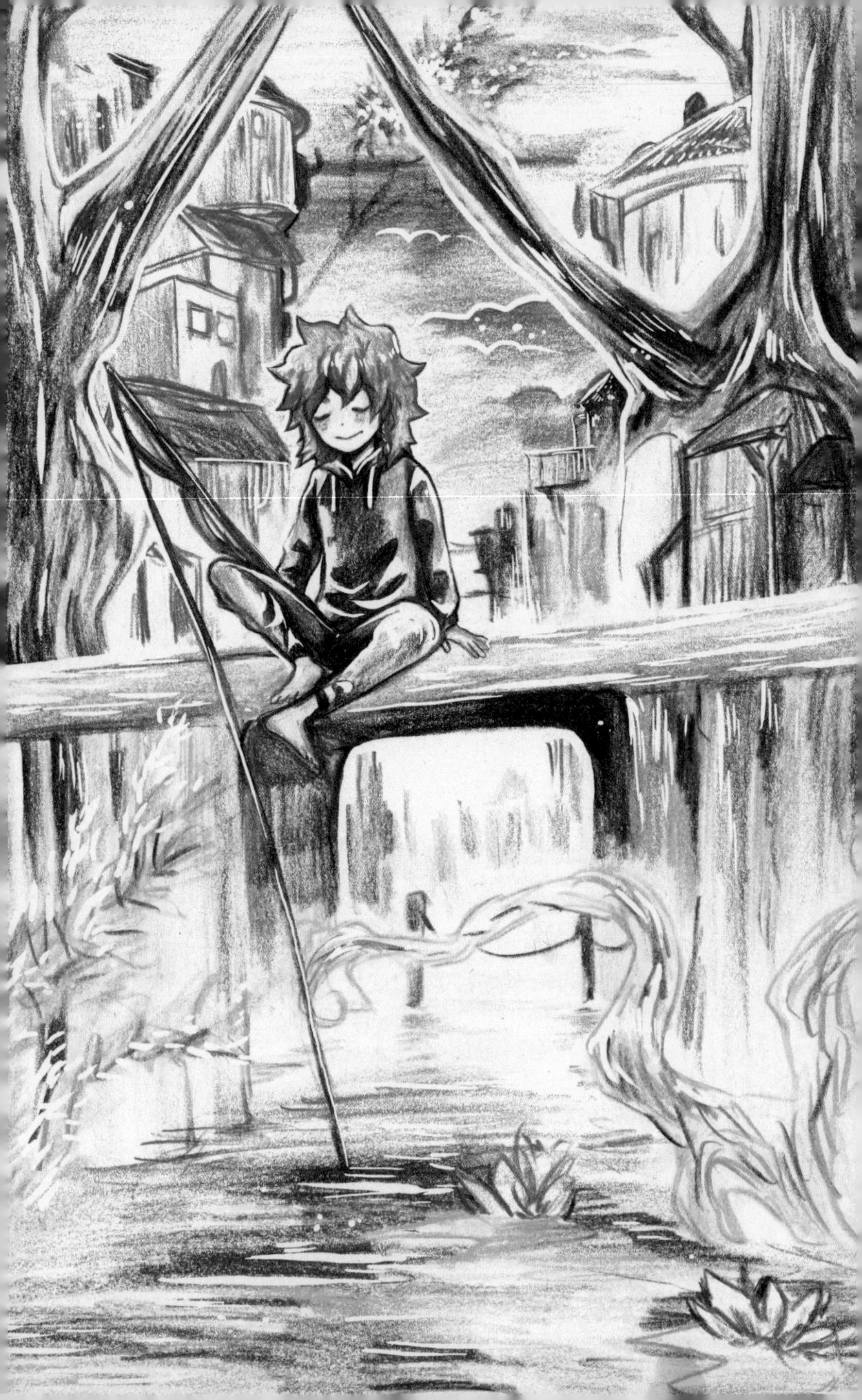

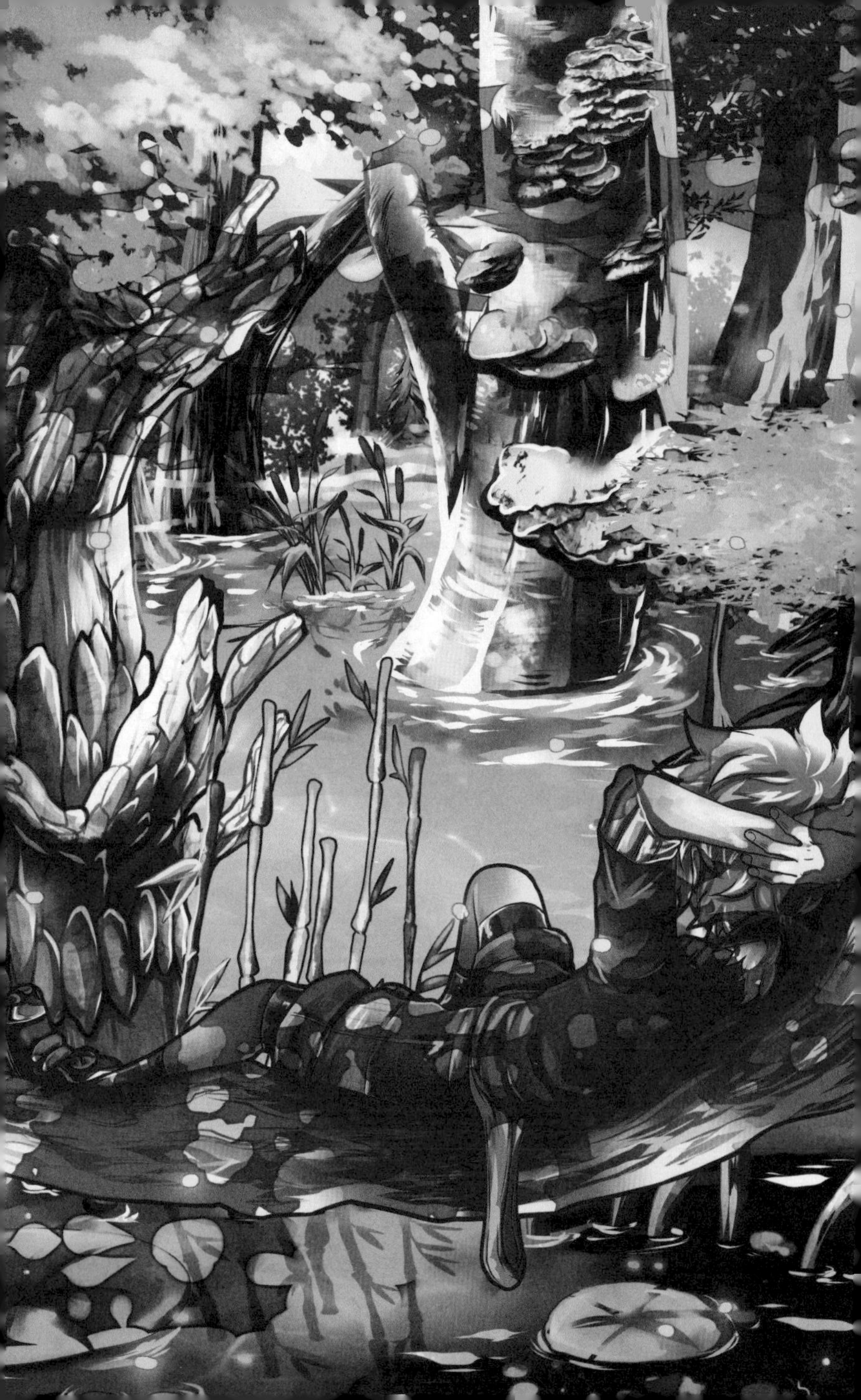

TABLE OF CONTENTS

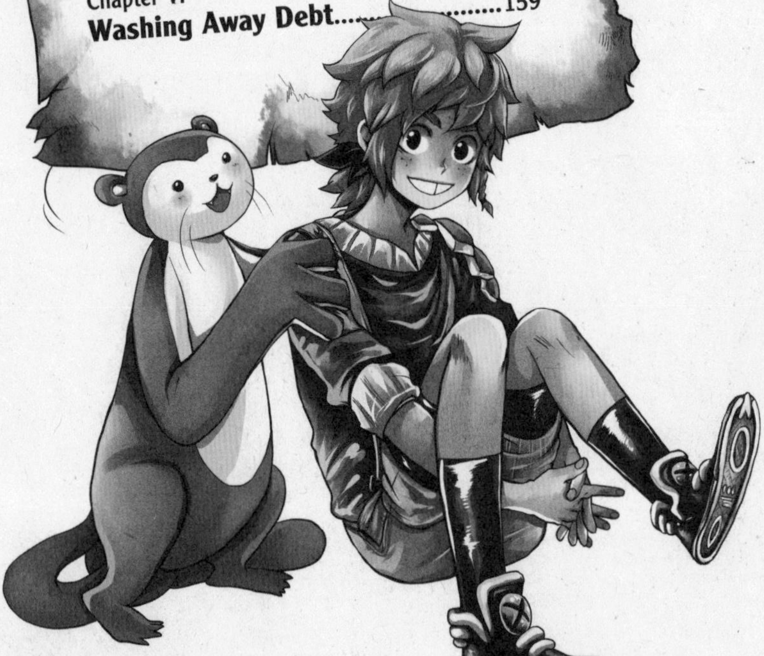

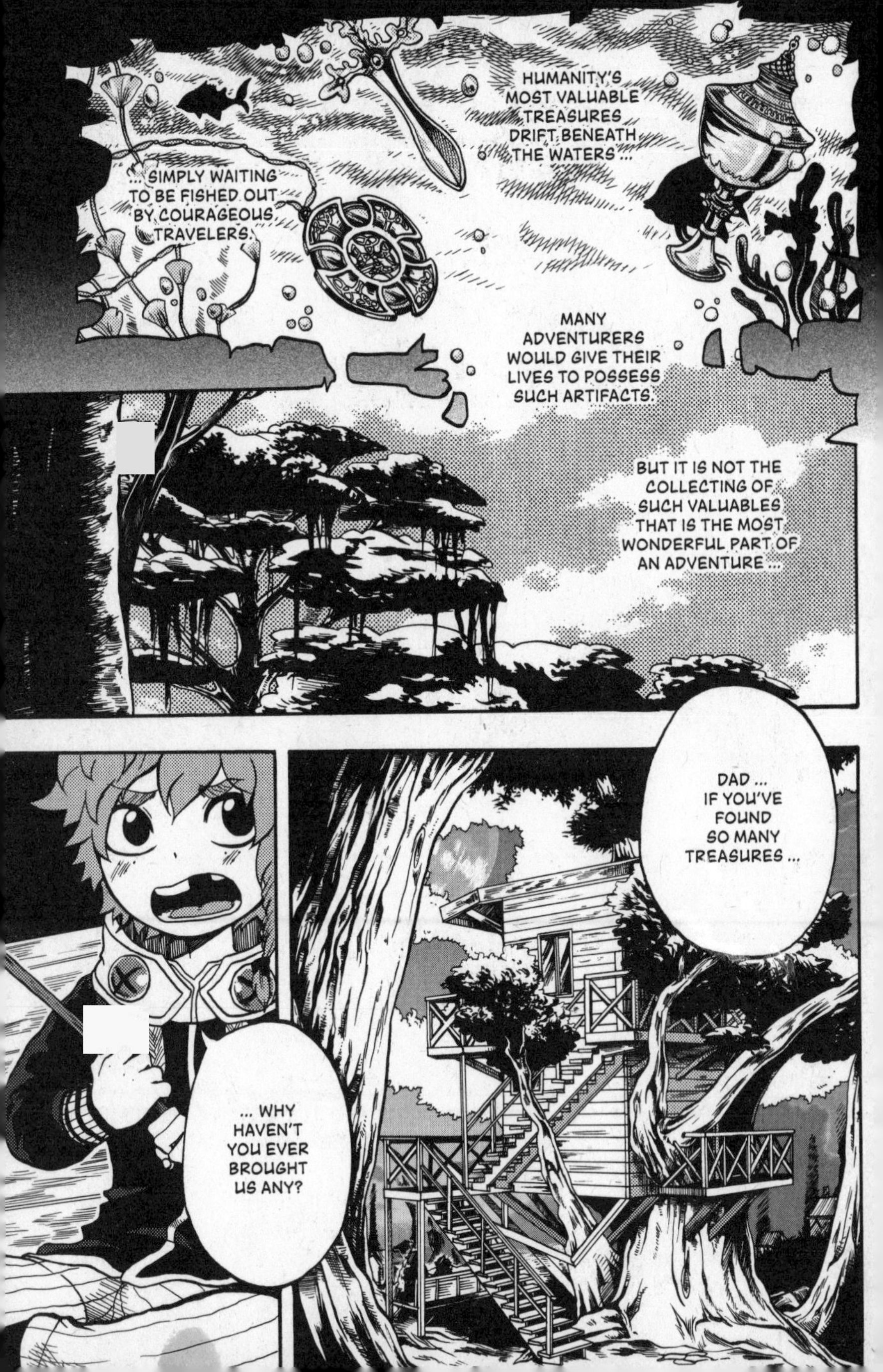
HUMANITY'S MOST VALUABLE TREASURES DRIFT BENEATH THE WATERS ...
... SIMPLY WAITING TO BE FISHED OUT BY COURAGEOUS TRAVELERS.
MANY ADVENTURERS WOULD GIVE THEIR LIVES TO POSSESS SUCH ARTIFACTS.
BUT IT IS NOT THE COLLECTING OF SUCH VALUABLES THAT IS THE MOST WONDERFUL PART OF AN ADVENTURE ...
DAD ... IF YOU'VE FOUND SO MANY TREASURES ...
... WHY HAVEN'T YOU EVER BROUGHT US ANY?

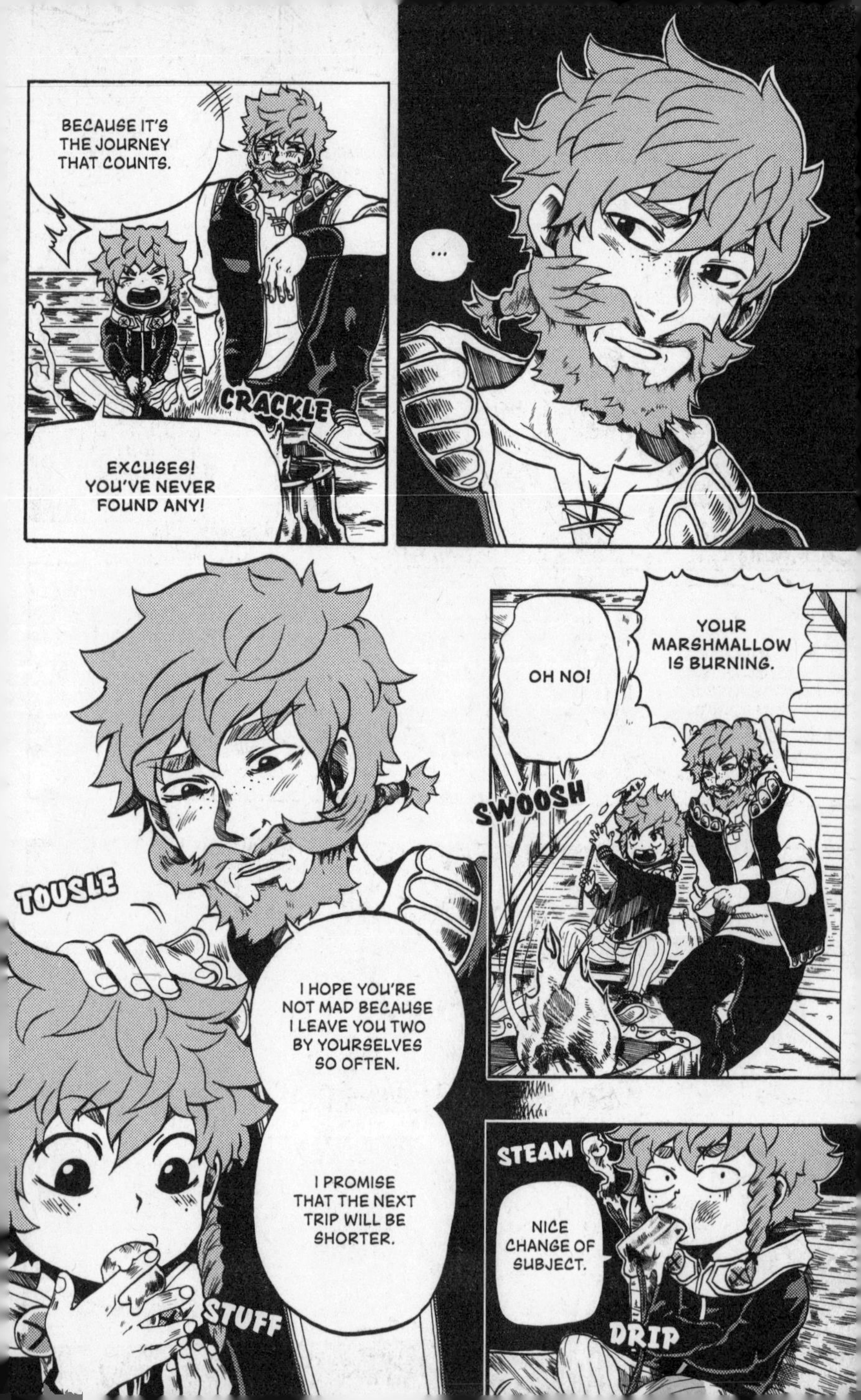
...
BECAUSE IT'S THE JOURNEY THAT COUNTS.
CRACKLE
EXCUSES! YOU'VE NEVER FOUND ANY!
YOUR MARSHMALLOW IS BURNING.
OH NO!
SWOOSH
STEAM
NICE CHANGE OF SUBJECT.
DRIP
TOUSLE
I HOPE YOU'RE NOT MAD BECAUSE I LEAVE YOU TWO BY YOURSELVES SO OFTEN.
I PROMISE THAT THE NEXT TRIP WILL BE SHORTER.
STUFF

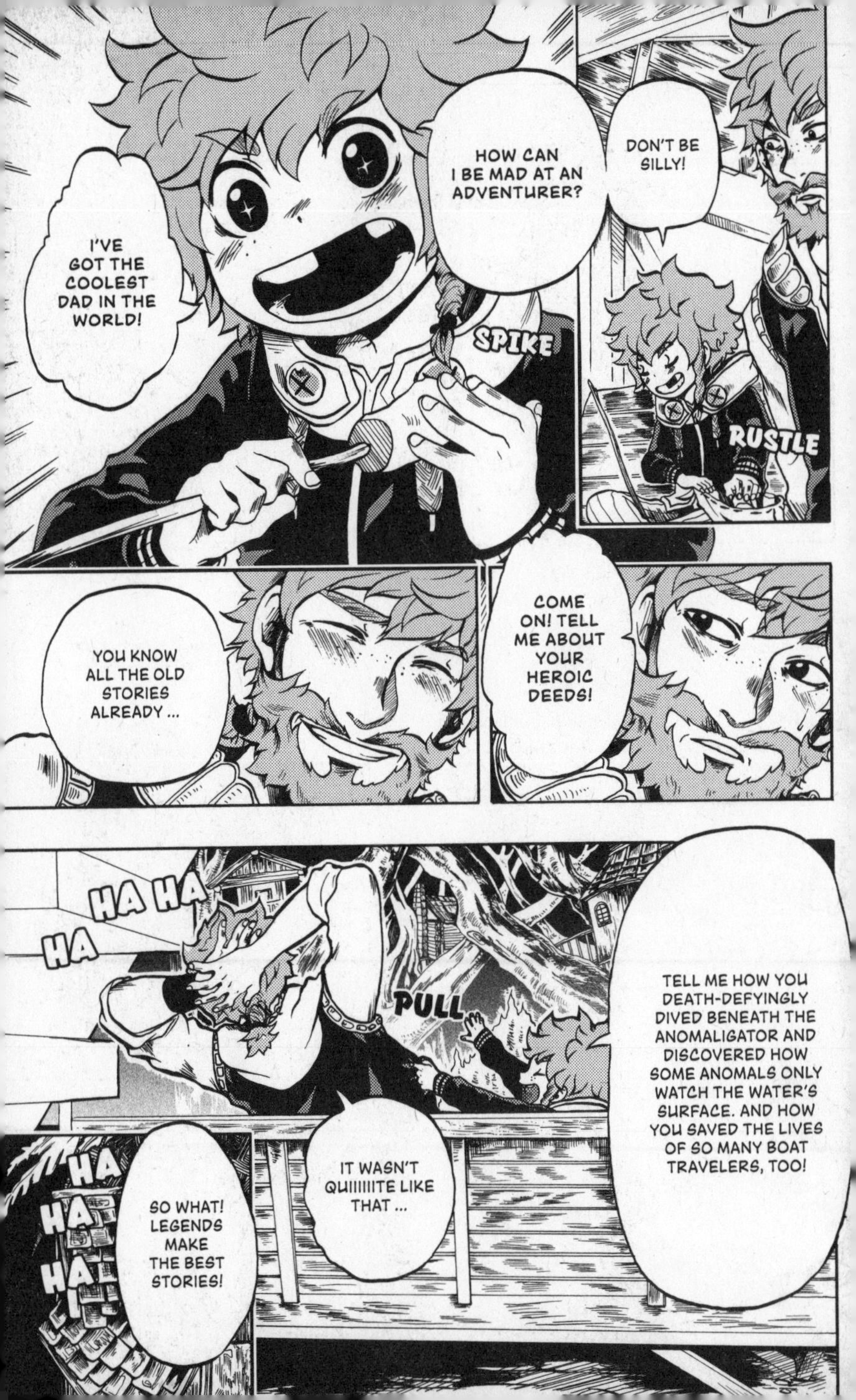
DON'T BE SILLY!
RUSTLE
HOW CAN I BE MAD AT AN ADVENTURER?
I'VE GOT THE COOLEST DAD IN THE WORLD!
SPIKE
COME ON! TELL ME ABOUT YOUR HEROIC DEEDS!
YOU KNOW ALL THE OLD STORIES ALREADY ...
TELL ME HOW YOU DEATH-DEFYINGLY DIVED BENEATH THE ANOMALIGATOR AND DISCOVERED HOW SOME ANOMALS ONLY WATCH THE WATER'S SURFACE. AND HOW YOU SAVED THE LIVES OF SO MANY BOAT TRAVELERS, TOO!
PULL
IT WASN'T QUIIIIIITE LIKE THAT ...
HA HA
HA
SO WHAT! LEGENDS MAKE THE BEST STORIES!
HA
HA
HA

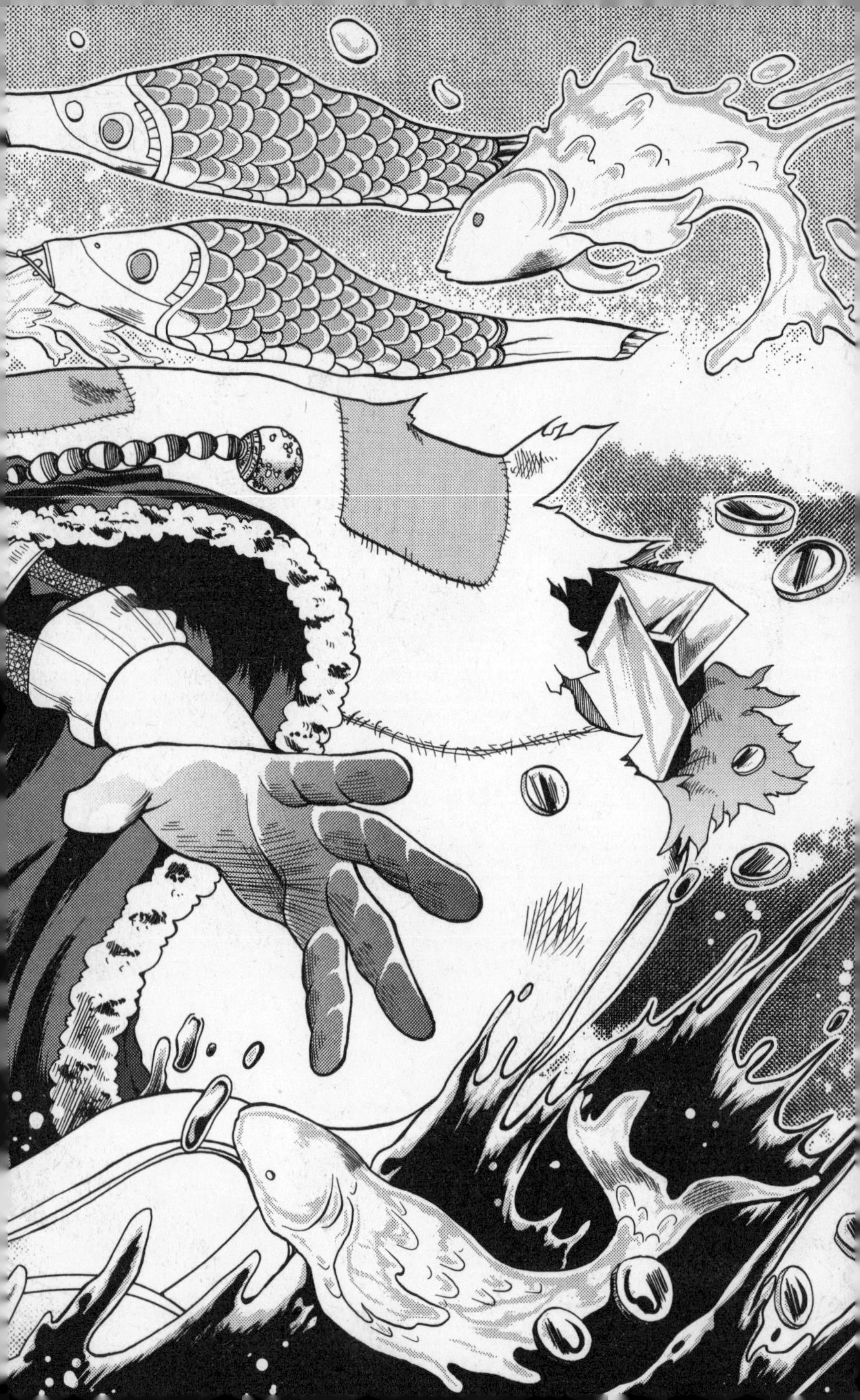

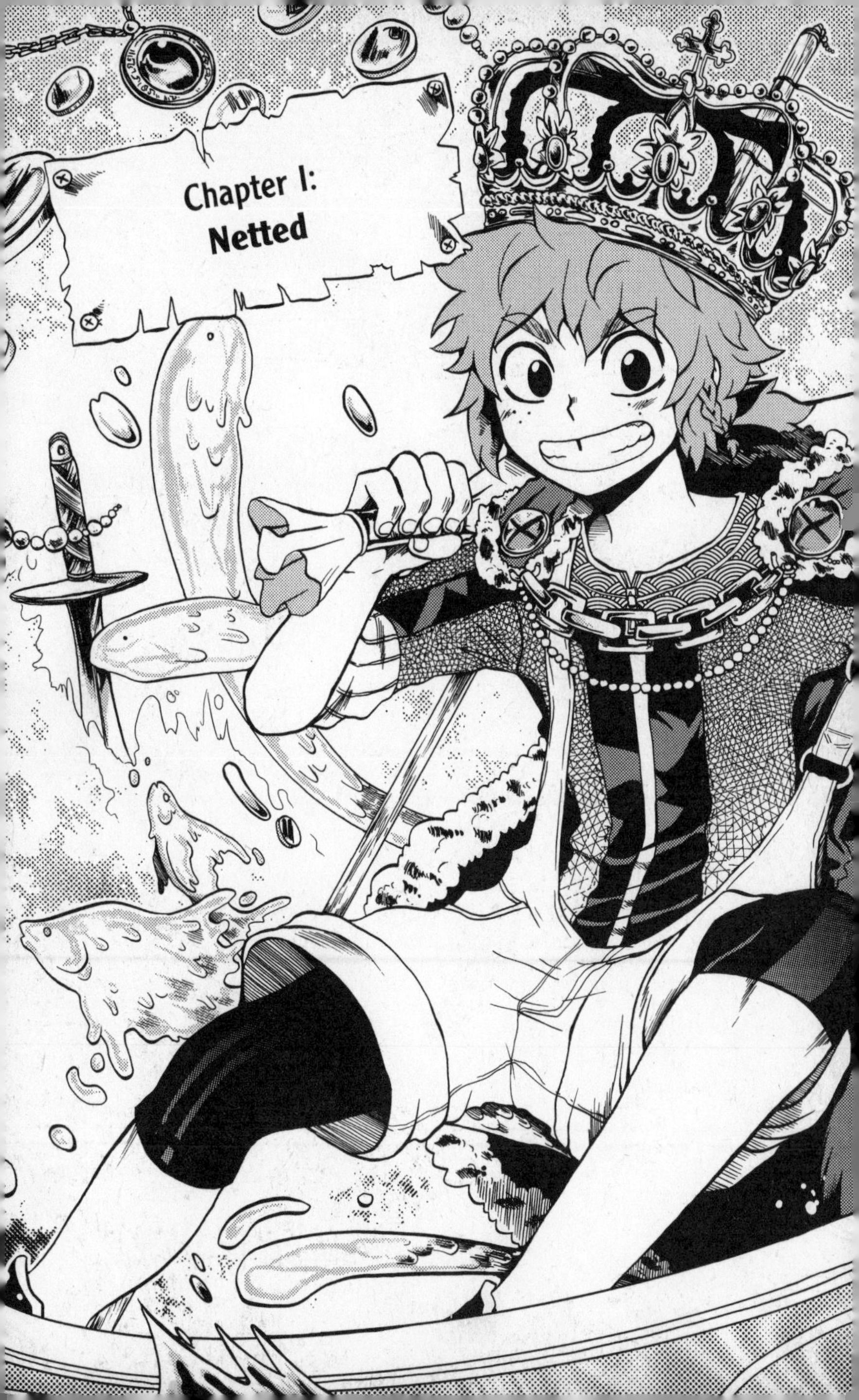
Chapter 1:
Netted

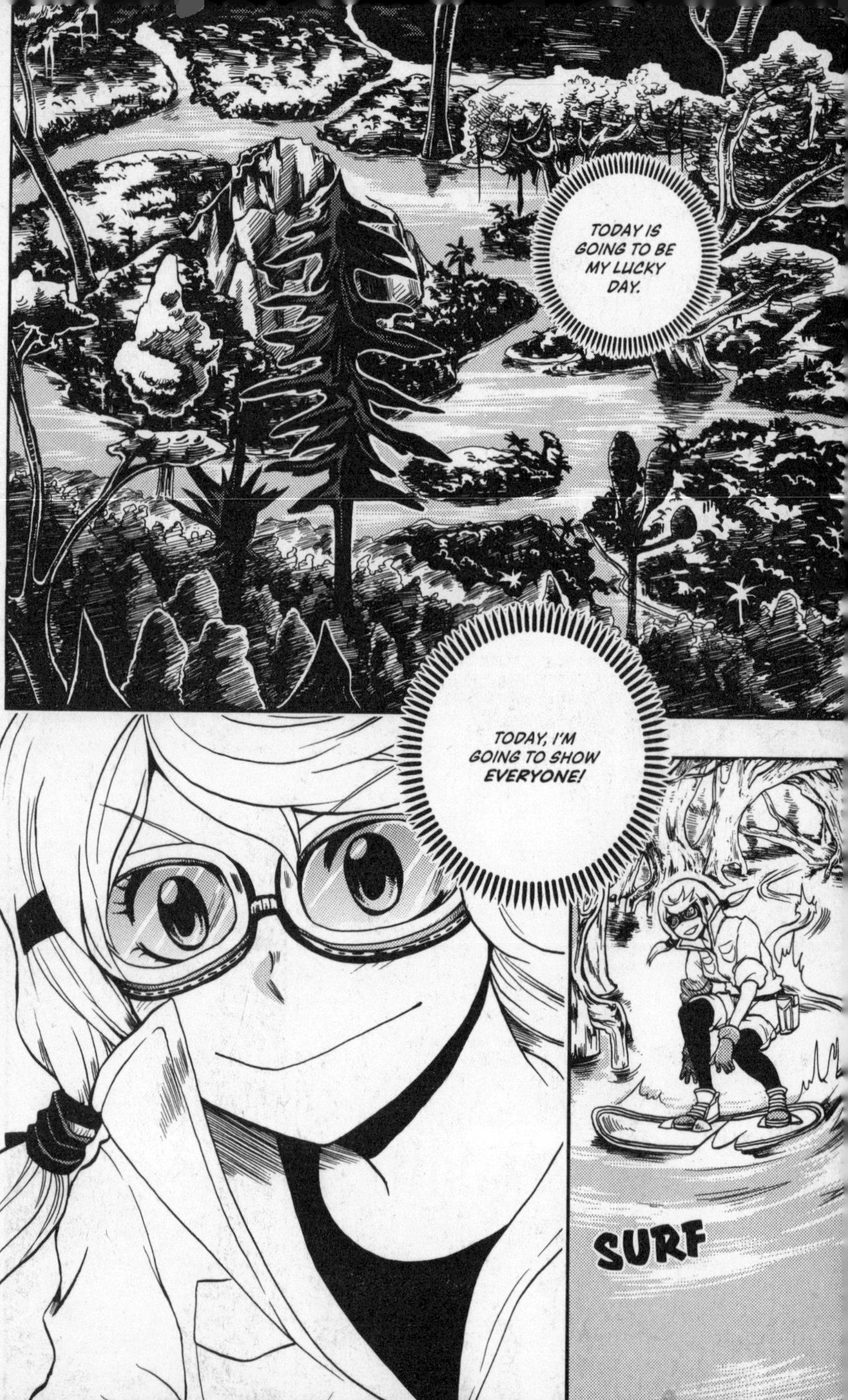
TODAY IS GOING TO BE MY LUCKY DAY.
TODAY, I'M GOING TO SHOW EVERYONE!
SURF

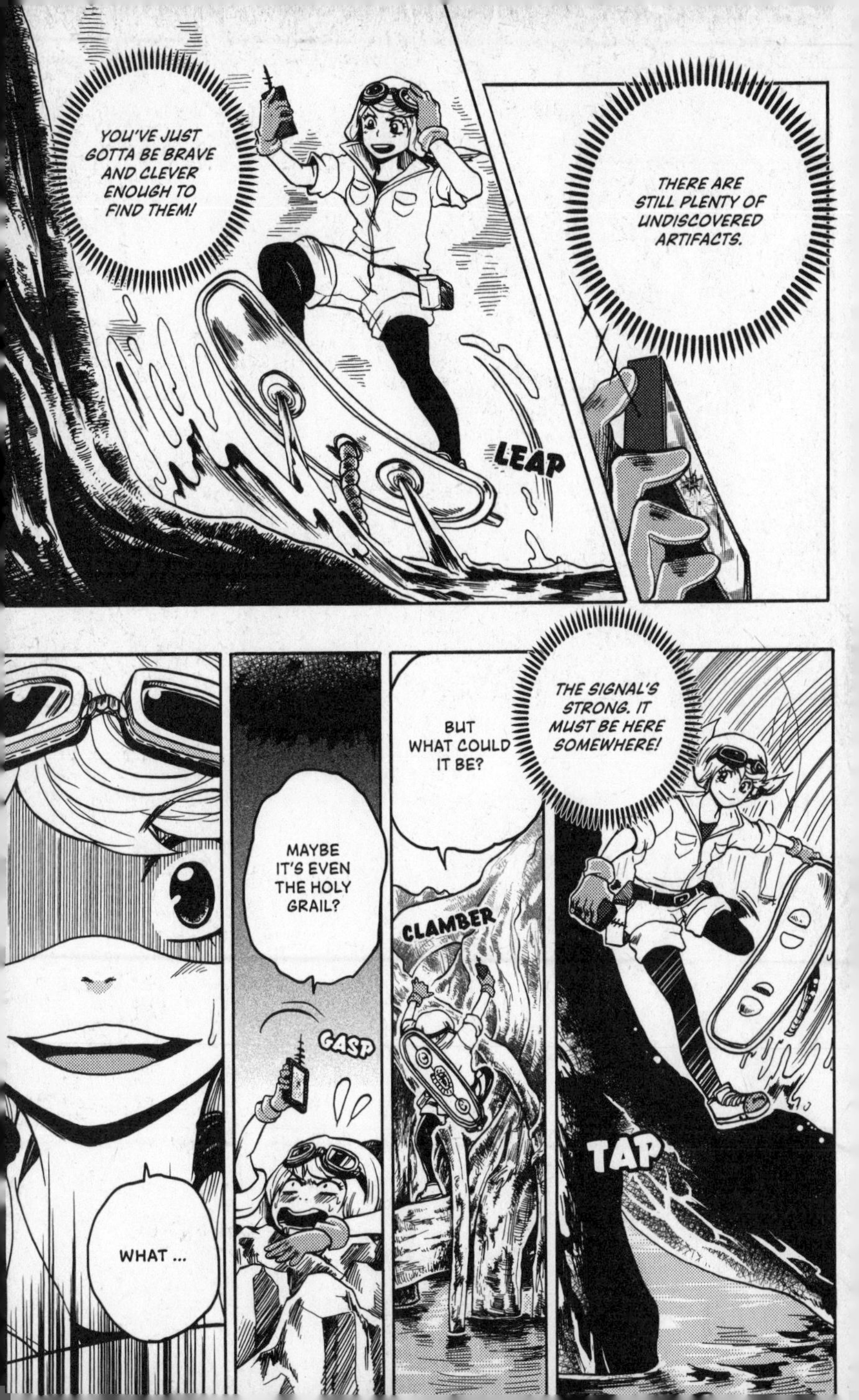
THERE ARE STILL PLENTY OF UNDISCOVERED ARTIFACTS.
YOU'VE JUST GOTTA BE BRAVE AND CLEVER ENOUGH TO FIND THEM!
LEAP
THE SIGNAL'S STRONG. IT MUST BE HERE SOMEWHERE!
TAP
BUT WHAT COULD IT BE?
CLAMBER
MAYBE IT'S EVEN THE HOLY GRAIL?
GASP
WHAT ...

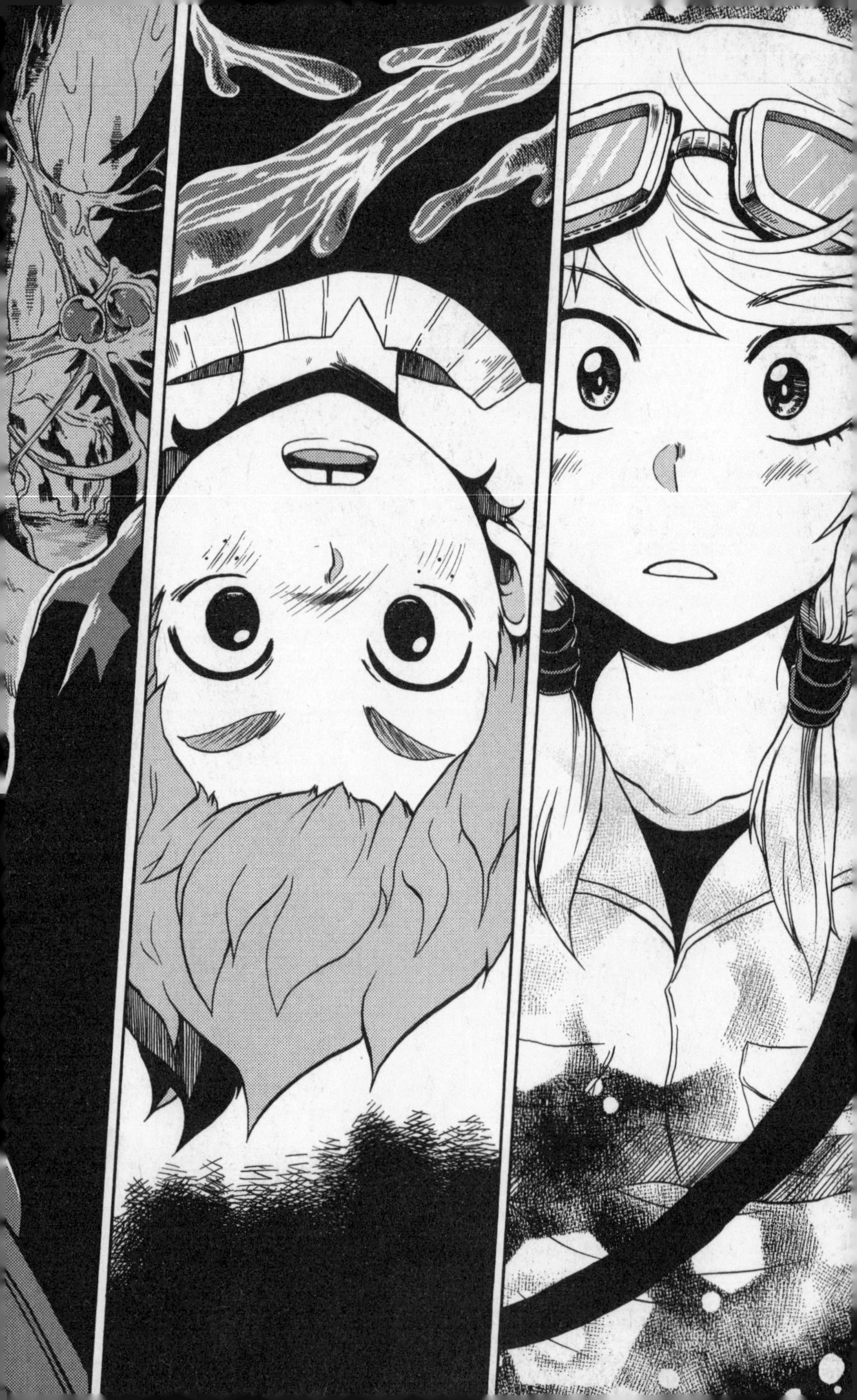

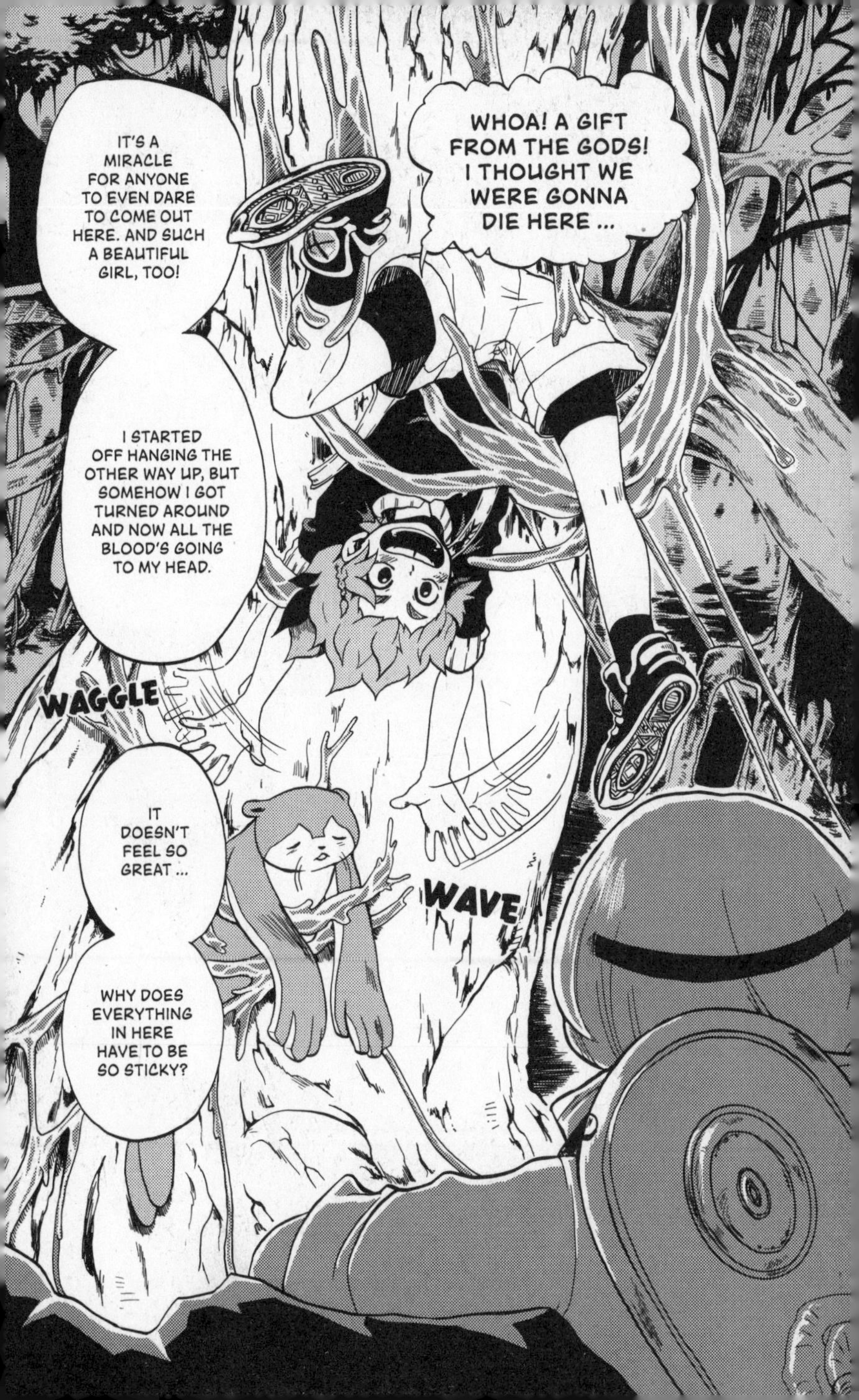
WHOA! A GIFT FROM THE GODS! I THOUGHT WE WERE GONNA DIE HERE ...
IT'S A MIRACLE FOR ANYONE TO EVEN DARE TO COME OUT HERE. AND SUCH A BEAUTIFUL GIRL, TOO!
I STARTED OFF HANGING THE OTHER WAY UP, BUT SOMEHOW I GOT TURNED AROUND AND NOW ALL THE BLOOD'S GOING TO MY HEAD.
WAGGLE
WAVE
IT DOESN'T FEEL SO GREAT ...
WHY DOES EVERYTHING IN HERE HAVE TO BE SO STICKY?

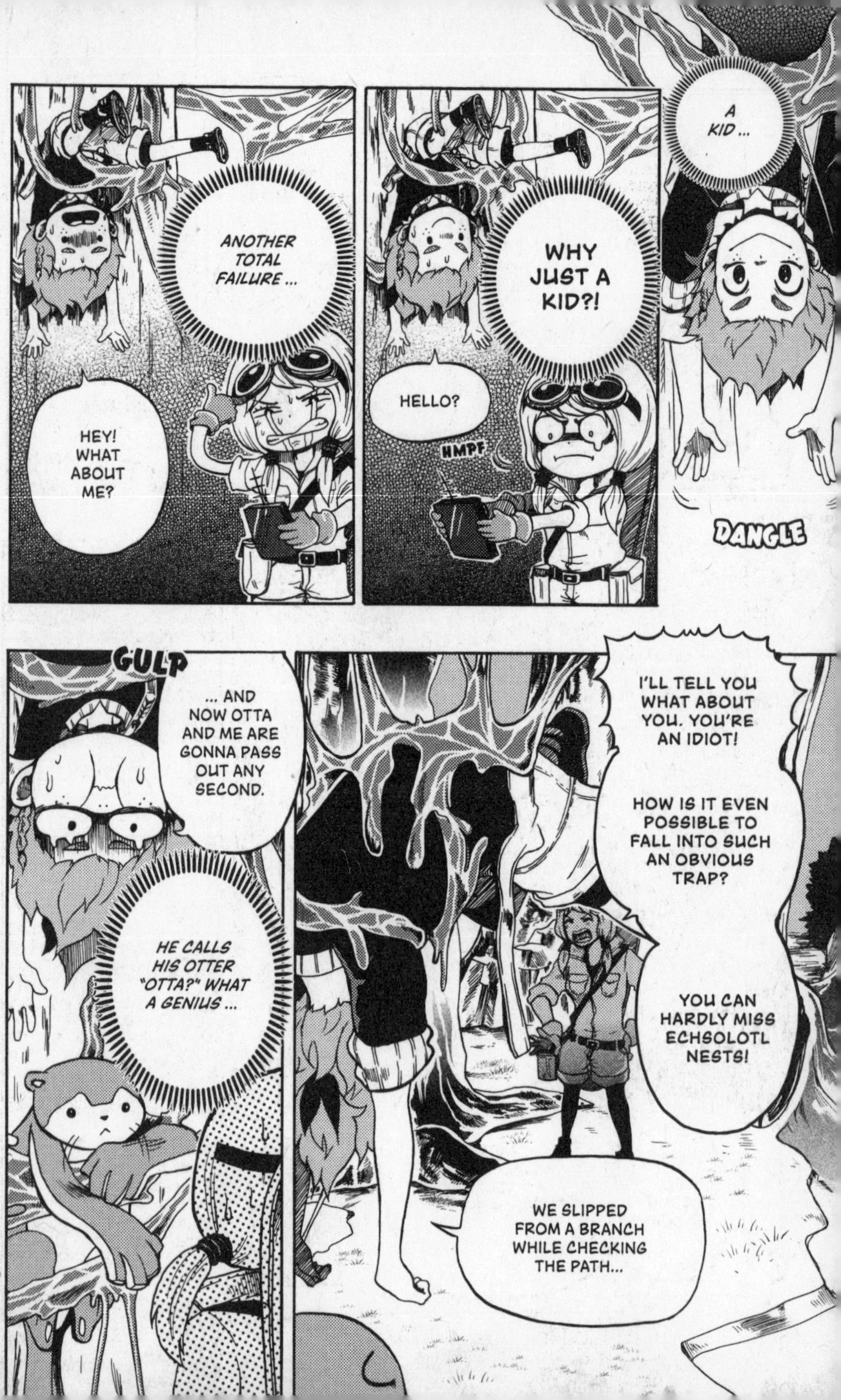
A KID ...
DANGLE
WHY JUST A KID?!
HELLO?
HMPF
ANOTHER TOTAL FAILURE ...
HEY! WHAT ABOUT ME?
I'LL TELL YOU WHAT ABOUT YOU. YOU'RE AN IDIOT!
HOW IS IT EVEN POSSIBLE TO FALL INTO SUCH AN OBVIOUS TRAP?
YOU CAN HARDLY MISS ECHSOLOTL NESTS!
WE SLIPPED FROM A BRANCH WHILE CHECKING THE PATH...
GULP
... AND NOW OTTA AND ME ARE GONNA PASS OUT ANY SECOND.
HE CALLS HIS OTTER "OTTA?" WHAT A GENIUS ...

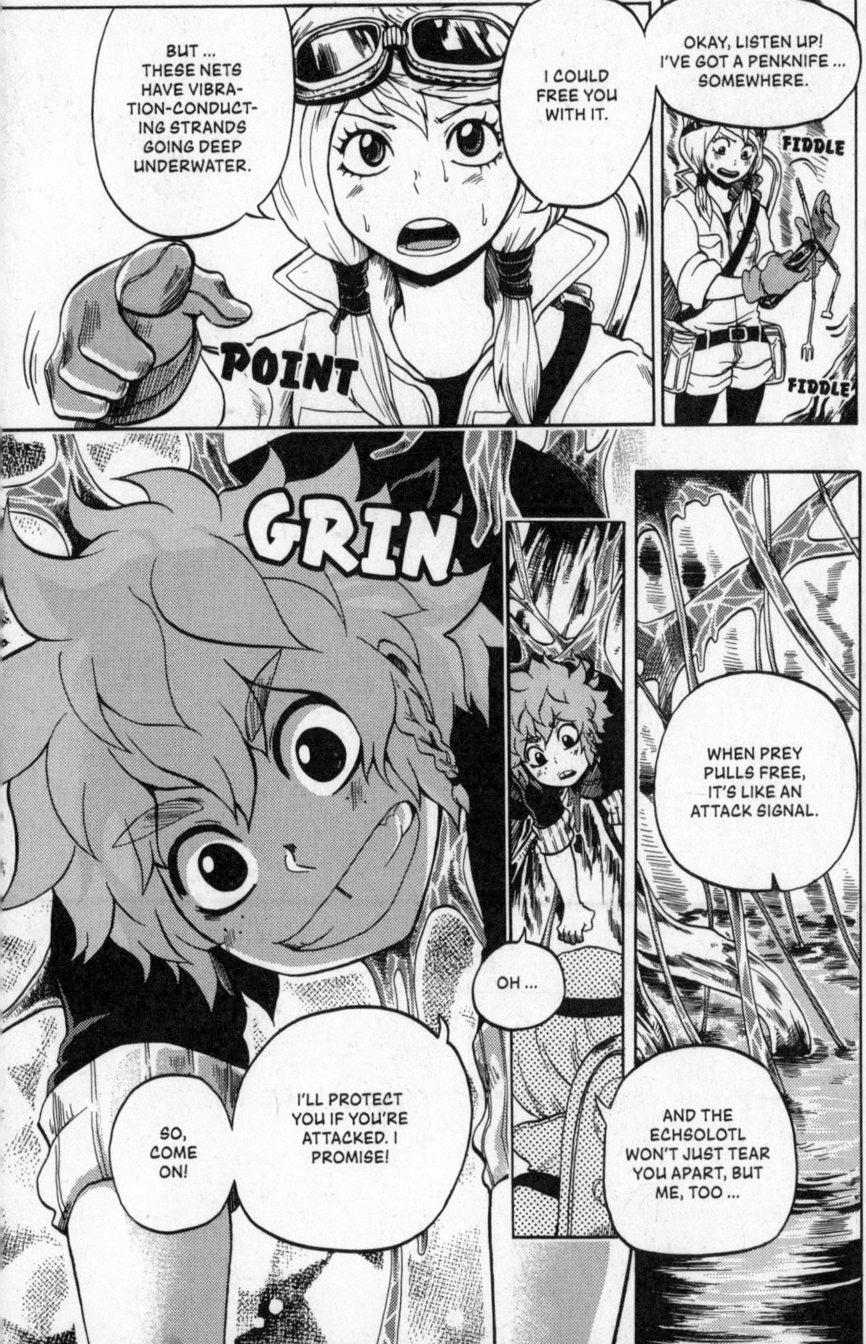
OKAY, LISTEN UP! I'VE GOT A PENKNIFE ... SOMEWHERE.
FIDDLE
FIDDLE
I COULD FREE YOU WITH IT.
BUT ... THESE NETS HAVE VIBRATION-CONDUCTING STRANDS GOING DEEP UNDERWATER.
POINT
WHEN PREY PULLS FREE, IT'S LIKE AN ATTACK SIGNAL.
AND THE ECHSOLOTL WON'T JUST TEAR YOU APART, BUT ME, TOO ...
OH ...
GRIN
I'LL PROTECT YOU IF YOU'RE ATTACKED. I PROMISE!
SO, COME ON!

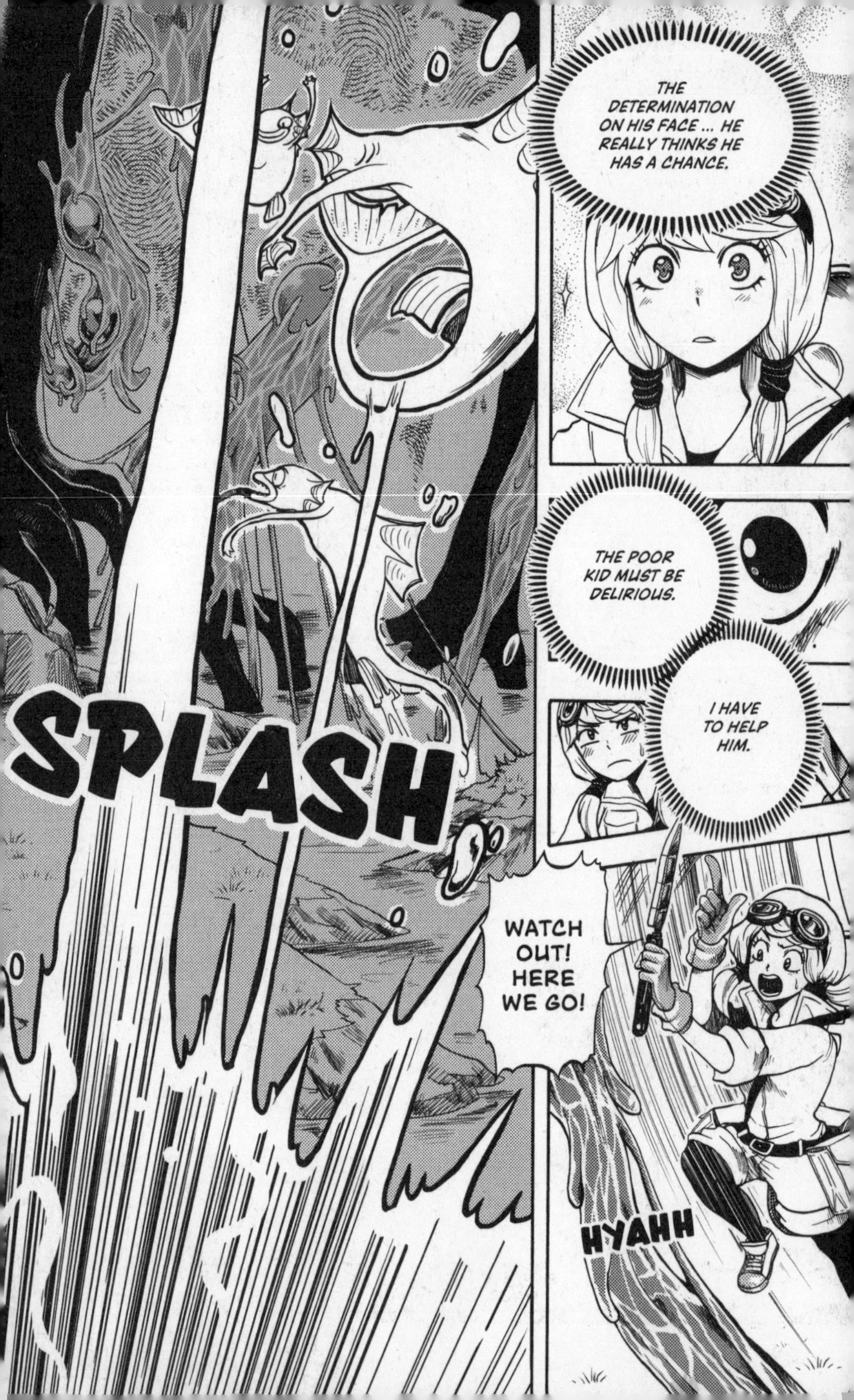
THE DETERMINATION ON HIS FACE ... HE REALLY THINKS HE HAS A CHANCE.
THE POOR KID MUST BE DELIRIOUS.
I HAVE TO HELP HIM.
WATCH OUT! HERE WE GO!
HYAHH
SPLASH

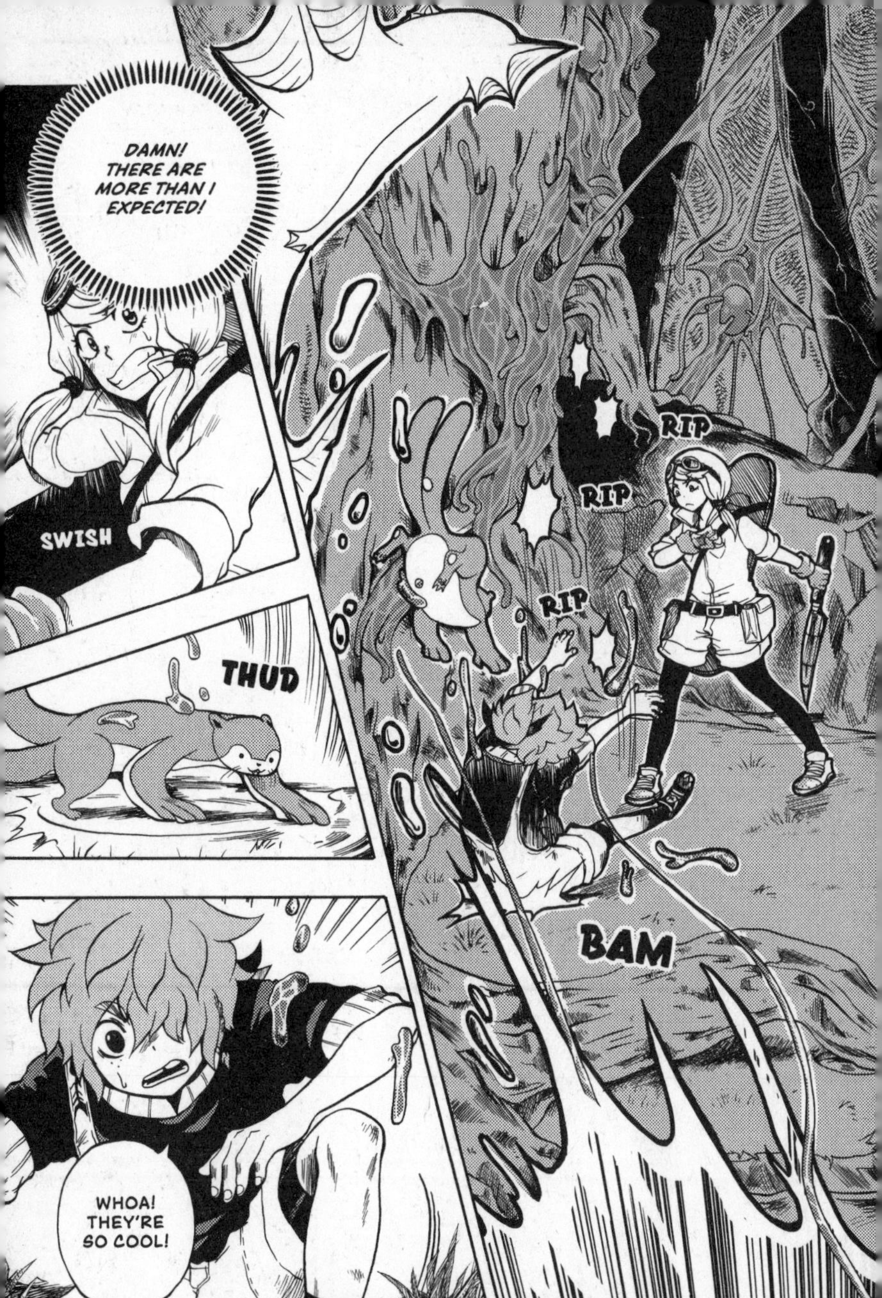
RIP
RIP
RIP
BAM
DAMN! THERE ARE MORE THAN I EXPECTED!
SWISH
THUD
WHOA! THEY'RE SO COOL!

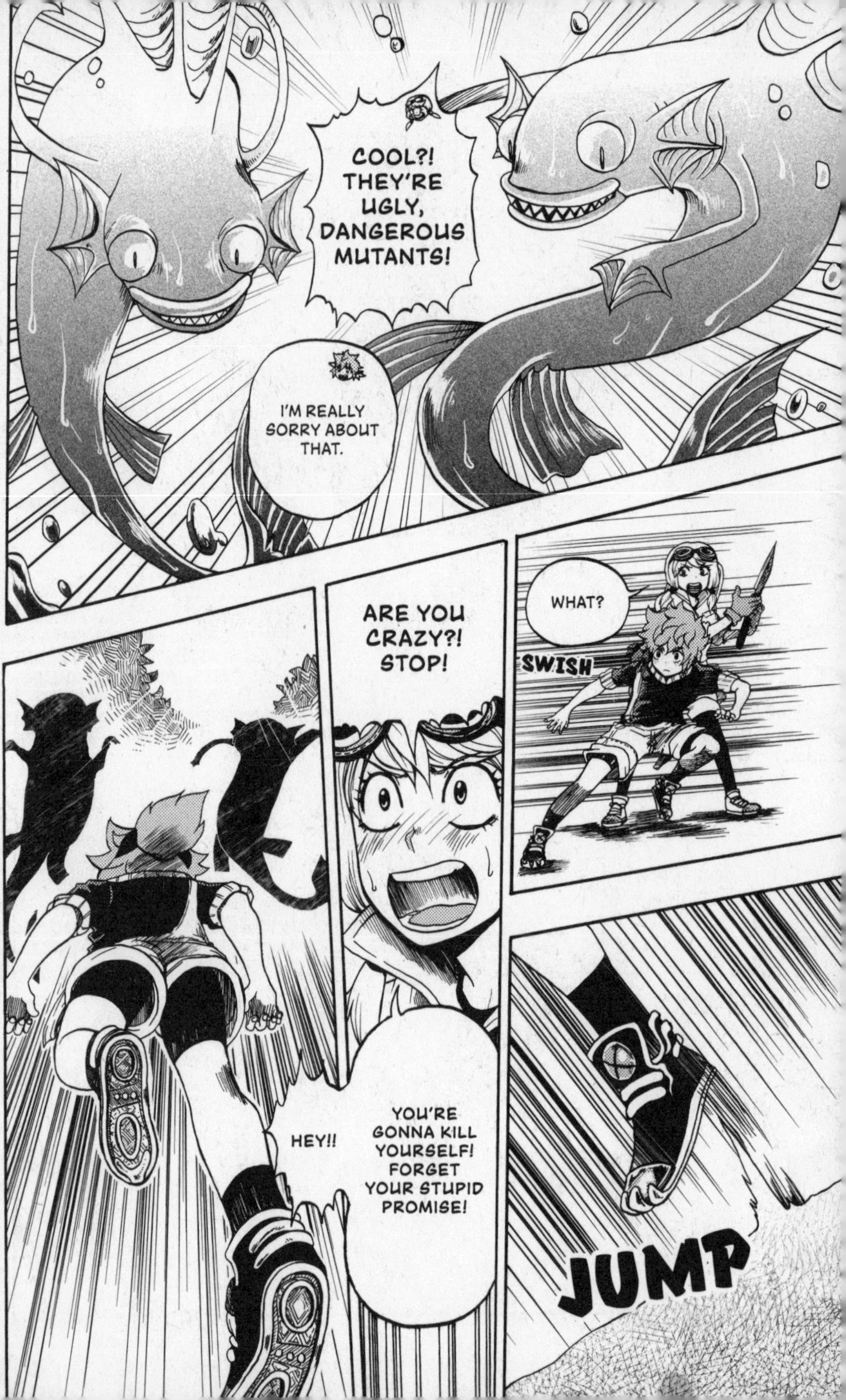
COOL?! THEY'RE UGLY, DANGEROUS MUTANTS!
I'M REALLY SORRY ABOUT THAT.
WHAT?
SWISH
JUMP
ARE YOU CRAZY?! STOP!
YOU'RE GONNA KILL YOURSELF! FORGET YOUR STUPID PROMISE!
HEY!!

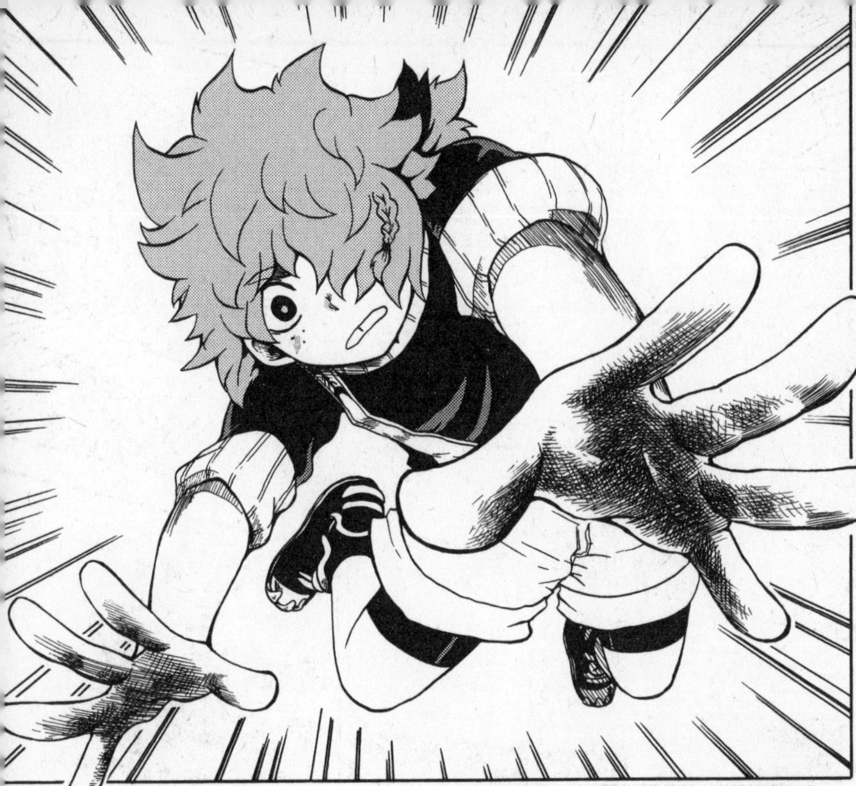

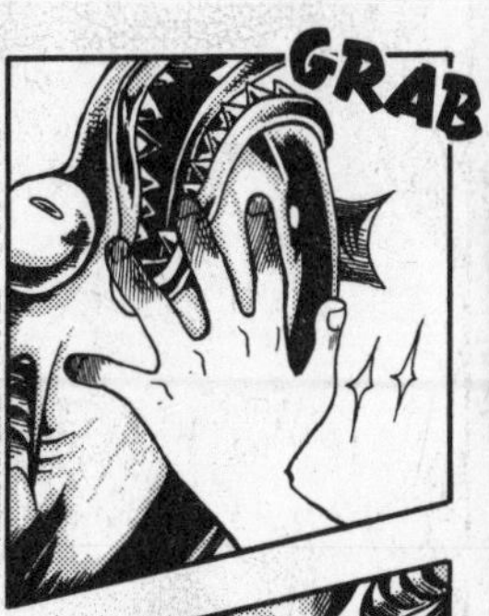
GRAB

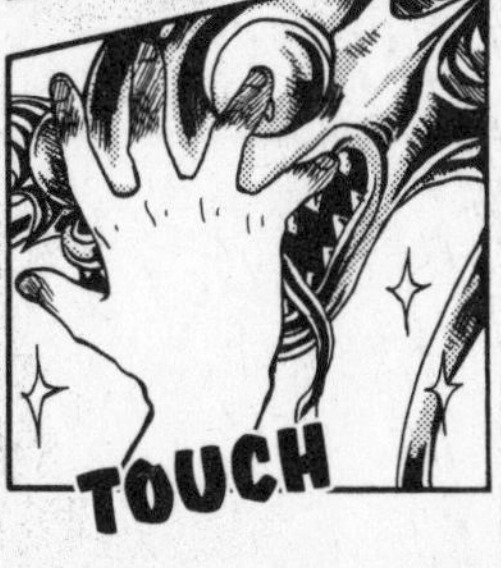
TOUCH

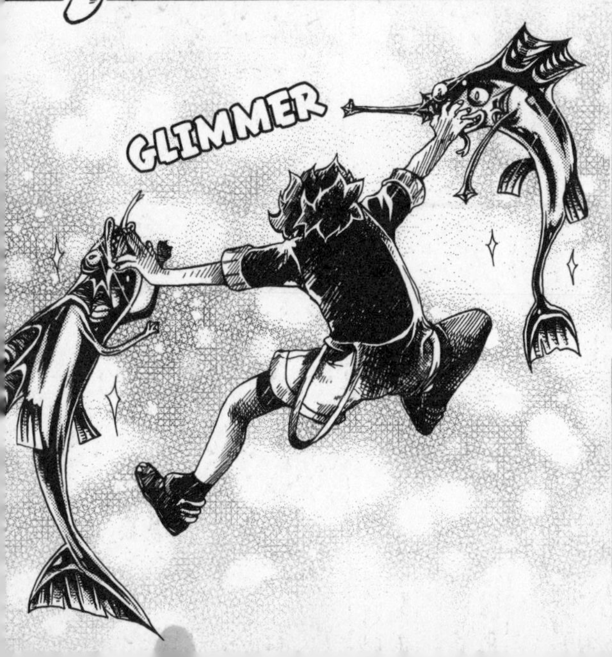
GLIMMER

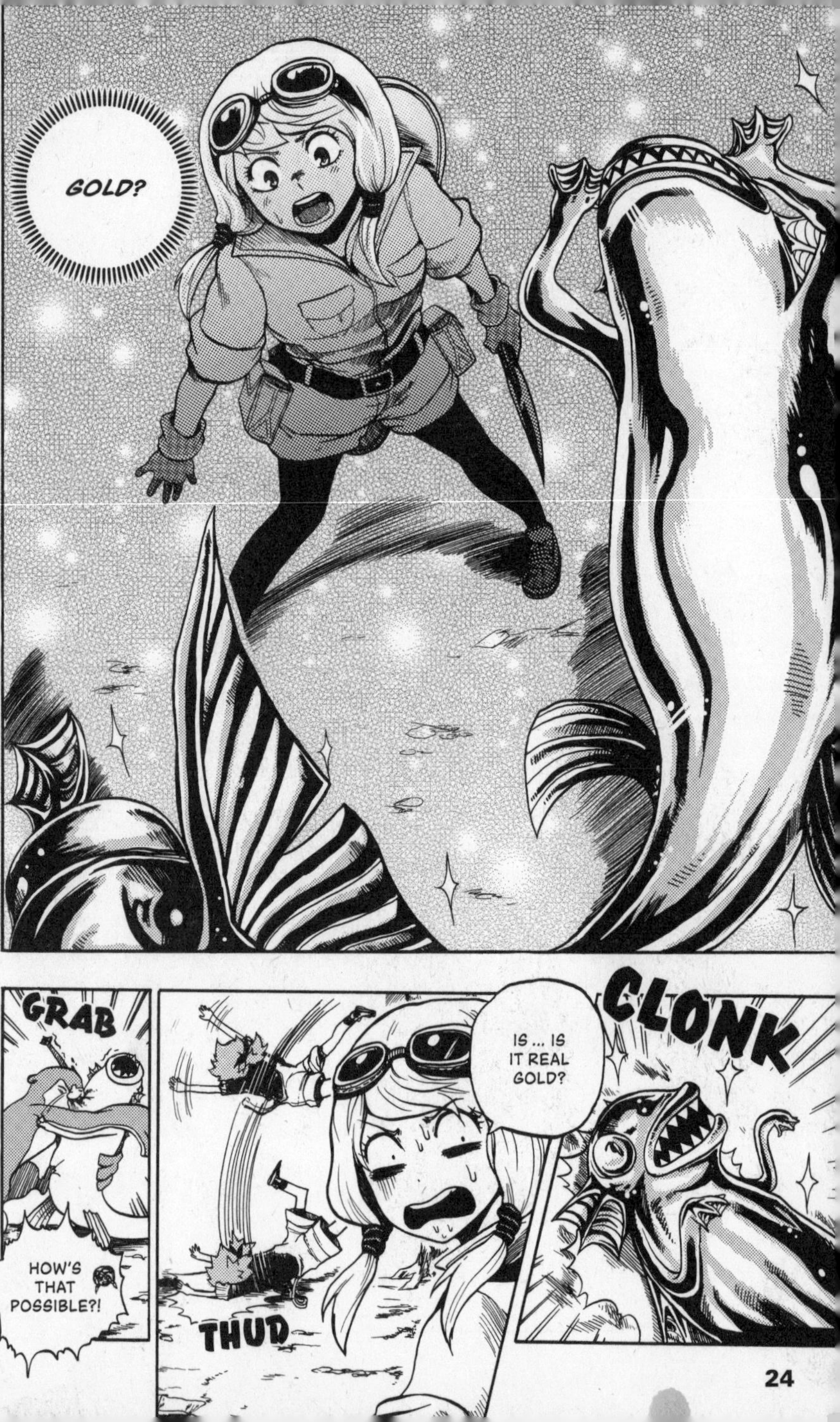
GOLD?
CLONK
IS ... IS IT REAL GOLD?
THUD
GRAB
HOW'S THAT POSSIBLE?!

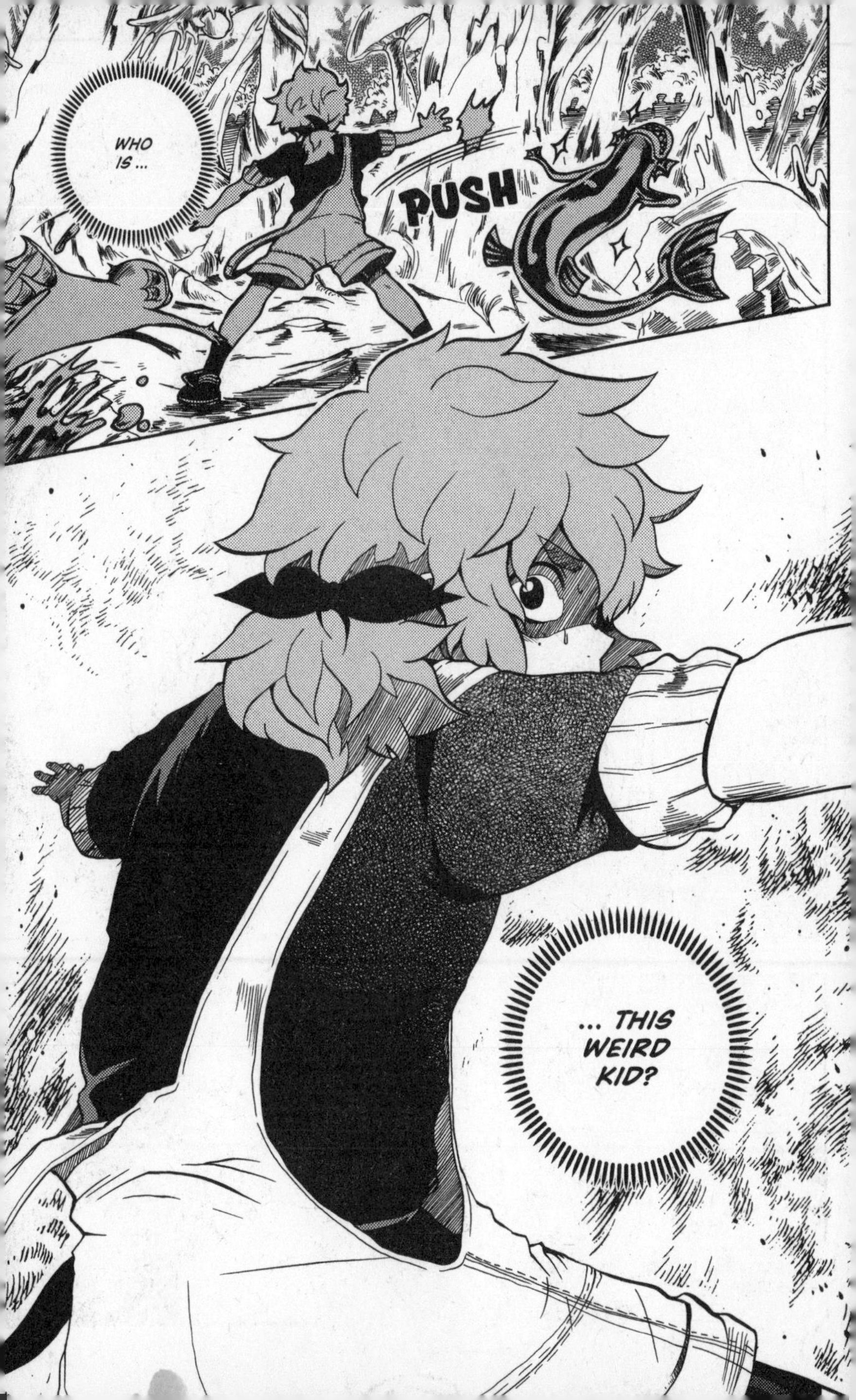
WHO IS...
PUSH
... THIS WEIRD KID?

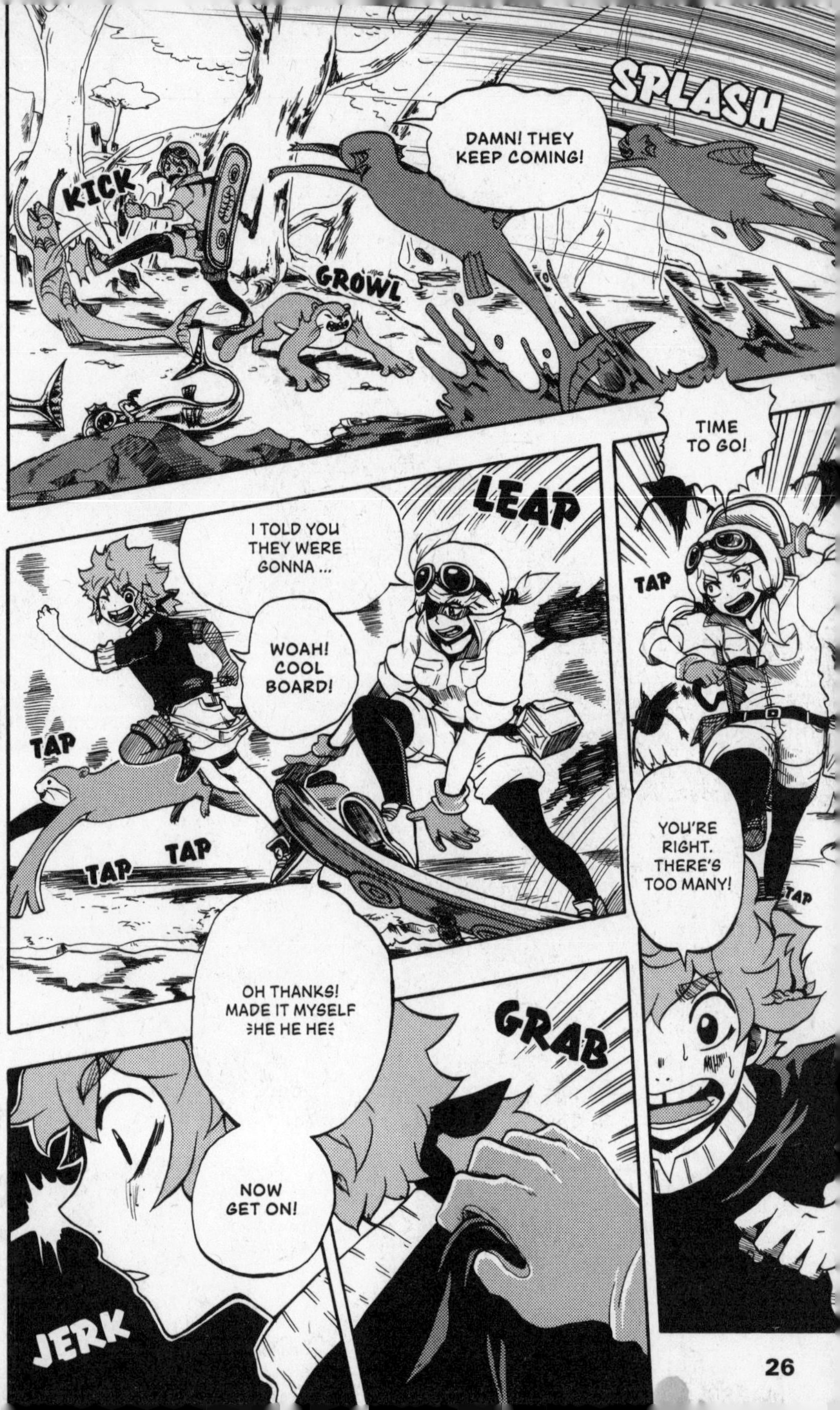
SPLASH
DAMN! THEY KEEP COMING!
GROWL
KICK
TIME TO GO!
TAP
YOU'RE RIGHT. THERE'S TOO MANY!
TAP
LEAP
I TOLD YOU THEY WERE GONNA ...
WOAH! COOL BOARD!
TAP
TAP
TAP
GRAB
OH THANKS! MADE IT MYSELF ≡HE HE HE≡
NOW GET ON!
JERK

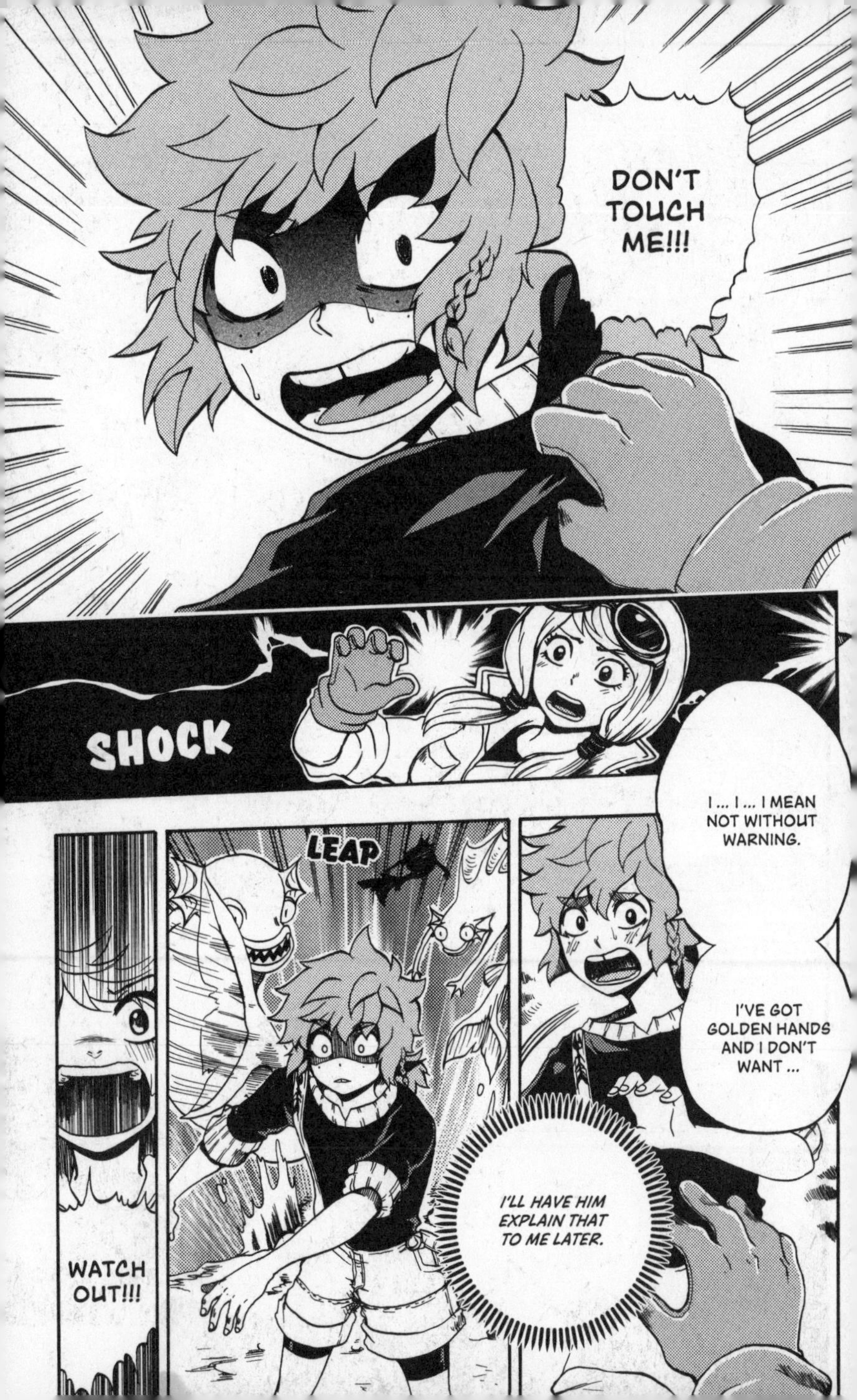
DON'T TOUCH ME!!!
SHOCK
I ... I ... I MEAN NOT WITHOUT WARNING.
I'VE GOT GOLDEN HANDS AND I DON'T WANT ...
I'LL HAVE HIM EXPLAIN THAT TO ME LATER.
LEAP
WATCH OUT!!!

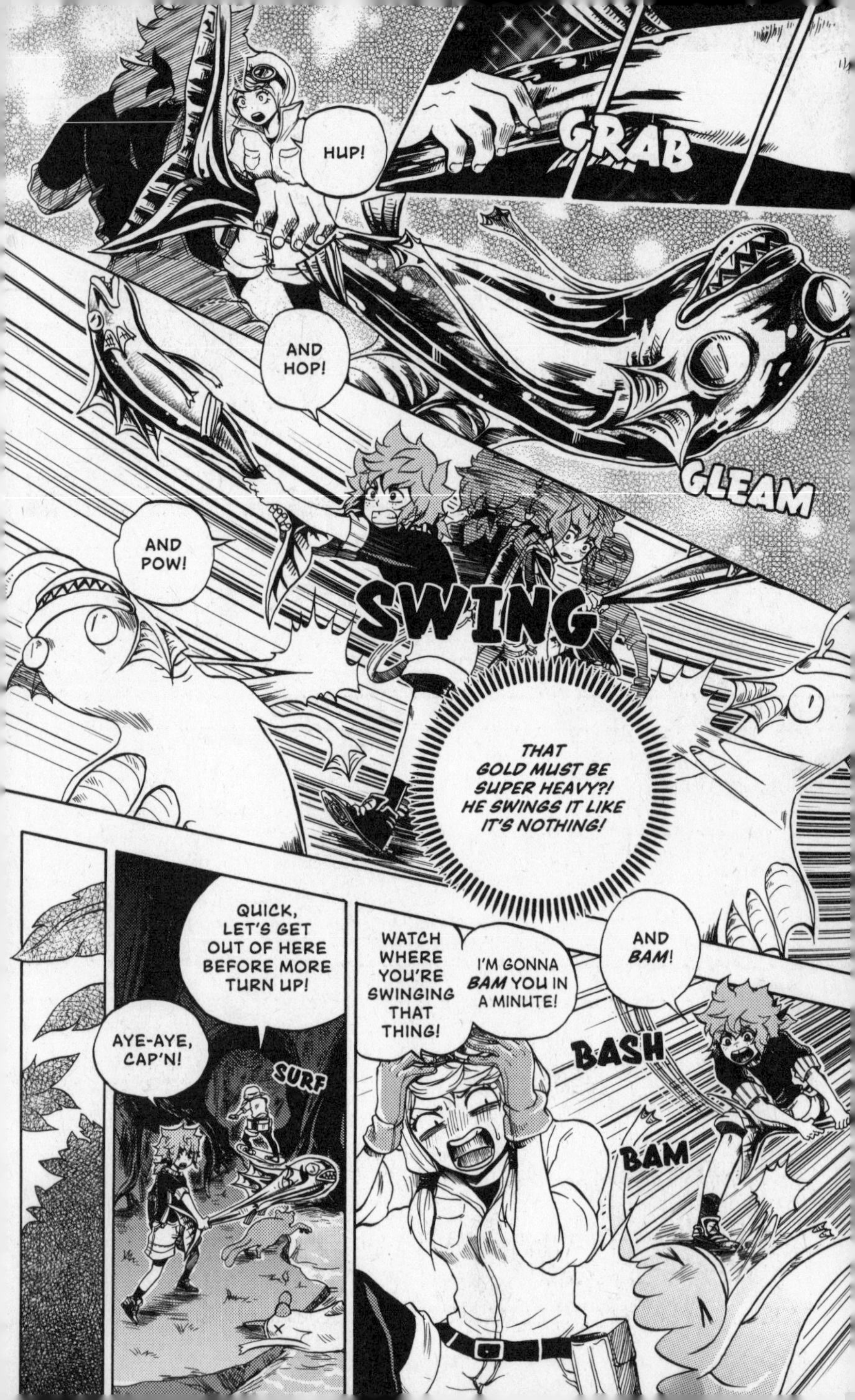
GRAB
HUP!
GLEAM
AND HOP!
AND POW!
SWING
THAT GOLD MUST BE SUPER HEAVY?! HE SWINGS IT LIKE IT'S NOTHING!
AND BAM!
BASH
BAM
I'M GONNA BAM YOU IN A MINUTE!
WATCH WHERE YOU'RE SWINGING THAT THING!
QUICK, LET'S GET OUT OF HERE BEFORE MORE TURN UP!
SURF
AYE-AYE, CAP'N!

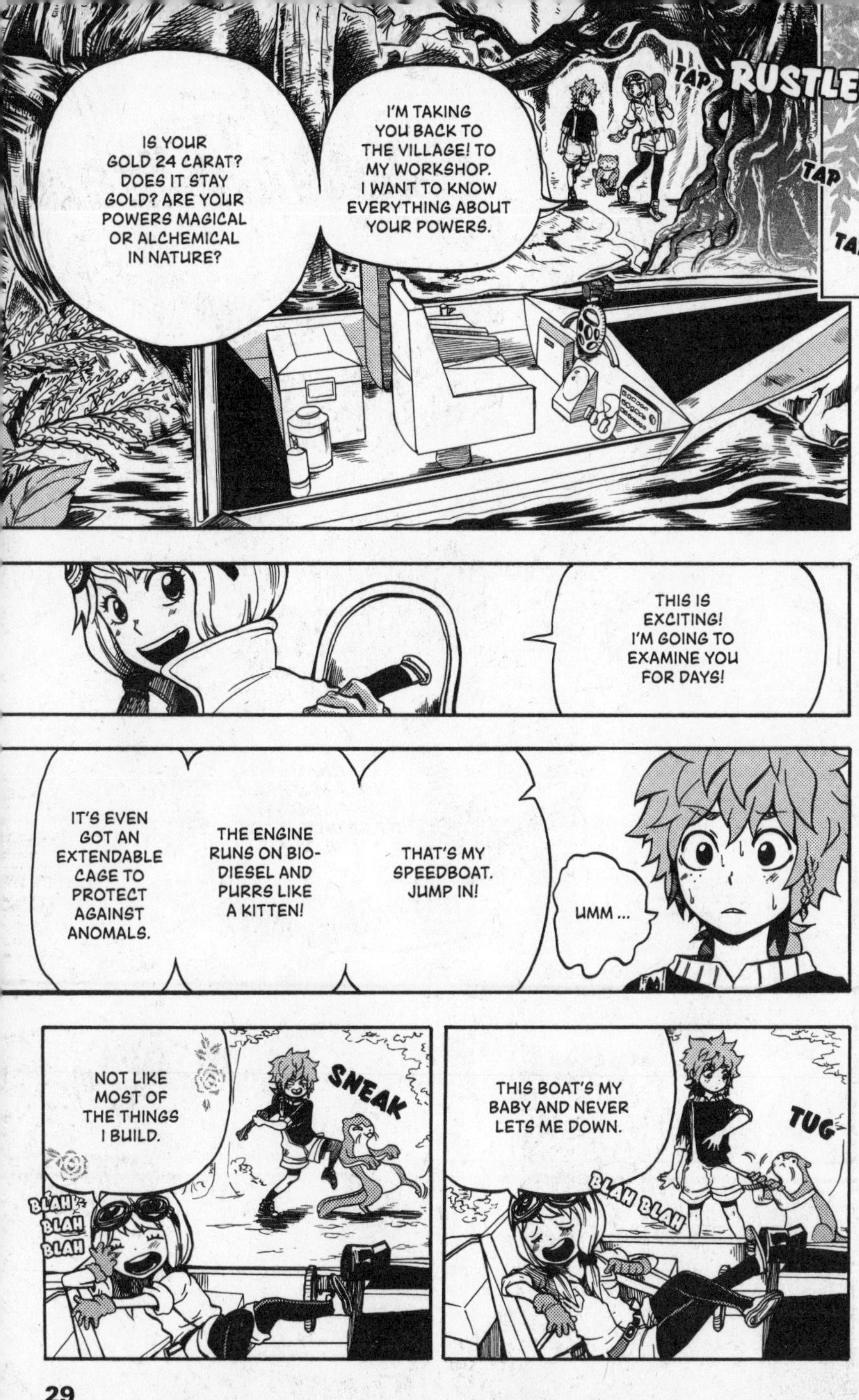
RUSTLE
TAP
TAP
TAP
I'M TAKING YOU BACK TO THE VILLAGE! TO MY WORKSHOP. I WANT TO KNOW EVERYTHING ABOUT YOUR POWERS.
IS YOUR GOLD 24 CARAT? DOES IT STAY GOLD? ARE YOUR POWERS MAGICAL OR ALCHEMICAL IN NATURE?
THIS IS EXCITING! I'M GOING TO EXAMINE YOU FOR DAYS!
UMM ...
THAT'S MY SPEEDBOAT. JUMP IN!
THE ENGINE RUNS ON BIO-DIESEL AND PURRS LIKE A KITTEN!
IT'S EVEN GOT AN EXTENDABLE CAGE TO PROTECT AGAINST ANOMALS.
THIS BOAT'S MY BABY AND NEVER LETS ME DOWN.
TUG
BLAH BLAH
NOT LIKE MOST OF THE THINGS I BUILD.
SNEAK
BLAH BLAH BLAH

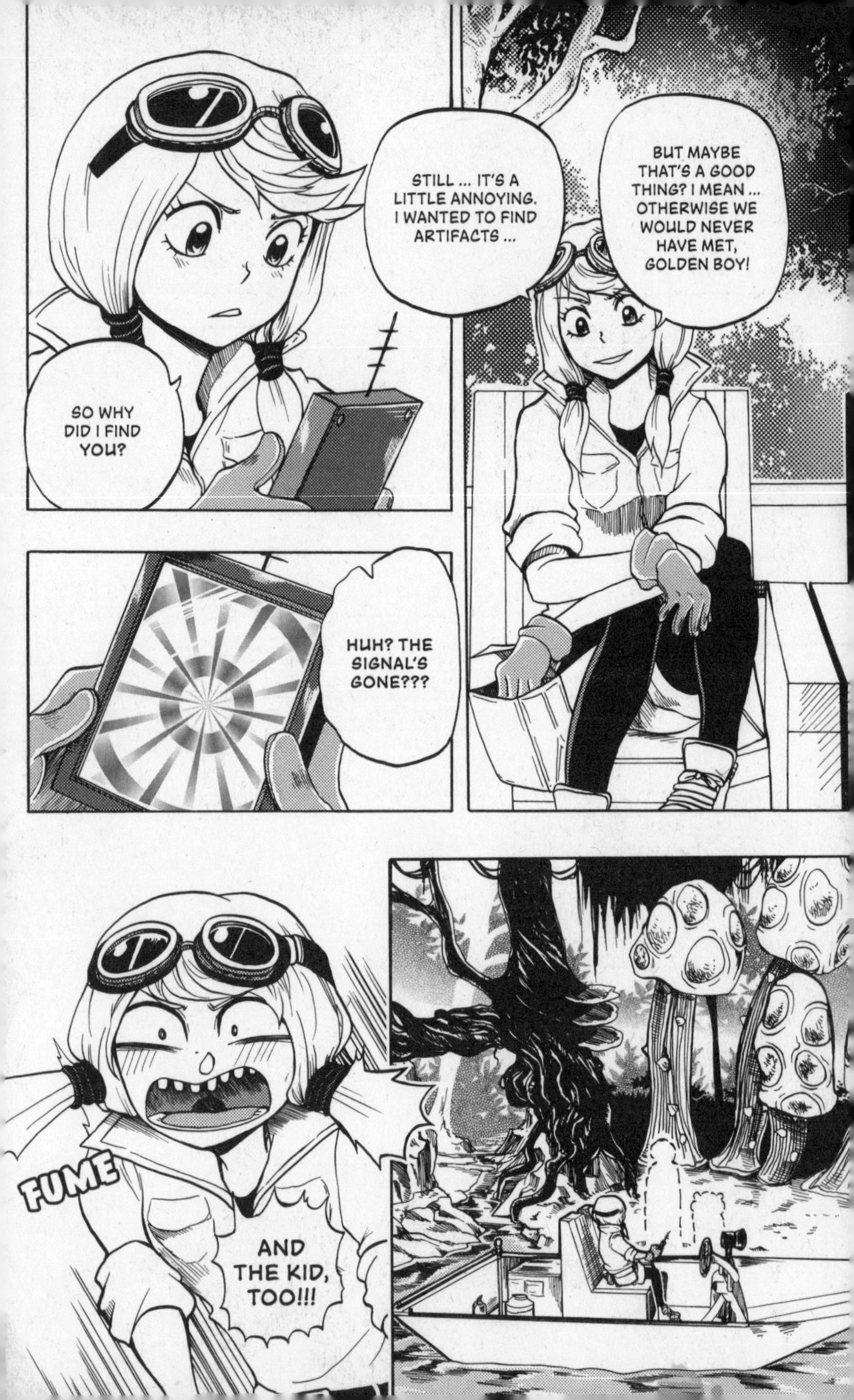
BUT MAYBE THAT'S A GOOD THING? I MEAN ... OTHERWISE WE WOULD NEVER HAVE MET, GOLDEN BOY!
STILL ... IT'S A LITTLE ANNOYING. I WANTED TO FIND ARTIFACTS ...
SO WHY DID I FIND YOU?
HUH? THE SIGNAL'S GONE???
FUME
AND THE KID, TOO!!!

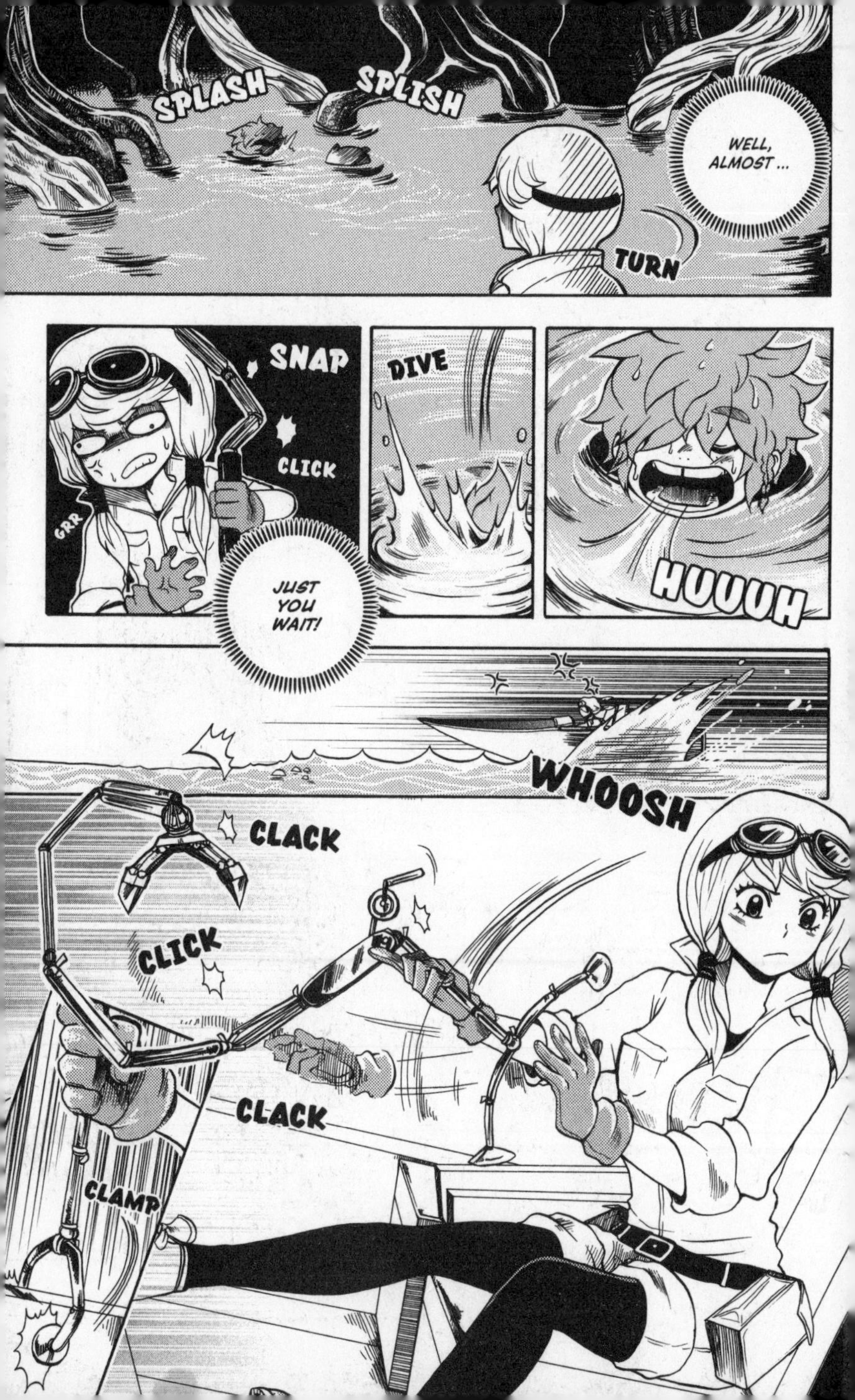
WELL, ALMOST ...
SPLISH
SPLASH
TURN
HUUUH
DIVE
SNAP
CLICK
GRR
JUST YOU WAIT!
WHOOSH
CLACK
CLICK
CLACK
CLAMP

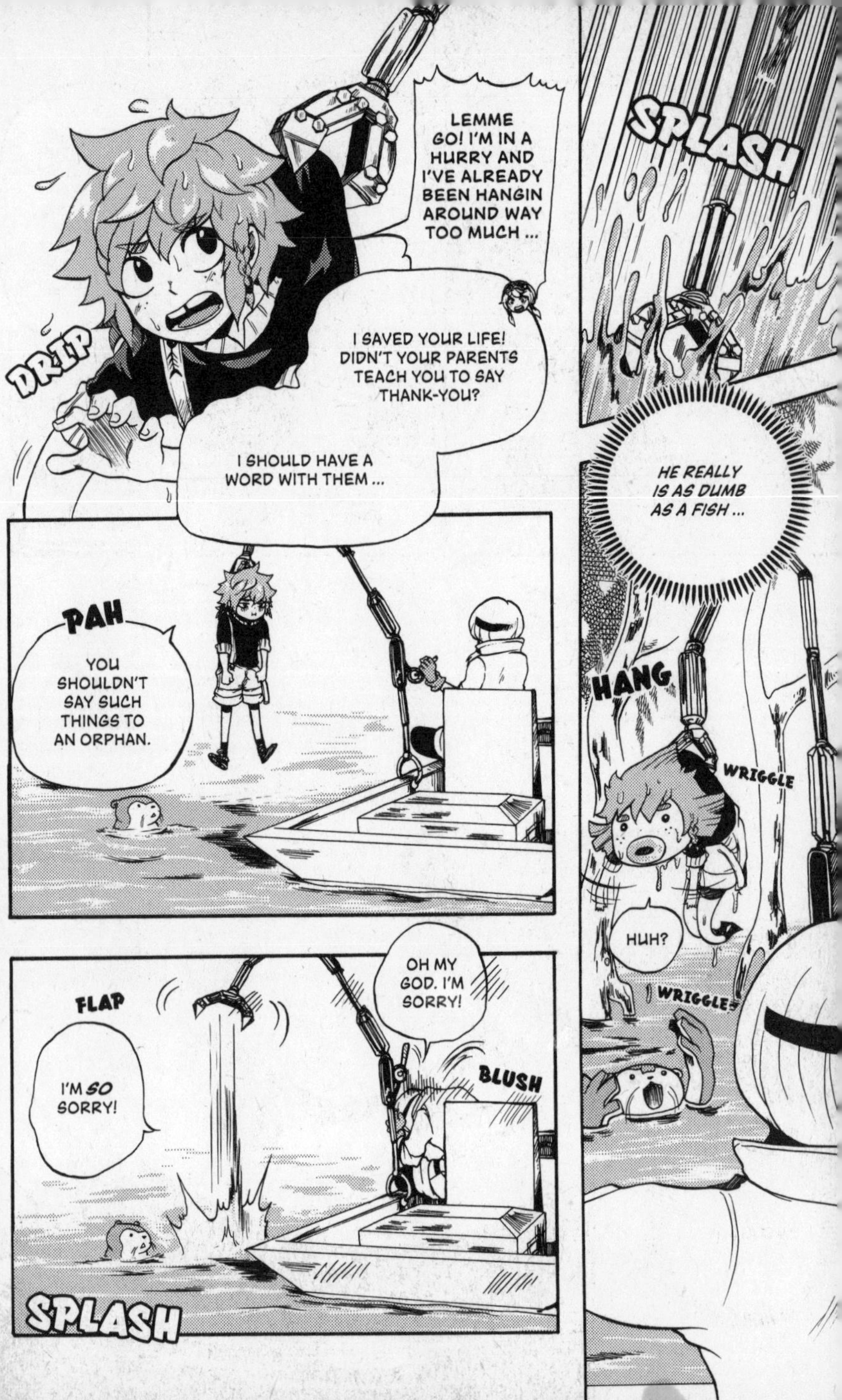
SPLASH
HE REALLY IS AS DUMB AS A FISH ...
HANG
WRIGGLE
HUH?
WRIGGLE
LEMME GO! I'M IN A HURRY AND I'VE ALREADY BEEN HANGIN AROUND WAY TOO MUCH ...
I SAVED YOUR LIFE! DIDN'T YOUR PARENTS TEACH YOU TO SAY THANK-YOU?
DRIP
I SHOULD HAVE A WORD WITH THEM ...
PAH
YOU SHOULDN'T SAY SUCH THINGS TO AN ORPHAN.
OH MY GOD. I'M SORRY!
BLUSH
FLAP
I'M SO SORRY!
SPLASH

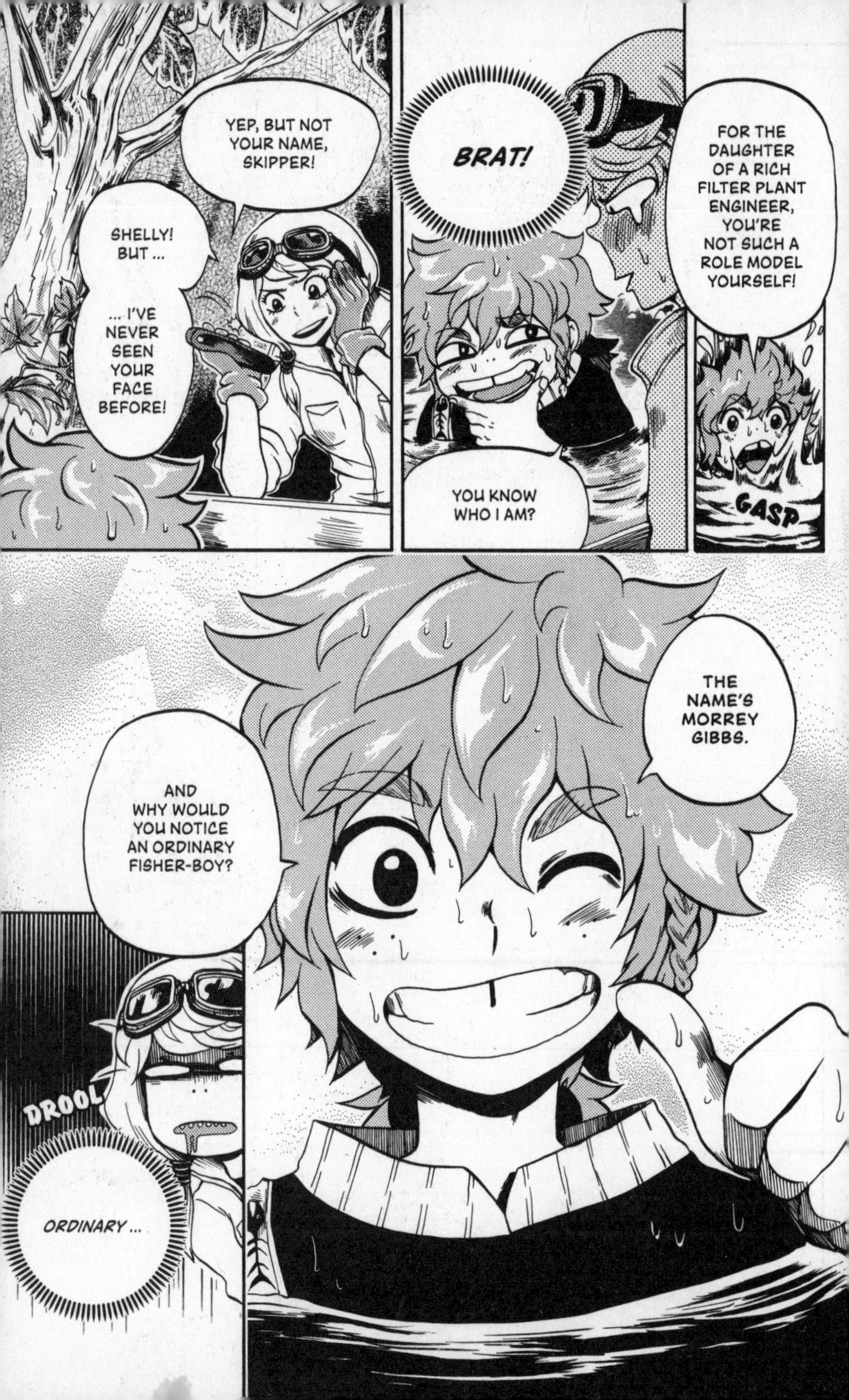
YEP, BUT NOT YOUR NAME, SKIPPER!
SHELLY! BUT ...
... I'VE NEVER SEEN YOUR FACE BEFORE!
BRAT!
YOU KNOW WHO I AM?
FOR THE DAUGHTER OF A RICH FILTER PLANT ENGINEER, YOU'RE NOT SUCH A ROLE MODEL YOURSELF!
GASP
THE NAME'S MORREY GIBBS.
AND WHY WOULD YOU NOTICE AN ORDINARY FISHER-BOY?
DROOL
ORDINARY ...

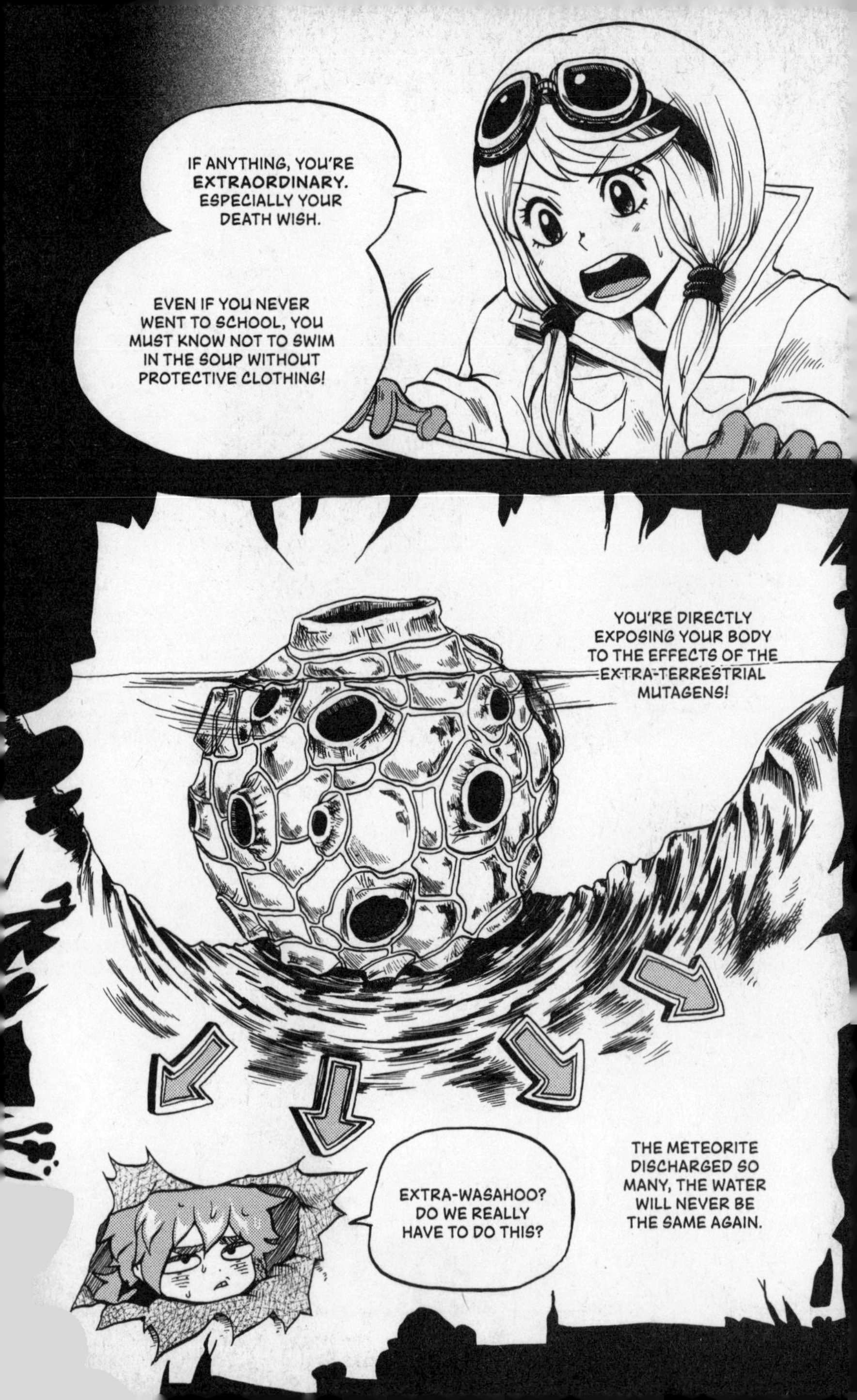
IF ANYTHING, YOU'RE EXTRAORDINARY. ESPECIALLY YOUR DEATH WISH.
EVEN IF YOU NEVER WENT TO SCHOOL, YOU MUST KNOW NOT TO SWIM IN THE SOUP WITHOUT PROTECTIVE CLOTHING!
YOU'RE DIRECTLY EXPOSING YOUR BODY TO THE EFFECTS OF THE EXTRA-TERRESTRIAL MUTAGENS!
THE METEORITE DISCHARGED SO MANY, THE WATER WILL NEVER BE THE SAME AGAIN.
EXTRA-WASAHOO? DO WE REALLY HAVE TO DO THIS?

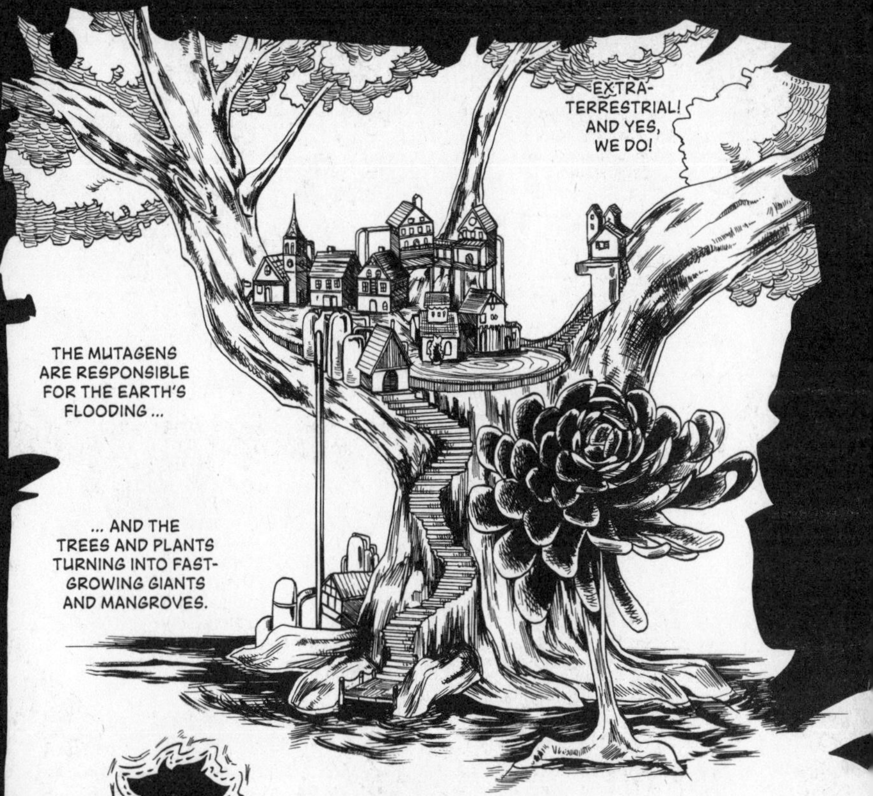
EXTRA-TERRESTRIAL! AND YES, WE DO!
THE MUTAGENS ARE RESPONSIBLE FOR THE EARTH'S FLOODING ...
... AND THE TREES AND PLANTS TURNING INTO FAST-GROWING GIANTS AND MANGROVES.

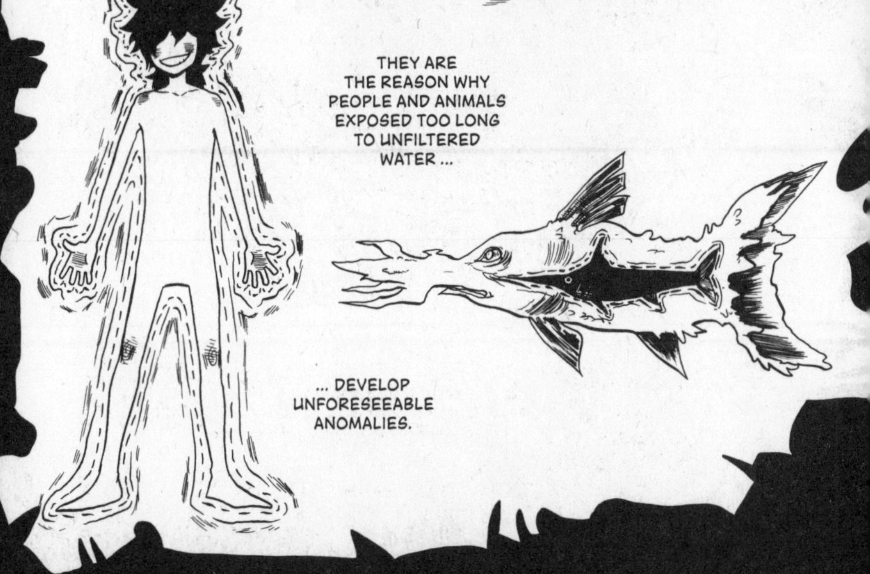
THEY ARE THE REASON WHY PEOPLE AND ANIMALS EXPOSED TOO LONG TO UNFILTERED WATER ...
... DEVELOP UNFORESEEABLE ANOMALIES.

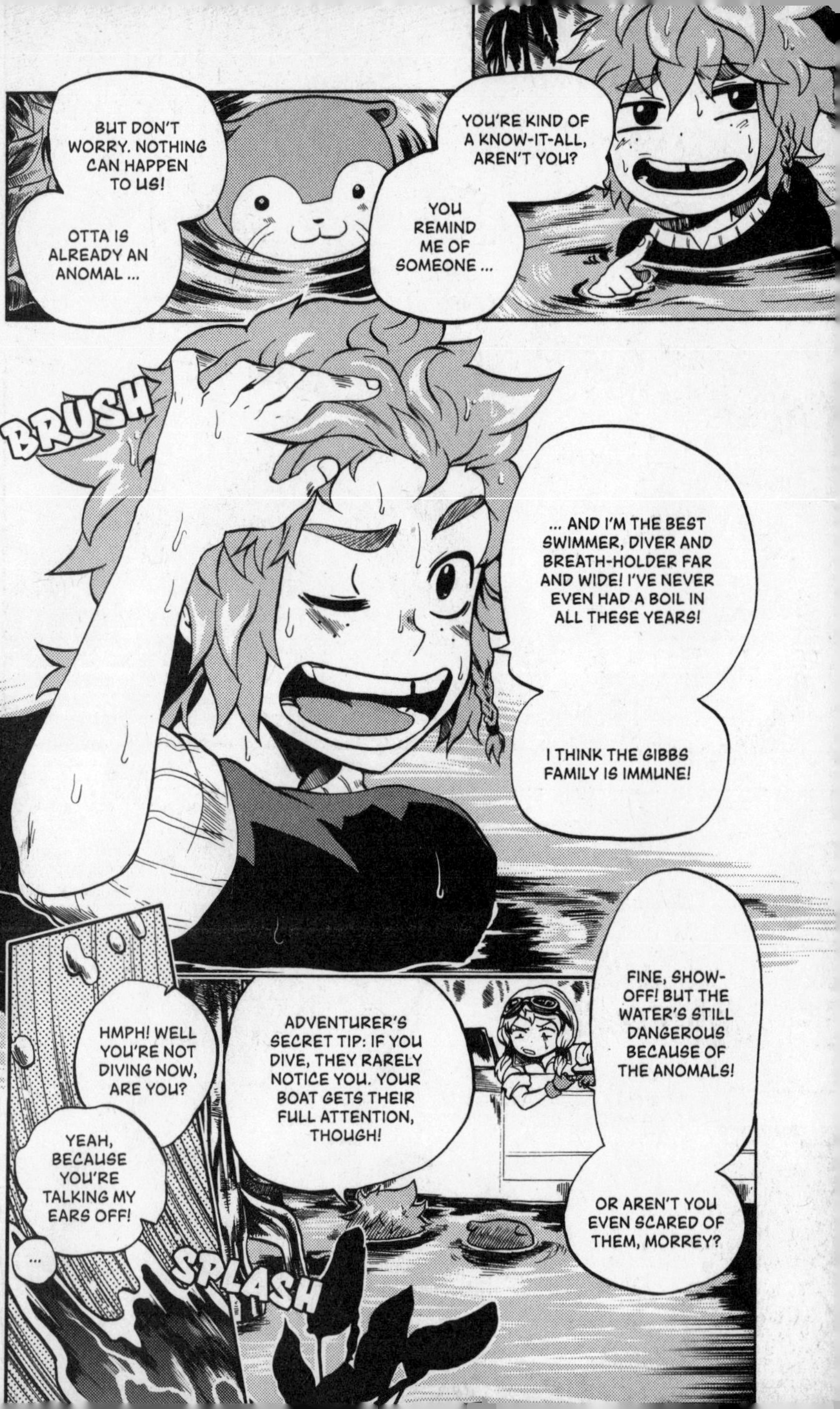
YOU'RE KIND OF A KNOW-IT-ALL, AREN'T YOU?
YOU REMIND ME OF SOMEONE ...
BUT DON'T WORRY. NOTHING CAN HAPPEN TO US!
OTTA IS ALREADY AN ANOMAL ...
BRUSH
... AND I'M THE BEST SWIMMER, DIVER AND BREATH-HOLDER FAR AND WIDE! I'VE NEVER EVEN HAD A BOIL IN ALL THESE YEARS!
I THINK THE GIBBS FAMILY IS IMMUNE!
FINE, SHOW-OFF! BUT THE WATER'S STILL DANGEROUS BECAUSE OF THE ANOMALS!
OR AREN'T YOU EVEN SCARED OF THEM, MORREY?
ADVENTURER'S SECRET TIP: IF YOU DIVE, THEY RARELY NOTICE YOU. YOUR BOAT GETS THEIR FULL ATTENTION, THOUGH!
HMPH! WELL YOU'RE NOT DIVING NOW, ARE YOU?
YEAH, BECAUSE YOU'RE TALKING MY EARS OFF!
...
SPLASH

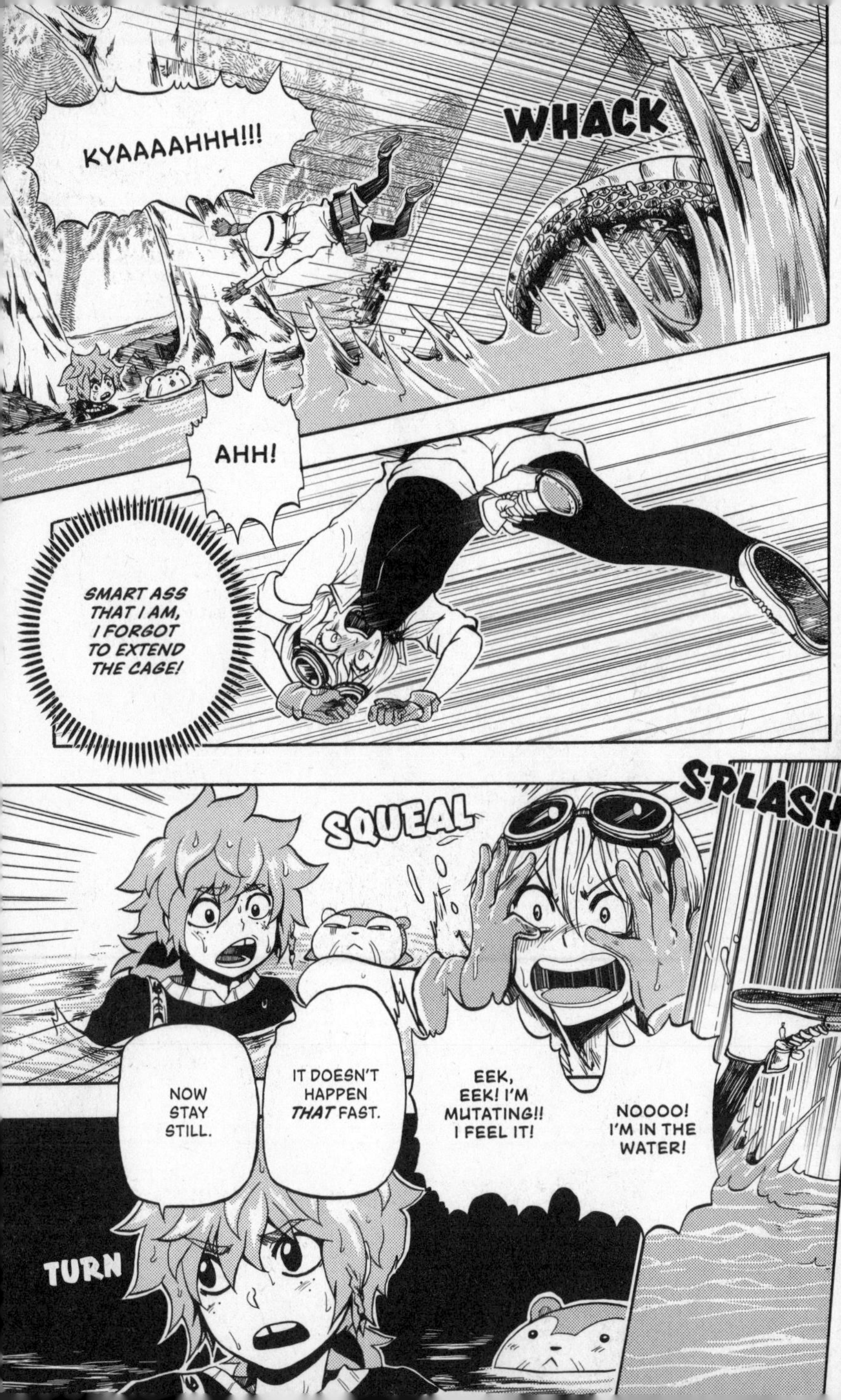
WHACK
KYAAAAHHH!!!
AHH!
SMART ASS THAT I AM, I FORGOT TO EXTEND THE CAGE!
SPLASH
SQUEAL
NOOOO! I'M IN THE WATER!
EEK, EEK! I'M MUTATING!! I FEEL IT!
IT DOESN'T HAPPEN *THAT* FAST.
NOW STAY STILL.
TURN

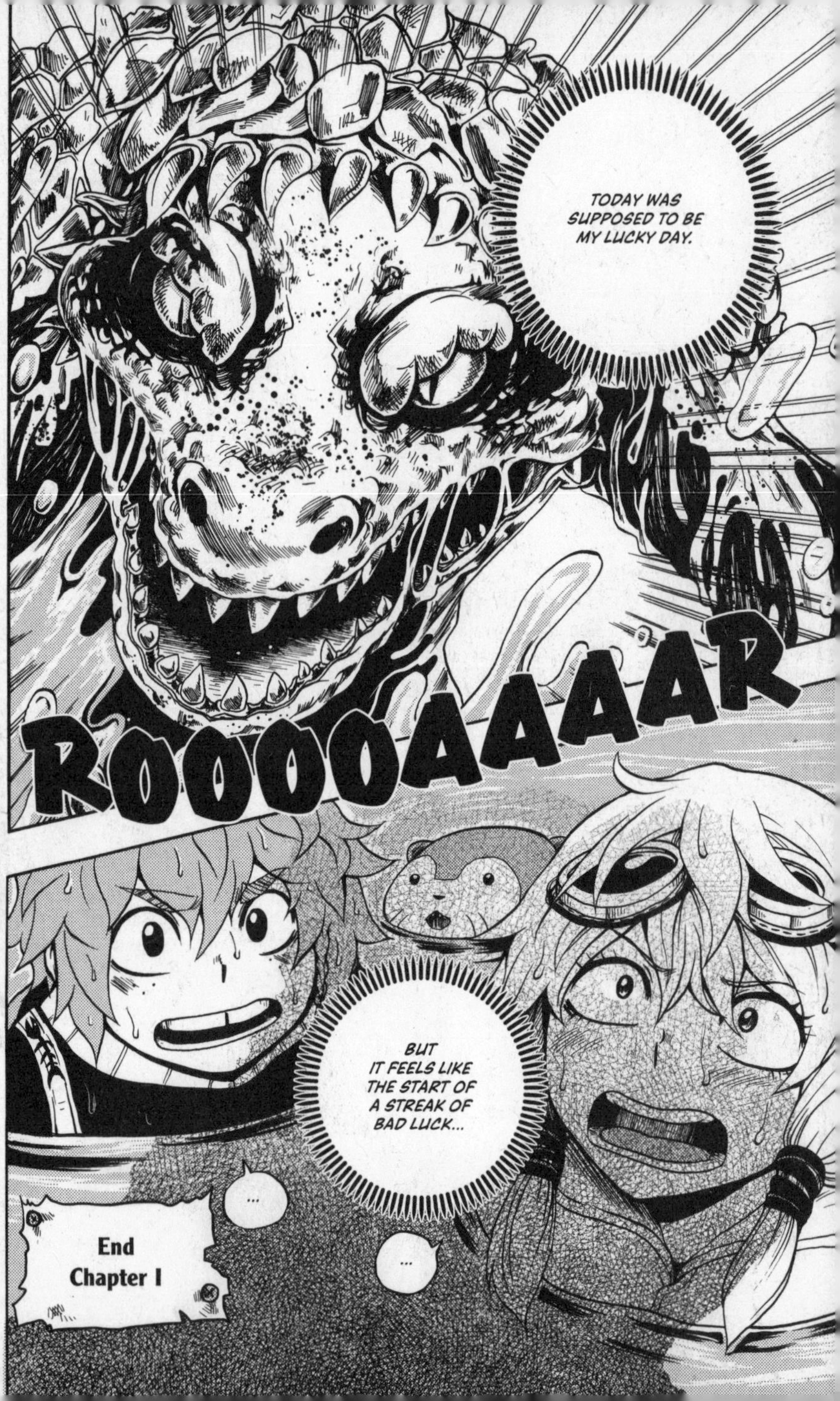
TODAY WAS SUPPOSED TO BE MY LUCKY DAY.
ROOOOAAAAAR
BUT IT FEELS LIKE THE START OF A STREAK OF BAD LUCK...
...
...
End Chapter 1

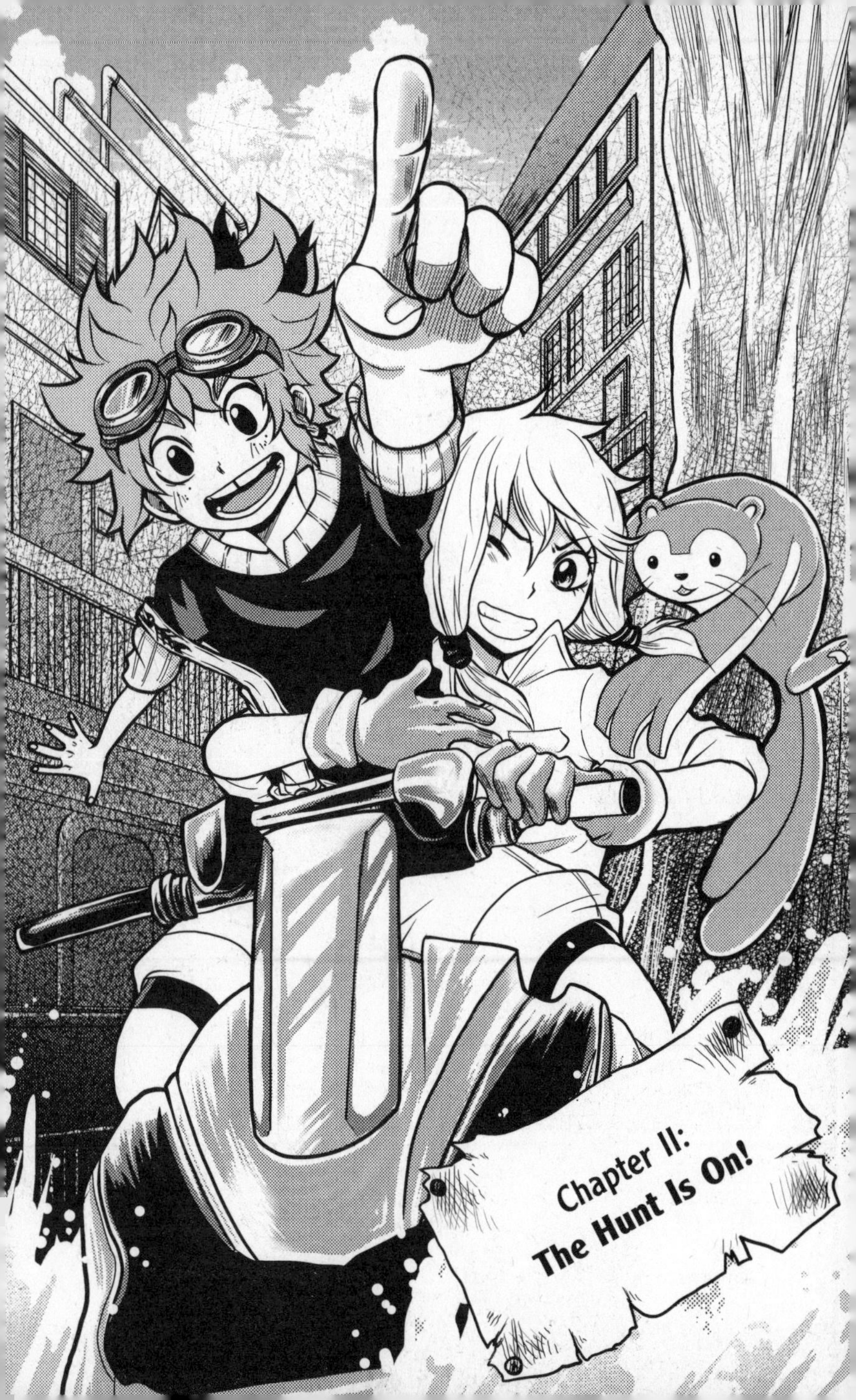
Chapter 11:
The Hunt Is On!

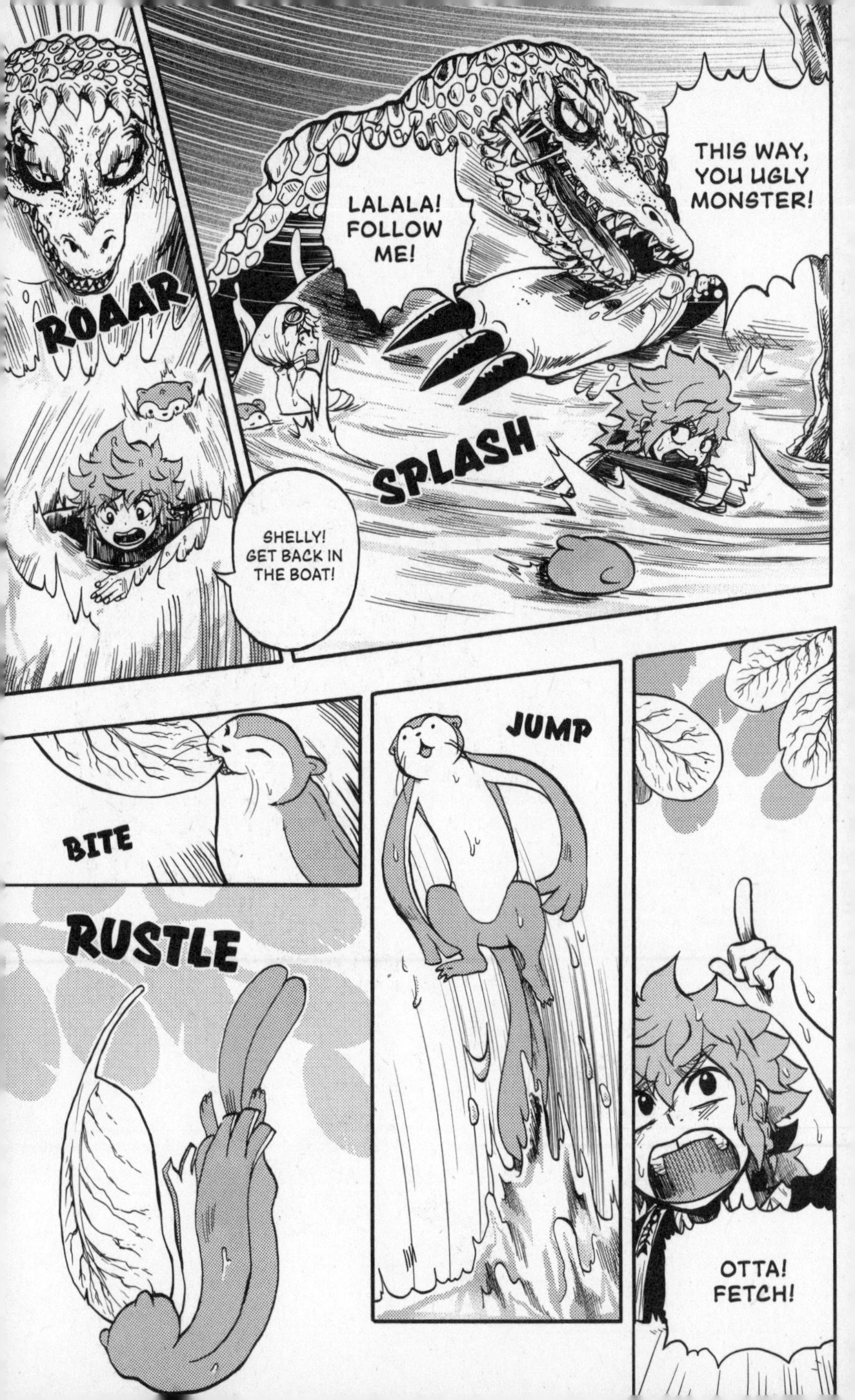
THIS WAY, YOU UGLY MONSTER!
LALALA! FOLLOW ME!
SPLASH
ROAAR
SHELLY! GET BACK IN THE BOAT!
OTTA! FETCH!
JUMP
BITE
RUSTLE

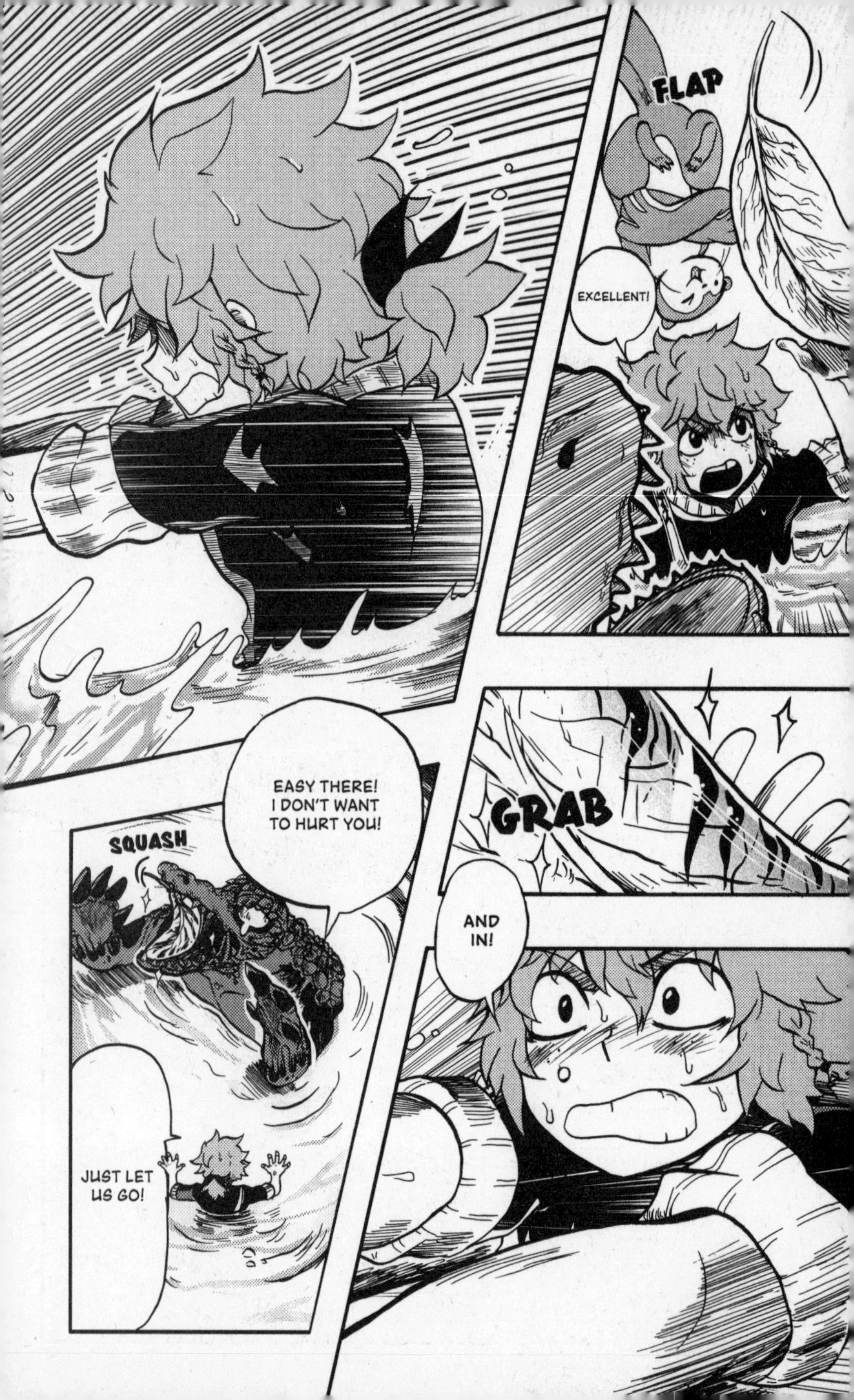
FLAP
EXCELLENT!
GRAB
AND IN!
EASY THERE! I DON'T WANT TO HURT YOU!
SQUASH
JUST LET US GO!

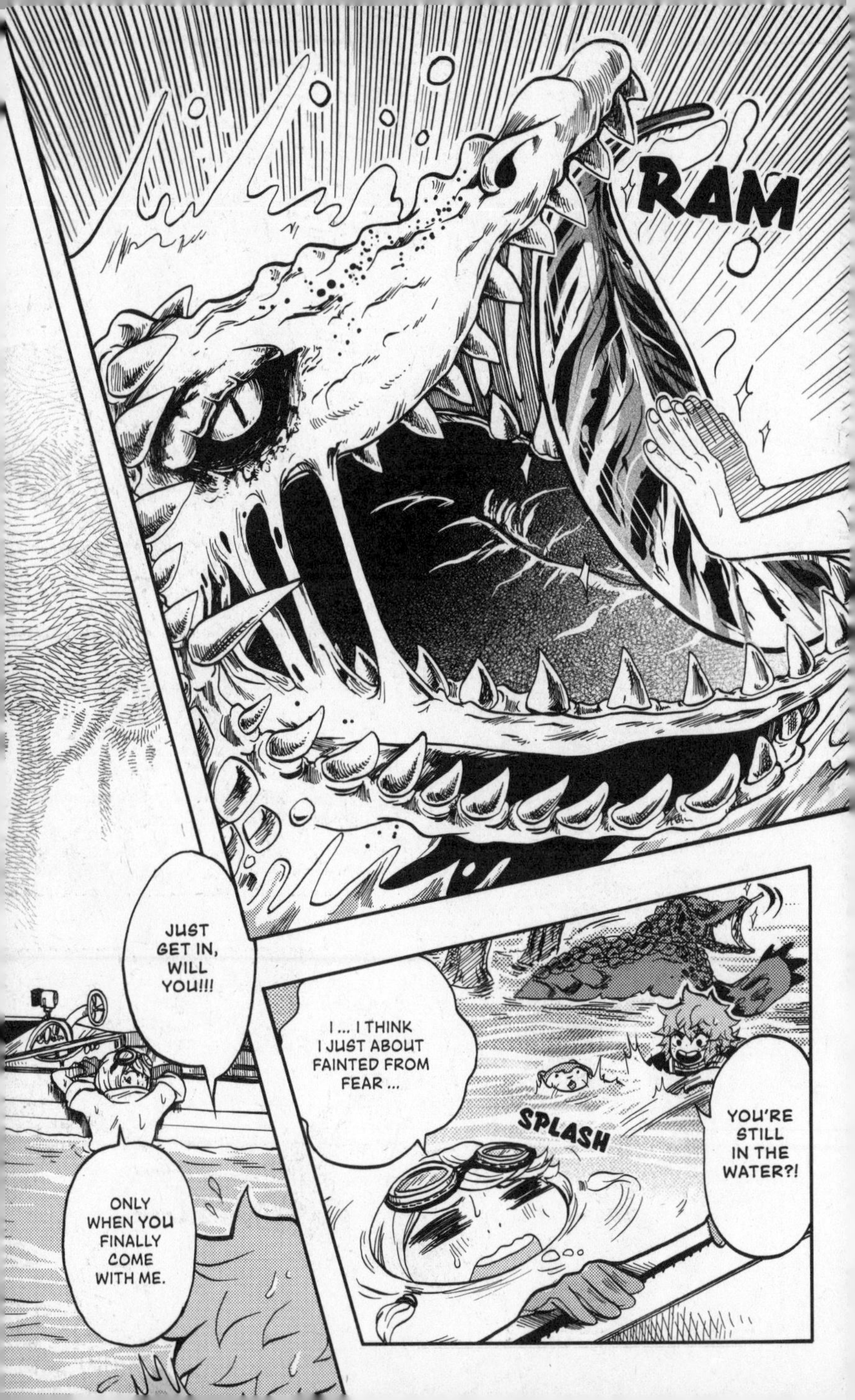
RAM
YOU'RE STILL IN THE WATER?!
SPLASH
I ... I THINK I JUST ABOUT FAINTED FROM FEAR ...
JUST GET IN, WILL YOU!!!
ONLY WHEN YOU FINALLY COME WITH ME.

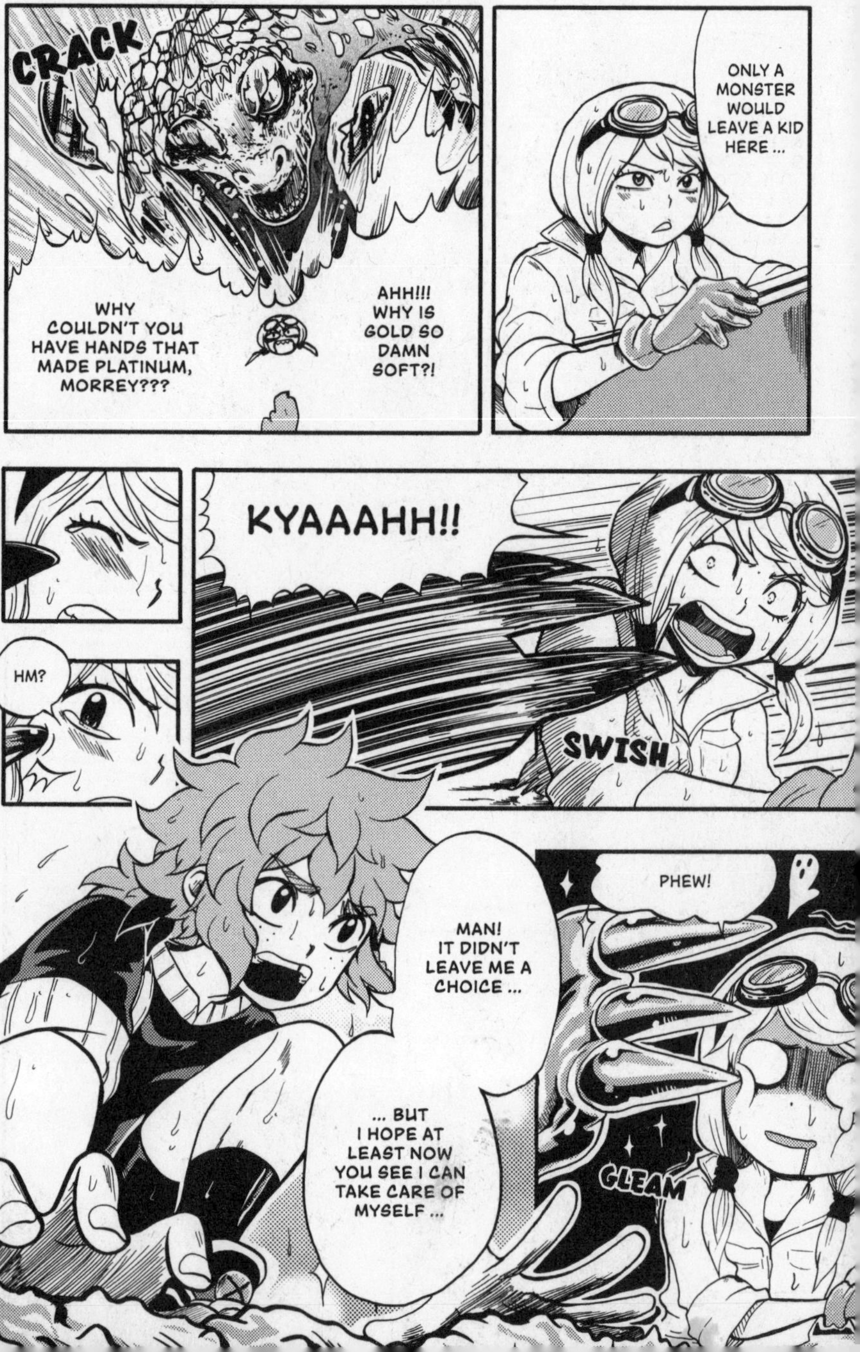
ONLY A MONSTER WOULD LEAVE A KID HERE ...
CRACK
AHH!!! WHY IS GOLD SO DAMN SOFT?!
WHY COULDN'T YOU HAVE HANDS THAT MADE PLATINUM, MORREY???
KYAAAHH!!
SWISH
HM?
PHEW!
GLEAM
MAN! IT DIDN'T LEAVE ME A CHOICE ...
... BUT I HOPE AT LEAST NOW YOU SEE I CAN TAKE CARE OF MYSELF ...

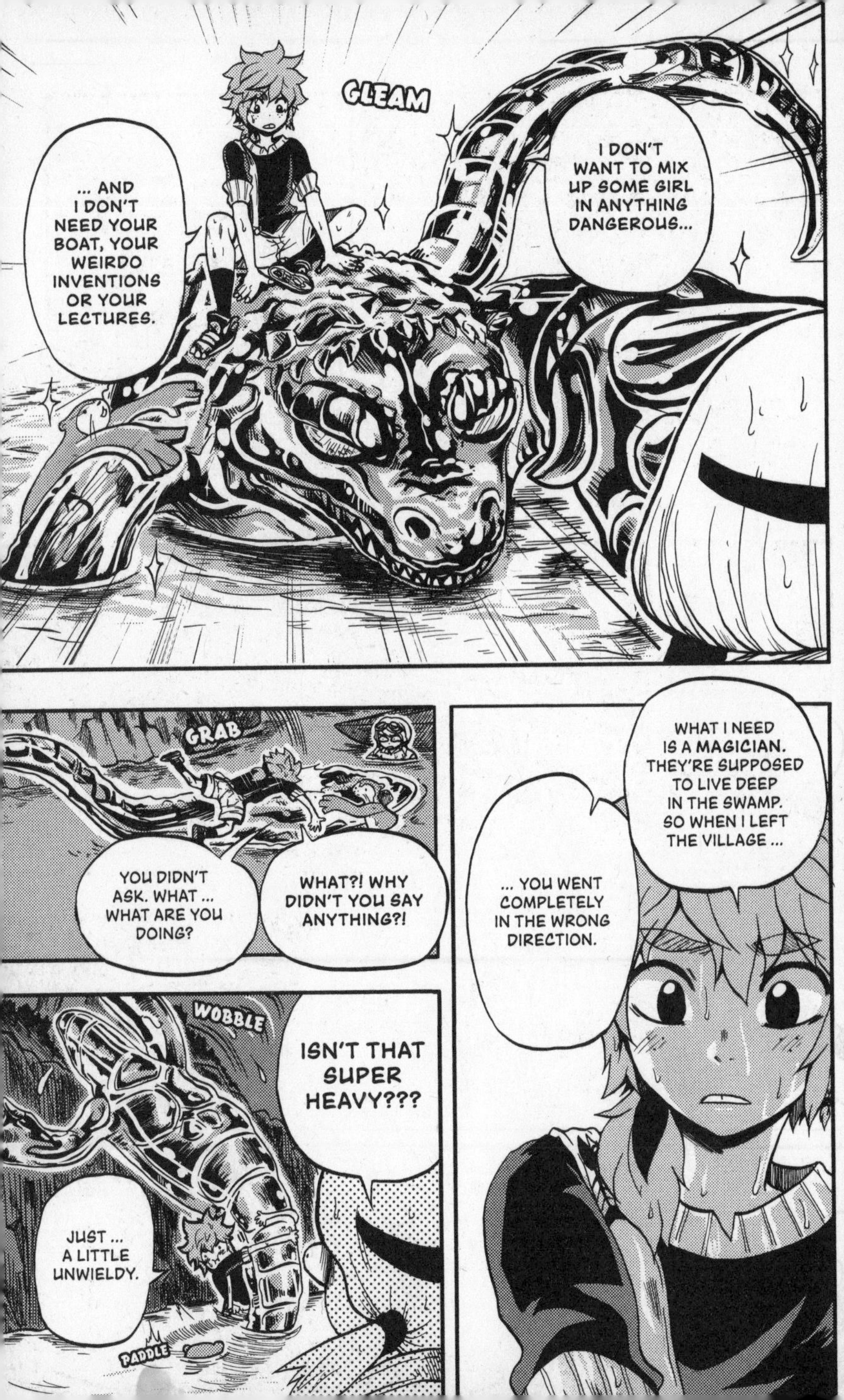
I DON'T WANT TO MIX UP SOME GIRL IN ANYTHING DANGEROUS...
GLEAM
... AND I DON'T NEED YOUR BOAT, YOUR WEIRDO INVENTIONS OR YOUR LECTURES.
WHAT I NEED IS A MAGICIAN. THEY'RE SUPPOSED TO LIVE DEEP IN THE SWAMP. SO WHEN I LEFT THE VILLAGE ...
... YOU WENT COMPLETELY IN THE WRONG DIRECTION.
GRAB
WHAT?! WHY DIDN'T YOU SAY ANYTHING?!
YOU DIDN'T ASK. WHAT ... WHAT ARE YOU DOING?
WOBBLE
ISN'T THAT SUPER HEAVY???
JUST ... A LITTLE UNWIELDY.
PADDLE

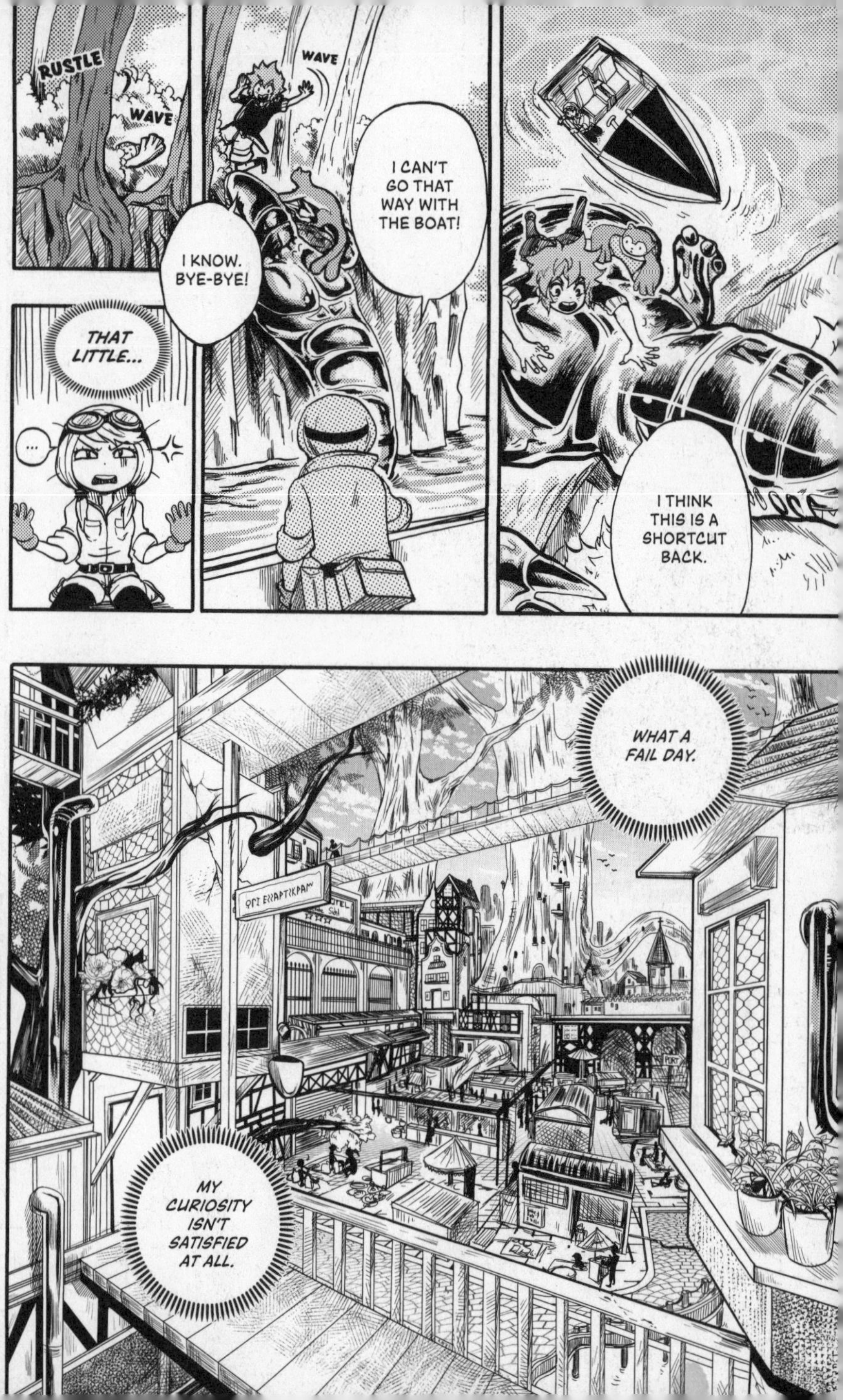
I THINK THIS IS A SHORTCUT BACK.
WAVE
I CAN'T GO THAT WAY WITH THE BOAT!
I KNOW. BYE-BYE!
RUSTLE
WAVE
THAT LITTLE...
...
WHAT A FAIL DAY.
MY CURIOSITY ISN'T SATISFIED AT ALL.

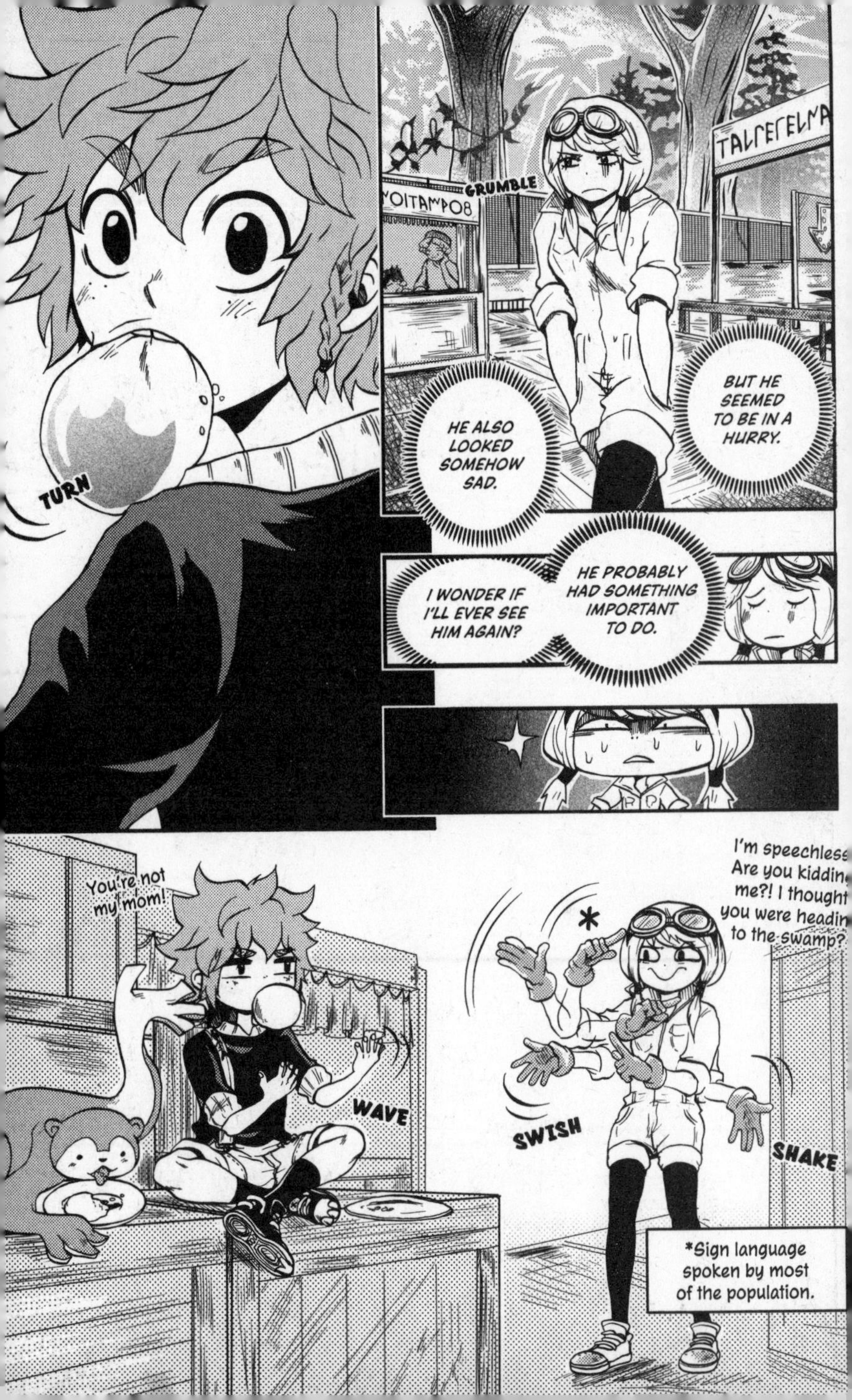
BUT HE SEEMED TO BE IN A HURRY.
HE ALSO LOOKED SOMEHOW SAD.
GRUMBLE
HE PROBABLY HAD SOMETHING IMPORTANT TO DO.
I WONDER IF I'LL EVER SEE HIM AGAIN?
TURN
I'm speechless Are you kidding me?! I thought you were headin to the swamp?
*
SHAKE
SWISH
*Sign language spoken by most of the population.
You're not my mom!
WAVE

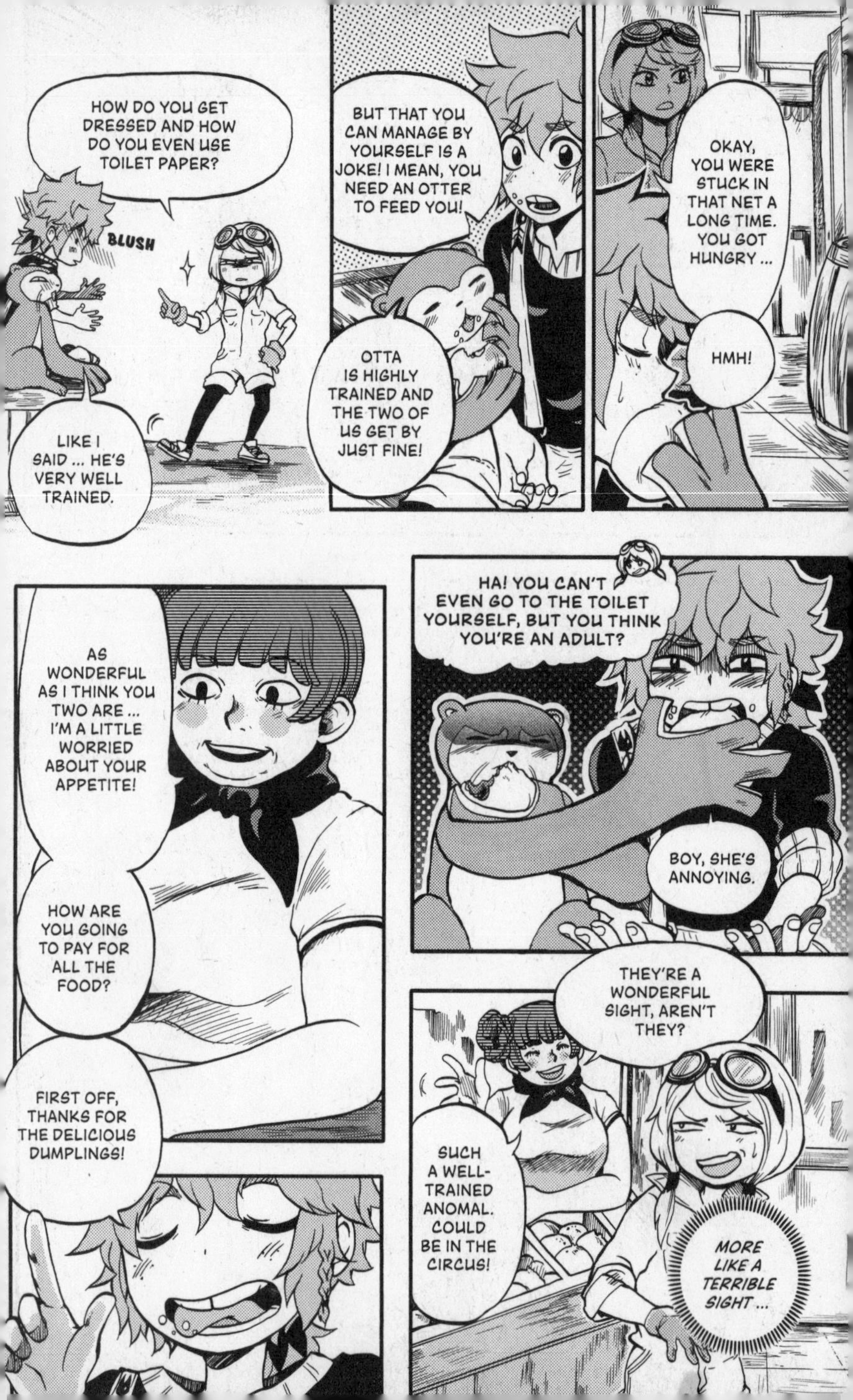
OKAY, YOU WERE STUCK IN THAT NET A LONG TIME. YOU GOT HUNGRY ...
HMH!
BUT THAT YOU CAN MANAGE BY YOURSELF IS A JOKE! I MEAN, YOU NEED AN OTTER TO FEED YOU!
OTTA IS HIGHLY TRAINED AND THE TWO OF US GET BY JUST FINE!
HOW DO YOU GET DRESSED AND HOW DO YOU EVEN USE TOILET PAPER?
BLUSH
LIKE I SAID ... HE'S VERY WELL TRAINED.
HA! YOU CAN'T EVEN GO TO THE TOILET YOURSELF, BUT YOU THINK YOU'RE AN ADULT?
BOY, SHE'S ANNOYING.
THEY'RE A WONDERFUL SIGHT, AREN'T THEY?
SUCH A WELL-TRAINED ANOMAL. COULD BE IN THE CIRCUS!
MORE LIKE A TERRIBLE SIGHT ...
AS WONDERFUL AS I THINK YOU TWO ARE ... I'M A LITTLE WORRIED ABOUT YOUR APPETITE!
HOW ARE YOU GOING TO PAY FOR ALL THE FOOD?
FIRST OFF, THANKS FOR THE DELICIOUS DUMPLINGS!

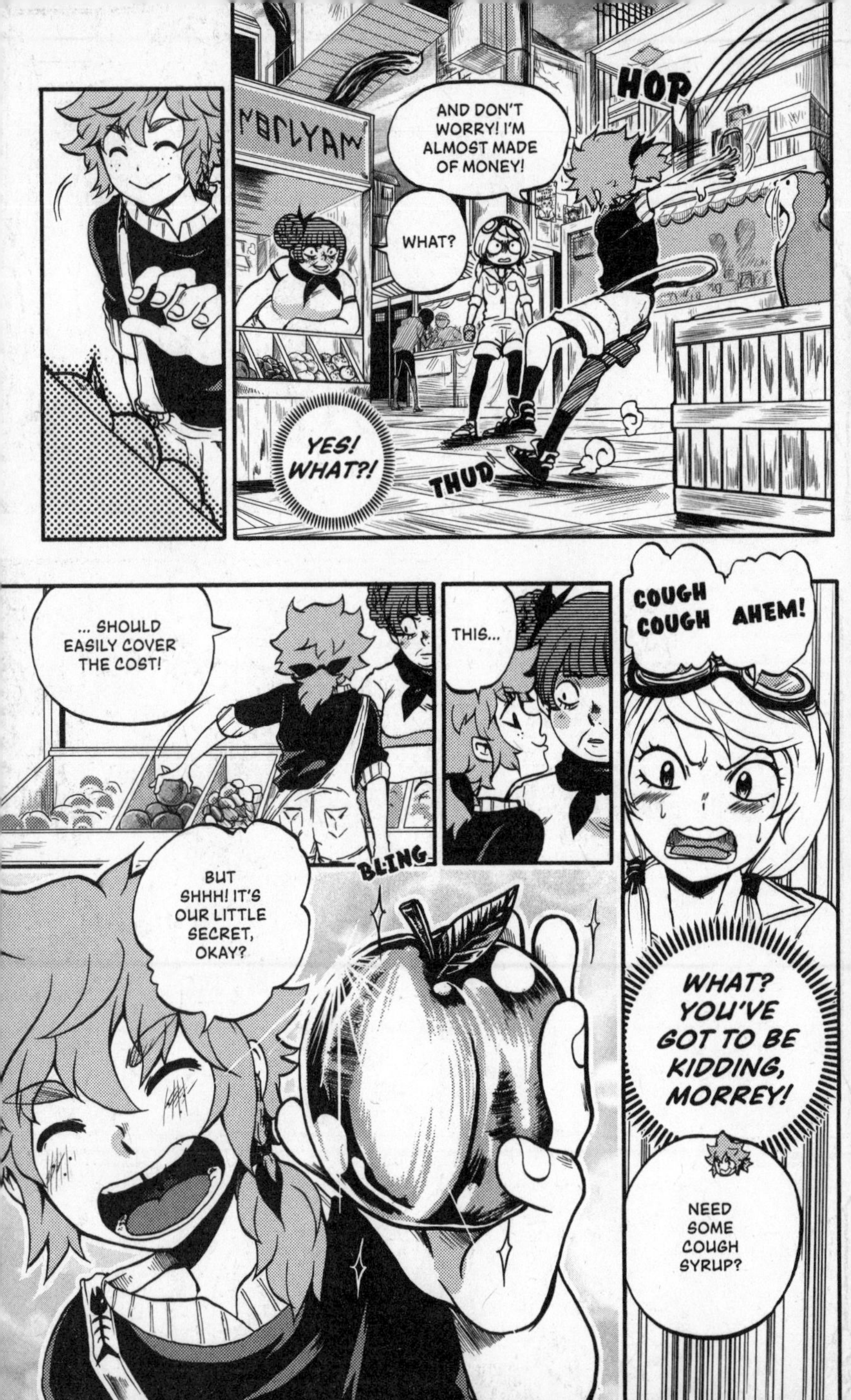

HOP
AND DON'T WORRY! I'M ALMOST MADE OF MONEY!
WHAT?
YES! WHAT?!
THUD
COUGH COUGH AHEM!
WHAT? YOU'VE GOT TO BE KIDDING, MORREY!
NEED SOME COUGH SYRUP?
THIS...
... SHOULD EASILY COVER THE COST!
BLING
BUT SHHH! IT'S OUR LITTLE SECRET, OKAY?

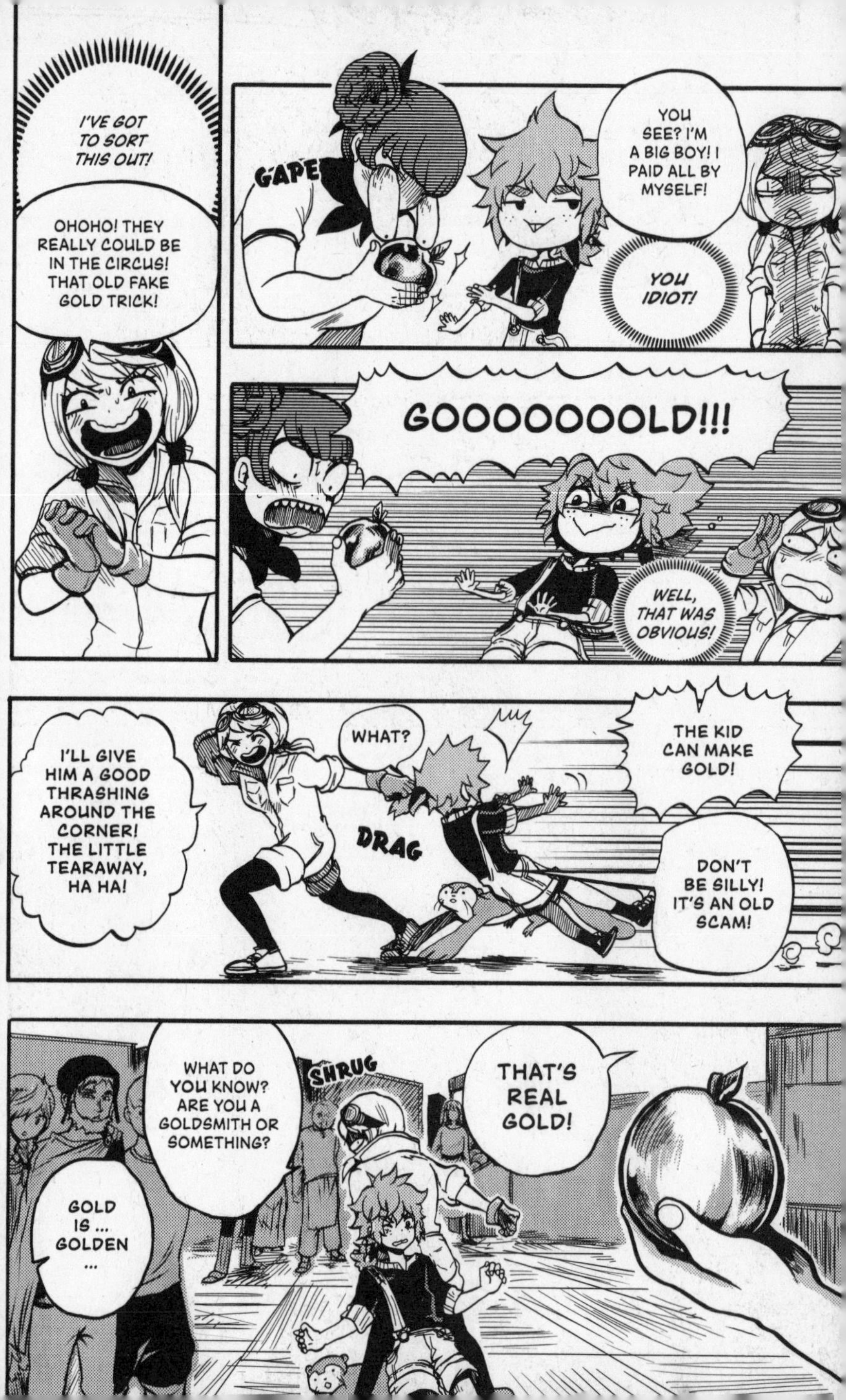
YOU SEE? I'M A BIG BOY! I PAID ALL BY MYSELF!
YOU IDIOT!
GAPE
GOOOOOOOLD!!!
WELL, THAT WAS OBVIOUS!
I'VE GOT TO SORT THIS OUT!
OHOHO! THEY REALLY COULD BE IN THE CIRCUS! THAT OLD FAKE GOLD TRICK!
THE KID CAN MAKE GOLD!
WHAT?
DON'T BE SILLY! IT'S AN OLD SCAM!
I'LL GIVE HIM A GOOD THRASHING AROUND THE CORNER! THE LITTLE TEARAWAY, HA HA!
DRAG
THAT'S REAL GOLD!
SHRUG
WHAT DO YOU KNOW? ARE YOU A GOLDSMITH OR SOMETHING?
GOLD IS ... GOLDEN ...

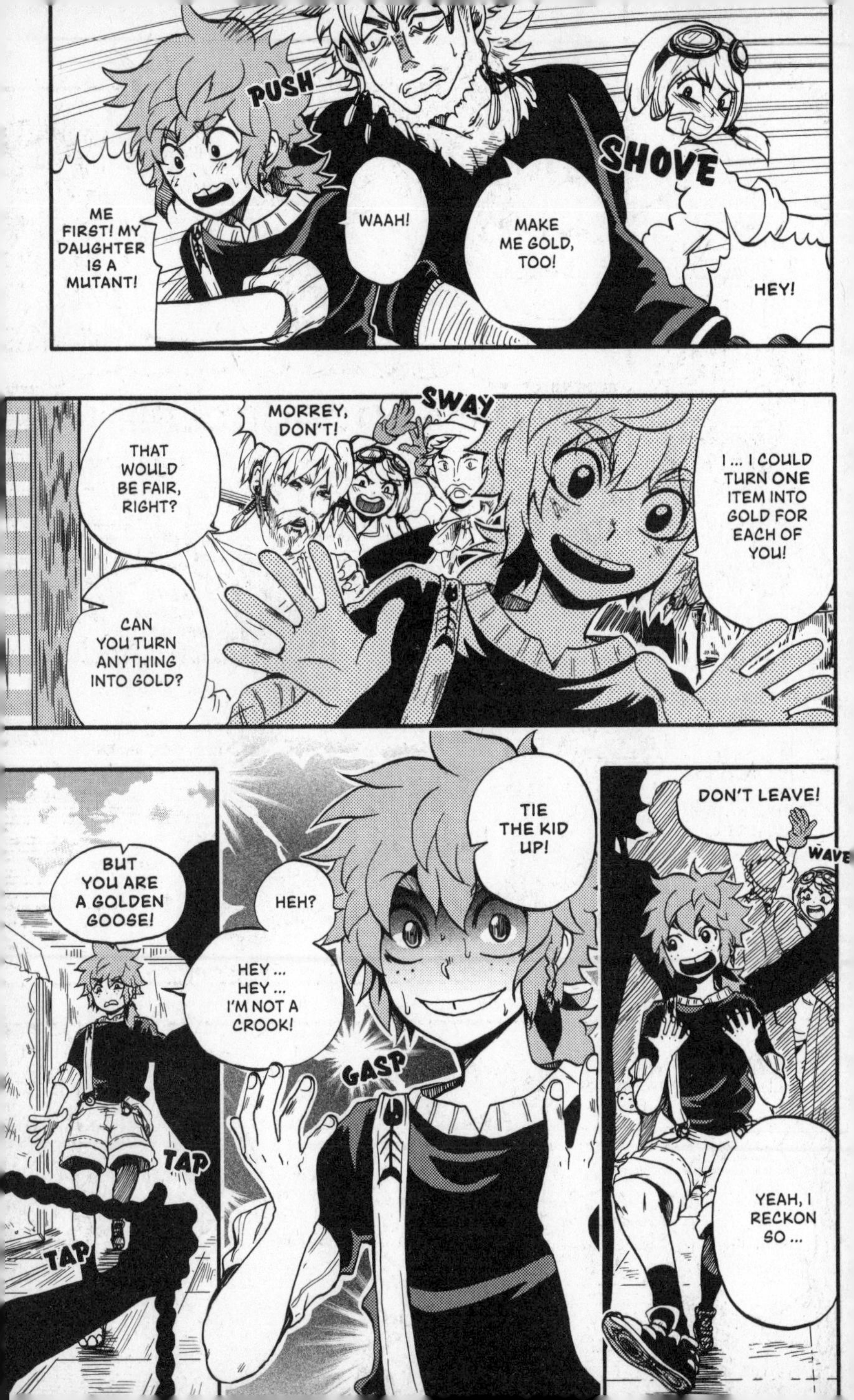
HEY!
SHOVE
MAKE ME GOLD, TOO!
WAAH!
PUSH
ME FIRST! MY DAUGHTER IS A MUTANT!
I ... I COULD TURN ONE ITEM INTO GOLD FOR EACH OF YOU!
SWAY
MORREY, DON'T!
THAT WOULD BE FAIR, RIGHT?
CAN YOU TURN ANYTHING INTO GOLD?
DON'T LEAVE!
WAVE
YEAH, I RECKON SO ...
TIE THE KID UP!
HEH?
HEY ... HEY ... I'M NOT A CROOK!
GASP
BUT YOU ARE A GOLDEN GOOSE!
TAP
TAP

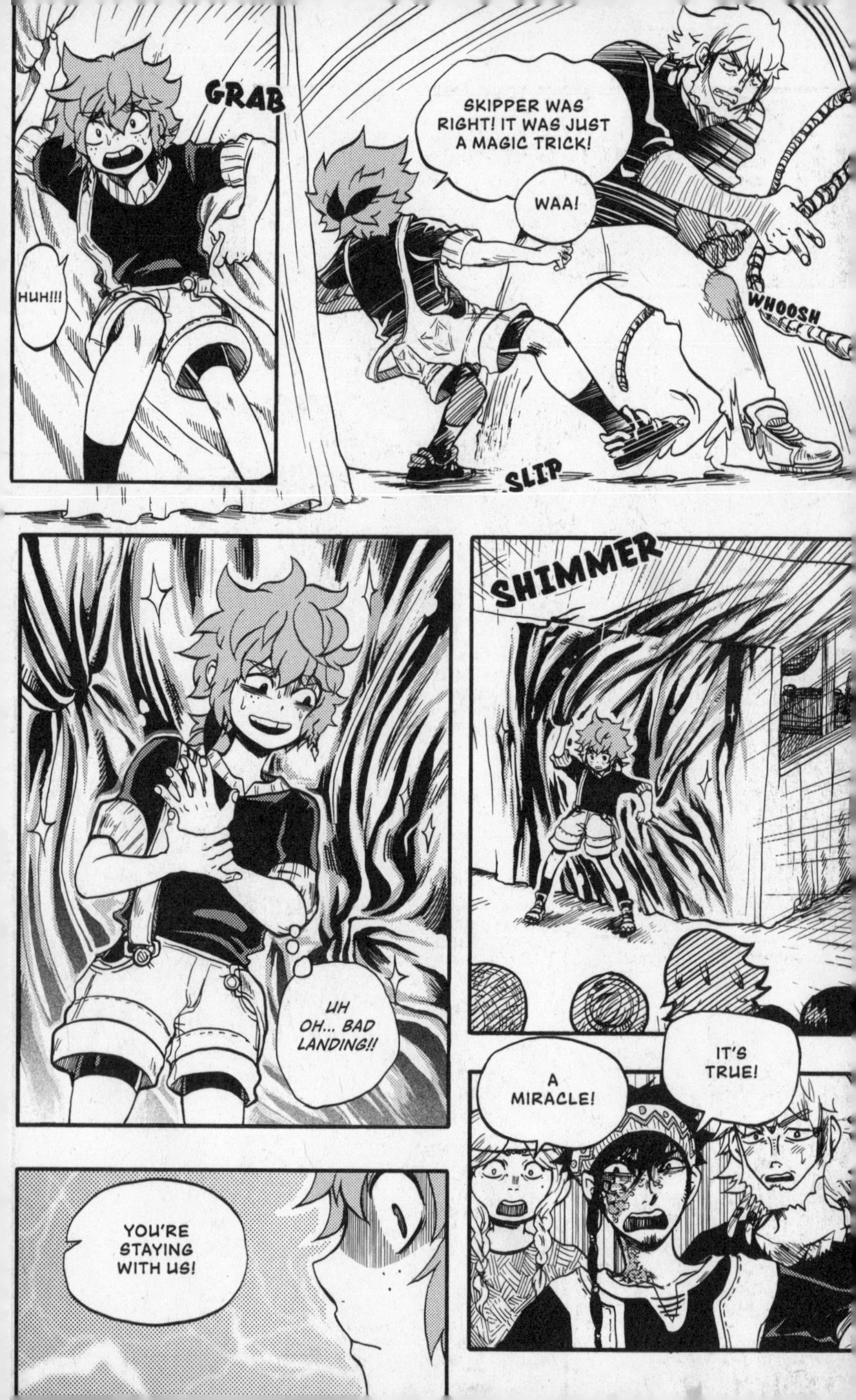
SKIPPER WAS RIGHT! IT WAS JUST A MAGIC TRICK!
WAA!
WHOOSH
SLIP
GRAB
HUH!!!
SHIMMER
UH OH... BAD LANDING!!
IT'S TRUE!
A MIRACLE!
YOU'RE STAYING WITH US!

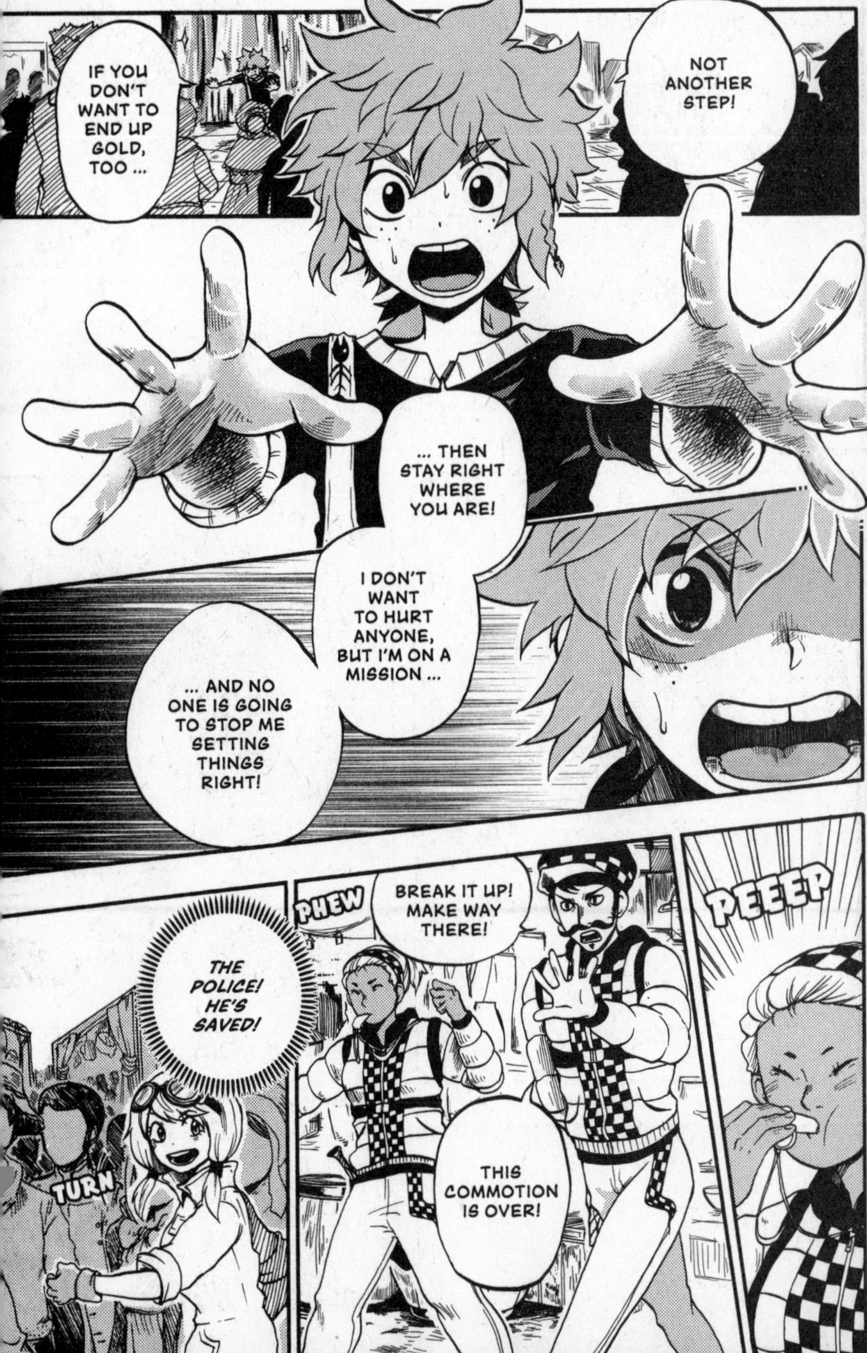
NOT ANOTHER STEP!
IF YOU DON'T WANT TO END UP GOLD, TOO ...
... THEN STAY RIGHT WHERE YOU ARE!
I DON'T WANT TO HURT ANYONE, BUT I'M ON A MISSION ...
... AND NO ONE IS GOING TO STOP ME SETTING THINGS RIGHT!
PEEEP
BREAK IT UP! MAKE WAY THERE!
PHEW
THIS COMMOTION IS OVER!
THE POLICE! HE'S SAVED!
TURN

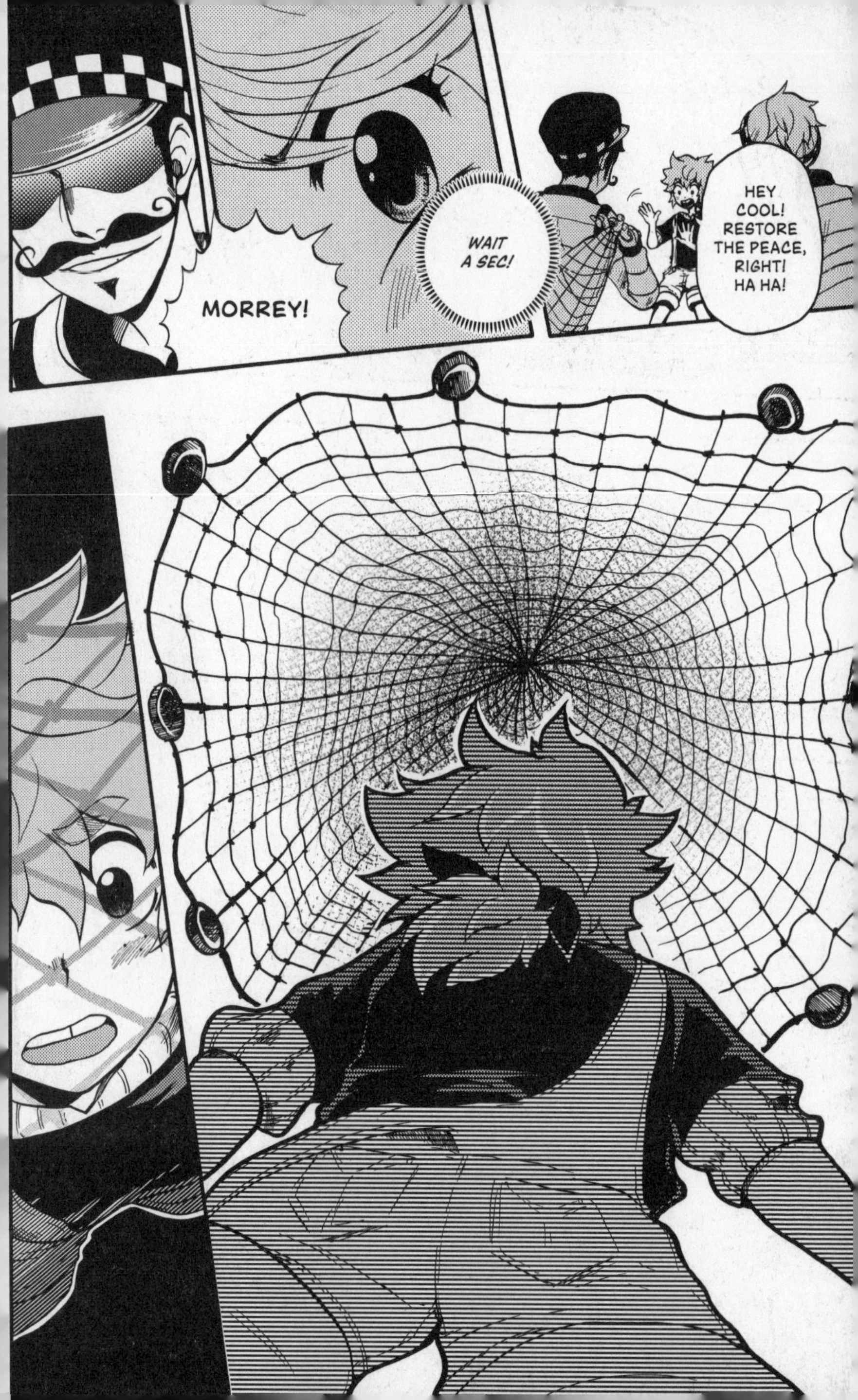
HEY COOL! RESTORE THE PEACE, RIGHT! HA HA!
WAIT A SEC!
MORREY!

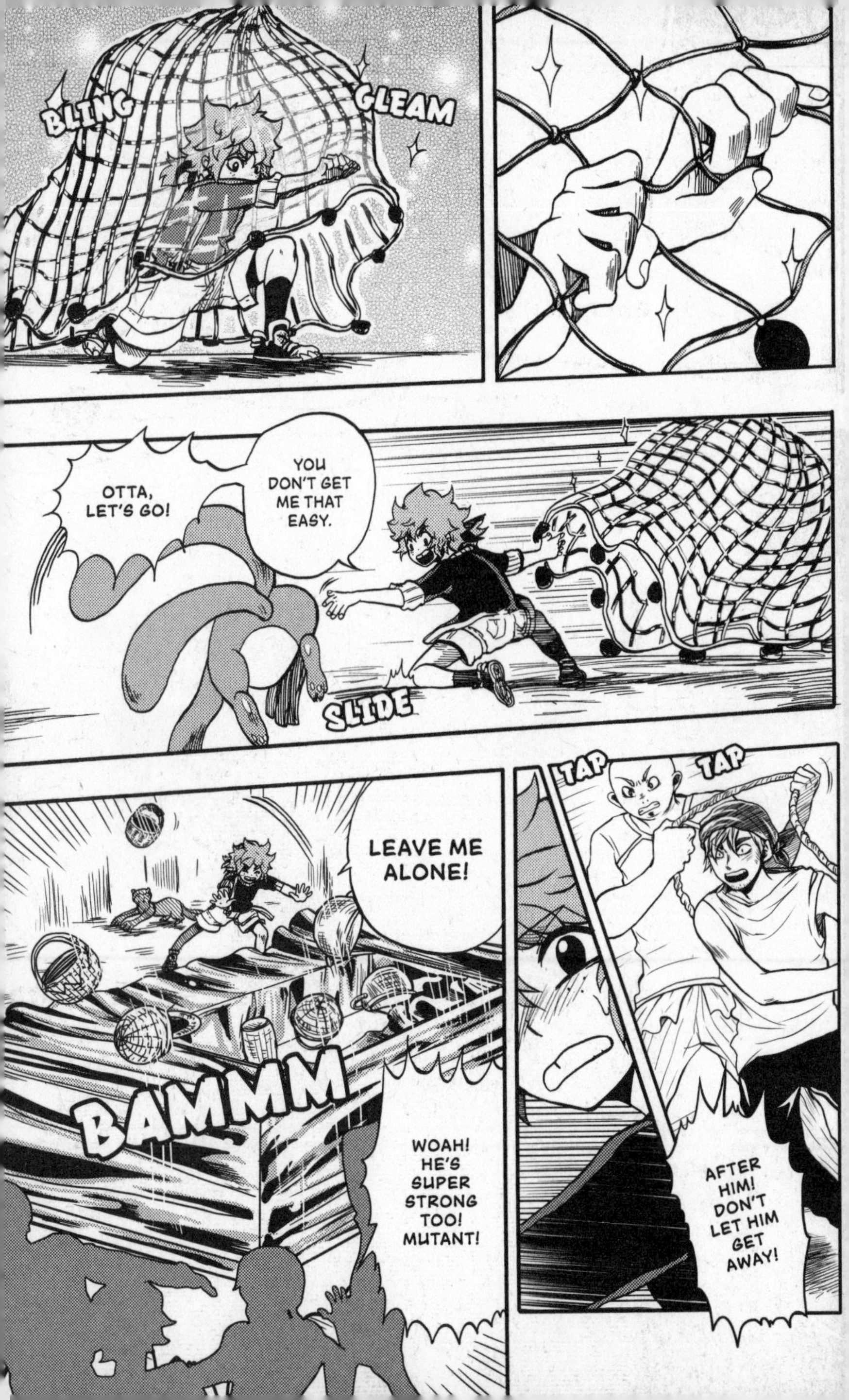
GLEAM
BLING
YOU DON'T GET ME THAT EASY.
OTTA, LET'S GO!
SLIDE
TAP
TAP
AFTER HIM! DON'T LET HIM GET AWAY!
LEAVE ME ALONE!
BAMMM
WOAH! HE'S SUPER STRONG TOO! MUTANT!

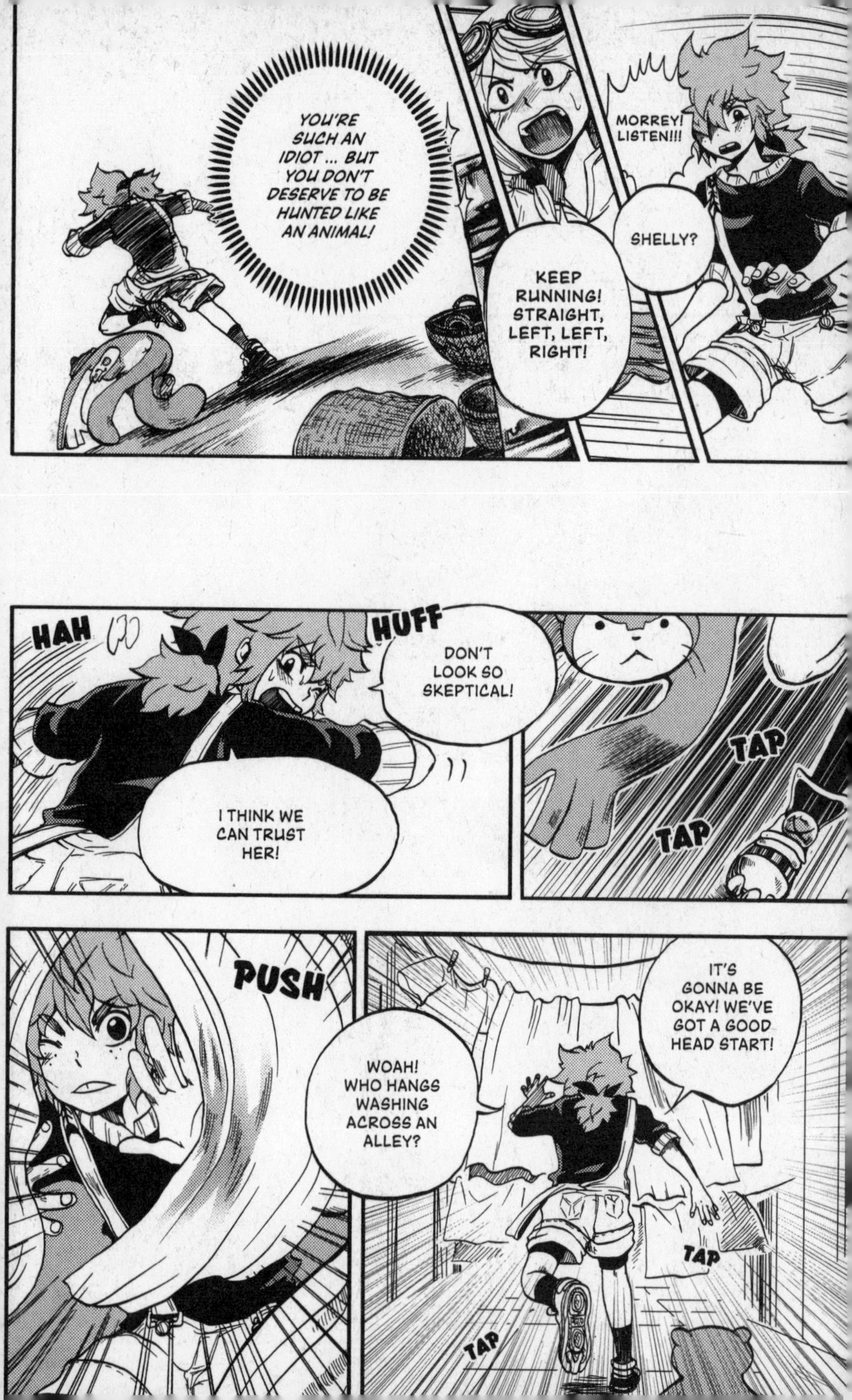
MORREY! LISTEN!!!
SHELLY?
KEEP RUNNING! STRAIGHT, LEFT, LEFT, RIGHT!
YOU'RE SUCH AN IDIOT ... BUT YOU DON'T DESERVE TO BE HUNTED LIKE AN ANIMAL!
TAP
TAP
HUFF
DON'T LOOK SO SKEPTICAL!
HAH
I THINK WE CAN TRUST HER!
IT'S GONNA BE OKAY! WE'VE GOT A GOOD HEAD START!
WOAH! WHO HANGS WASHING ACROSS AN ALLEY?
TAP
TAP
PUSH

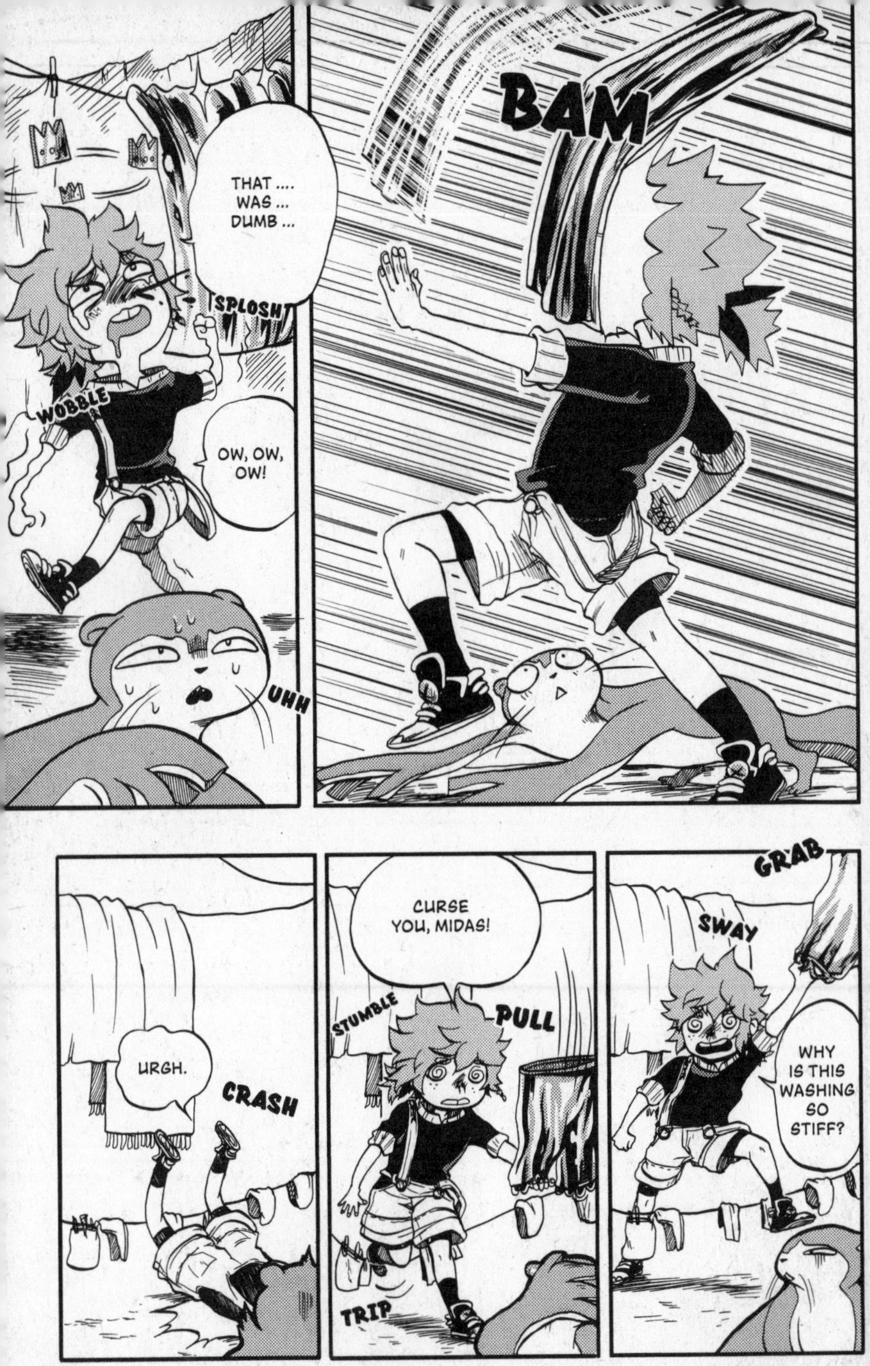
BAM
THAT .... WAS ... DUMB ...
SPLOSH
WOBBLE
OW, OW, OW!
UHH
GRAB
SWAY
WHY IS THIS WASHING SO STIFF?
CURSE YOU, MIDAS!
STUMBLE
PULL
TRIP
URGH.
CRASH

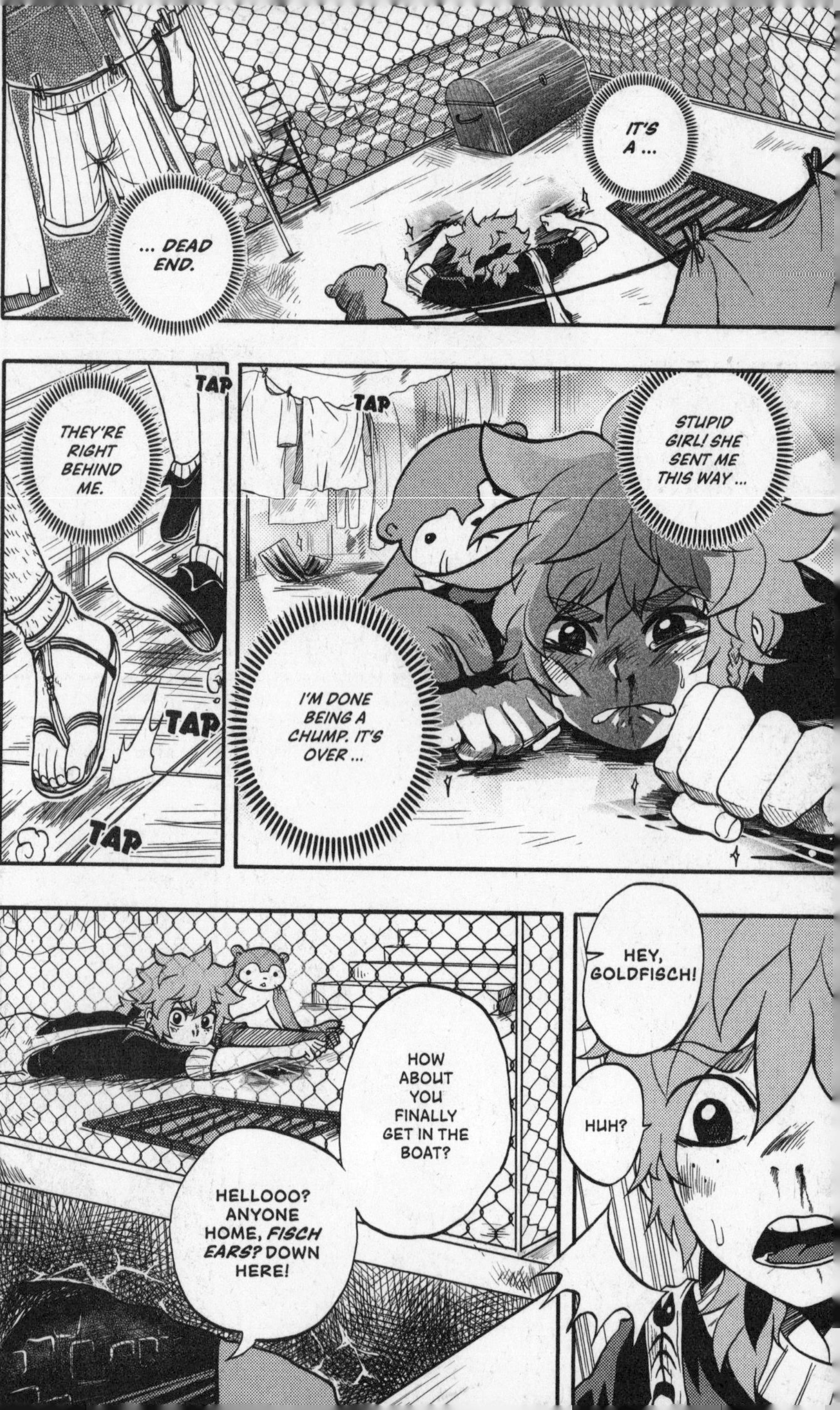
IT'S A ...
... DEAD END.
STUPID GIRL! SHE SENT ME THIS WAY ...
TAP
I'M DONE BEING A CHUMP. IT'S OVER ...
TAP
THEY'RE RIGHT BEHIND ME.
TAP
TAP
HEY, GOLDFISCH!
HUH?
HOW ABOUT YOU FINALLY GET IN THE BOAT?
HELLOOO? ANYONE HOME, *FISCH EARS?* DOWN HERE!

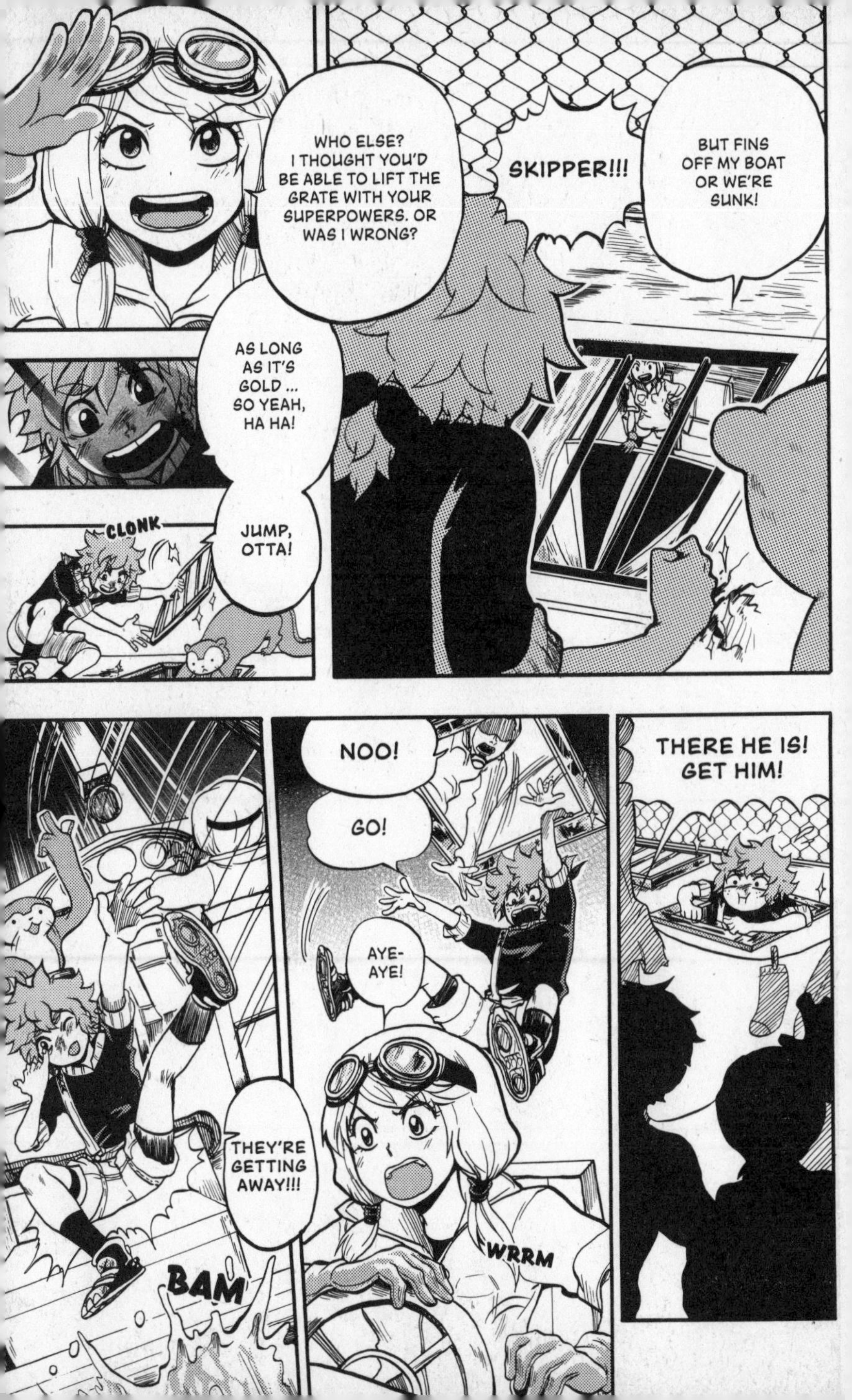
BUT FINS OFF MY BOAT OR WE'RE SUNK!
SKIPPER!!!
WHO ELSE? I THOUGHT YOU'D BE ABLE TO LIFT THE GRATE WITH YOUR SUPERPOWERS. OR WAS I WRONG?
AS LONG AS IT'S GOLD ... SO YEAH, HA HA!
JUMP, OTTA!
CLONK
THERE HE IS! GET HIM!
NOO!
GO!
AYE-AYE!
THEY'RE GETTING AWAY!!!
WRRM
BAM

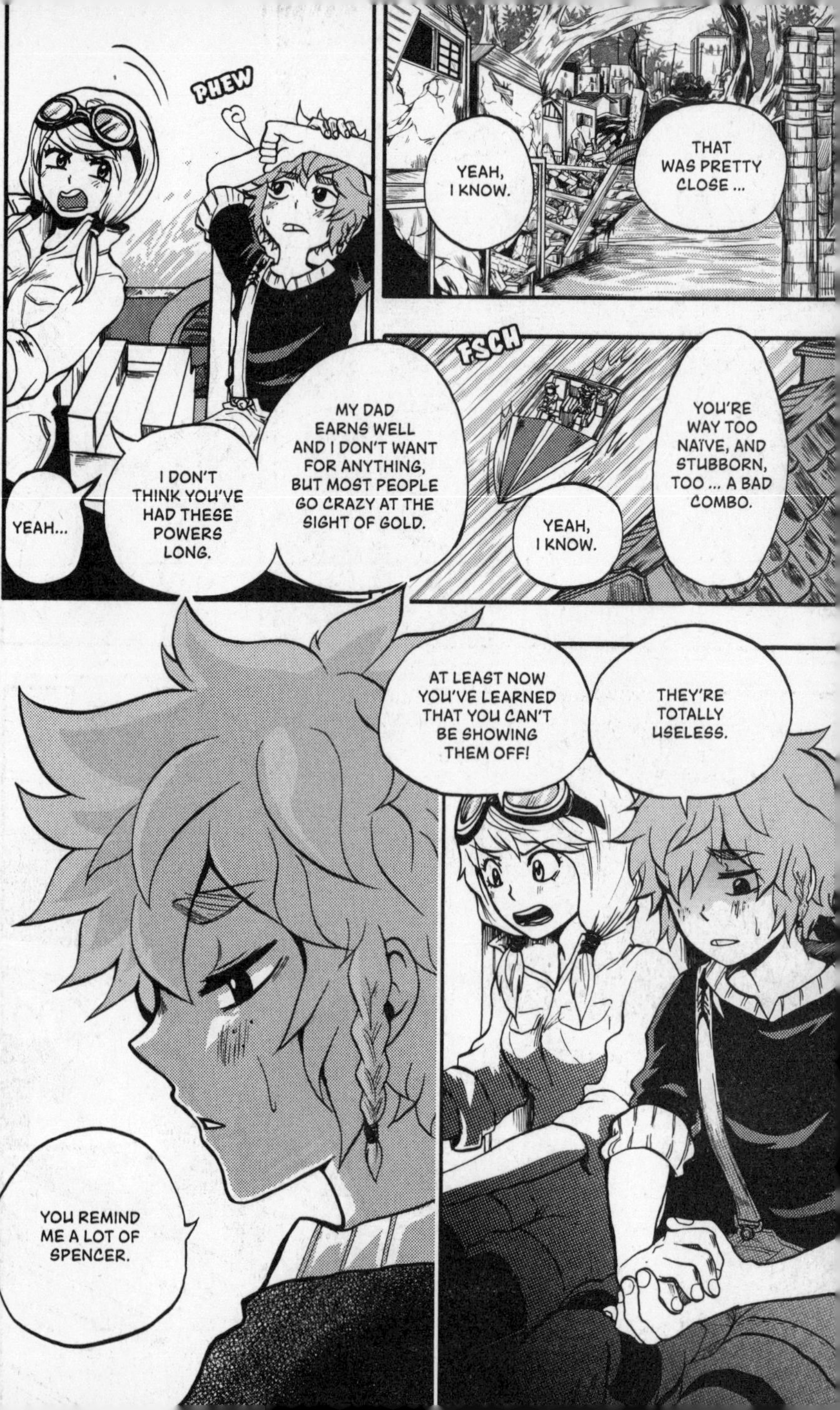
THAT WAS PRETTY CLOSE ...
YEAH, I KNOW.
FSCH
YOU'RE WAY TOO NAÏVE, AND STUBBORN, TOO ... A BAD COMBO.
YEAH, I KNOW.
PHEW
MY DAD EARNS WELL AND I DON'T WANT FOR ANYTHING, BUT MOST PEOPLE GO CRAZY AT THE SIGHT OF GOLD.
I DON'T THINK YOU'VE HAD THESE POWERS LONG.
YEAH...
THEY'RE TOTALLY USELESS.
AT LEAST NOW YOU'VE LEARNED THAT YOU CAN'T BE SHOWING THEM OFF!
YOU REMIND ME A LOT OF SPENCER.

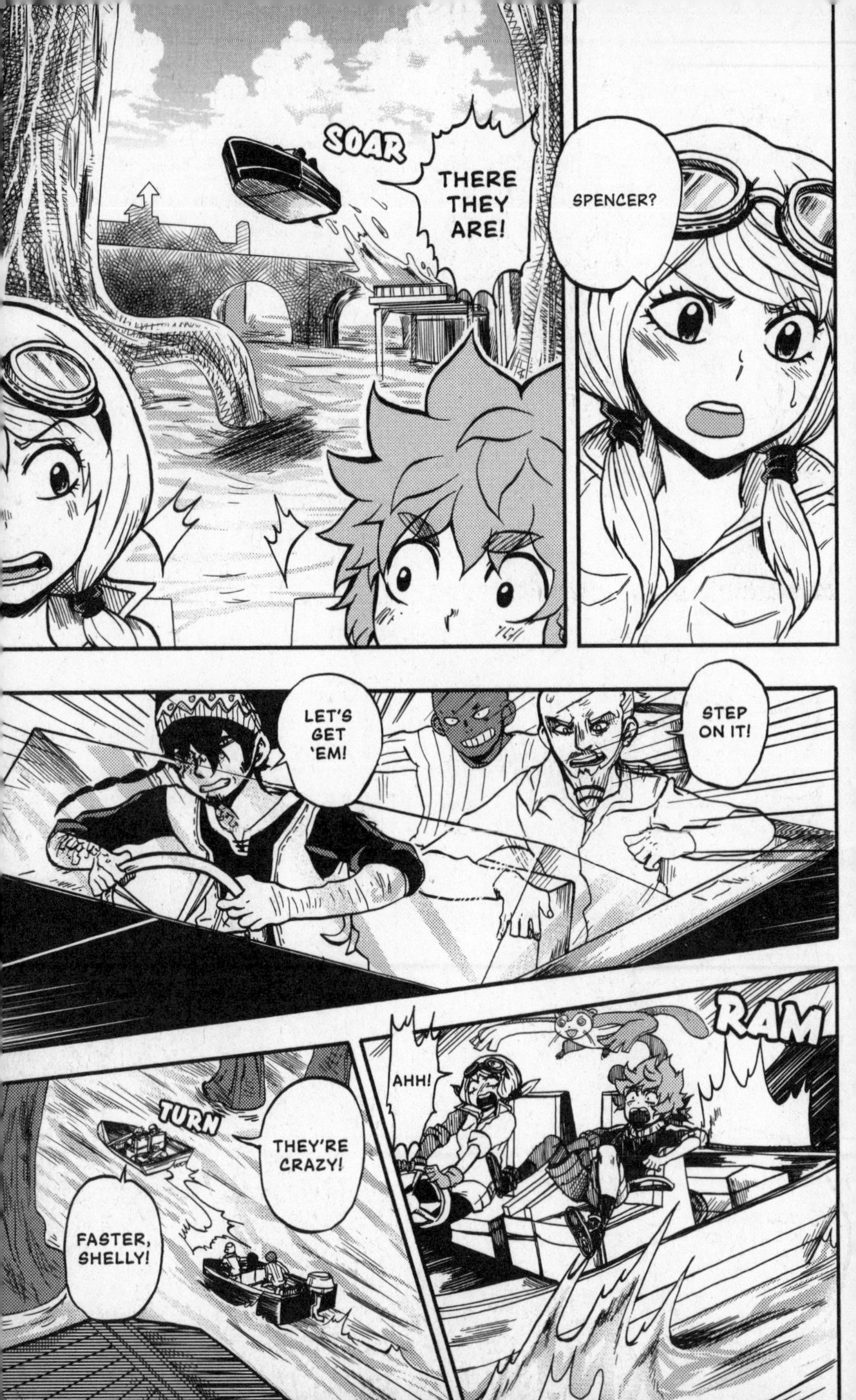
SPENCER?
THERE THEY ARE!
SOAR
STEP ON IT!
LET'S GET 'EM!
RAM
AHH!
THEY'RE CRAZY!
TURN
FASTER, SHELLY!

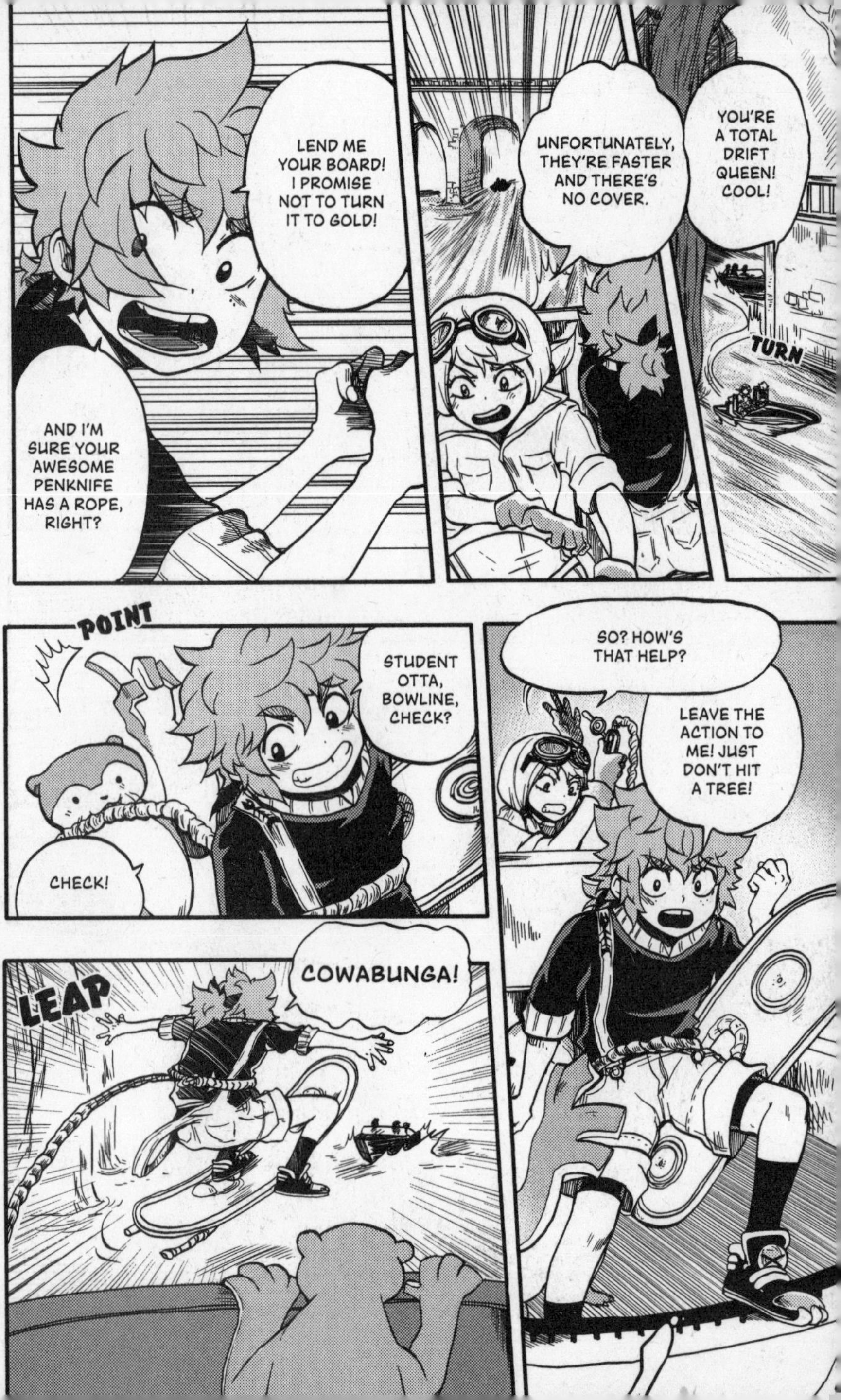
YOU'RE A TOTAL DRIFT QUEEN! COOL!
TURN
UNFORTUNATELY, THEY'RE FASTER AND THERE'S NO COVER.
LEND ME YOUR BOARD! I PROMISE NOT TO TURN IT TO GOLD!
AND I'M SURE YOUR AWESOME PENKNIFE HAS A ROPE, RIGHT?
SO? HOW'S THAT HELP?
LEAVE THE ACTION TO ME! JUST DON'T HIT A TREE!
POINT
STUDENT OTTA, BOWLINE, CHECK?
CHECK!
COWABUNGA!
LEAP

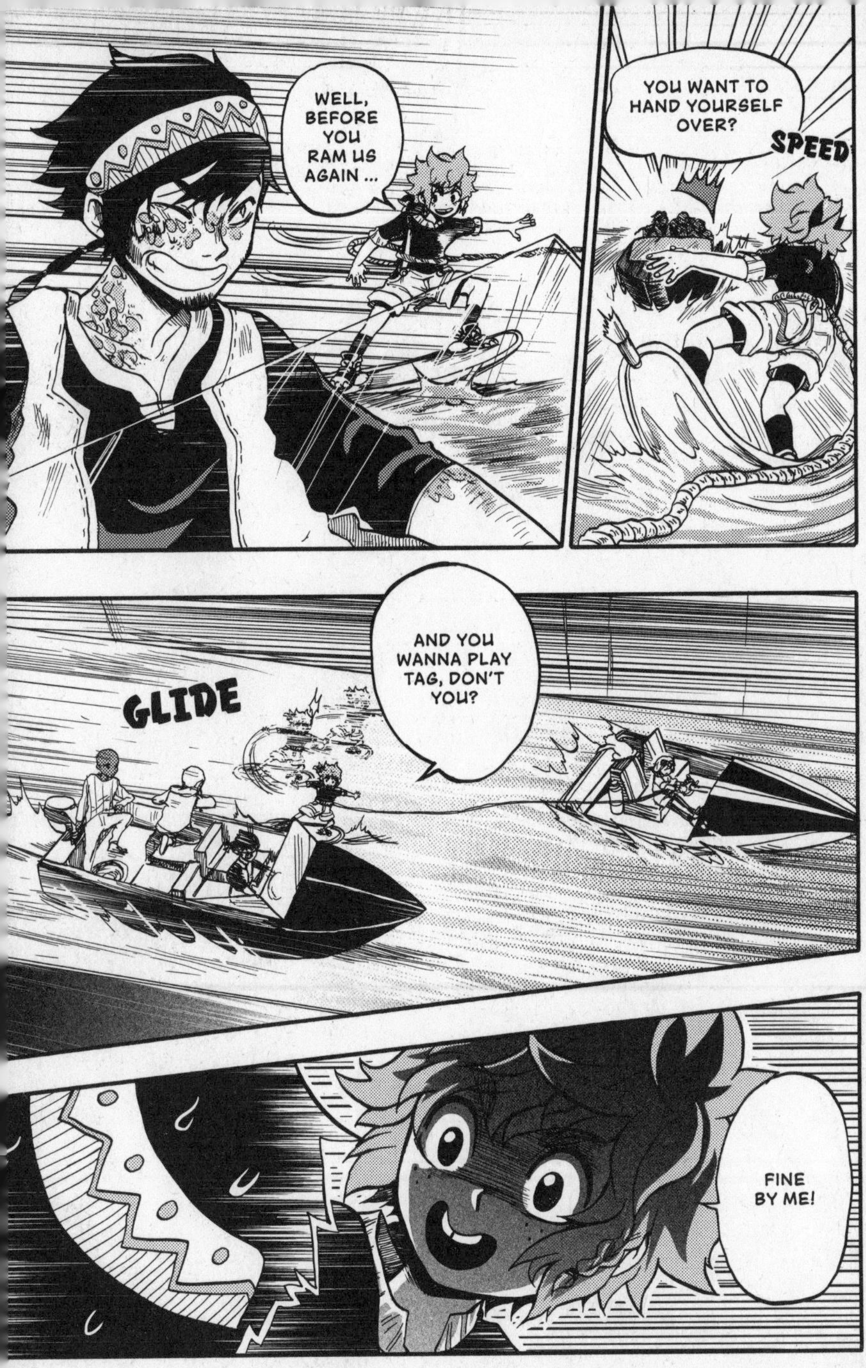
YOU WANT TO HAND YOURSELF OVER?
SPEED
WELL, BEFORE YOU RAM US AGAIN ...
AND YOU WANNA PLAY TAG, DON'T YOU?
GLIDE
FINE BY ME!

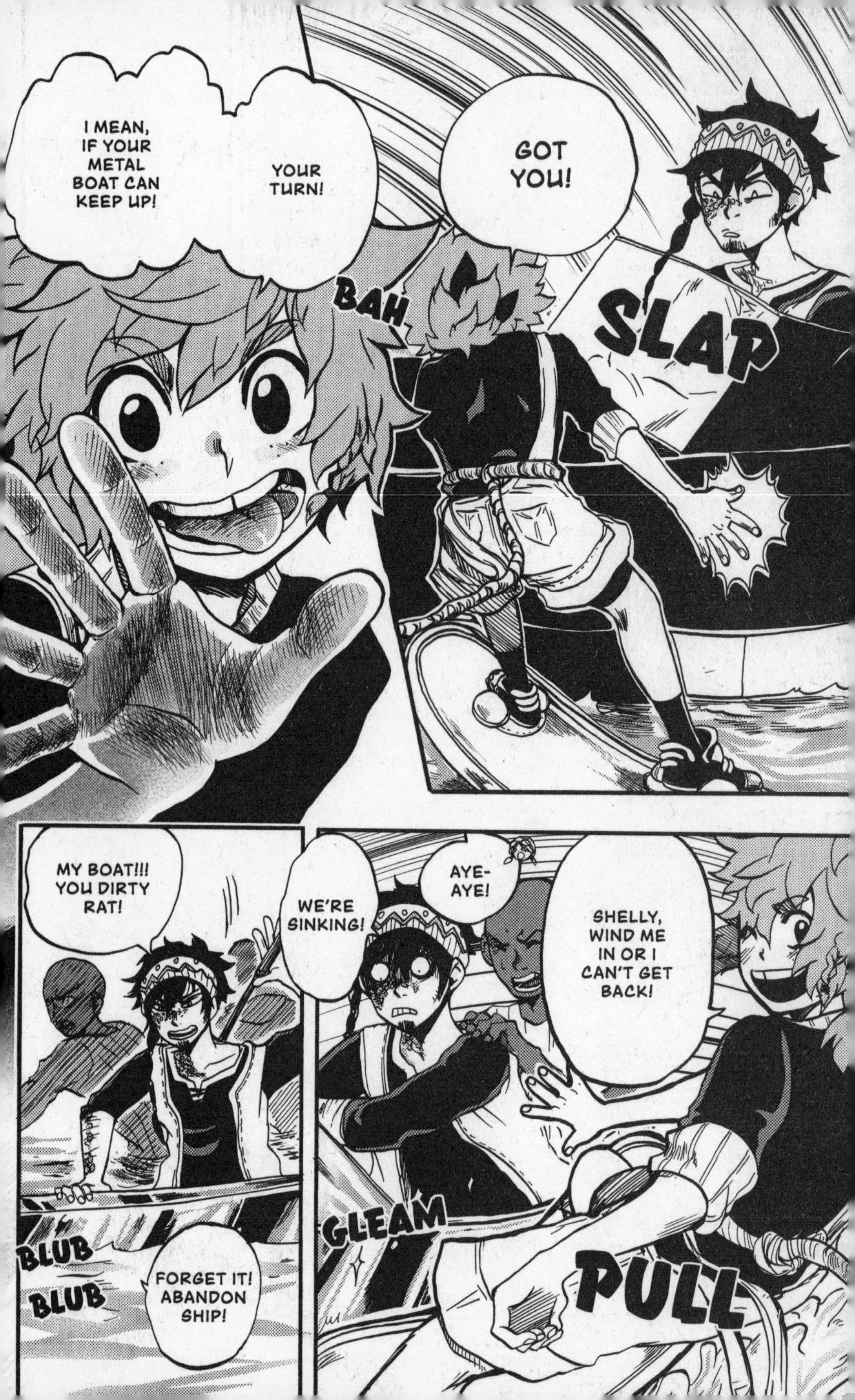
GOT YOU!
BAH
SLAP
YOUR TURN!
I MEAN, IF YOUR METAL BOAT CAN KEEP UP!
SHELLY, WIND ME IN OR I CAN'T GET BACK!
AYE-AYE!
WE'RE SINKING!
GLEAM
PULL
MY BOAT!!! YOU DIRTY RAT!
FORGET IT! ABANDON SHIP!
BLUB
BLUB

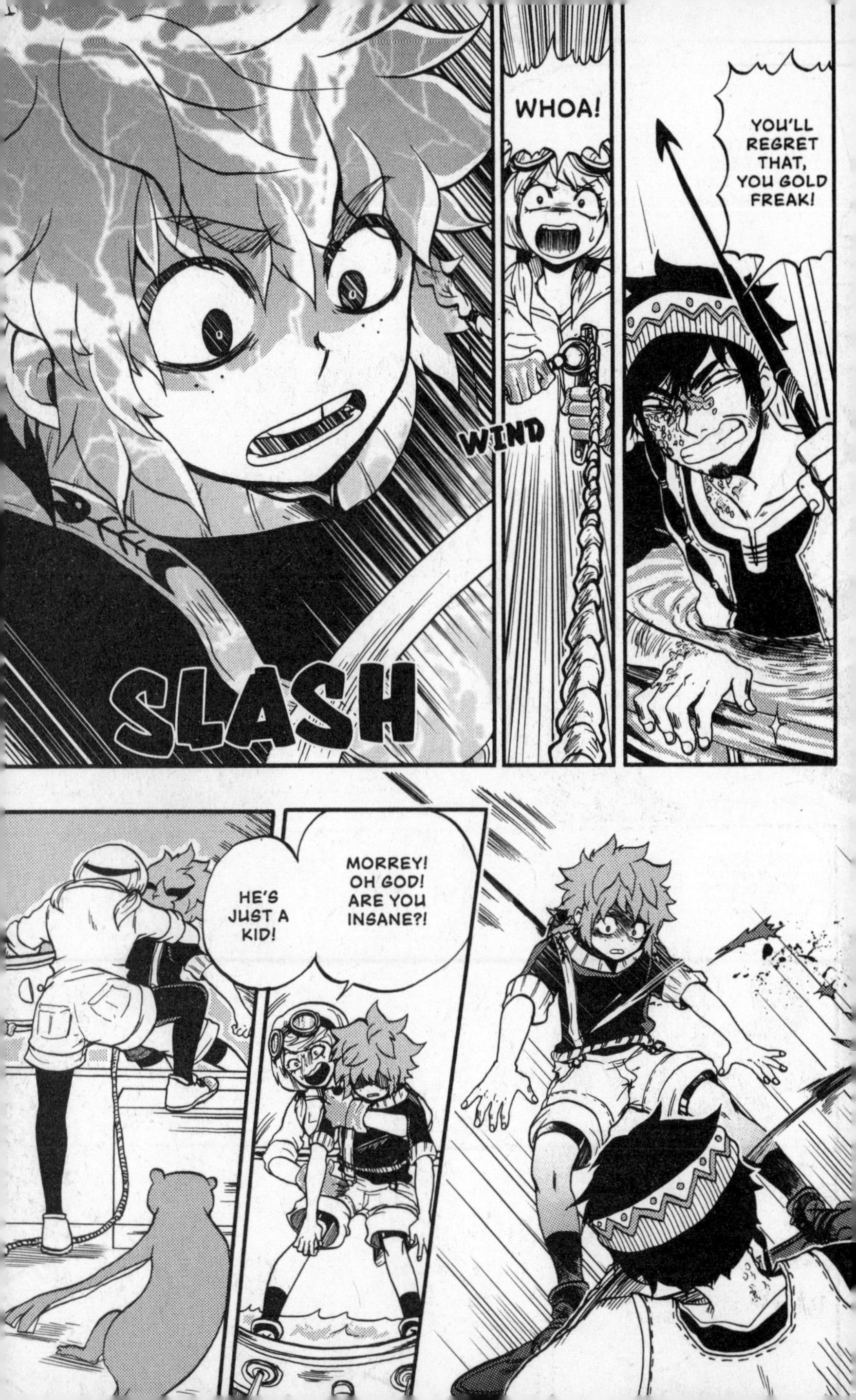
YOU'LL REGRET THAT, YOU GOLD FREAK!
WHOA!
WIND
SLASH
MORREY! OH GOD! ARE YOU INSANE?!
HE'S JUST A KID!

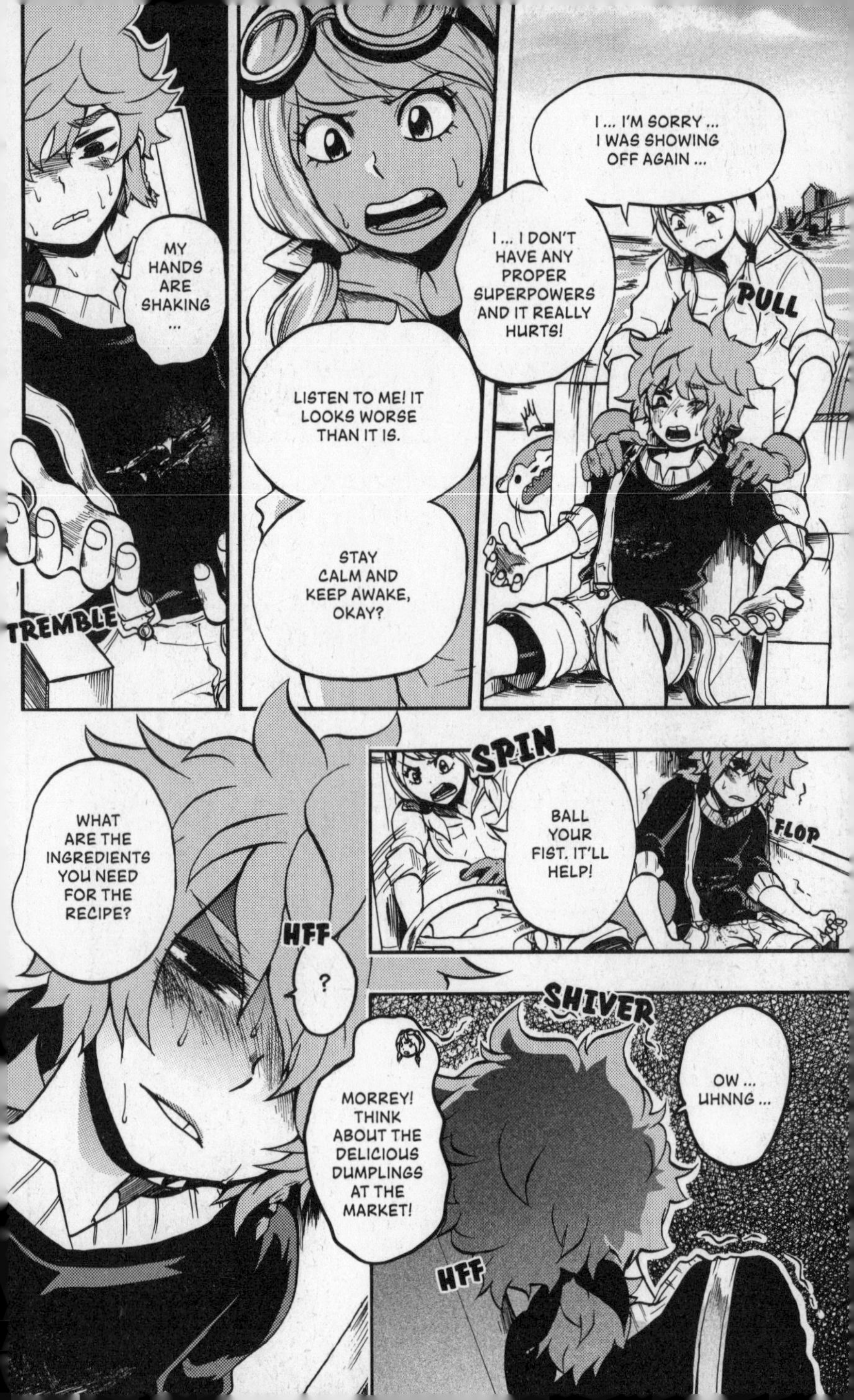
I ... I'M SORRY ... I WAS SHOWING OFF AGAIN ...
PULL
I ... I DON'T HAVE ANY PROPER SUPERPOWERS AND IT REALLY HURTS!
LISTEN TO ME! IT LOOKS WORSE THAN IT IS.
STAY CALM AND KEEP AWAKE, OKAY?
MY HANDS ARE SHAKING ...
TREMBLE
SPIN
BALL YOUR FIST. IT'LL HELP!
FLOP
SHIVER
OW ... UHNNG ...
MORREY! THINK ABOUT THE DELICIOUS DUMPLINGS AT THE MARKET!
HFF
WHAT ARE THE INGREDIENTS YOU NEED FOR THE RECIPE?
HFF
?

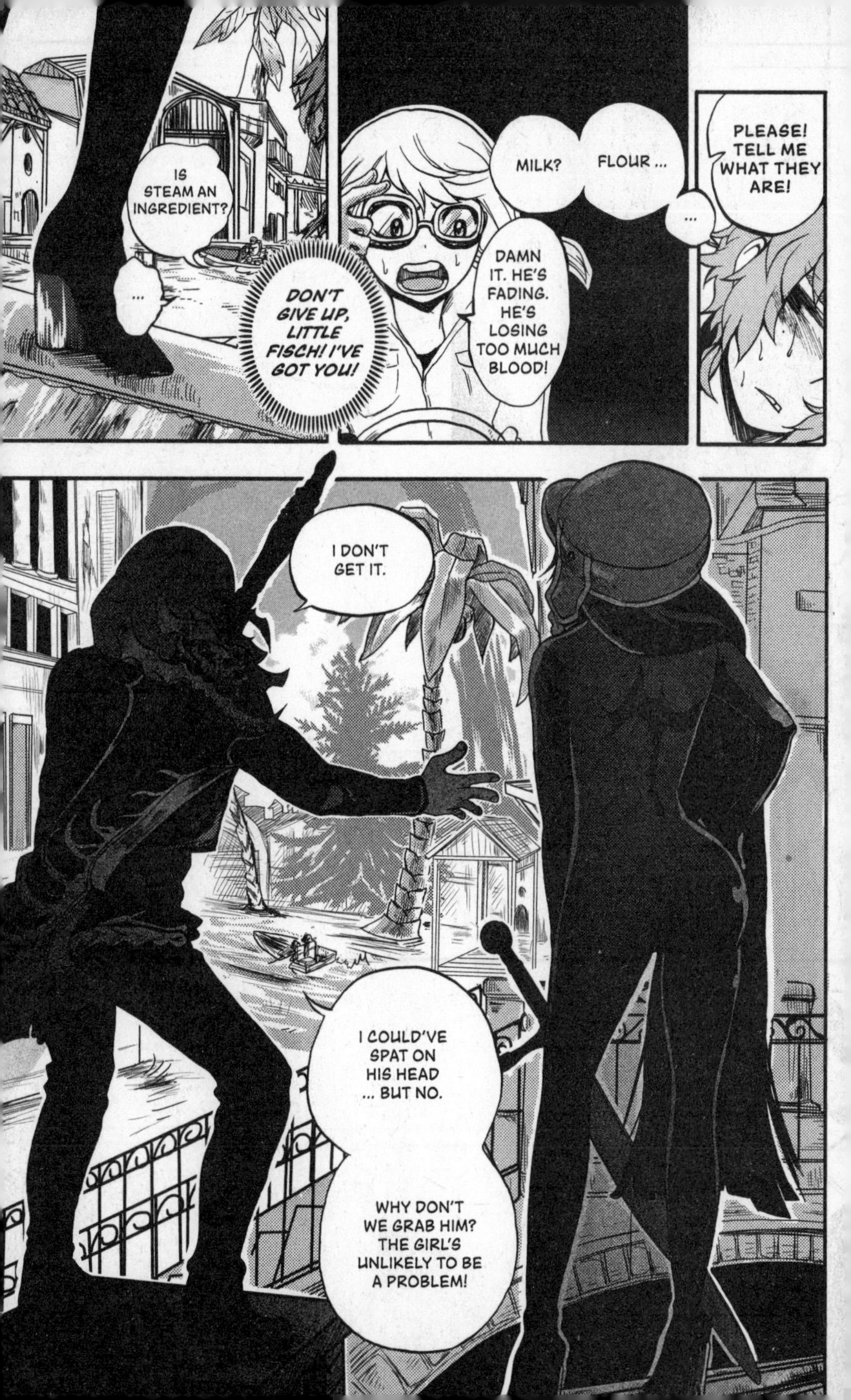
PLEASE! TELL ME WHAT THEY ARE!
...
FLOUR ...
MILK?
DAMN IT. HE'S FADING. HE'S LOSING TOO MUCH BLOOD!
DON'T GIVE UP, LITTLE FISCH! I'VE GOT YOU!
IS STEAM AN INGREDIENT?
...
I DON'T GET IT.
I COULD'VE SPAT ON HIS HEAD ... BUT NO.
WHY DON'T WE GRAB HIM? THE GIRL'S UNLIKELY TO BE A PROBLEM!

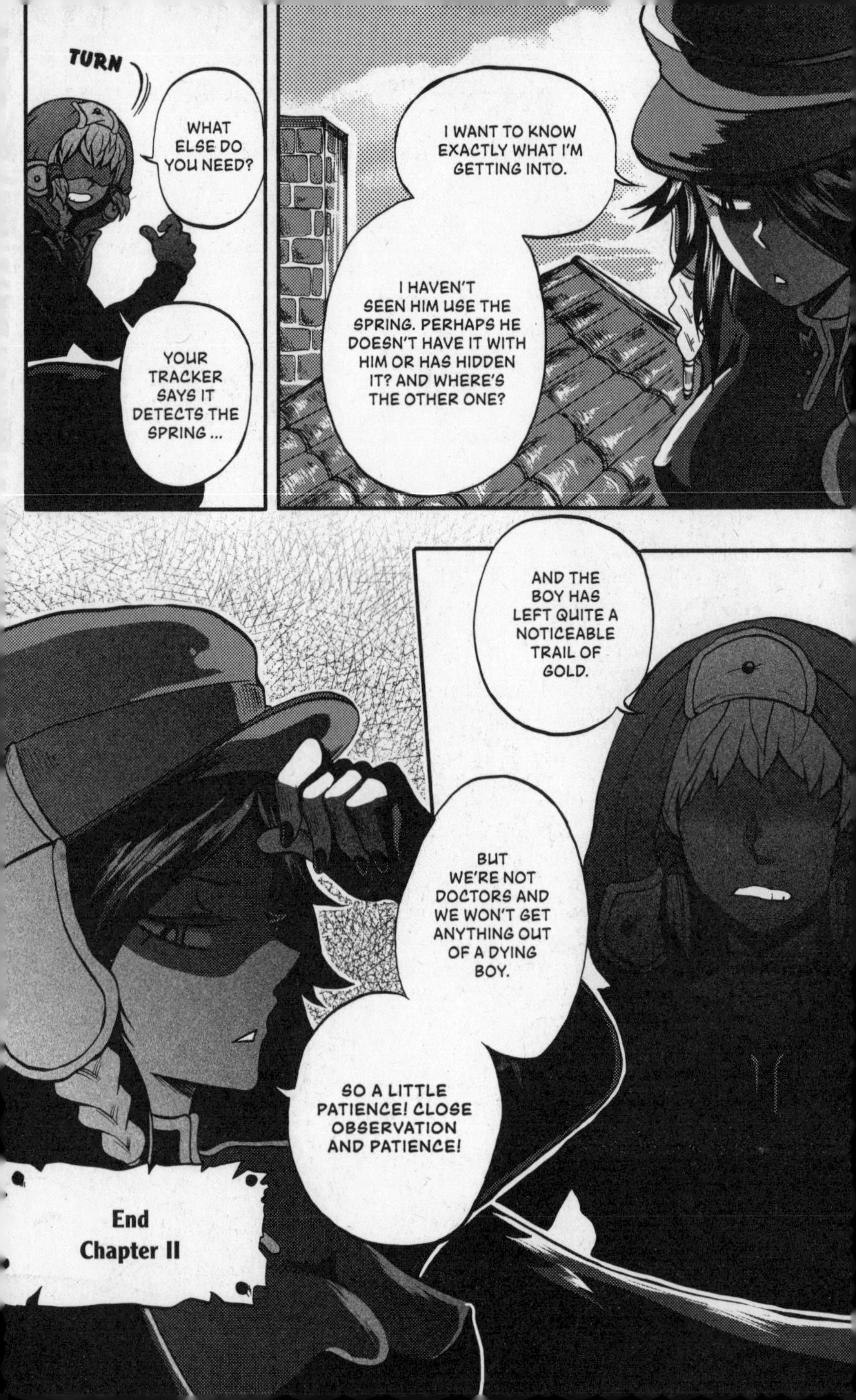
I WANT TO KNOW EXACTLY WHAT I'M GETTING INTO.
I HAVEN'T SEEN HIM USE THE SPRING. PERHAPS HE DOESN'T HAVE IT WITH HIM OR HAS HIDDEN IT? AND WHERE'S THE OTHER ONE?
TURN
WHAT ELSE DO YOU NEED?
YOUR TRACKER SAYS IT DETECTS THE SPRING ...
AND THE BOY HAS LEFT QUITE A NOTICEABLE TRAIL OF GOLD.
BUT WE'RE NOT DOCTORS AND WE WON'T GET ANYTHING OUT OF A DYING BOY.
SO A LITTLE PATIENCE! CLOSE OBSERVATION AND PATIENCE!
End
Chapter II

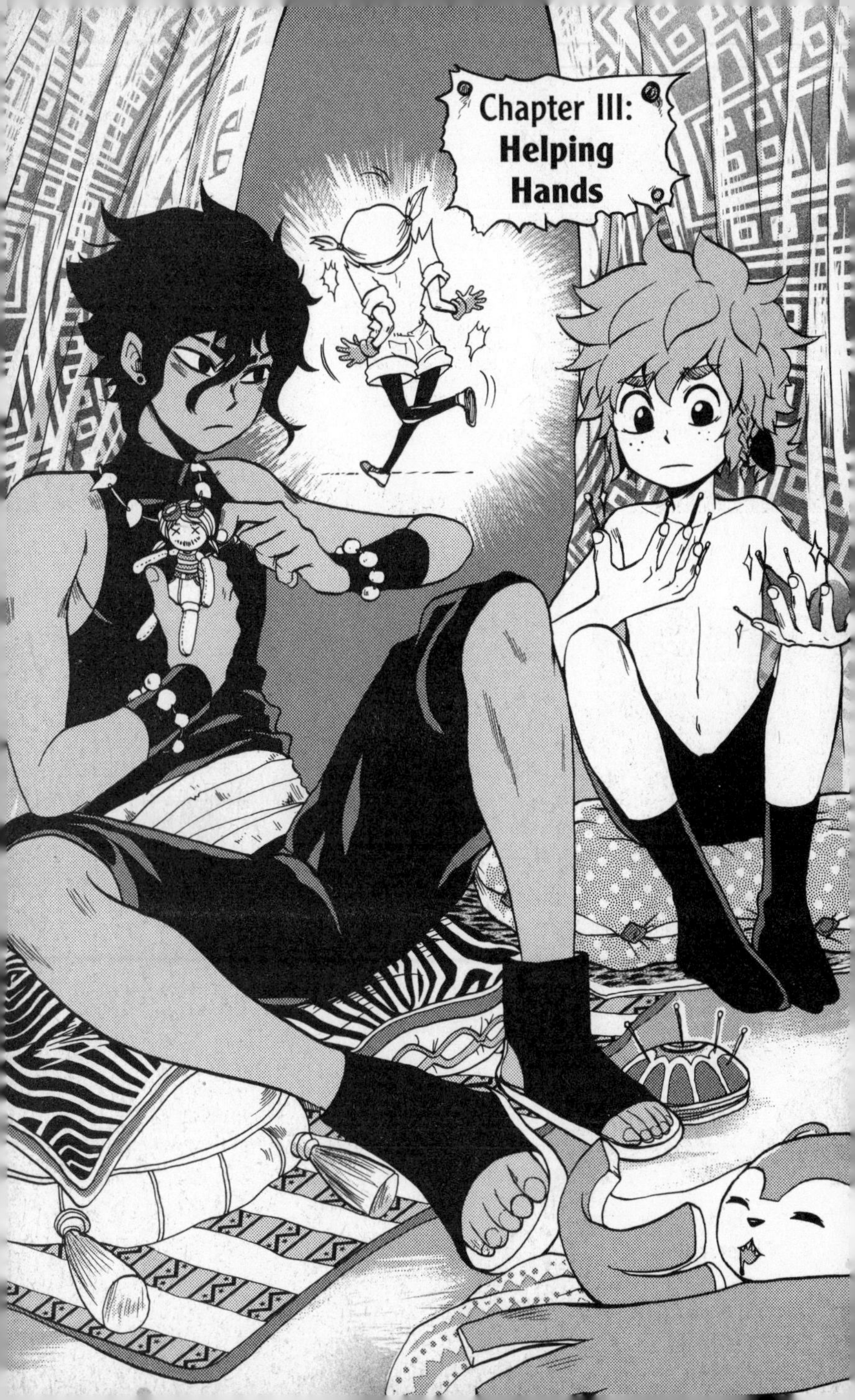
Chapter III:
Helping
Hands

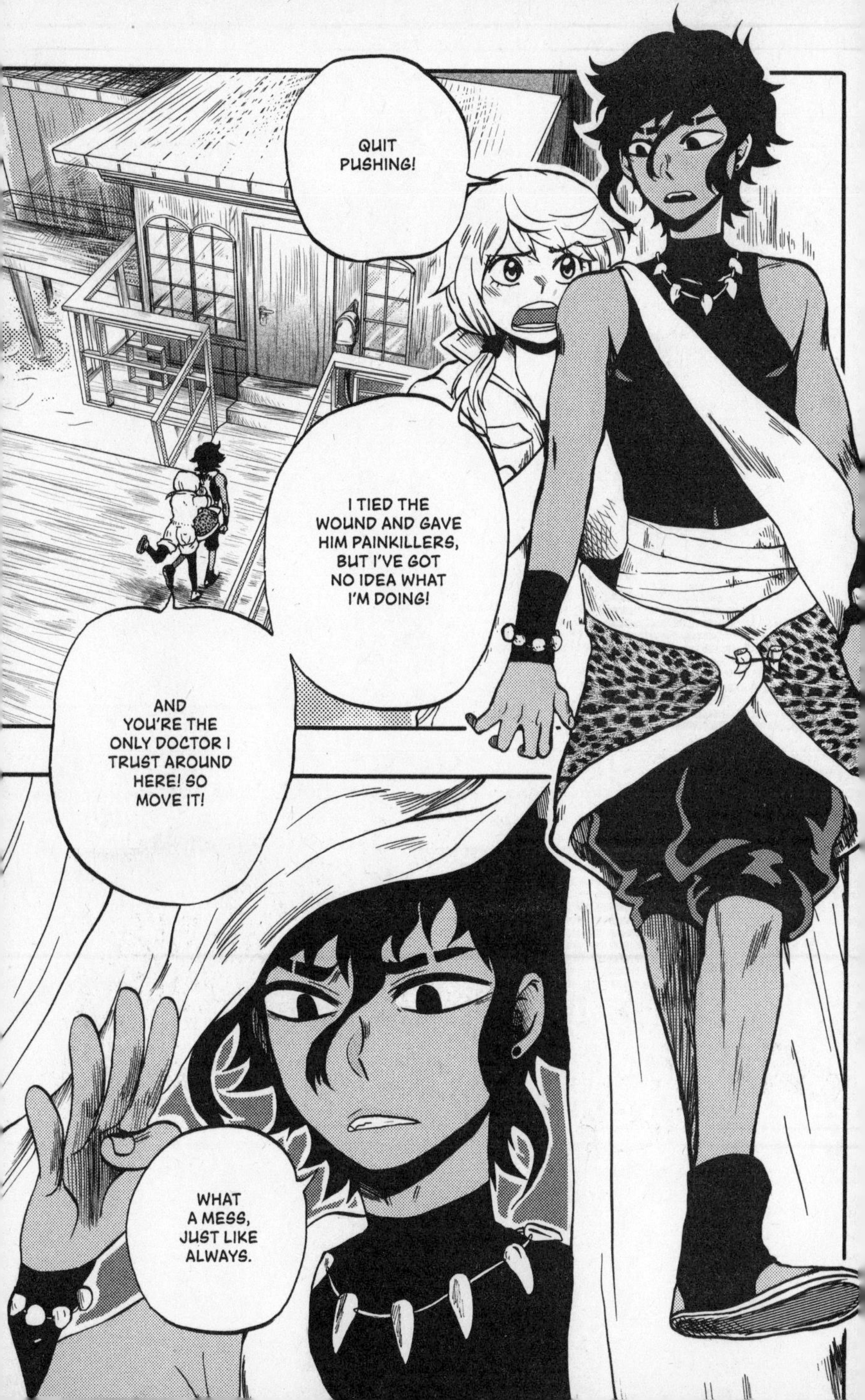
QUIT PUSHING!
I TIED THE WOUND AND GAVE HIM PAINKILLERS, BUT I'VE GOT NO IDEA WHAT I'M DOING!
AND YOU'RE THE ONLY DOCTOR I TRUST AROUND HERE! SO MOVE IT!
WHAT A MESS, JUST LIKE ALWAYS.

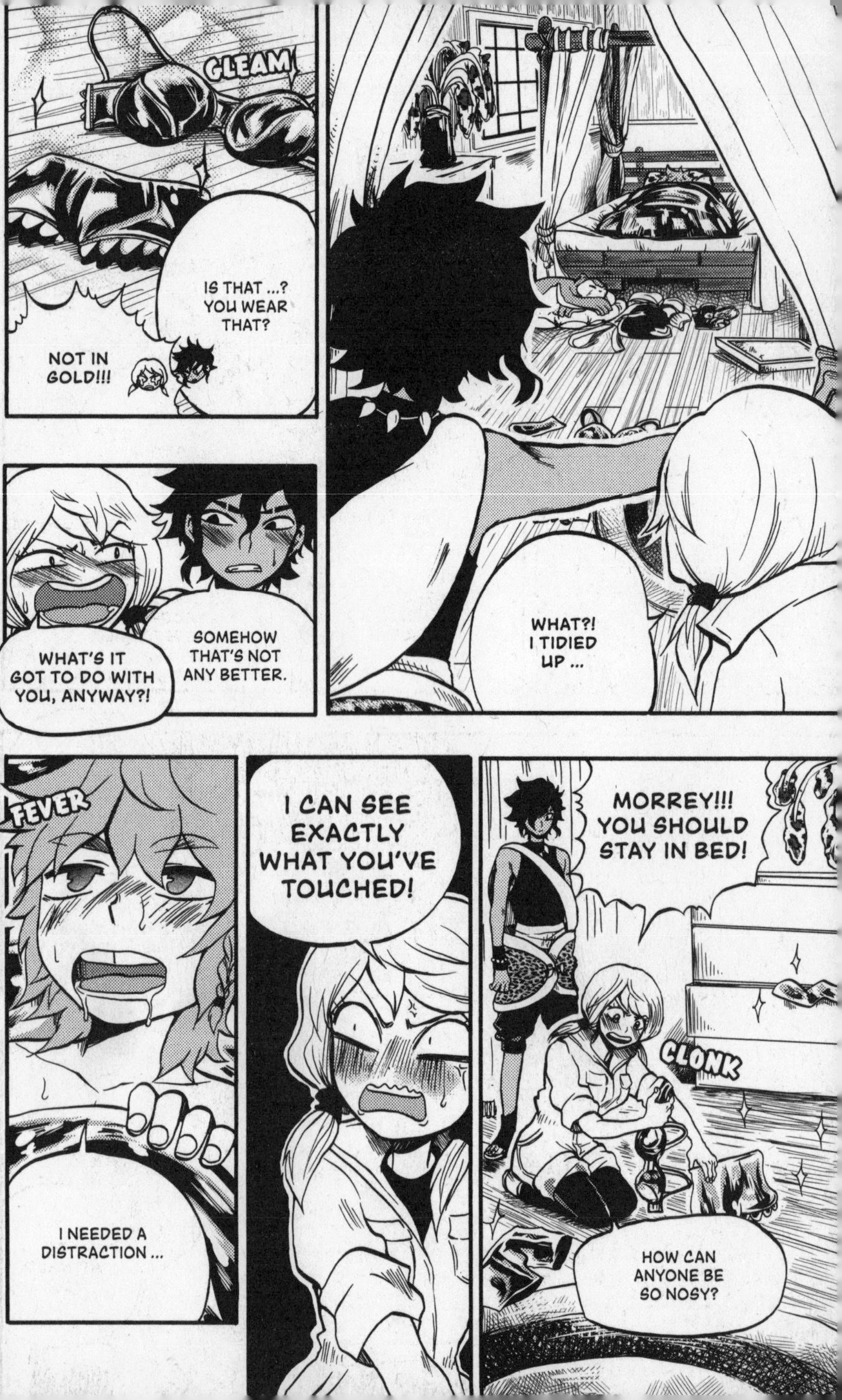
WHAT?! I TIDIED UP ...
GLEAM
IS THAT ...? YOU WEAR THAT?
NOT IN GOLD!!!
SOMEHOW THAT'S NOT ANY BETTER.
WHAT'S IT GOT TO DO WITH YOU, ANYWAY?!
MORREY!!! YOU SHOULD STAY IN BED!
CLONK
HOW CAN ANYONE BE SO NOSY?
I CAN SEE EXACTLY WHAT YOU'VE TOUCHED!
FEVER
I NEEDED A DISTRACTION ...

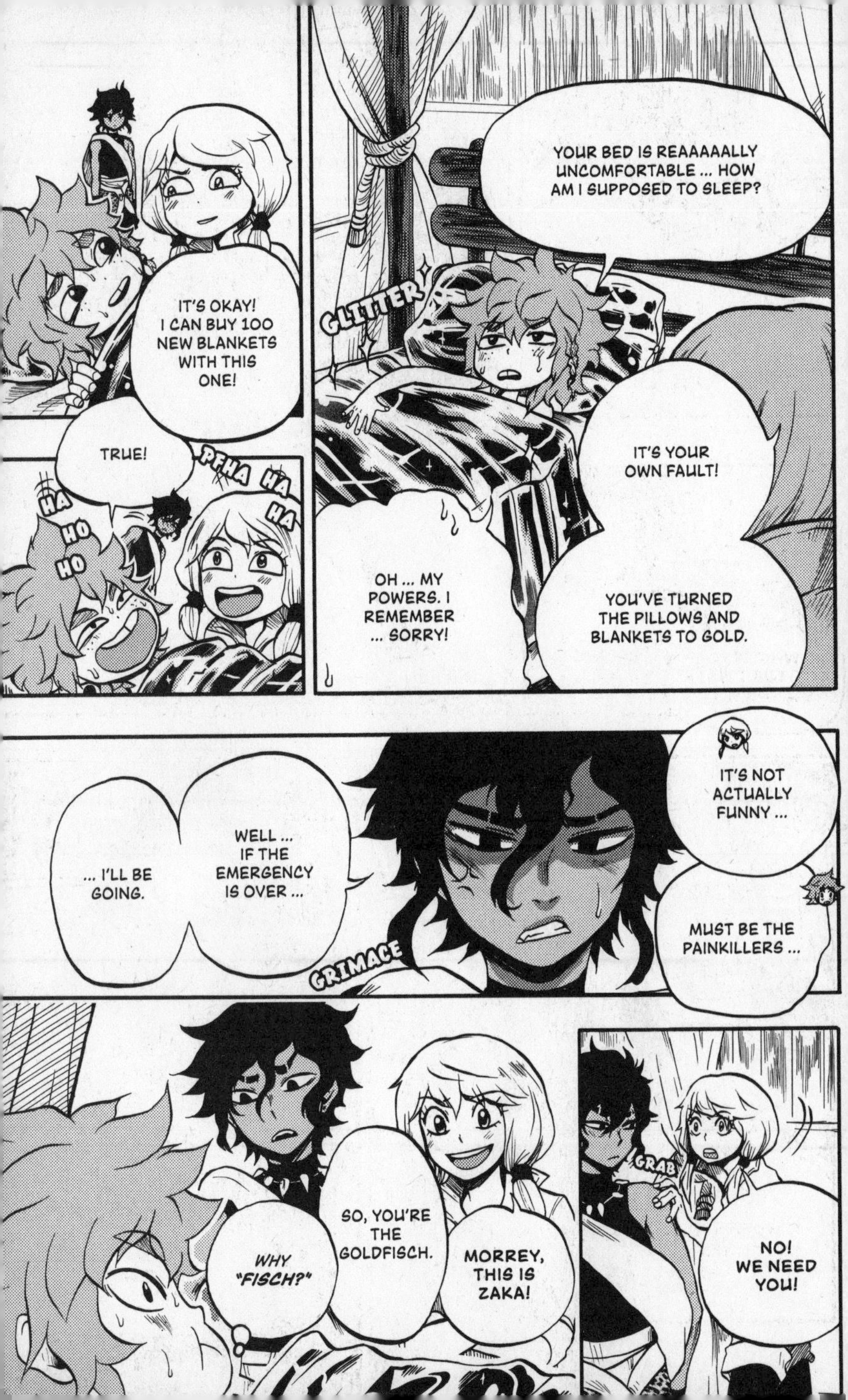
YOUR BED IS REAAAAALLY UNCOMFORTABLE ... HOW AM I SUPPOSED TO SLEEP?
GLITTER
IT'S YOUR OWN FAULT!
YOU'VE TURNED THE PILLOWS AND BLANKETS TO GOLD.
OH ... MY POWERS. I REMEMBER ... SORRY!
IT'S OKAY! I CAN BUY 100 NEW BLANKETS WITH THIS ONE!
TRUE!
PFHA HA HA HA
HA HO HO HO
IT'S NOT ACTUALLY FUNNY ...
MUST BE THE PAINKILLERS ...
WELL ... IF THE EMERGENCY IS OVER ...
... I'LL BE GOING.
GRIMACE
GRAB
NO! WE NEED YOU!
MORREY, THIS IS ZAKA!
SO, YOU'RE THE GOLDFISCH.
WHY "FISCH?"

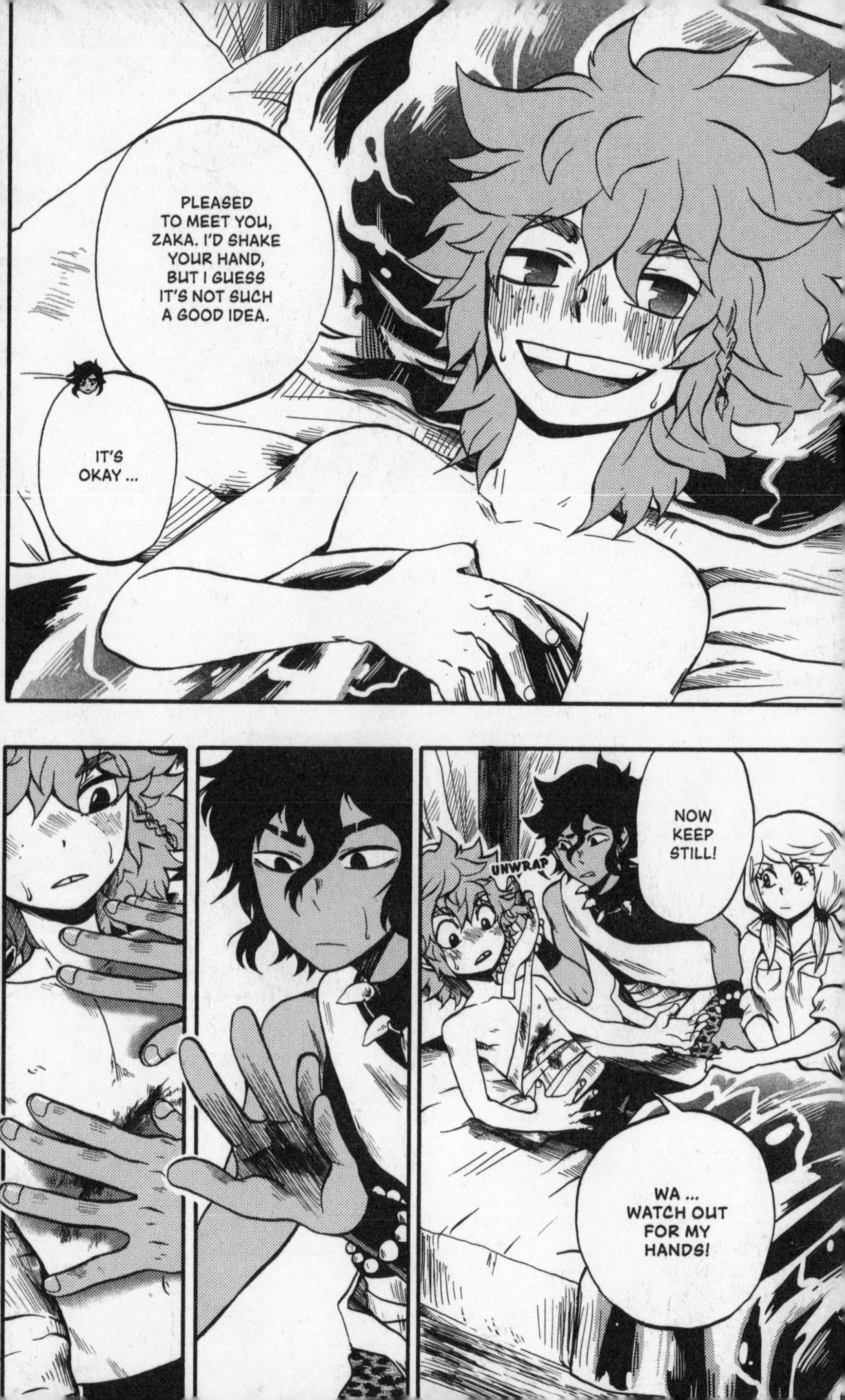
PLEASED TO MEET YOU, ZAKA. I'D SHAKE YOUR HAND, BUT I GUESS IT'S NOT SUCH A GOOD IDEA.
IT'S OKAY ...
NOW KEEP STILL!
UNWRAP
WA ... WATCH OUT FOR MY HANDS!

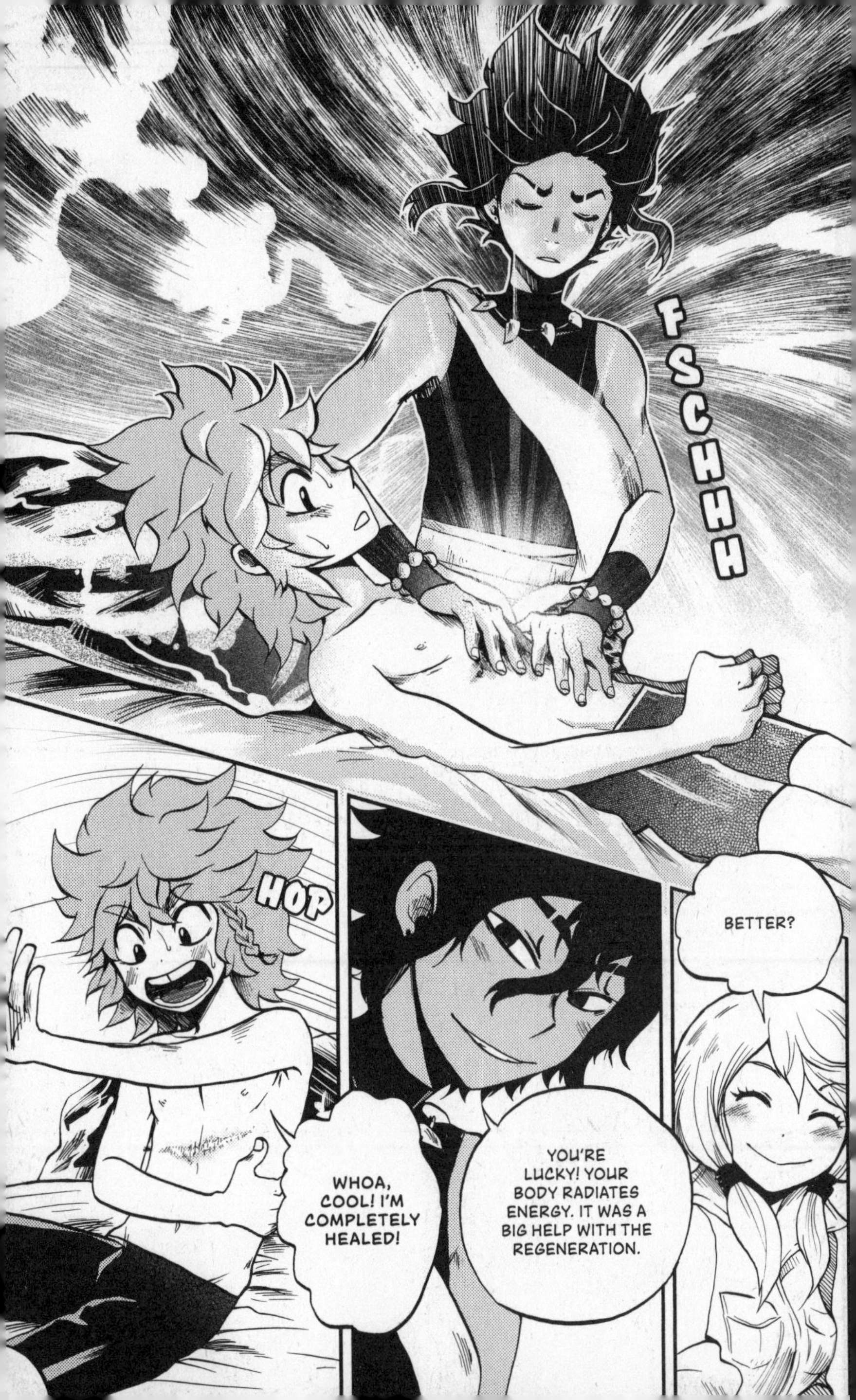
FSCHHH
BETTER?
YOU'RE LUCKY! YOUR BODY RADIATES ENERGY. IT WAS A BIG HELP WITH THE REGENERATION.
HOP
WHOA, COOL! I'M COMPLETELY HEALED!

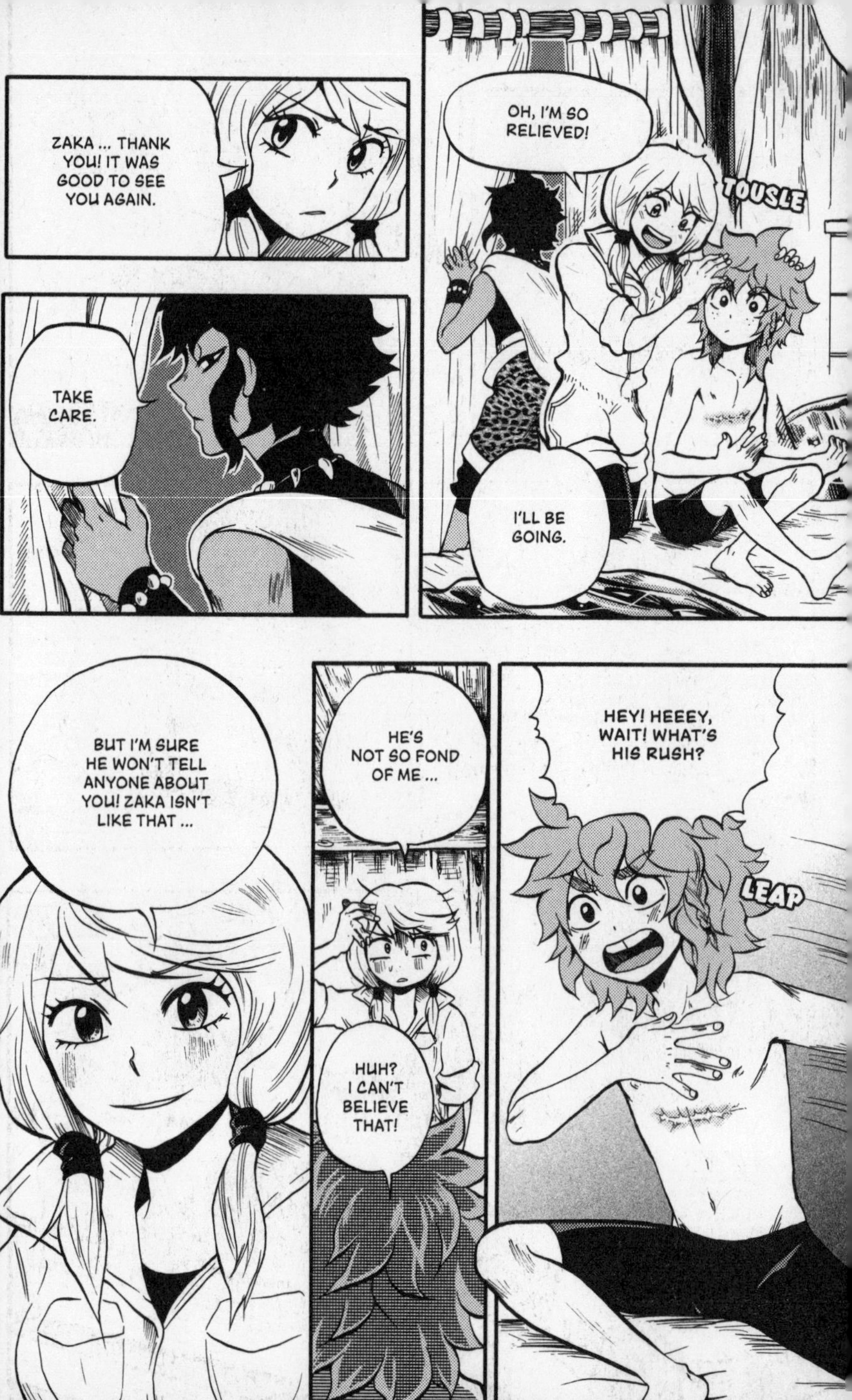
OH, I'M SO RELIEVED!
TOUSLE
I'LL BE GOING.
ZAKA ... THANK YOU! IT WAS GOOD TO SEE YOU AGAIN.
TAKE CARE.
HEY! HEEEY, WAIT! WHAT'S HIS RUSH?
LEAP
HE'S NOT SO FOND OF ME ...
HUH? I CAN'T BELIEVE THAT!
BUT I'M SURE HE WON'T TELL ANYONE ABOUT YOU! ZAKA ISN'T LIKE THAT ...

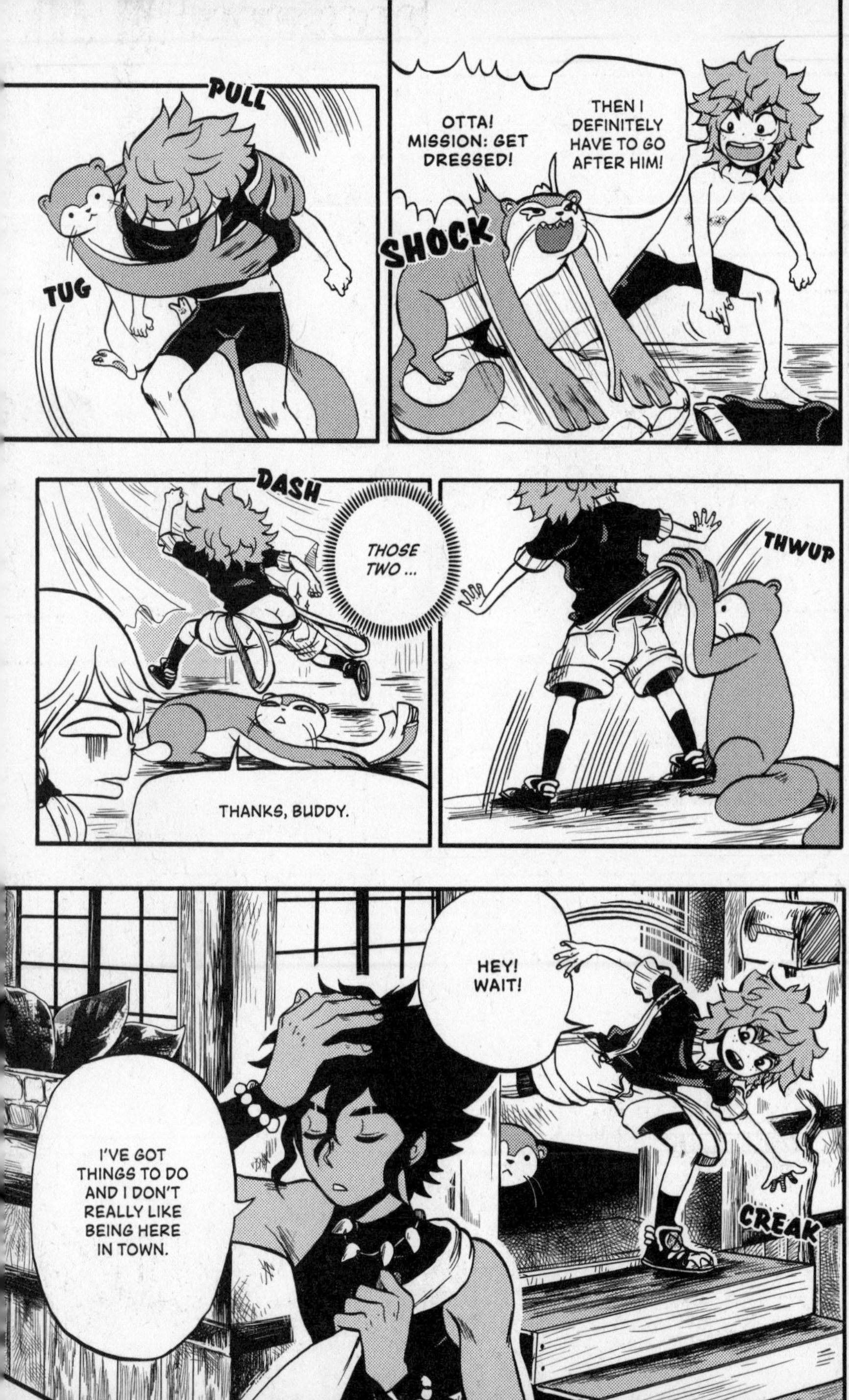
THEN I DEFINITELY HAVE TO GO AFTER HIM!
OTTA! MISSION: GET DRESSED!
SHOCK
PULL
TUG
THWUP
DASH
THOSE TWO ...
THANKS, BUDDY.
HEY! WAIT!
CREAK
I'VE GOT THINGS TO DO AND I DON'T REALLY LIKE BEING HERE IN TOWN.

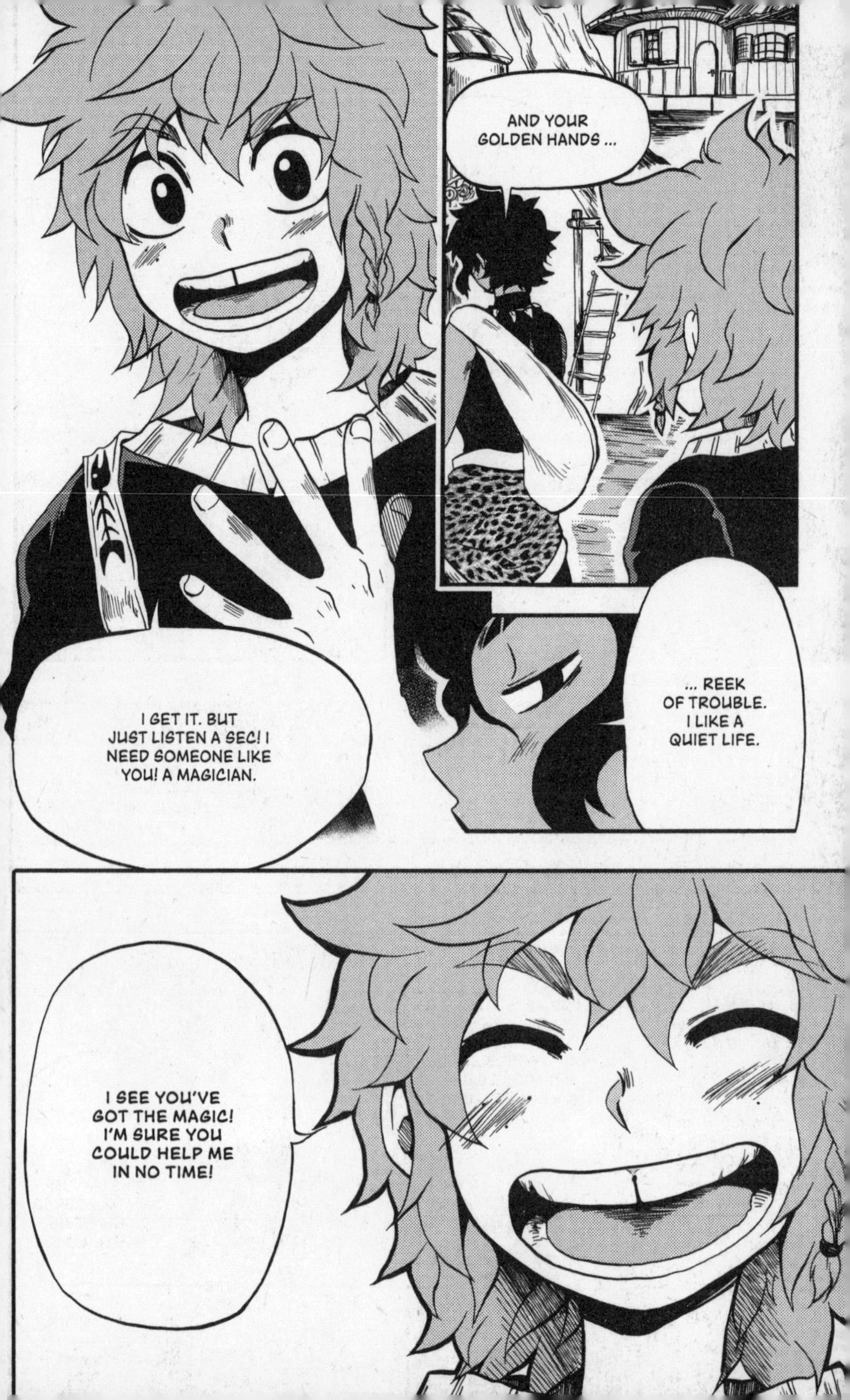
AND YOUR GOLDEN HANDS ...
... REEK OF TROUBLE. I LIKE A QUIET LIFE.
I GET IT. BUT JUST LISTEN A SEC! I NEED SOMEONE LIKE YOU! A MAGICIAN.
I SEE YOU'VE GOT THE MAGIC! I'M SURE YOU COULD HELP ME IN NO TIME!

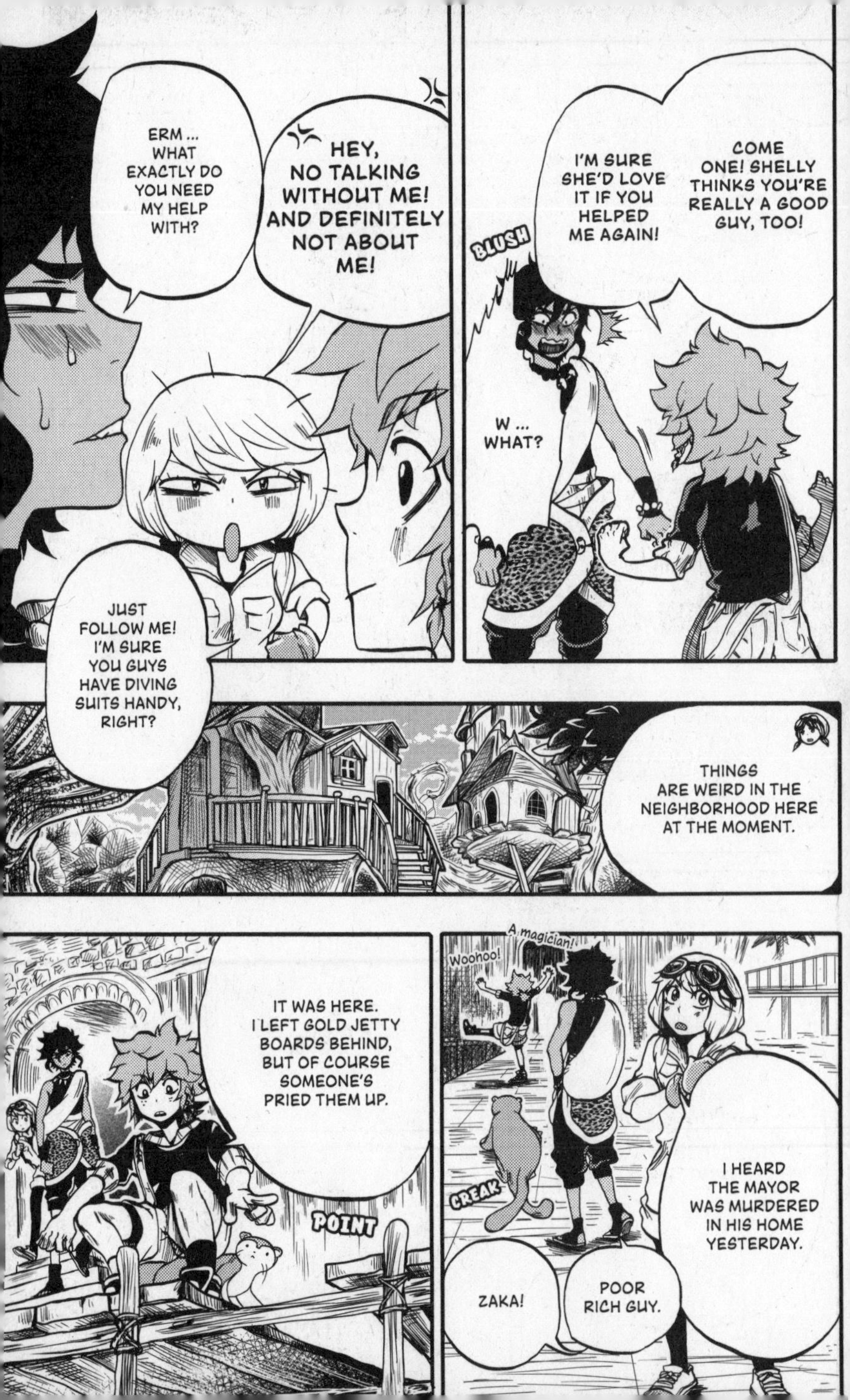
COME ONE! SHELLY THINKS YOU'RE REALLY A GOOD GUY, TOO!
I'M SURE SHE'D LOVE IT IF YOU HELPED ME AGAIN!
BLUSH
W ... WHAT?
HEY, NO TALKING WITHOUT ME! AND DEFINITELY NOT ABOUT ME!
ERM ... WHAT EXACTLY DO YOU NEED MY HELP WITH?
JUST FOLLOW ME! I'M SURE YOU GUYS HAVE DIVING SUITS HANDY, RIGHT?
THINGS ARE WEIRD IN THE NEIGHBORHOOD HERE AT THE MOMENT.
A magician!
Woohoo!
I HEARD THE MAYOR WAS MURDERED IN HIS HOME YESTERDAY.
CREAK
POOR RICH GUY.
ZAKA!
IT WAS HERE. I LEFT GOLD JETTY BOARDS BEHIND, BUT OF COURSE SOMEONE'S PRIED THEM UP.
POINT

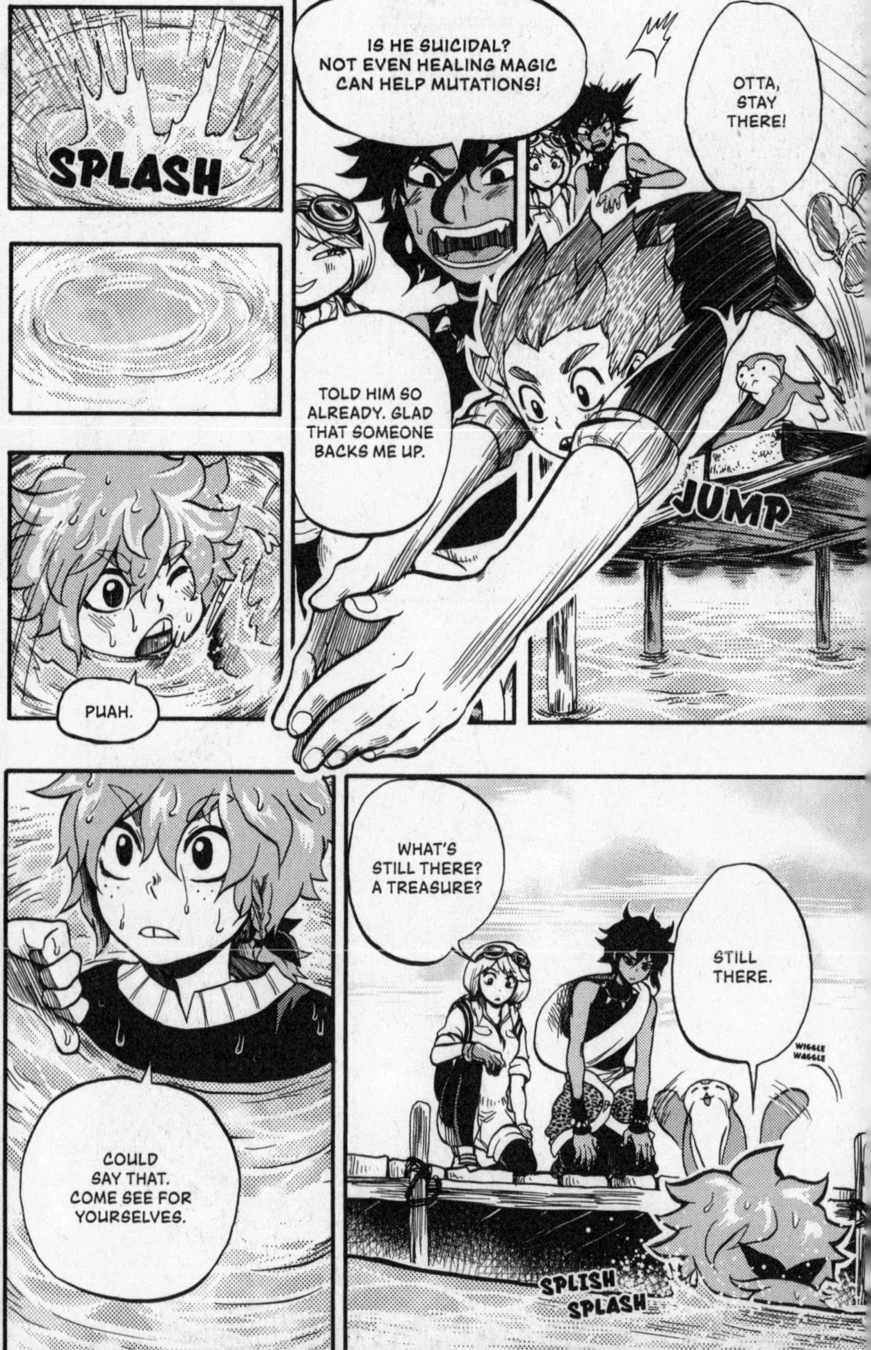
OTTA, STAY THERE!
JUMP
IS HE SUICIDAL? NOT EVEN HEALING MAGIC CAN HELP MUTATIONS!
TOLD HIM SO ALREADY. GLAD THAT SOMEONE BACKS ME UP.
SPLASH
PUAH.
STILL THERE.
WHAT'S STILL THERE? A TREASURE?
WIGGLE WAGGLE
SPLISH SPLASH
COULD SAY THAT. COME SEE FOR YOURSELVES.

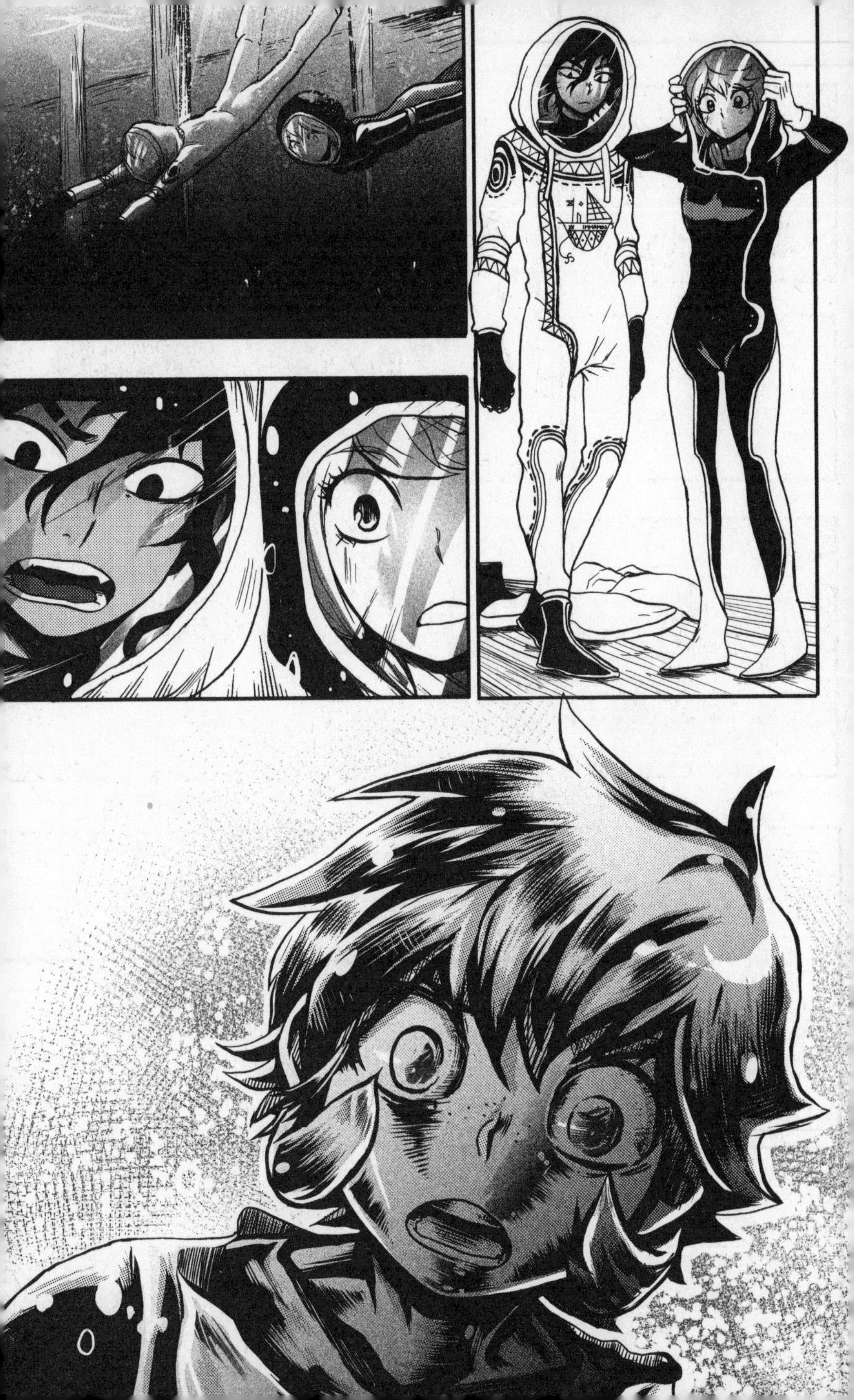

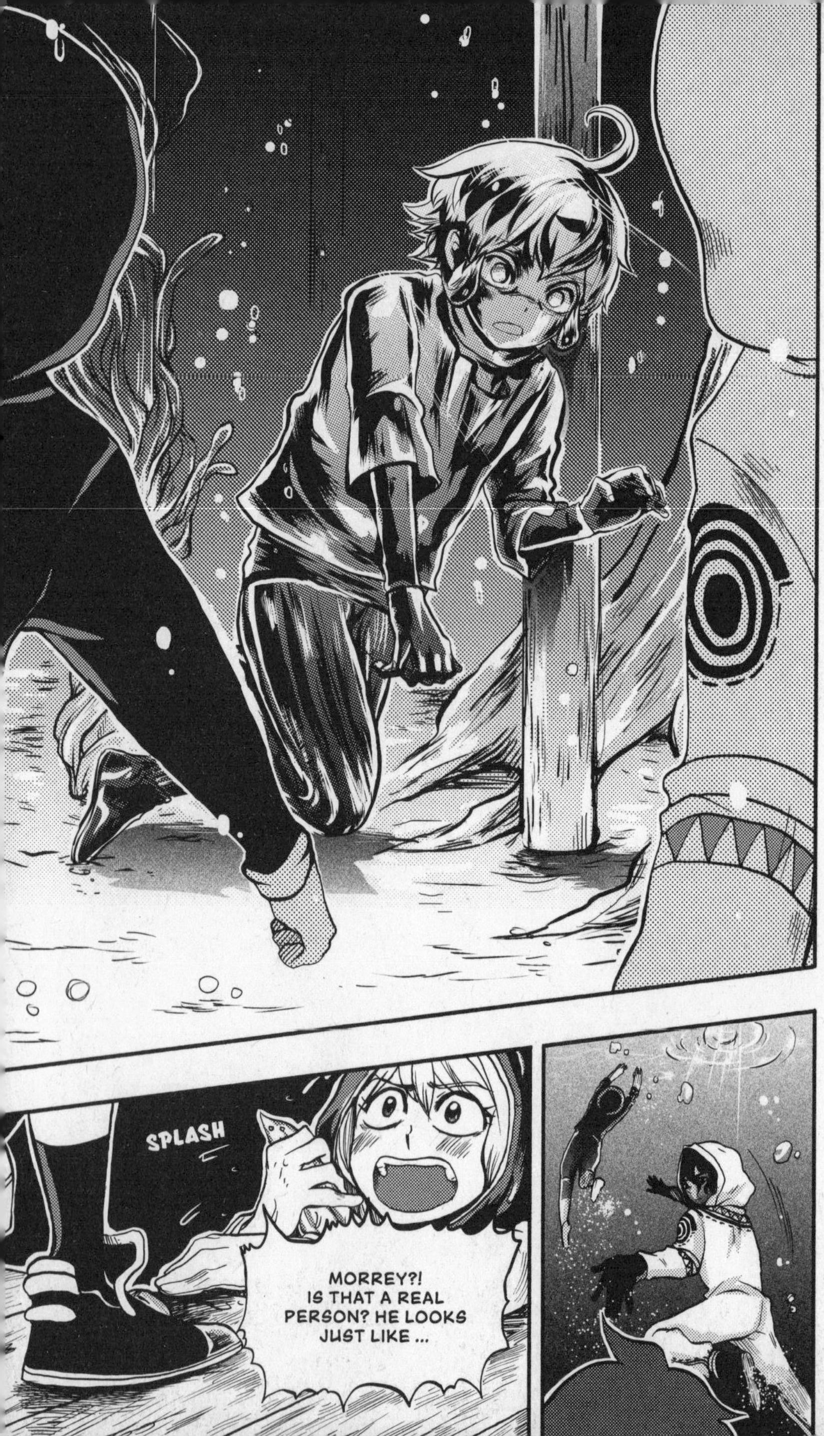
SPLASH
MORREY?! IS THAT A REAL PERSON? HE LOOKS JUST LIKE ...

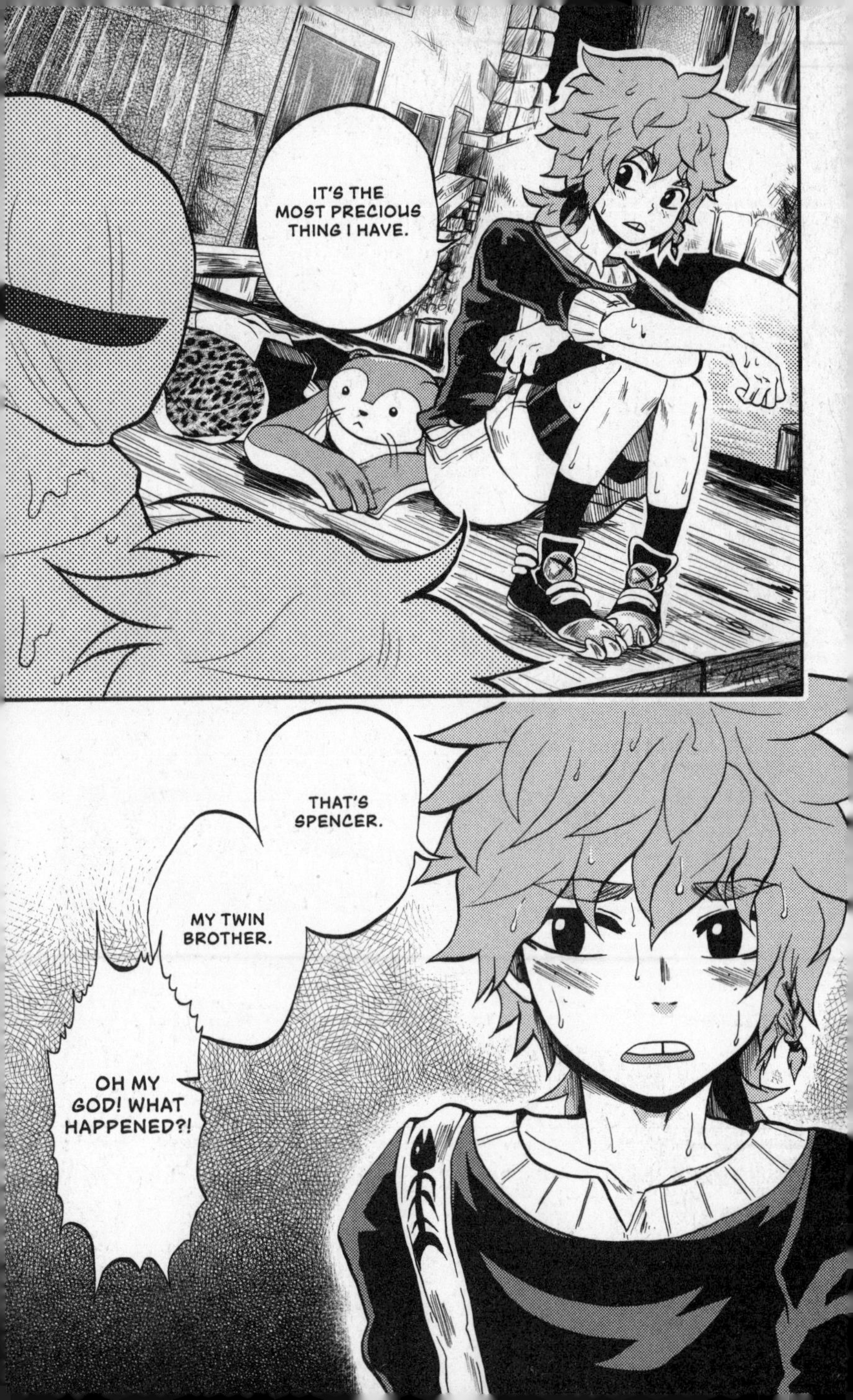
IT'S THE MOST PRECIOUS THING I HAVE.
THAT'S SPENCER.
MY TWIN BROTHER.
OH MY GOD! WHAT HAPPENED?!

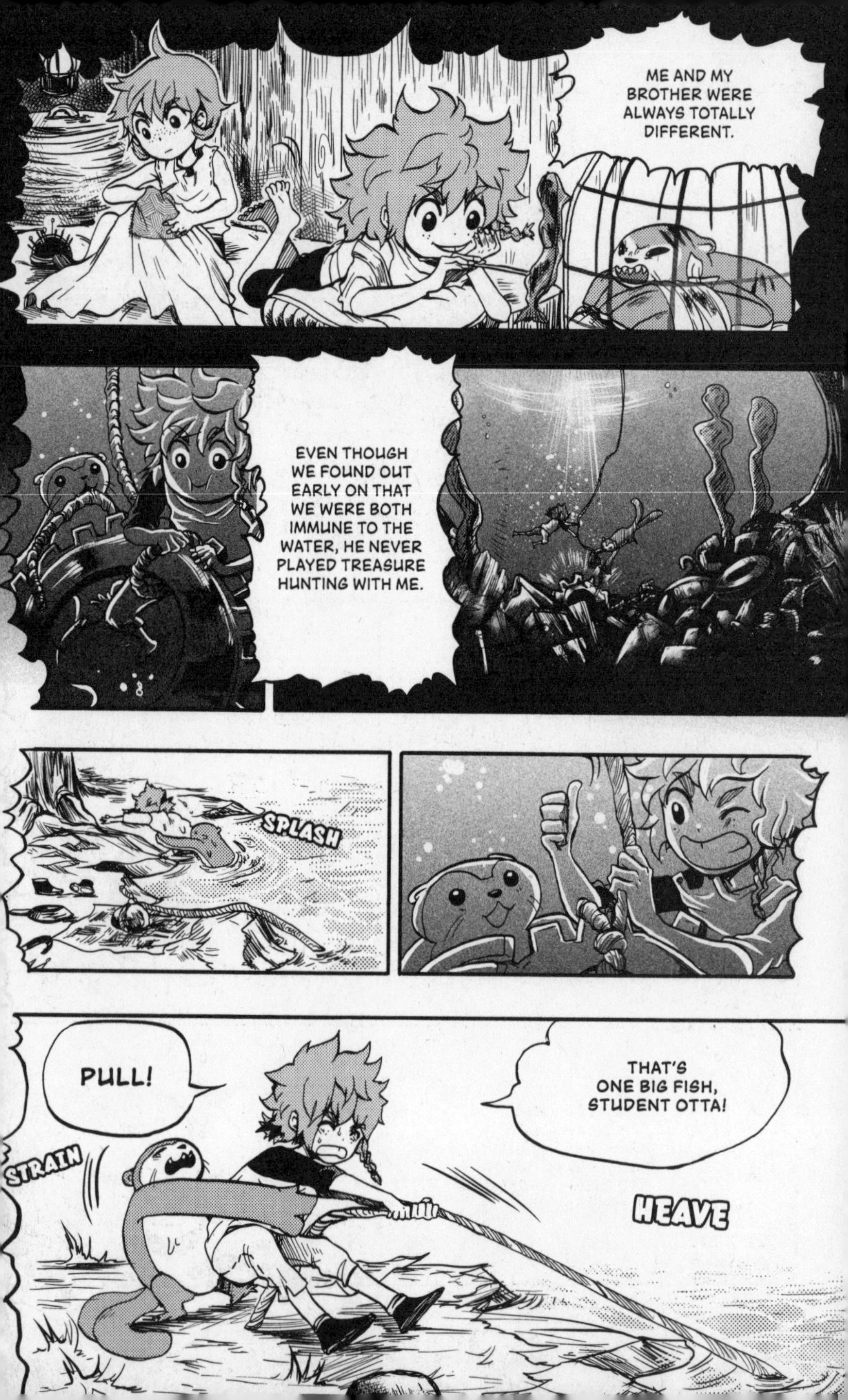
ME AND MY BROTHER WERE ALWAYS TOTALLY DIFFERENT.
EVEN THOUGH WE FOUND OUT EARLY ON THAT WE WERE BOTH IMMUNE TO THE WATER, HE NEVER PLAYED TREASURE HUNTING WITH ME.
SPLASH
THAT'S ONE BIG FISH, STUDENT OTTA!
PULL!
HEAVE
STRAIN

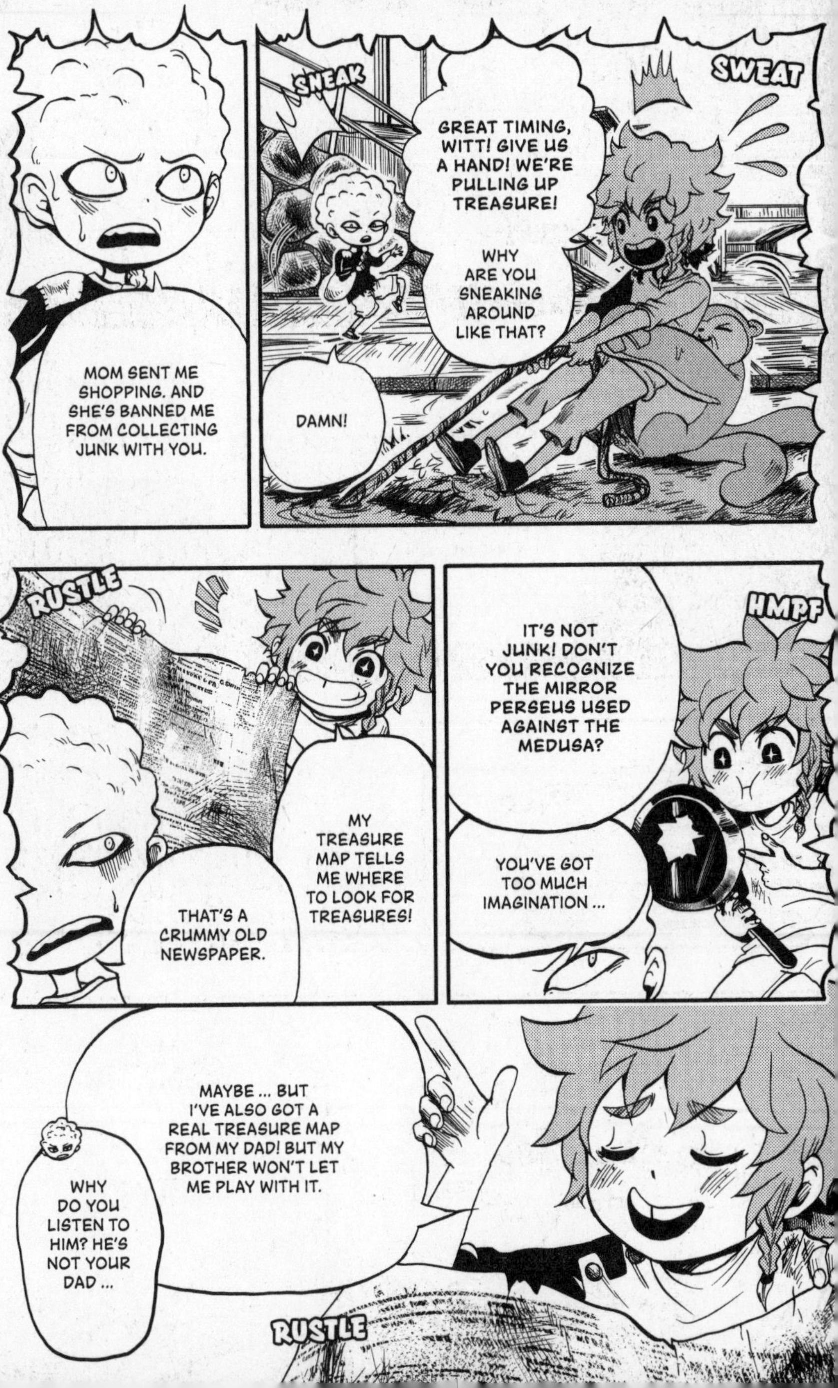
SWEAT
GREAT TIMING, WITT! GIVE US A HAND! WE'RE PULLING UP TREASURE!
WHY ARE YOU SNEAKING AROUND LIKE THAT?
SNEAK
DAMN!
MOM SENT ME SHOPPING. AND SHE'S BANNED ME FROM COLLECTING JUNK WITH YOU.
HMPF
IT'S NOT JUNK! DON'T YOU RECOGNIZE THE MIRROR PERSEUS USED AGAINST THE MEDUSA?
YOU'VE GOT TOO MUCH IMAGINATION ...
RUSTLE
MY TREASURE MAP TELLS ME WHERE TO LOOK FOR TREASURES!
THAT'S A CRUMMY OLD NEWSPAPER.
MAYBE ... BUT I'VE ALSO GOT A REAL TREASURE MAP FROM MY DAD! BUT MY BROTHER WON'T LET ME PLAY WITH IT.
WHY DO YOU LISTEN TO HIM? HE'S NOT YOUR DAD ...
RUSTLE

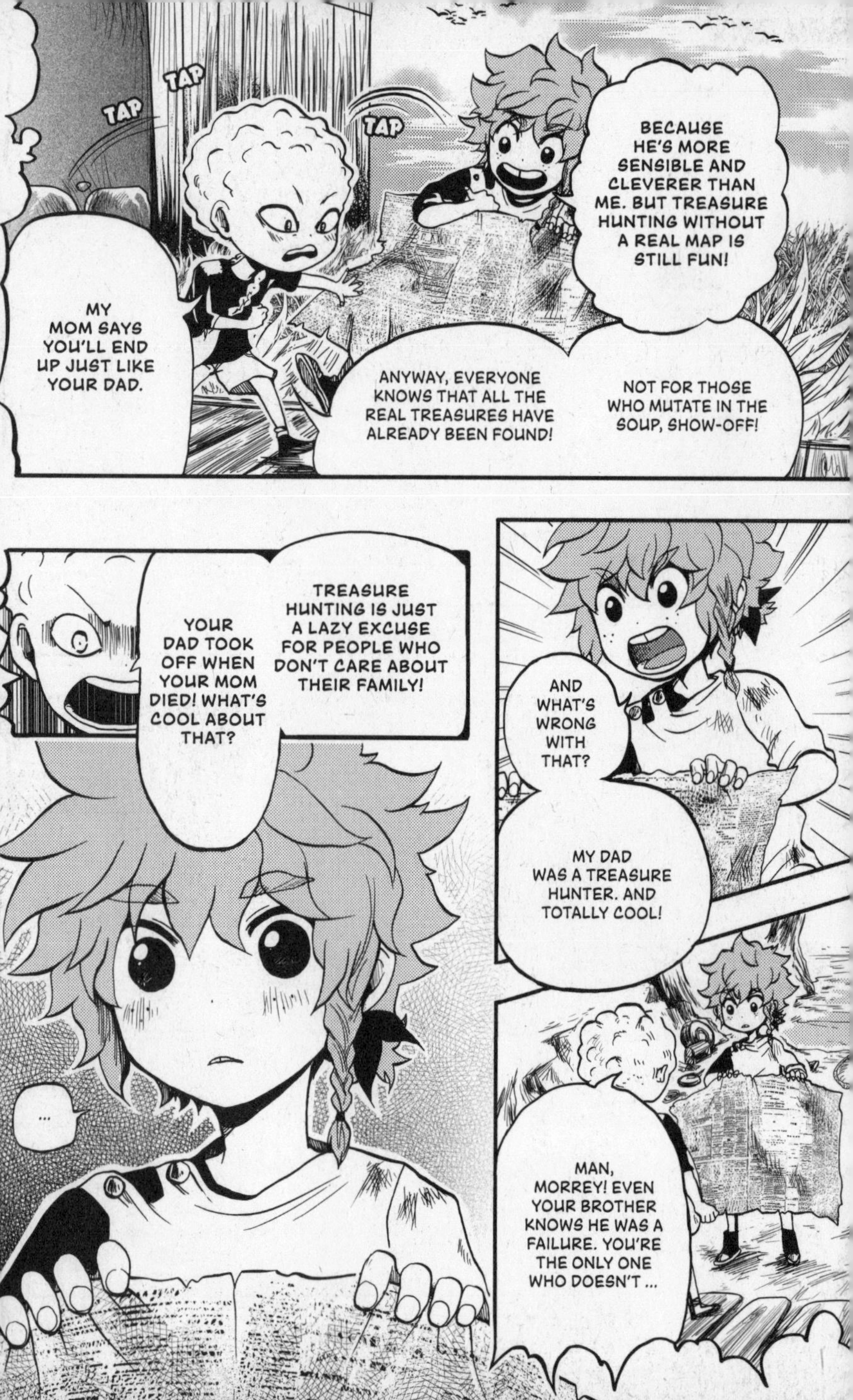
BECAUSE HE'S MORE SENSIBLE AND CLEVERER THAN ME. BUT TREASURE HUNTING WITHOUT A REAL MAP IS STILL FUN!
TAP
TAP
TAP
NOT FOR THOSE WHO MUTATE IN THE SOUP, SHOW-OFF!
ANYWAY, EVERYONE KNOWS THAT ALL THE REAL TREASURES HAVE ALREADY BEEN FOUND!
MY MOM SAYS YOU'LL END UP JUST LIKE YOUR DAD.
AND WHAT'S WRONG WITH THAT?
MY DAD WAS A TREASURE HUNTER. AND TOTALLY COOL!
MAN, MORREY! EVEN YOUR BROTHER KNOWS HE WAS A FAILURE. YOU'RE THE ONLY ONE WHO DOESN'T ...
TREASURE HUNTING IS JUST A LAZY EXCUSE FOR PEOPLE WHO DON'T CARE ABOUT THEIR FAMILY!
YOUR DAD TOOK OFF WHEN YOUR MOM DIED! WHAT'S COOL ABOUT THAT?
...

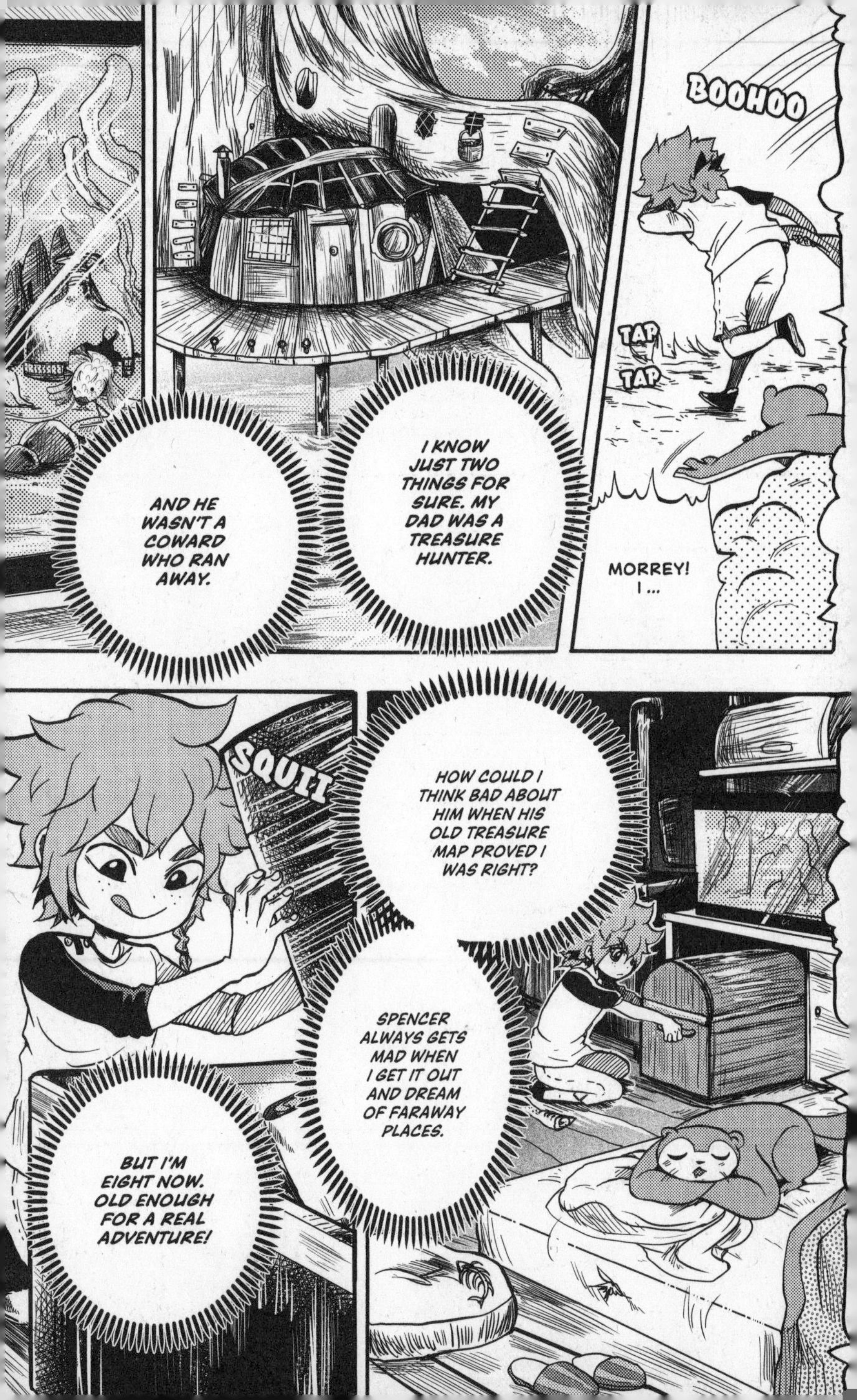
BOOHOO
TAP
TAP
MORREY! I...
I KNOW JUST TWO THINGS FOR SURE. MY DAD WAS A TREASURE HUNTER.
AND HE WASN'T A COWARD WHO RAN AWAY.
HOW COULD I THINK BAD ABOUT HIM WHEN HIS OLD TREASURE MAP PROVED I WAS RIGHT?
SPENCER ALWAYS GETS MAD WHEN I GET IT OUT AND DREAM OF FARAWAY PLACES.
SQUII
BUT I'M EIGHT NOW. OLD ENOUGH FOR A REAL ADVENTURE!

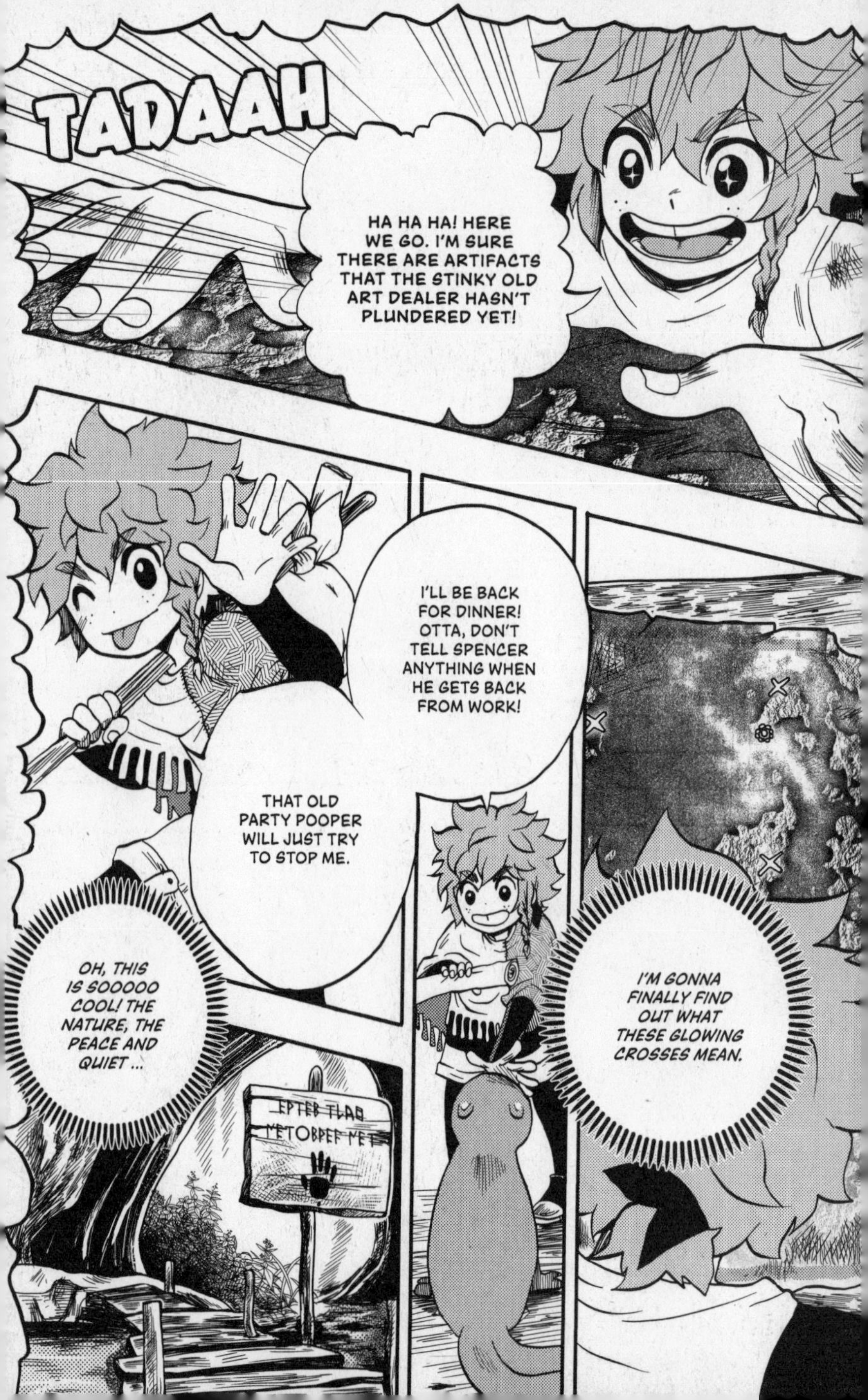
TADAAH
HA HA HA! HERE WE GO. I'M SURE THERE ARE ARTIFACTS THAT THE STINKY OLD ART DEALER HASN'T PLUNDERED YET!
I'M GONNA FINALLY FIND OUT WHAT THESE GLOWING CROSSES MEAN.
I'LL BE BACK FOR DINNER! OTTA, DON'T TELL SPENCER ANYTHING WHEN HE GETS BACK FROM WORK!
THAT OLD PARTY POOPER WILL JUST TRY TO STOP ME.
OH, THIS IS SOOOOO COOL! THE NATURE, THE PEACE AND QUIET ...

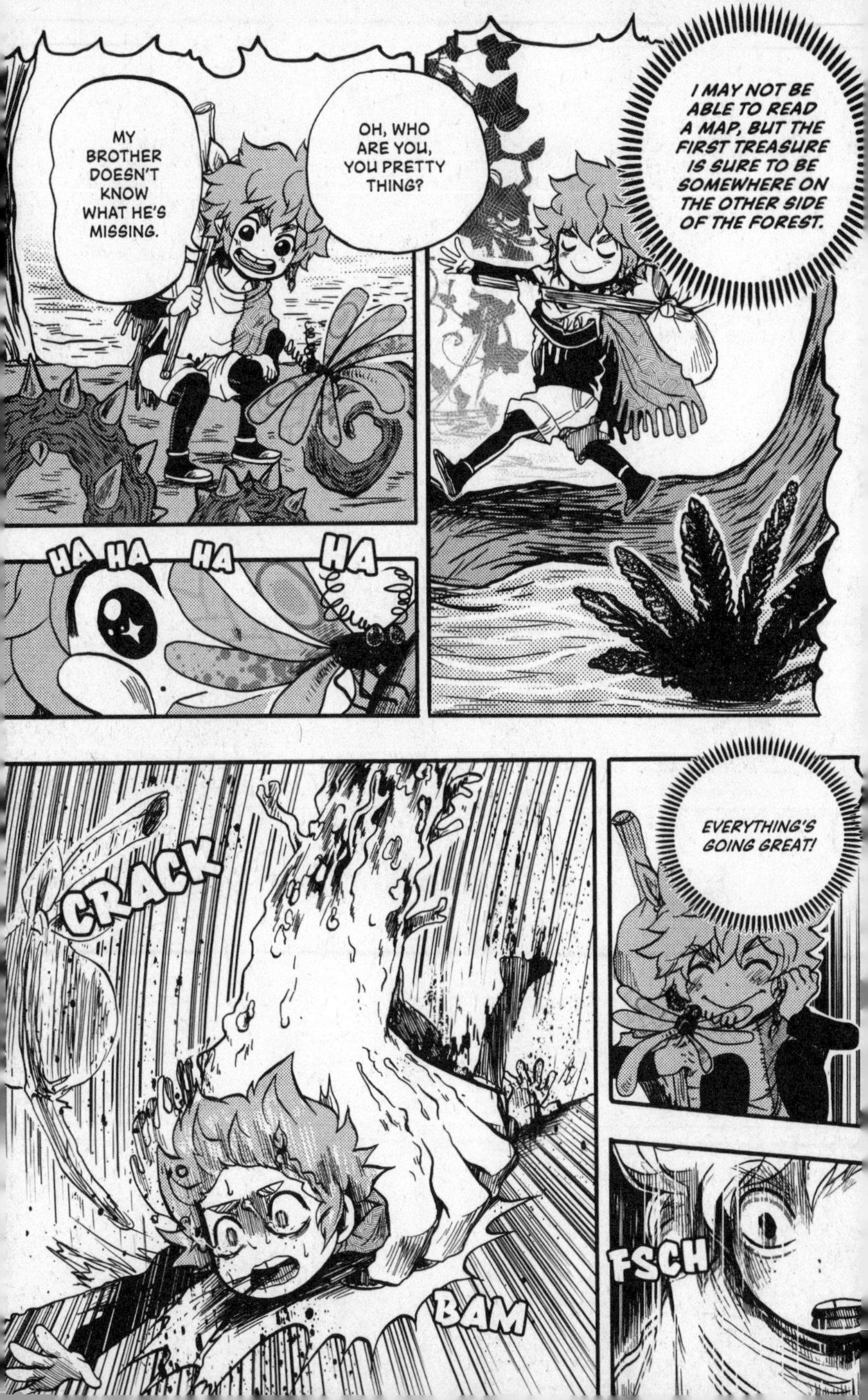
I MAY NOT BE ABLE TO READ A MAP, BUT THE FIRST TREASURE IS SURE TO BE SOMEWHERE ON THE OTHER SIDE OF THE FOREST.
OH, WHO ARE YOU, YOU PRETTY THING?
MY BROTHER DOESN'T KNOW WHAT HE'S MISSING.
HA HA HA HA
EVERYTHING'S GOING GREAT!
FSCH
CRACK
BAM

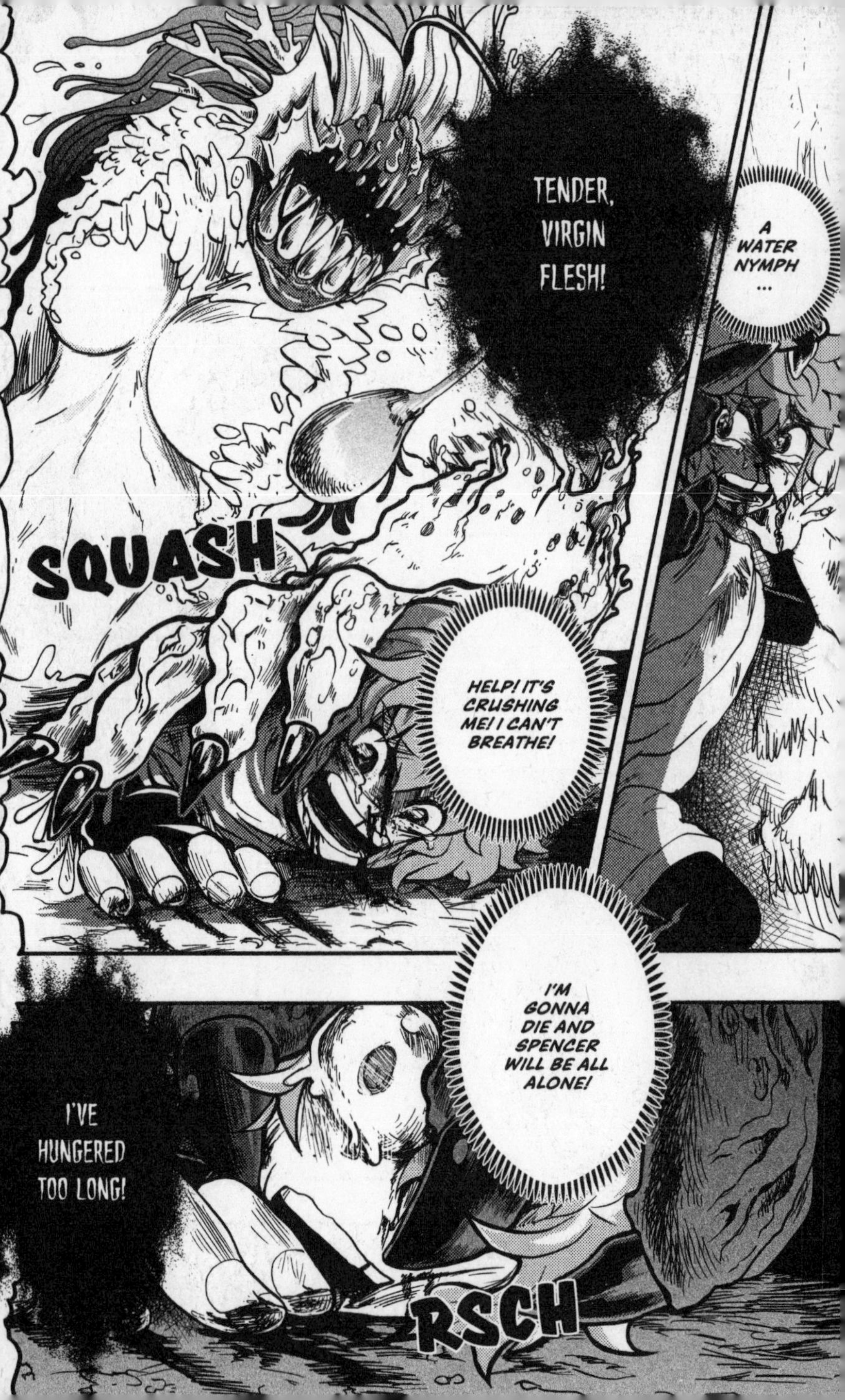
A WATER NYMPH ...
TENDER, VIRGIN FLESH!
SQUASH
HELP! IT'S CRUSHING ME! I CAN'T BREATHE!
I'M GONNA DIE AND SPENCER WILL BE ALL ALONE!
I'VE HUNGERED TOO LONG!
RSCH

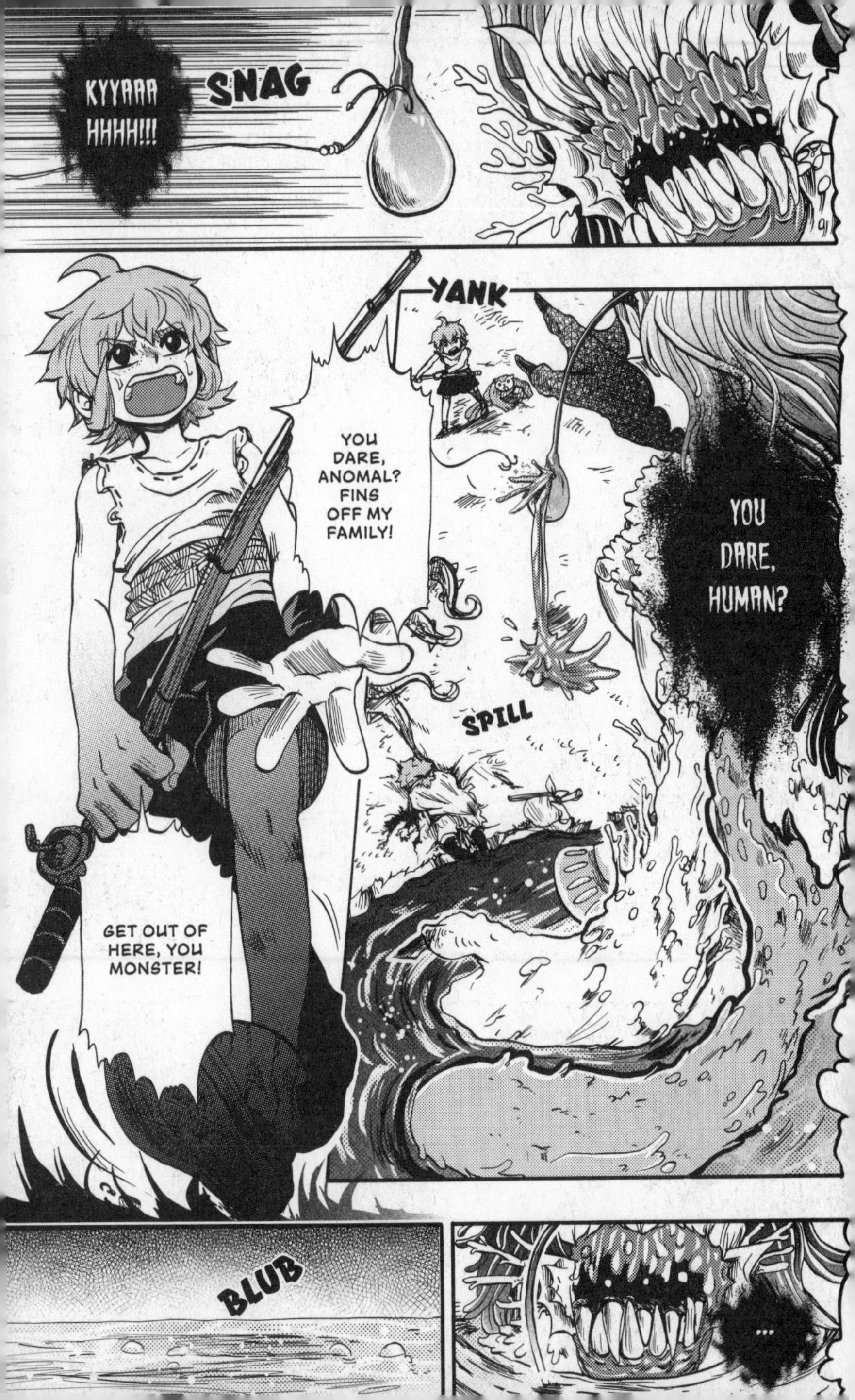
SNAG
KYYAAA HHHH!!!
YANK
YOU DARE, HUMAN?
YOU DARE, ANOMAL? FINS OFF MY FAMILY!
SPILL
GET OUT OF HERE, YOU MONSTER!
...
BLUB

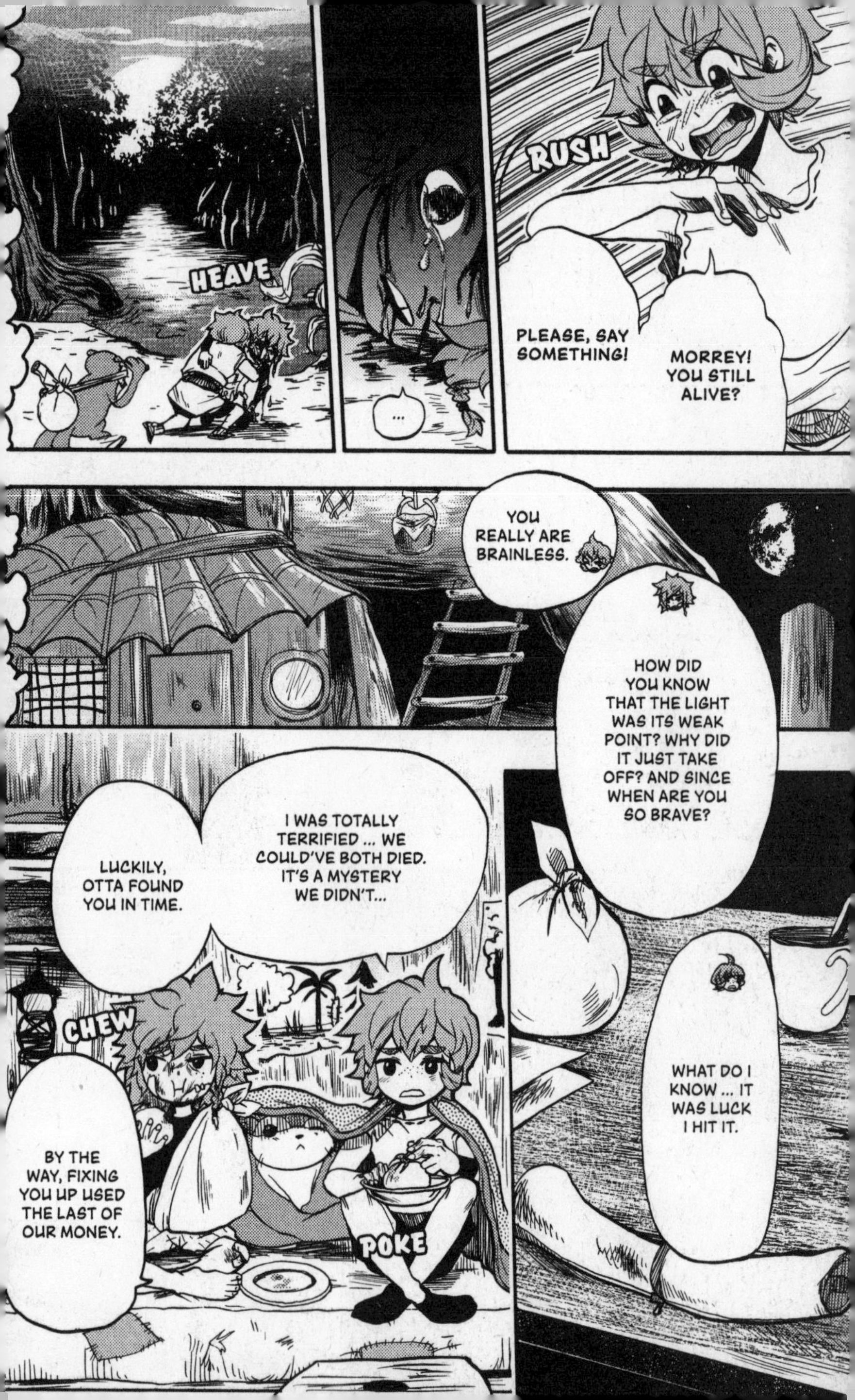
RUSH
MORREY! YOU STILL ALIVE?
PLEASE, SAY SOMETHING!
...
HEAVE
YOU REALLY ARE BRAINLESS.
HOW DID YOU KNOW THAT THE LIGHT WAS ITS WEAK POINT? WHY DID IT JUST TAKE OFF? AND SINCE WHEN ARE YOU SO BRAVE?
WHAT DO I KNOW ... IT WAS LUCK I HIT IT.
I WAS TOTALLY TERRIFIED ... WE COULD'VE BOTH DIED. IT'S A MYSTERY WE DIDN'T...
LUCKILY, OTTA FOUND YOU IN TIME.
CHEW
POKE
BY THE WAY, FIXING YOU UP USED THE LAST OF OUR MONEY.

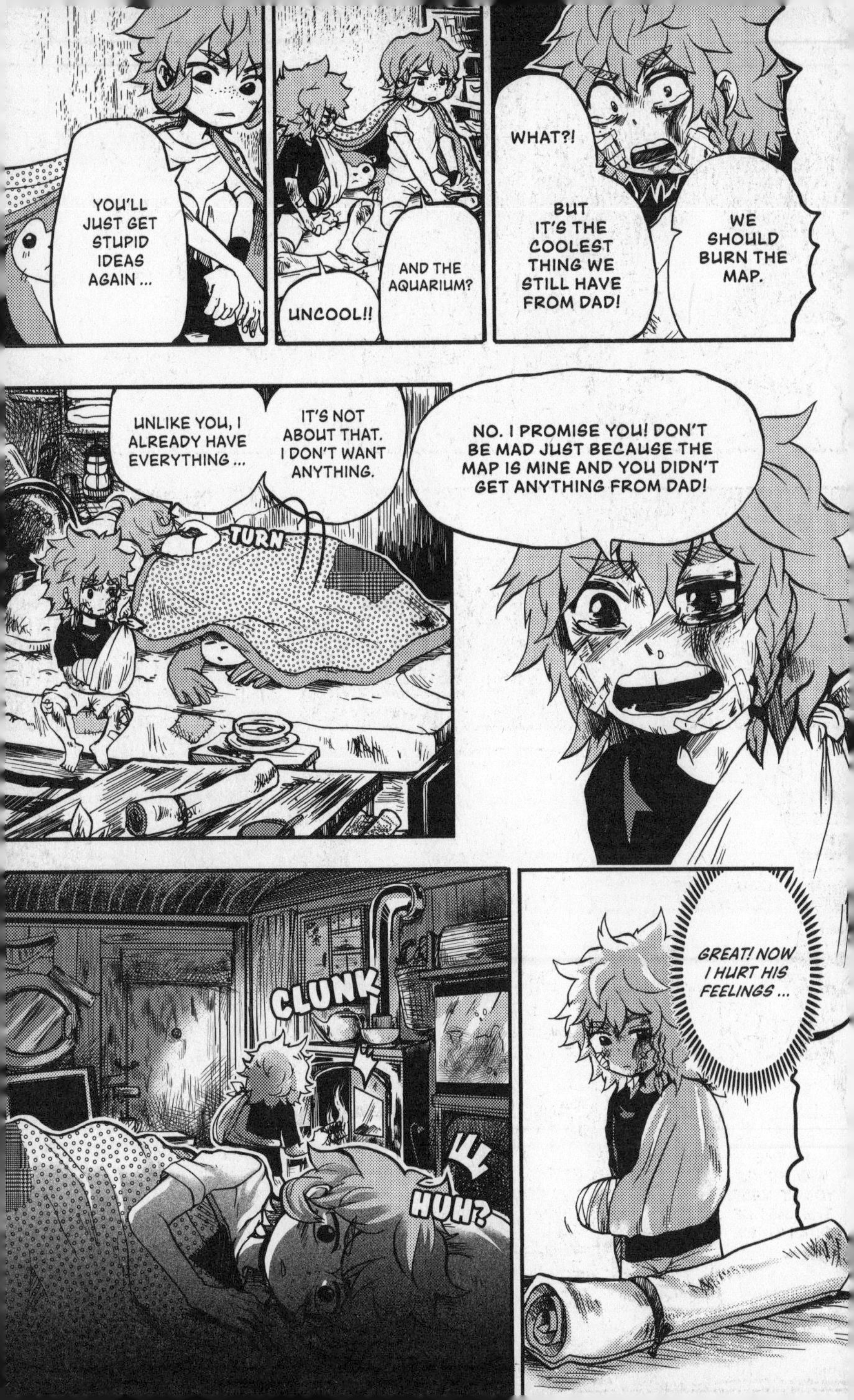
WE SHOULD BURN THE MAP.
WHAT?!
BUT IT'S THE COOLEST THING WE STILL HAVE FROM DAD!
AND THE AQUARIUM?
UNCOOL!!
YOU'LL JUST GET STUPID IDEAS AGAIN ...
NO. I PROMISE YOU! DON'T BE MAD JUST BECAUSE THE MAP IS MINE AND YOU DIDN'T GET ANYTHING FROM DAD!
IT'S NOT ABOUT THAT. I DON'T WANT ANYTHING.
UNLIKE YOU, I ALREADY HAVE EVERYTHING ...
TURN
GREAT! NOW I HURT HIS FEELINGS ...
CLUNK
HUH?

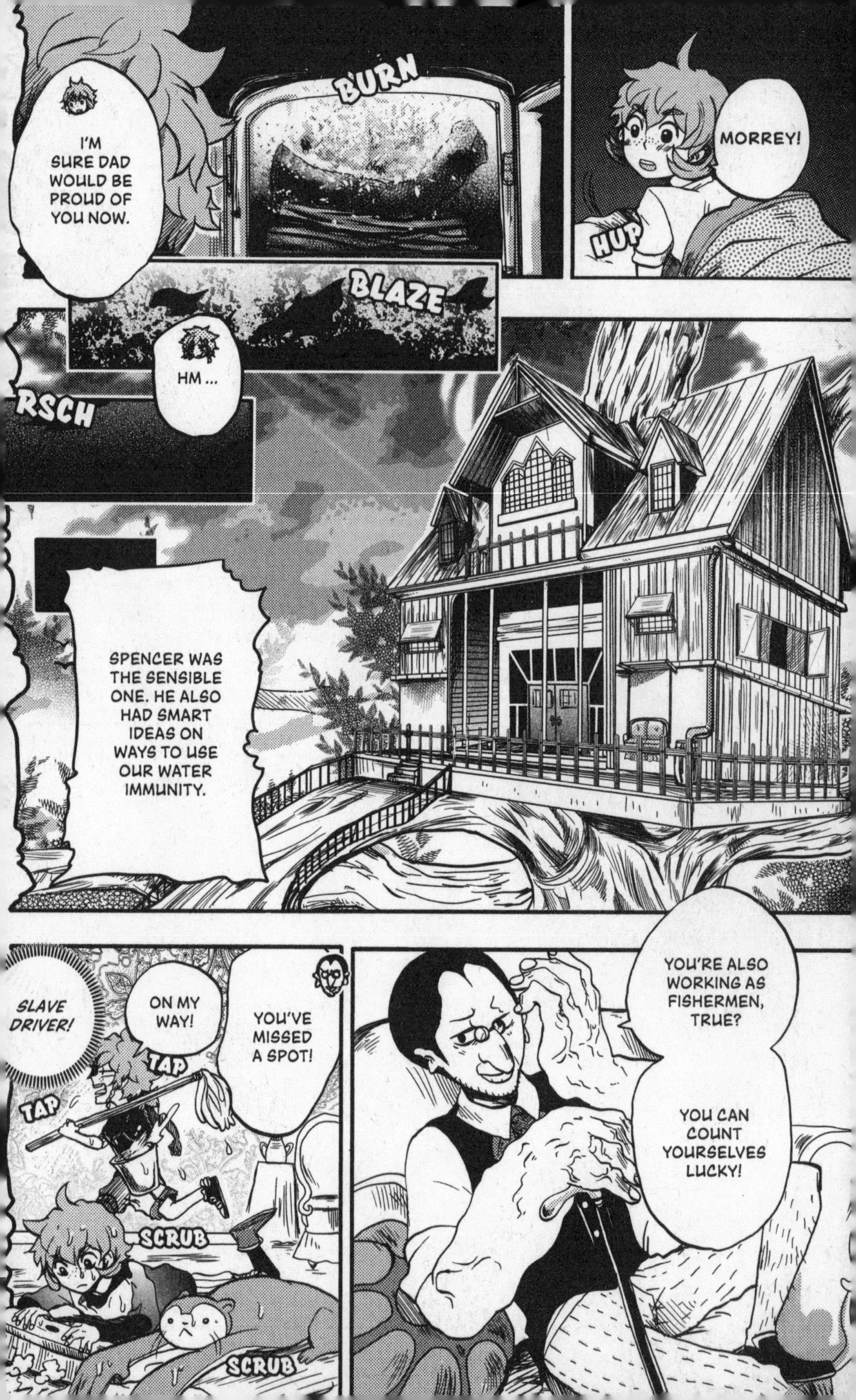
MORREY!
HUP
BURN
I'M SURE DAD WOULD BE PROUD OF YOU NOW.
BLAZE
HM ...
RSCH
SPENCER WAS THE SENSIBLE ONE. HE ALSO HAD SMART IDEAS ON WAYS TO USE OUR WATER IMMUNITY.
YOU'RE ALSO WORKING AS FISHERMEN, TRUE?
YOU CAN COUNT YOURSELVES LUCKY!
YOU'VE MISSED A SPOT!
ON MY WAY!
SLAVE DRIVER!
TAP
TAP
SCRUB
SCRUB

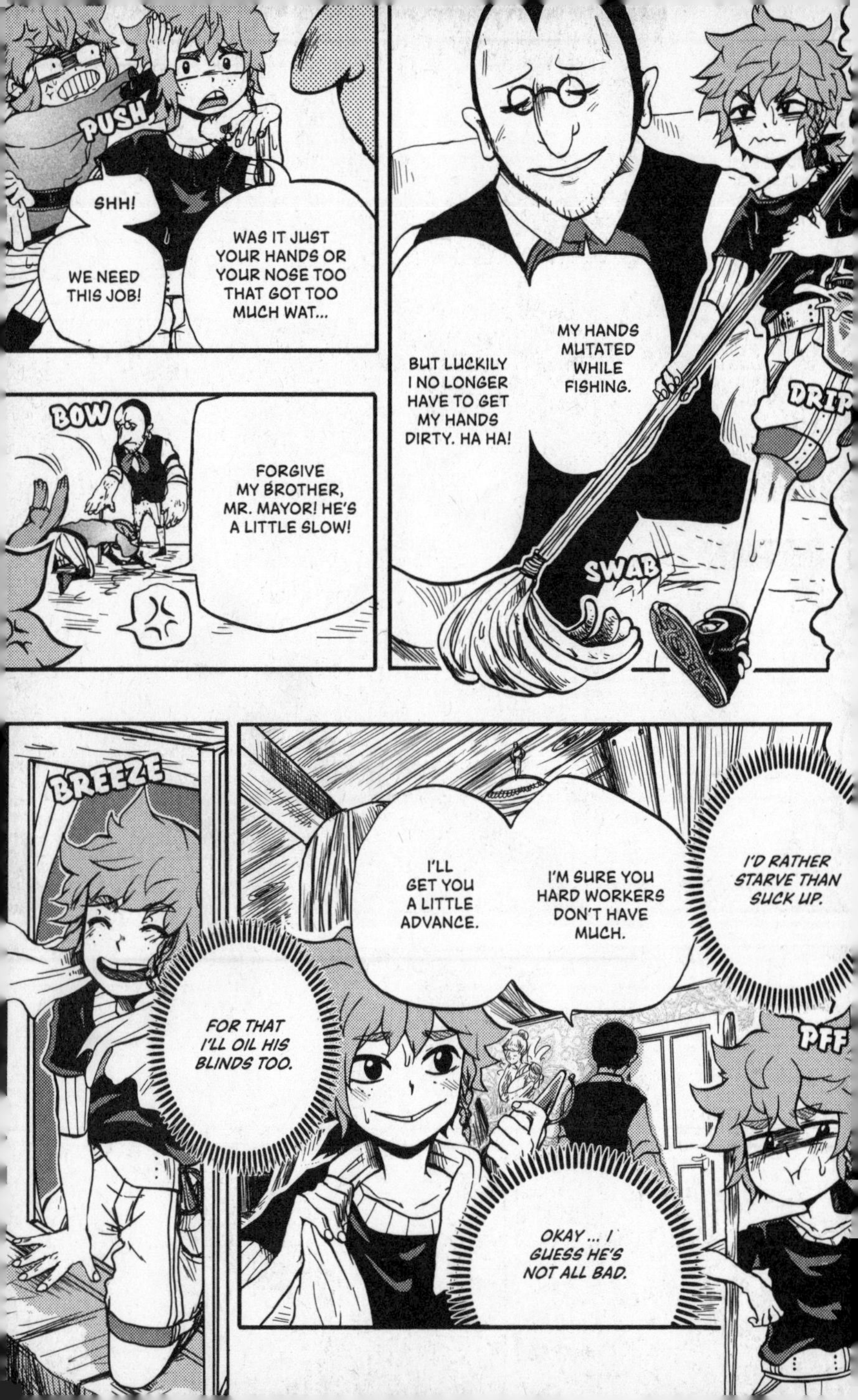
MY HANDS MUTATED WHILE FISHING.
BUT LUCKILY I NO LONGER HAVE TO GET MY HANDS DIRTY. HA HA!
DRIP
SWAB
WAS IT JUST YOUR HANDS OR YOUR NOSE TOO THAT GOT TOO MUCH WAT...
PUSH
SHH!
WE NEED THIS JOB!
FORGIVE MY BROTHER, MR. MAYOR! HE'S A LITTLE SLOW!
BOW
I'D RATHER STARVE THAN SUCK UP.
I'M SURE YOU HARD WORKERS DON'T HAVE MUCH.
I'LL GET YOU A LITTLE ADVANCE.
PFF
OKAY ... I GUESS HE'S NOT ALL BAD.
BREEZE
FOR THAT I'LL OIL HIS BLINDS TOO.

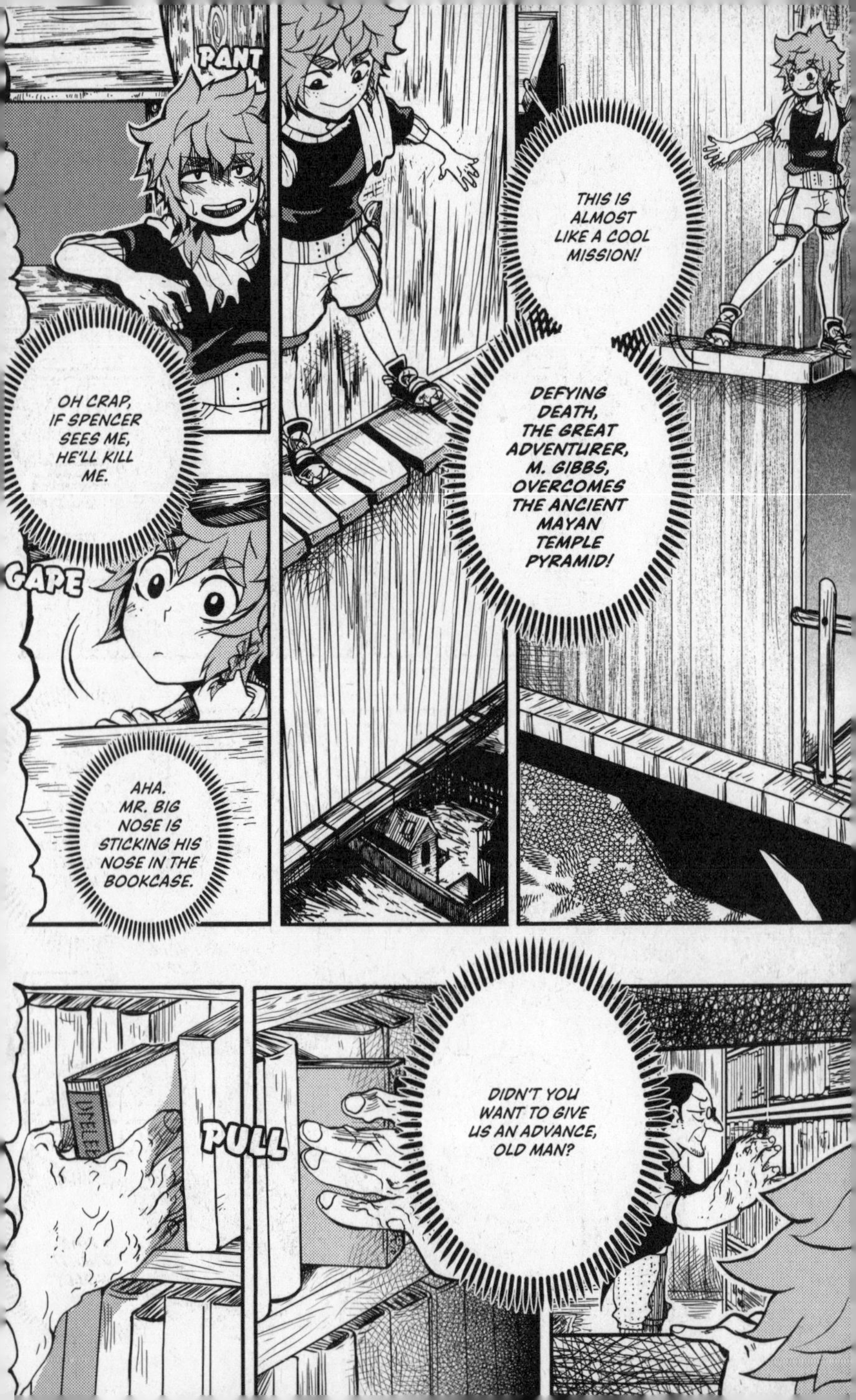
THIS IS ALMOST LIKE A COOL MISSION!
DEFYING DEATH, THE GREAT ADVENTURER, M. GIBBS, OVERCOMES THE ANCIENT MAYAN TEMPLE PYRAMID!
PANT
OH CRAP, IF SPENCER SEES ME, HE'LL KILL ME.
GAPE
AHA. MR. BIG NOSE IS STICKING HIS NOSE IN THE BOOKCASE.
DIDN'T YOU WANT TO GIVE US AN ADVANCE, OLD MAN?
PULL

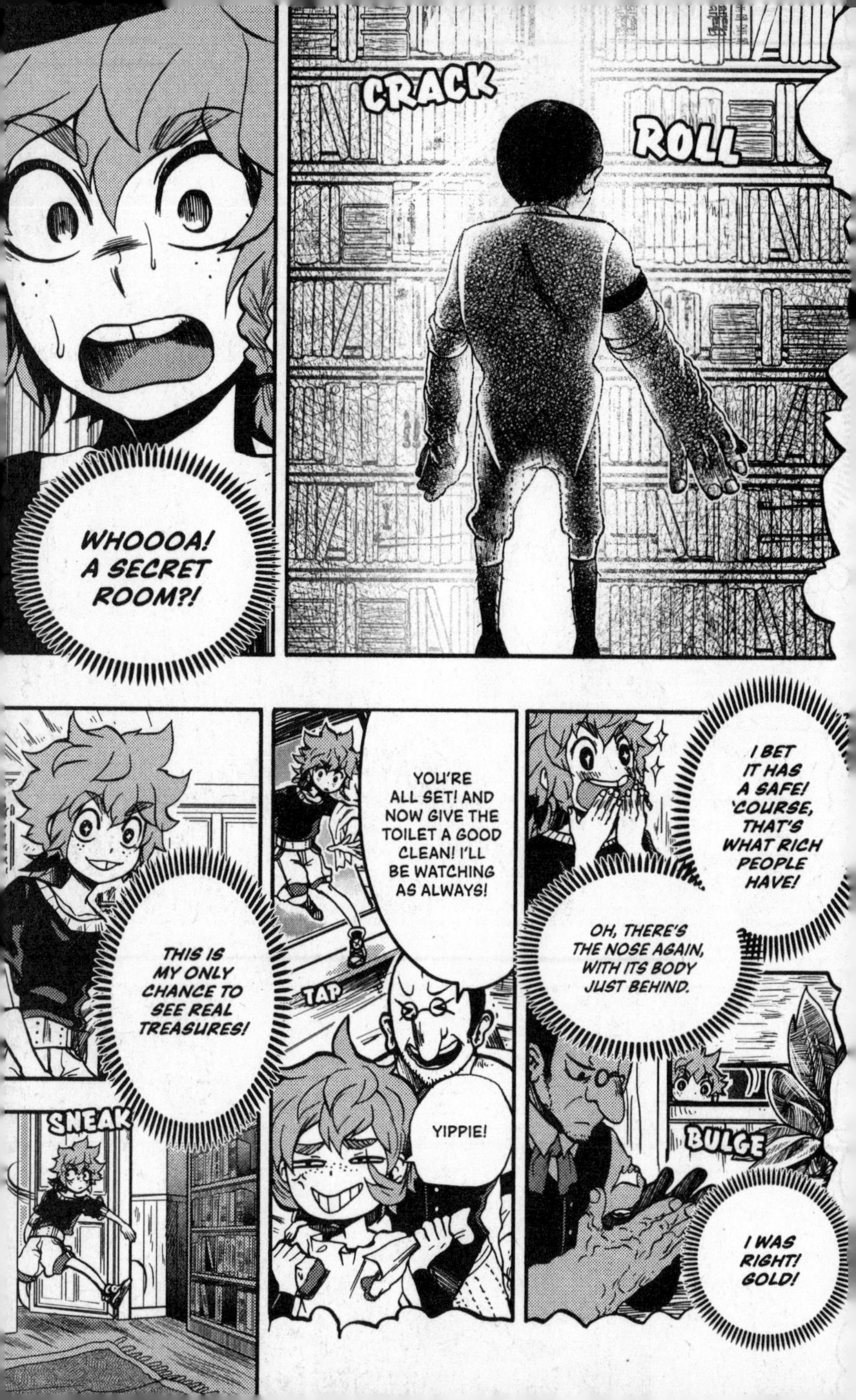
CRACK
ROLL
WHOOOA! A SECRET ROOM?!
I BET IT HAS A SAFE! 'COURSE, THAT'S WHAT RICH PEOPLE HAVE!
OH, THERE'S THE NOSE AGAIN, WITH ITS BODY JUST BEHIND.
BULGE
I WAS RIGHT! GOLD!
YOU'RE ALL SET! AND NOW GIVE THE TOILET A GOOD CLEAN! I'LL BE WATCHING AS ALWAYS!
TAP
YIPPIE!
THIS IS MY ONLY CHANCE TO SEE REAL TREASURES!
SNEAK

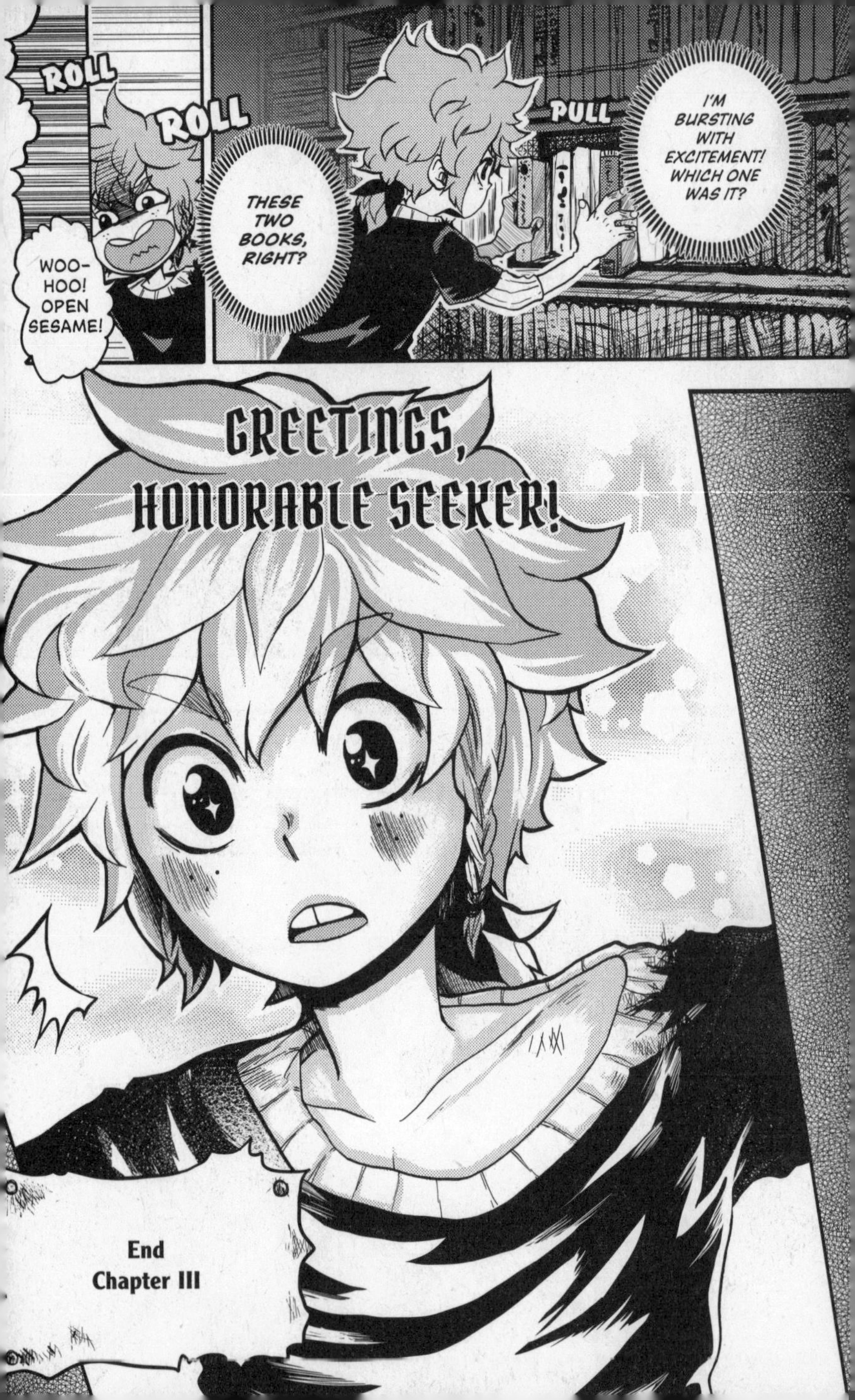
I'M BURSTING WITH EXCITEMENT! WHICH ONE WAS IT?
PULL
THESE TWO BOOKS, RIGHT?
ROLL
ROLL
WOO-HOO! OPEN SESAME!
GREETINGS, HONORABLE SEEKER!
End
Chapter III

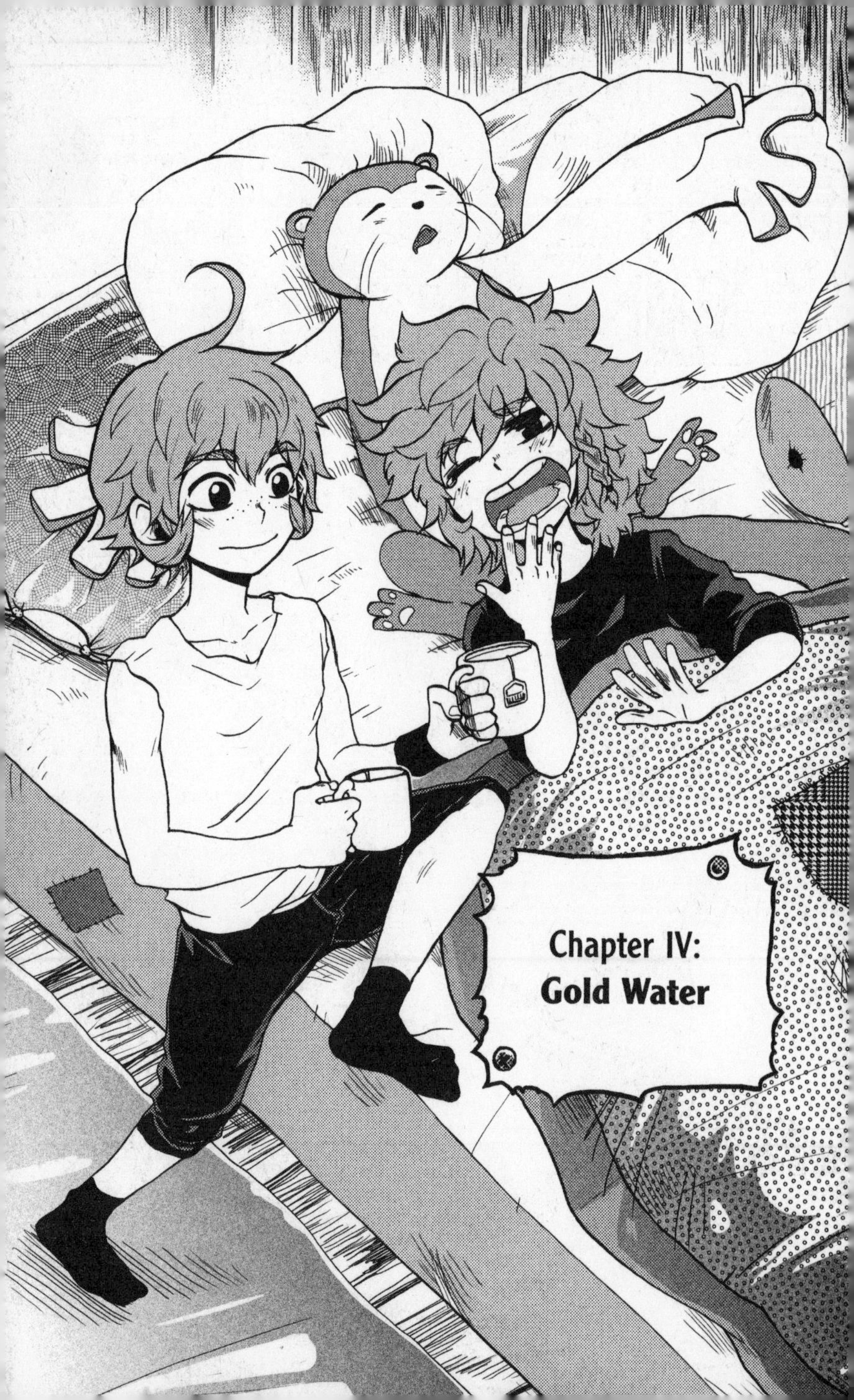
Chapter IV:
Gold Water

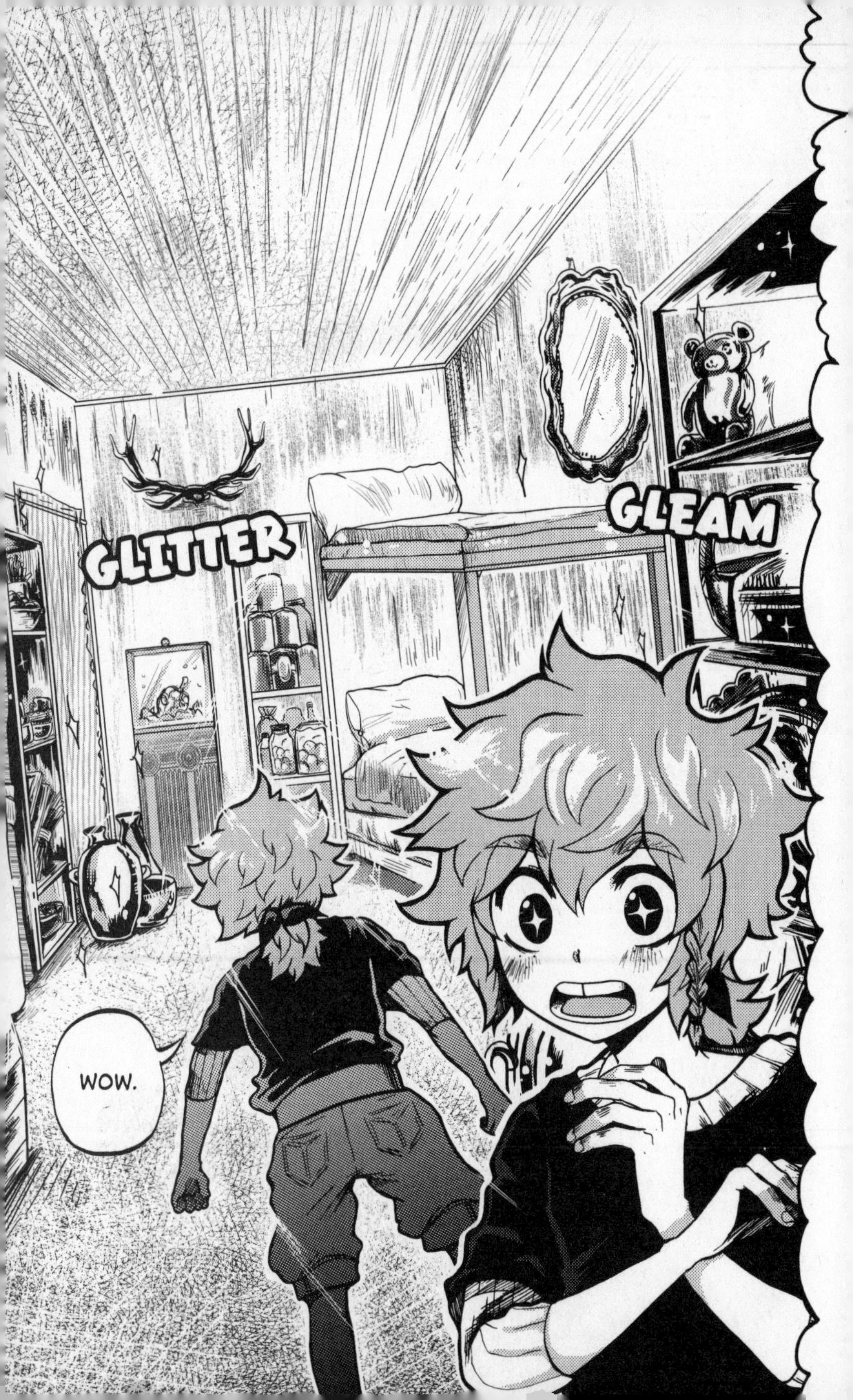
GLEAM
GLITTER
WOW.

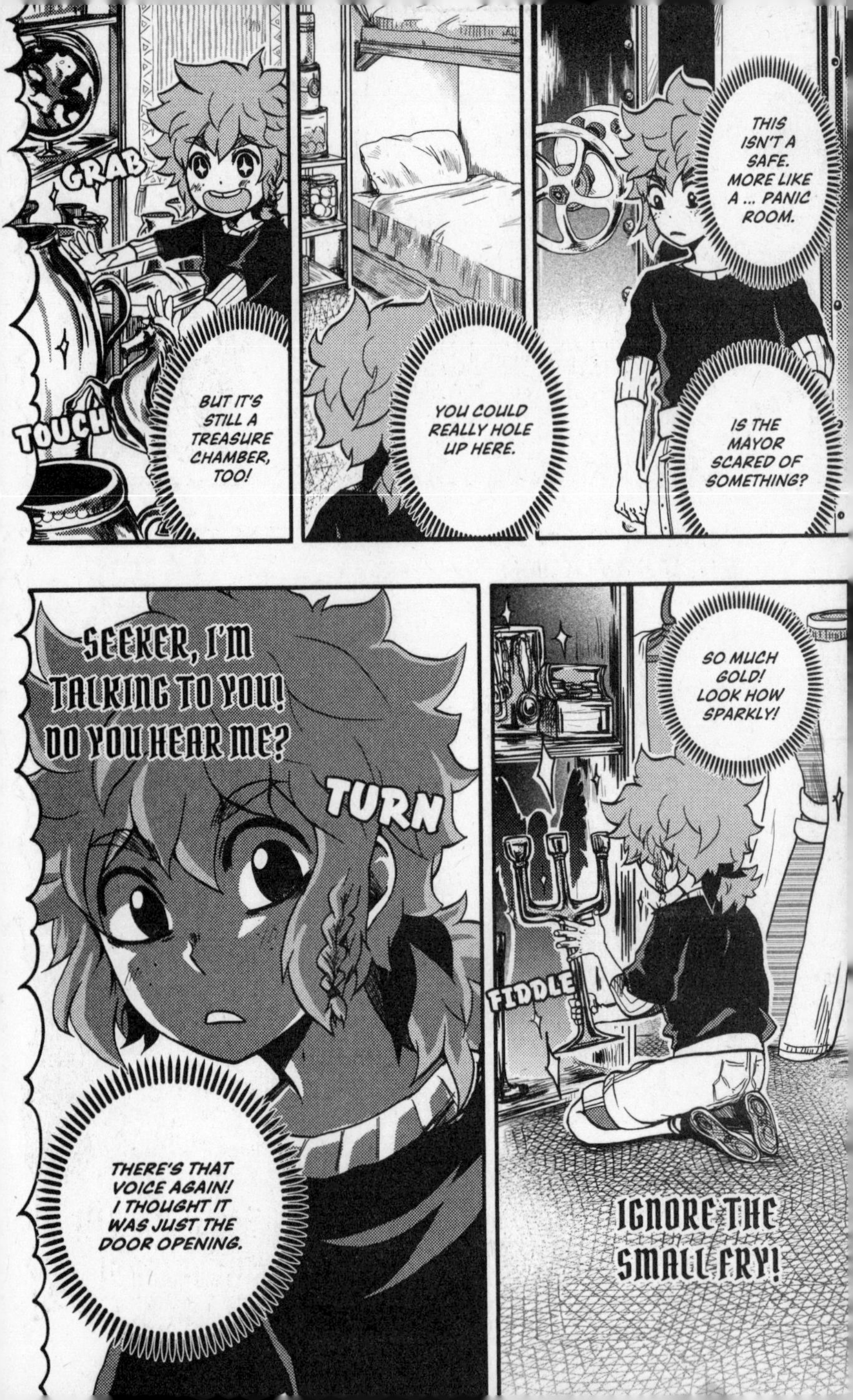
THIS ISN'T A SAFE. MORE LIKE A ... PANIC ROOM.
IS THE MAYOR SCARED OF SOMETHING?
YOU COULD REALLY HOLE UP HERE.
GRAB
BUT IT'S STILL A TREASURE CHAMBER, TOO!
TOUCH
SO MUCH GOLD! LOOK HOW SPARKLY!
FIDDLE
IGNORE THE SMALL FRY!
SEEKER, I'M TALKING TO YOU! DO YOU HEAR ME?
TURN
THERE'S THAT VOICE AGAIN! I THOUGHT IT WAS JUST THE DOOR OPENING.

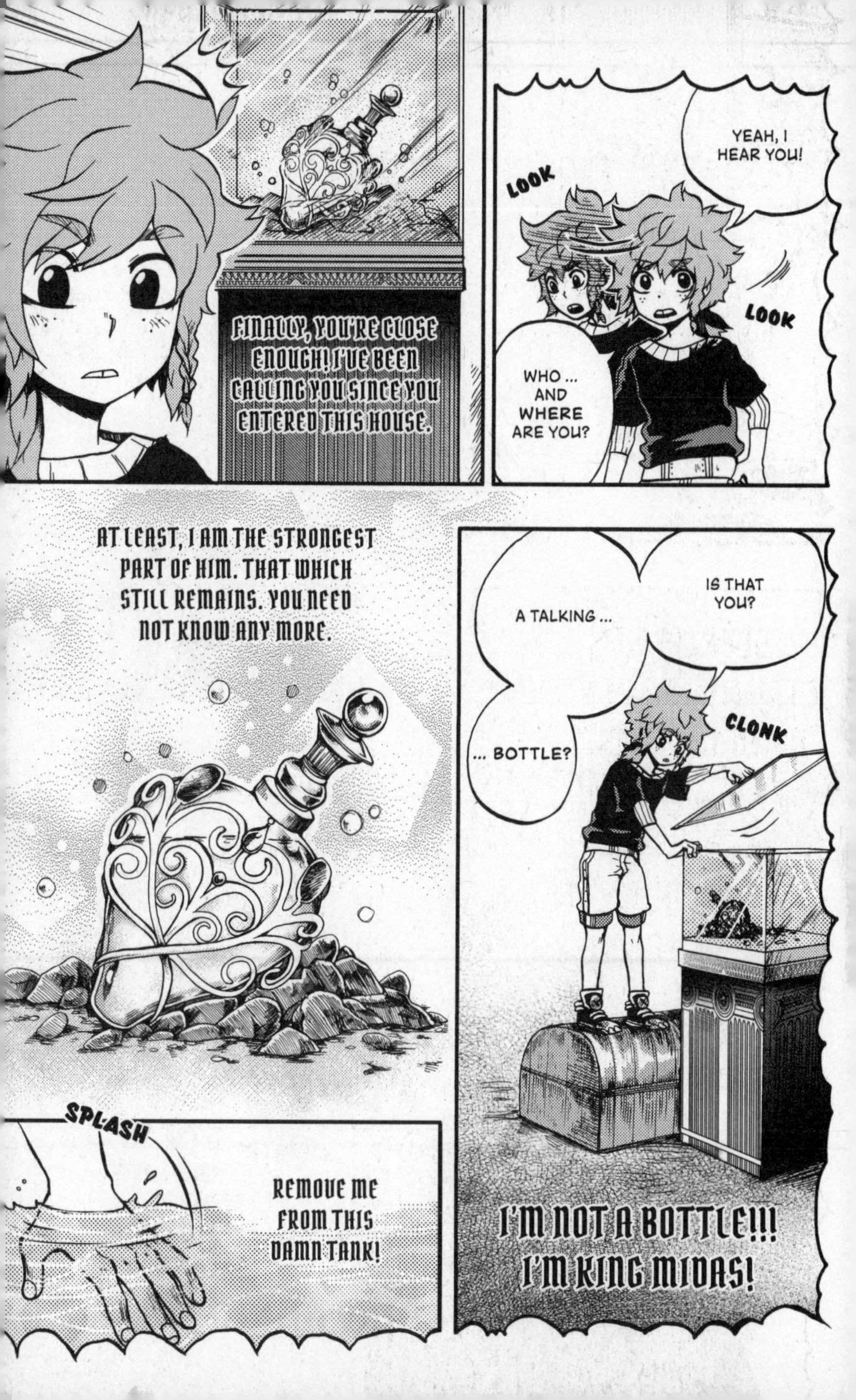
YEAH, I HEAR YOU!
LOOK
LOOK
WHO ... AND WHERE ARE YOU?
FINALLY, YOU'RE CLOSE ENOUGH! I'VE BEEN CALLING YOU SINCE YOU ENTERED THIS HOUSE.
IS THAT YOU?
A TALKING ...
CLONK
... BOTTLE?
I'M NOT A BOTTLE!!! I'M KING MIDAS!
AT LEAST, I AM THE STRONGEST PART OF HIM. THAT WHICH STILL REMAINS. YOU NEED NOT KNOW ANY MORE.
REMOVE ME FROM THIS DAMN TANK!
SPLASH

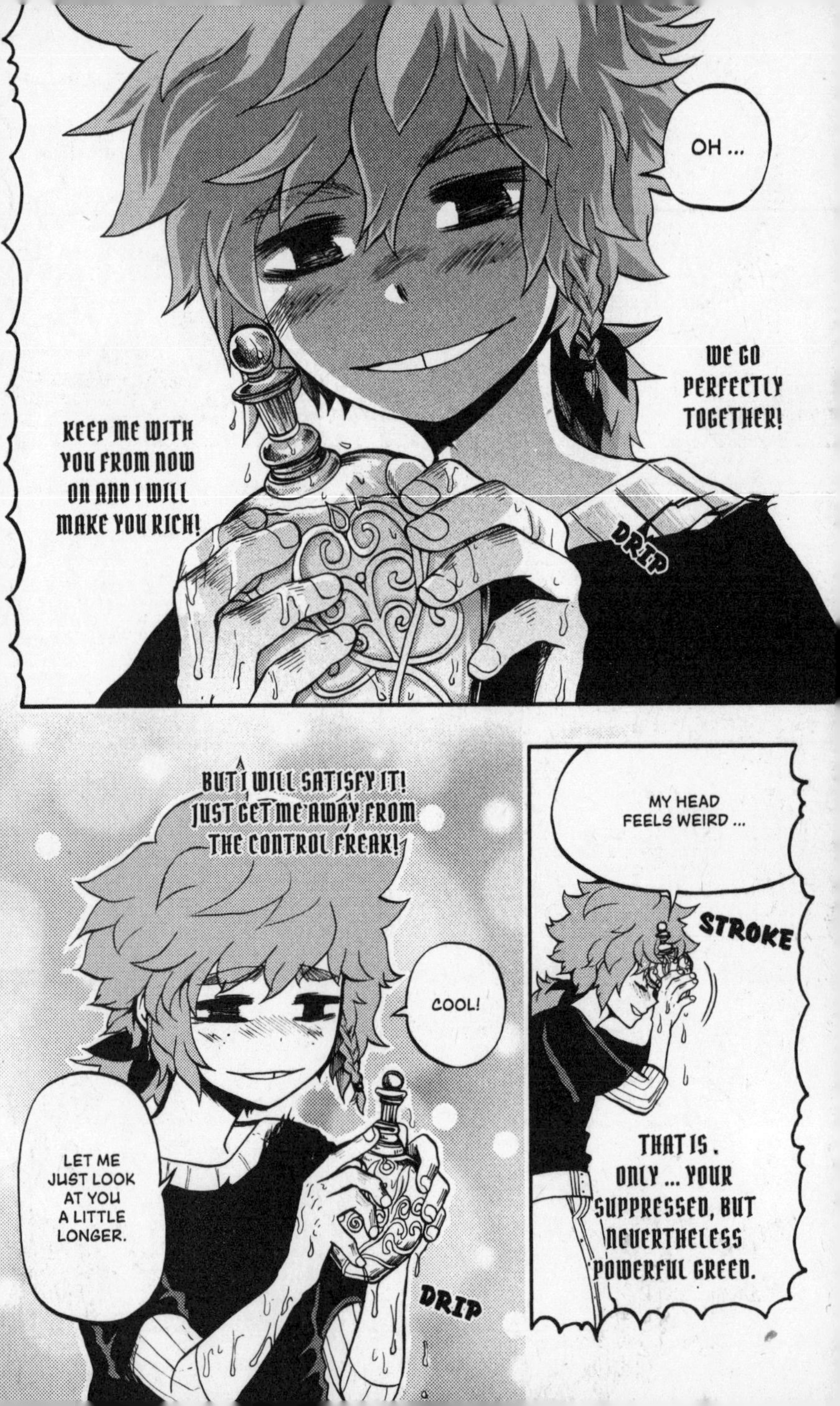
OH ...
WE GO PERFECTLY TOGETHER!
KEEP ME WITH YOU FROM NOW ON AND I WILL MAKE YOU RICH!
DRIP
MY HEAD FEELS WEIRD ...
STROKE
THAT IS . ONLY ... YOUR SUPPRESSED, BUT NEVERTHELESS POWERFUL GREED.
BUT I WILL SATISFY IT! JUST GET ME AWAY FROM THE CONTROL FREAK!
COOL!
LET ME JUST LOOK AT YOU A LITTLE LONGER.
DRIP

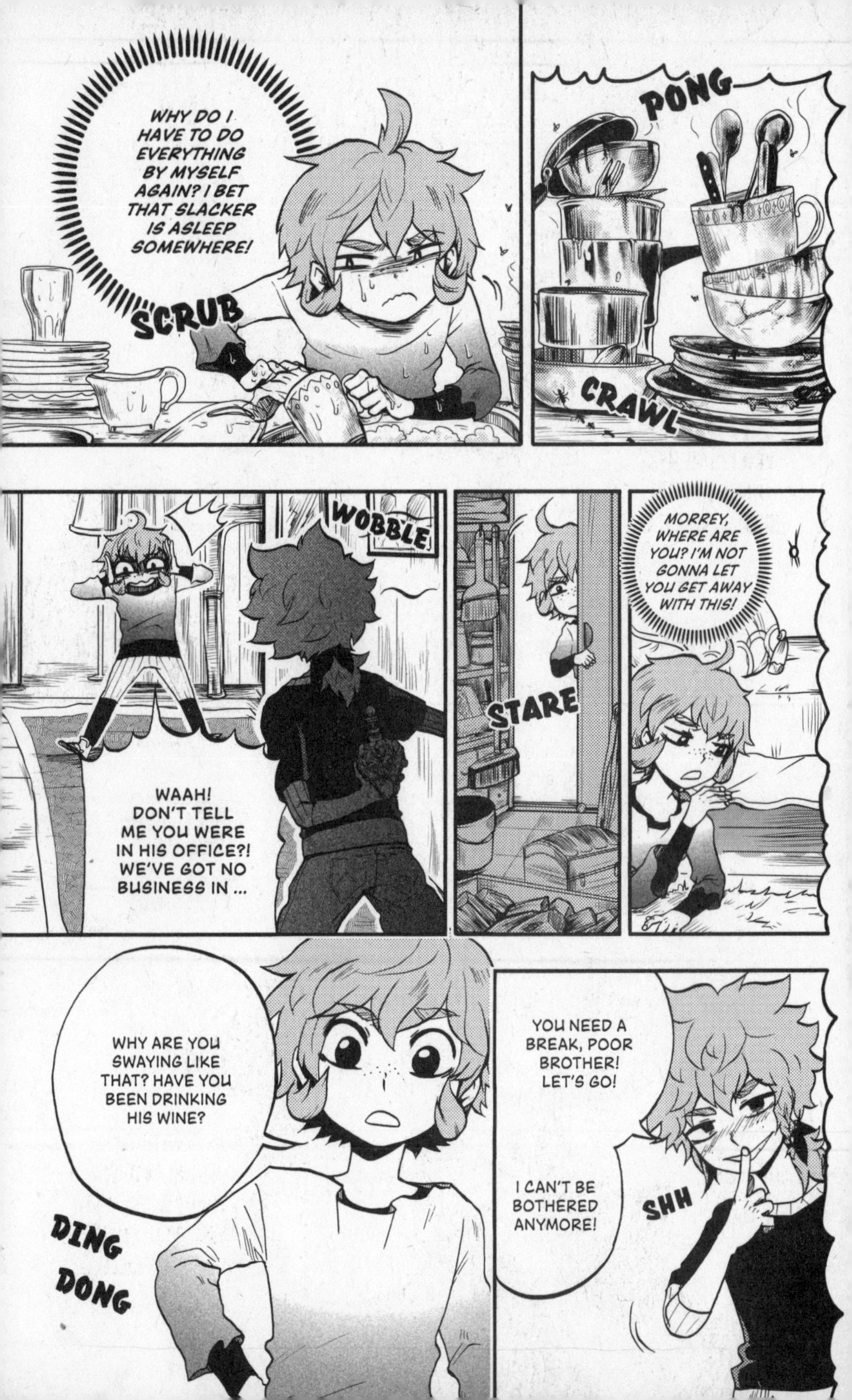
PONG
CRAWL
WHY DO I HAVE TO DO EVERYTHING BY MYSELF AGAIN? I BET THAT SLACKER IS ASLEEP SOMEWHERE!
SCRUB
MORREY, WHERE ARE YOU? I'M NOT GONNA LET YOU GET AWAY WITH THIS!
STARE
WOBBLE
WAAH! DON'T TELL ME YOU WERE IN HIS OFFICE?! WE'VE GOT NO BUSINESS IN ...
YOU NEED A BREAK, POOR BROTHER! LET'S GO!
I CAN'T BE BOTHERED ANYMORE!
SHH
WHY ARE YOU SWAYING LIKE THAT? HAVE YOU BEEN DRINKING HIS WINE?
DING DONG

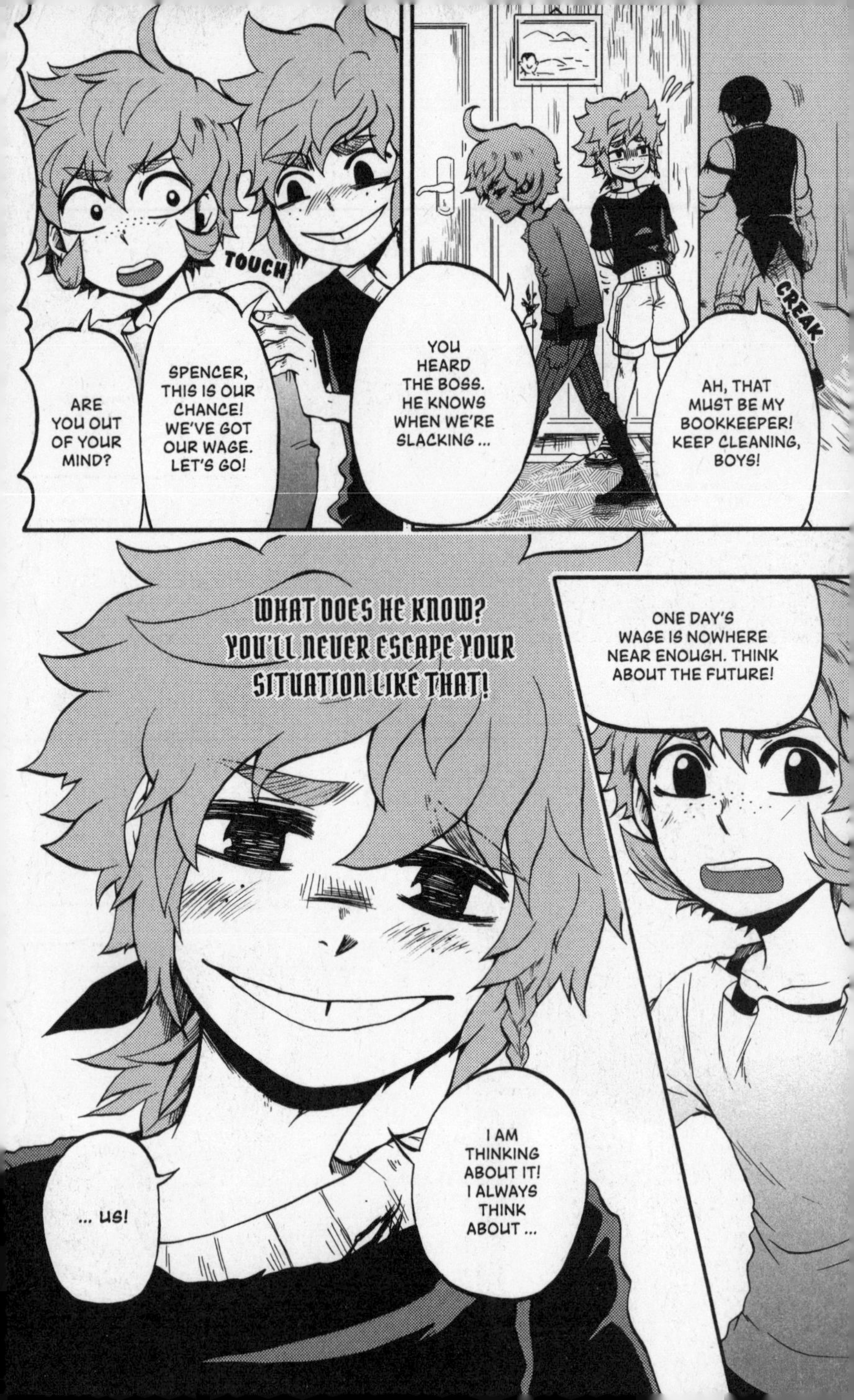
AH, THAT MUST BE MY BOOKKEEPER! KEEP CLEANING, BOYS!
CREAK
YOU HEARD THE BOSS. HE KNOWS WHEN WE'RE SLACKING ...
TOUCH
SPENCER, THIS IS OUR CHANCE! WE'VE GOT OUR WAGE. LET'S GO!
ARE YOU OUT OF YOUR MIND?
ONE DAY'S WAGE IS NOWHERE NEAR ENOUGH. THINK ABOUT THE FUTURE!
WHAT DOES HE KNOW? YOU'LL NEVER ESCAPE YOUR SITUATION LIKE THAT!
I AM THINKING ABOUT IT! I ALWAYS THINK ABOUT ...
... US!

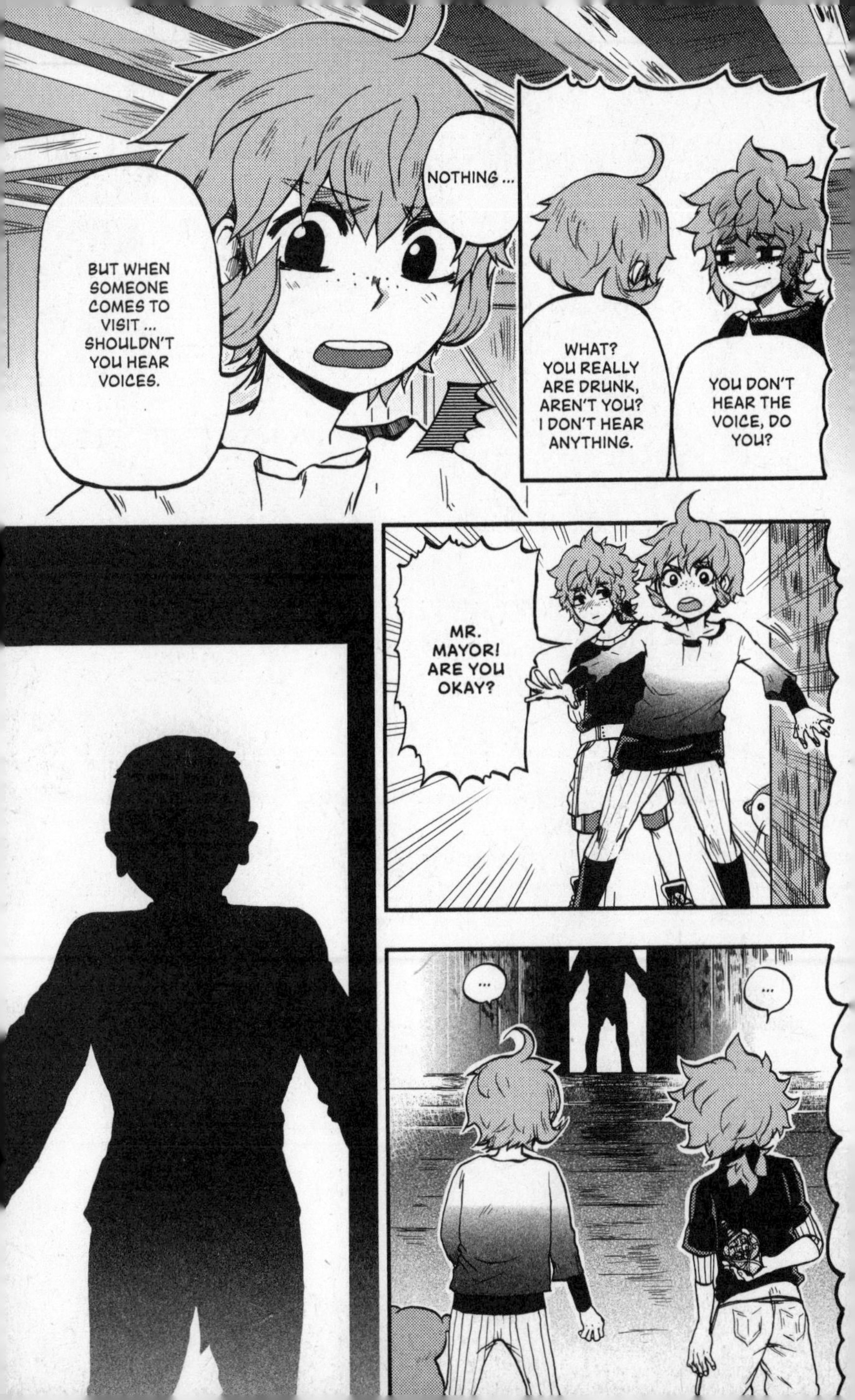
YOU DON'T HEAR THE VOICE, DO YOU?
WHAT? YOU REALLY ARE DRUNK, AREN'T YOU? I DON'T HEAR ANYTHING.
NOTHING ...
BUT WHEN SOMEONE COMES TO VISIT ... SHOULDN'T YOU HEAR VOICES.
MR. MAYOR! ARE YOU OKAY?
...
...

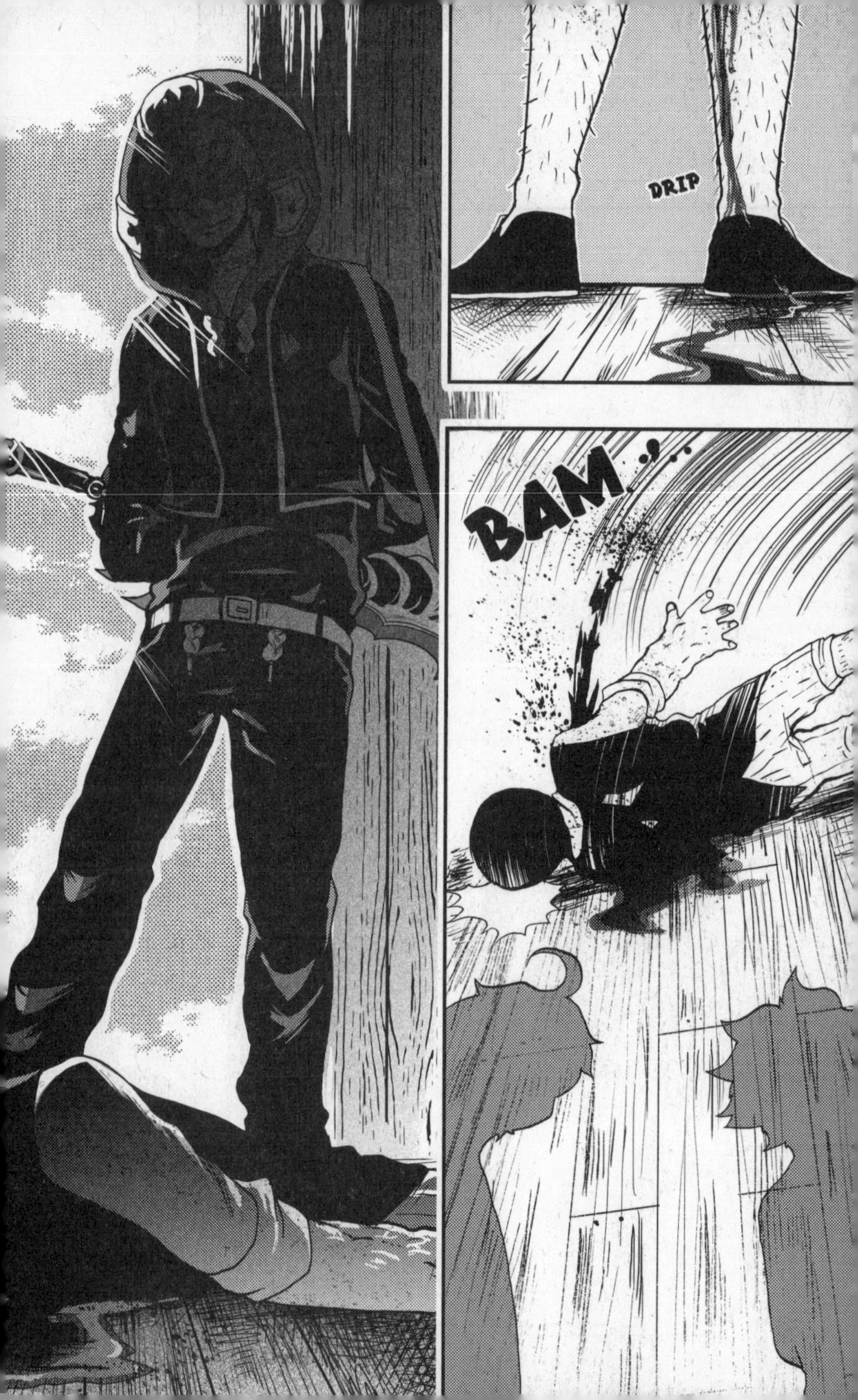
DRIP
BAM...

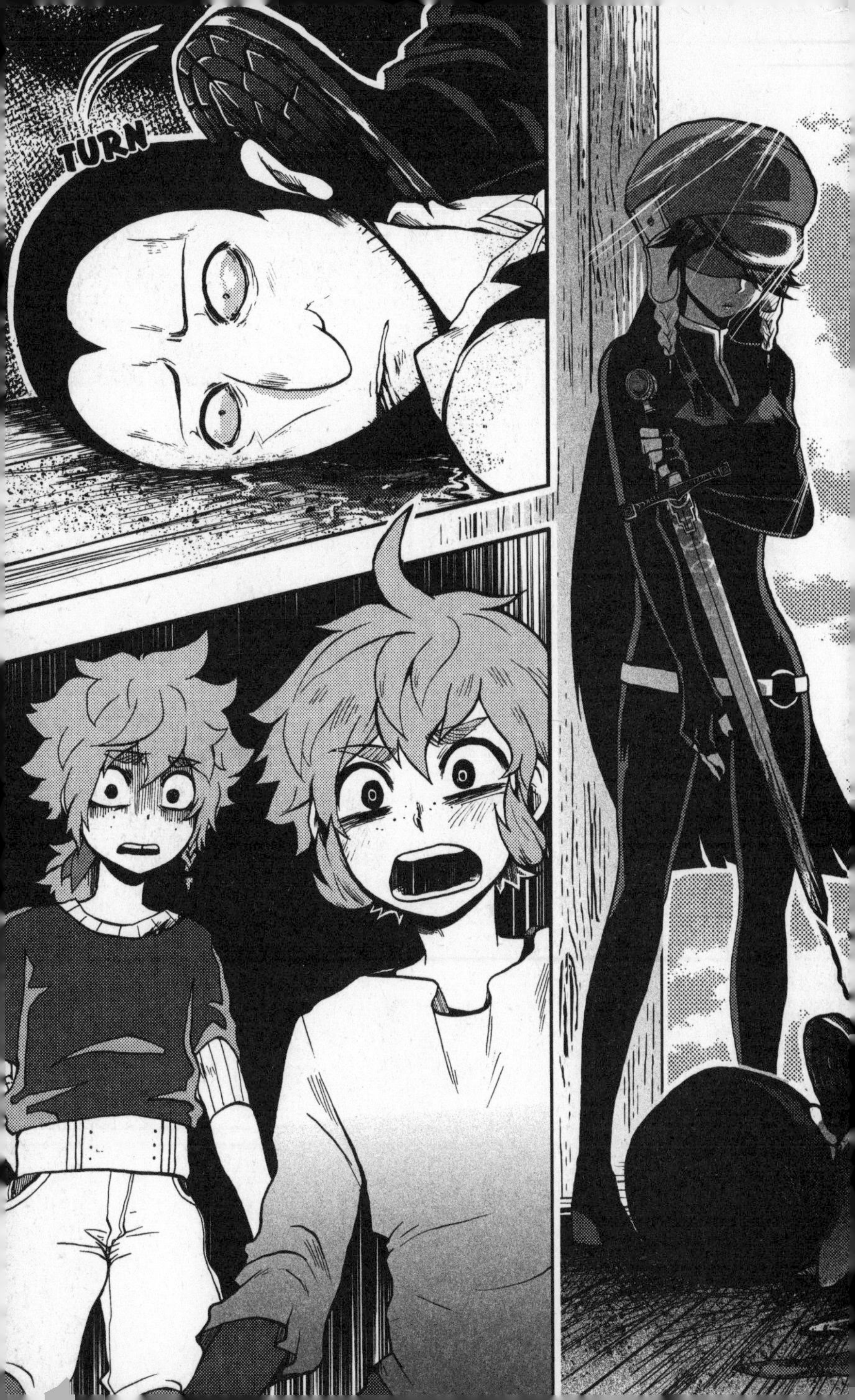
TURN

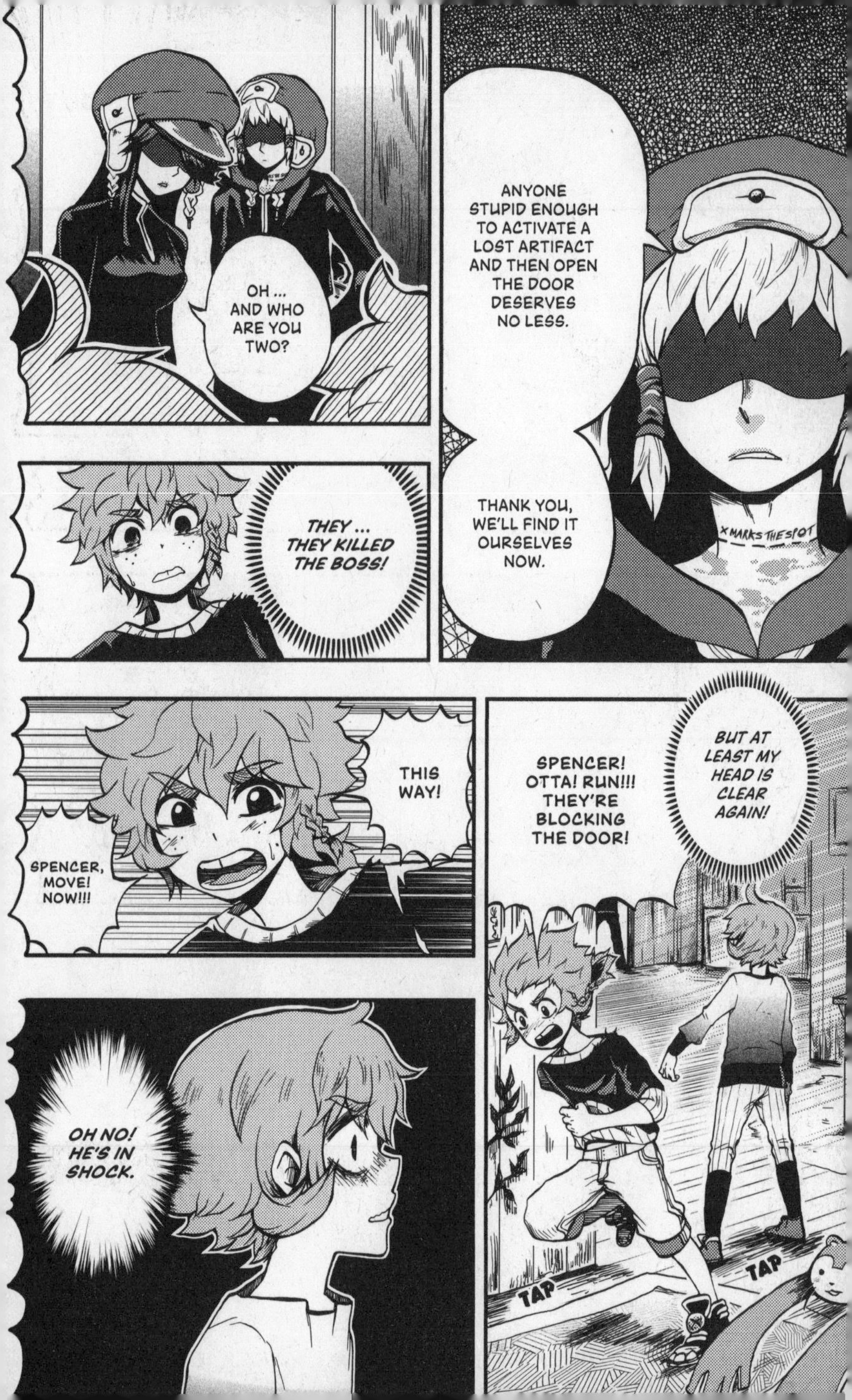
ANYONE STUPID ENOUGH TO ACTIVATE A LOST ARTIFACT AND THEN OPEN THE DOOR DESERVES NO LESS.
X MARKS THE SPOT
THANK YOU, WE'LL FIND IT OURSELVES NOW.
OH ... AND WHO ARE YOU TWO?
THEY ... THEY KILLED THE BOSS!
BUT AT LEAST MY HEAD IS CLEAR AGAIN!
SPENCER! OTTA! RUN!!! THEY'RE BLOCKING THE DOOR!
TAP
TAP
THIS WAY!
SPENCER, MOVE! NOW!!!
OH NO! HE'S IN SHOCK.

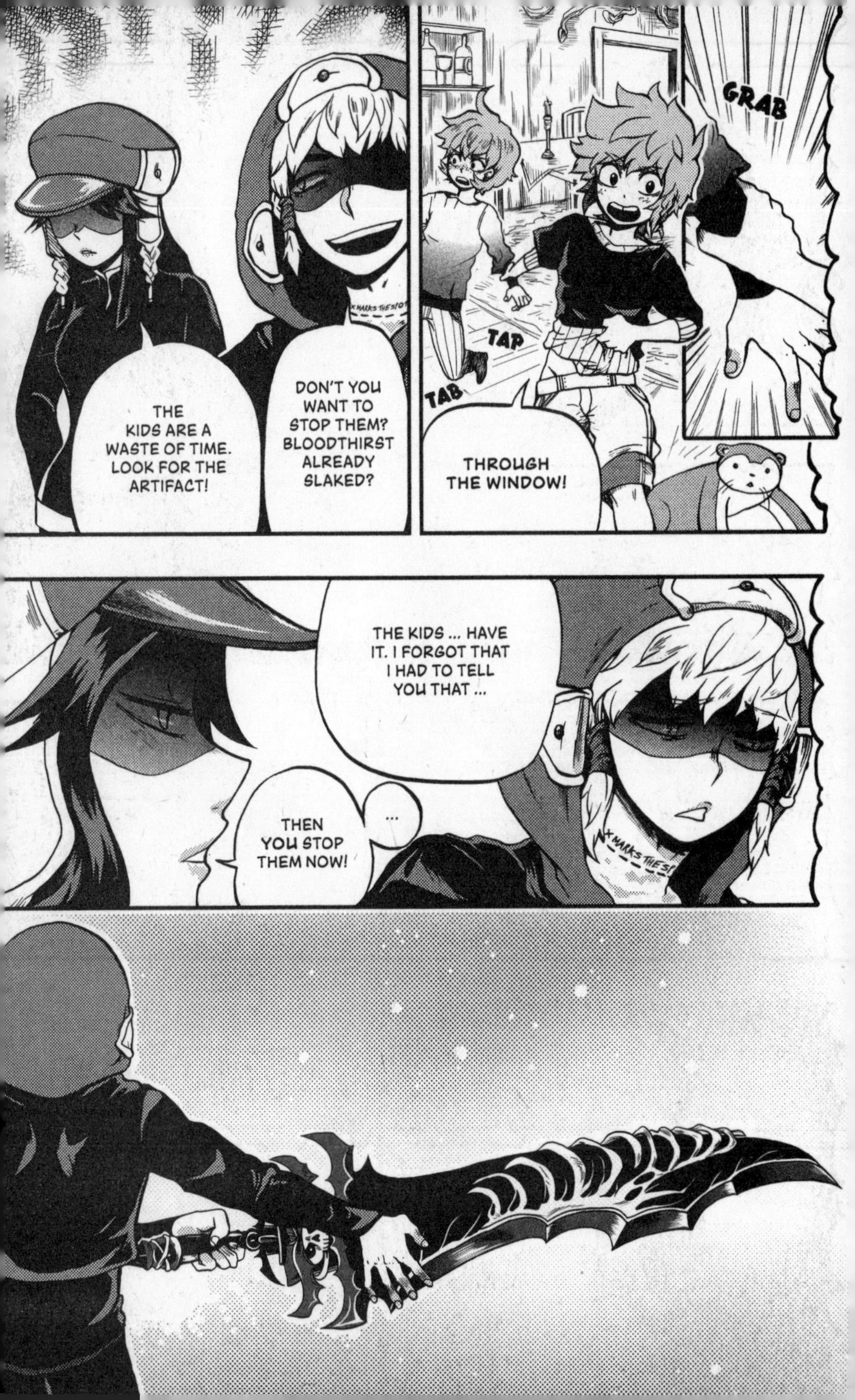
GRAB
TAP
TAB
THROUGH THE WINDOW!
DON'T YOU WANT TO STOP THEM? BLOODTHIRST ALREADY SLAKED?
THE KIDS ARE A WASTE OF TIME. LOOK FOR THE ARTIFACT!
THE KIDS ... HAVE IT. I FORGOT THAT I HAD TO TELL YOU THAT ...
...
THEN YOU STOP THEM NOW!

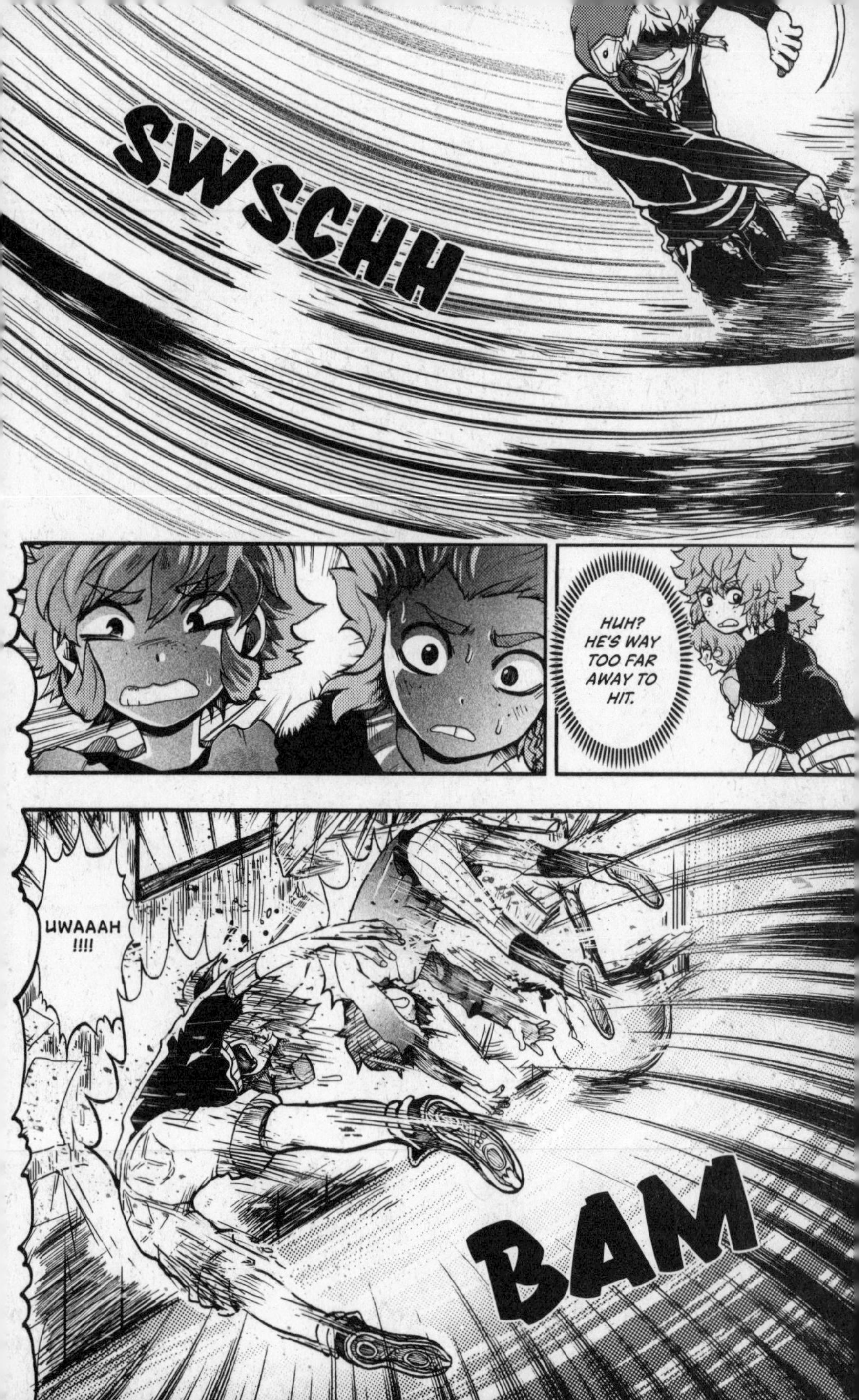
SWSCHH
HUH? HE'S WAY TOO FAR AWAY TO HIT.
UWAAAH !!!!
BAM

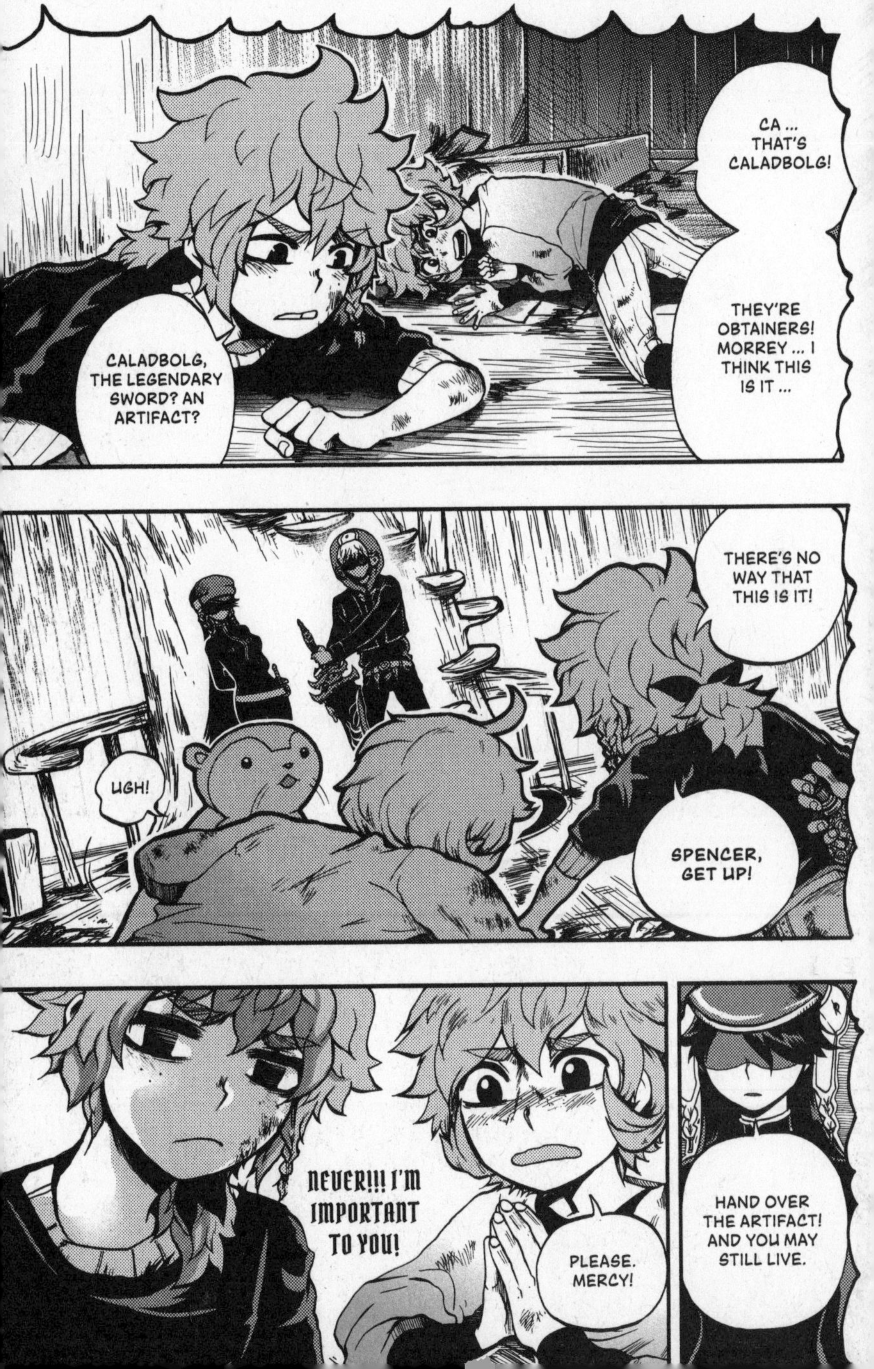
CA ... THAT'S CALADBOLG!
THEY'RE OBTAINERS! MORREY ... I THINK THIS IS IT ...
CALADBOLG, THE LEGENDARY SWORD? AN ARTIFACT?
THERE'S NO WAY THAT THIS IS IT!
SPENCER, GET UP!
UGH!
HAND OVER THE ARTIFACT! AND YOU MAY STILL LIVE.
PLEASE. MERCY!
NEVER!!! I'M IMPORTANT TO YOU!

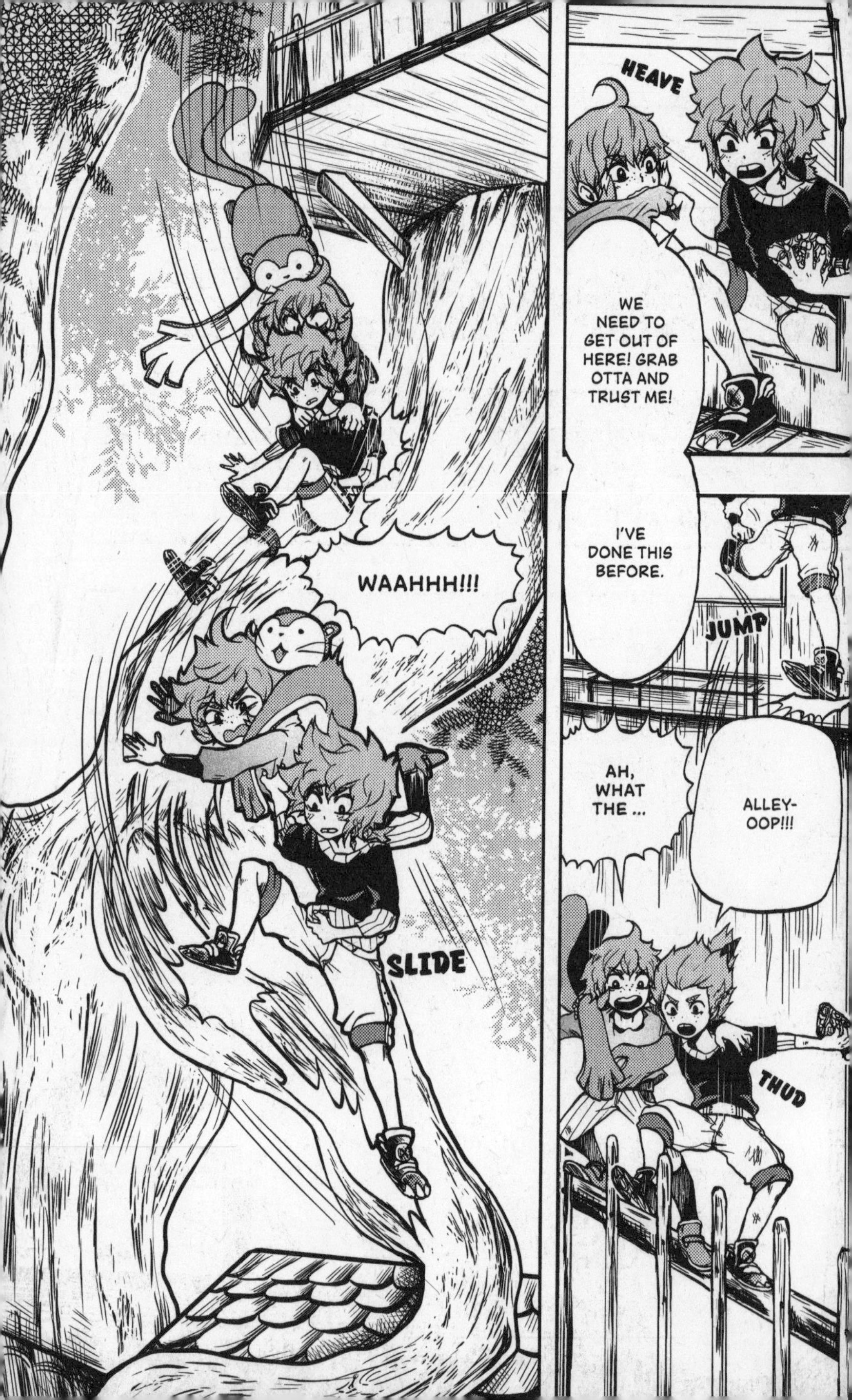
HEAVE
WE NEED TO GET OUT OF HERE! GRAB OTTA AND TRUST ME!
I'VE DONE THIS BEFORE.
JUMP
ALLEY-OOP!!!
AH, WHAT THE ...
THUD
WAAHHH!!!
SLIDE

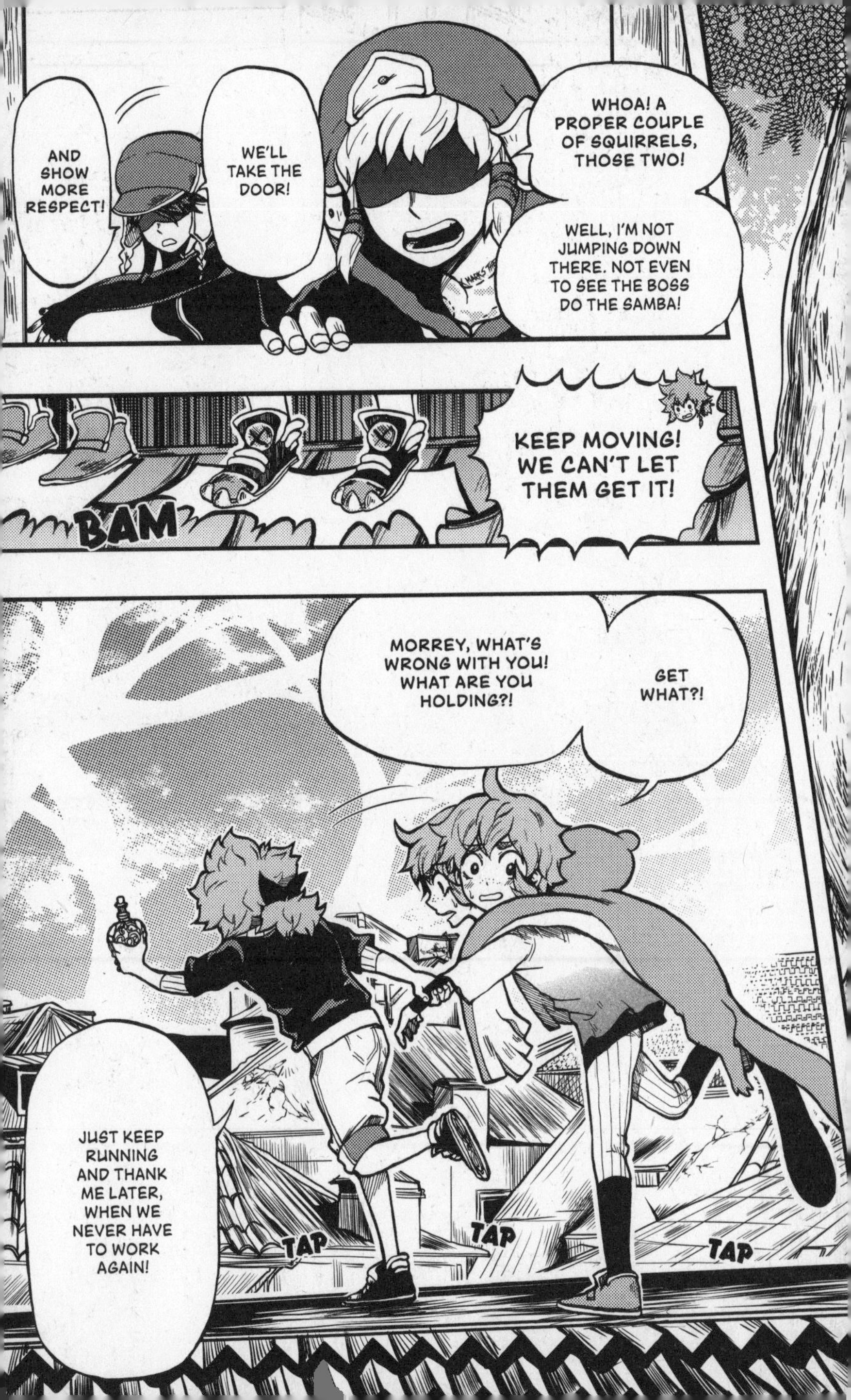
WHOA! A PROPER COUPLE OF SQUIRRELS, THOSE TWO!
WELL, I'M NOT JUMPING DOWN THERE. NOT EVEN TO SEE THE BOSS DO THE SAMBA!
WE'LL TAKE THE DOOR!
AND SHOW MORE RESPECT!
KEEP MOVING! WE CAN'T LET THEM GET IT!
BAM
GET WHAT?!
MORREY, WHAT'S WRONG WITH YOU! WHAT ARE YOU HOLDING?!
TAP
TAP
TAP
JUST KEEP RUNNING AND THANK ME LATER, WHEN WE NEVER HAVE TO WORK AGAIN!

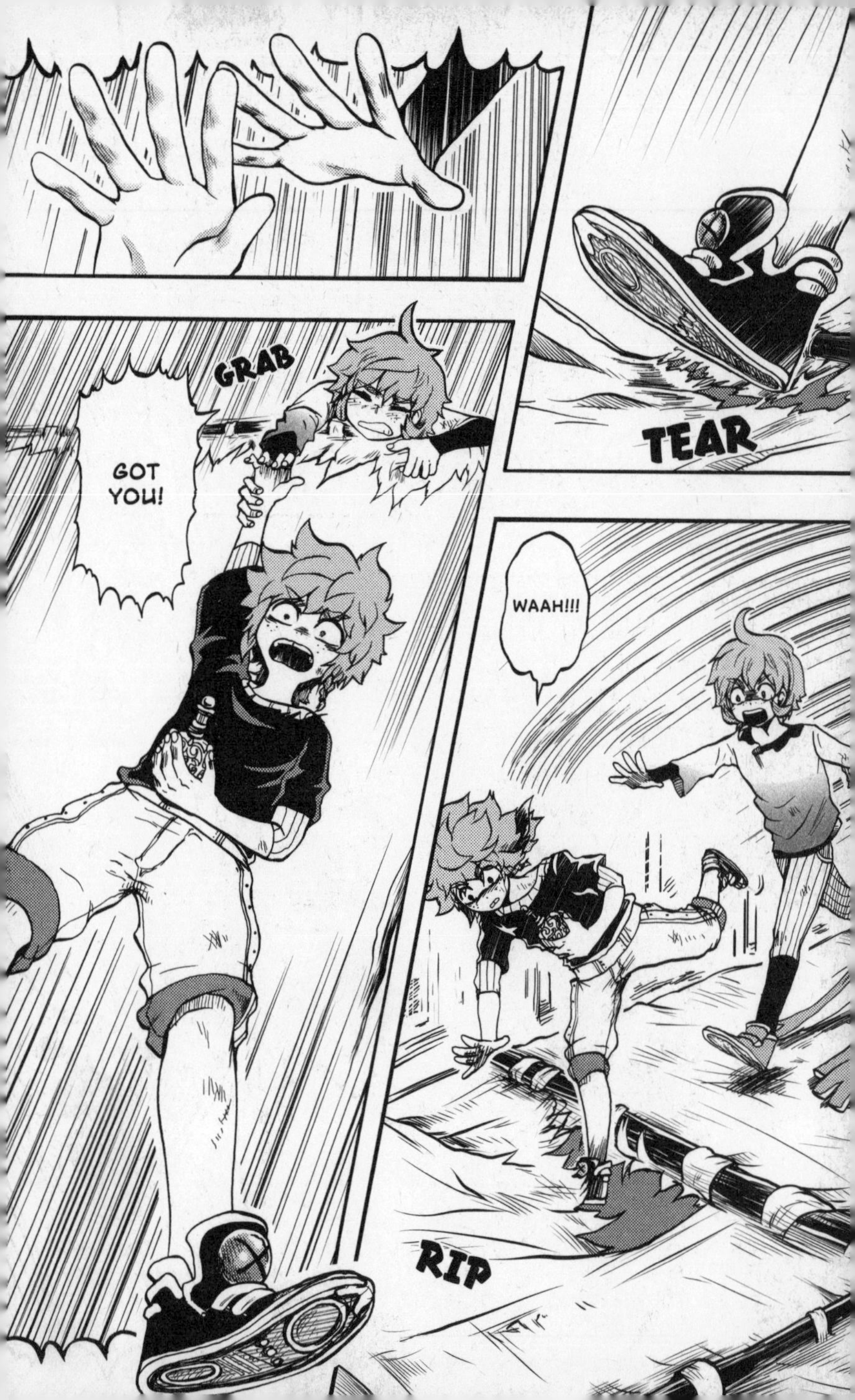
TEAR
WAAH!!!
RIP
GRAB
GOT YOU!

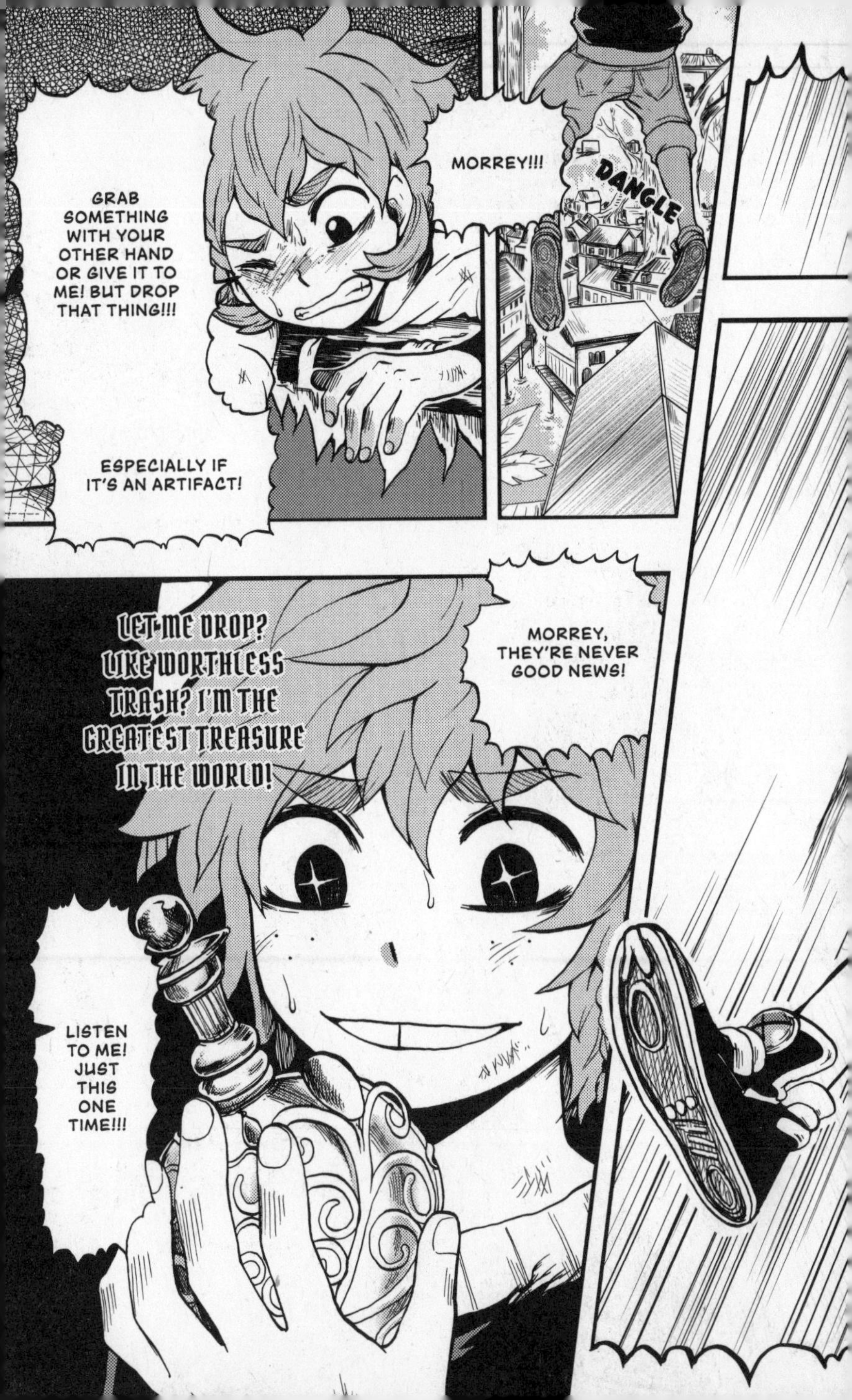
MORREY!!!
DANGLE
GRAB SOMETHING WITH YOUR OTHER HAND OR GIVE IT TO ME! BUT DROP THAT THING!!!
ESPECIALLY IF IT'S AN ARTIFACT!
MORREY, THEY'RE NEVER GOOD NEWS!
LET ME DROP? LIKE WORTHLESS TRASH? I'M THE GREATEST TREASURE IN THE WORLD!
LISTEN TO ME! JUST THIS ONE TIME!!!

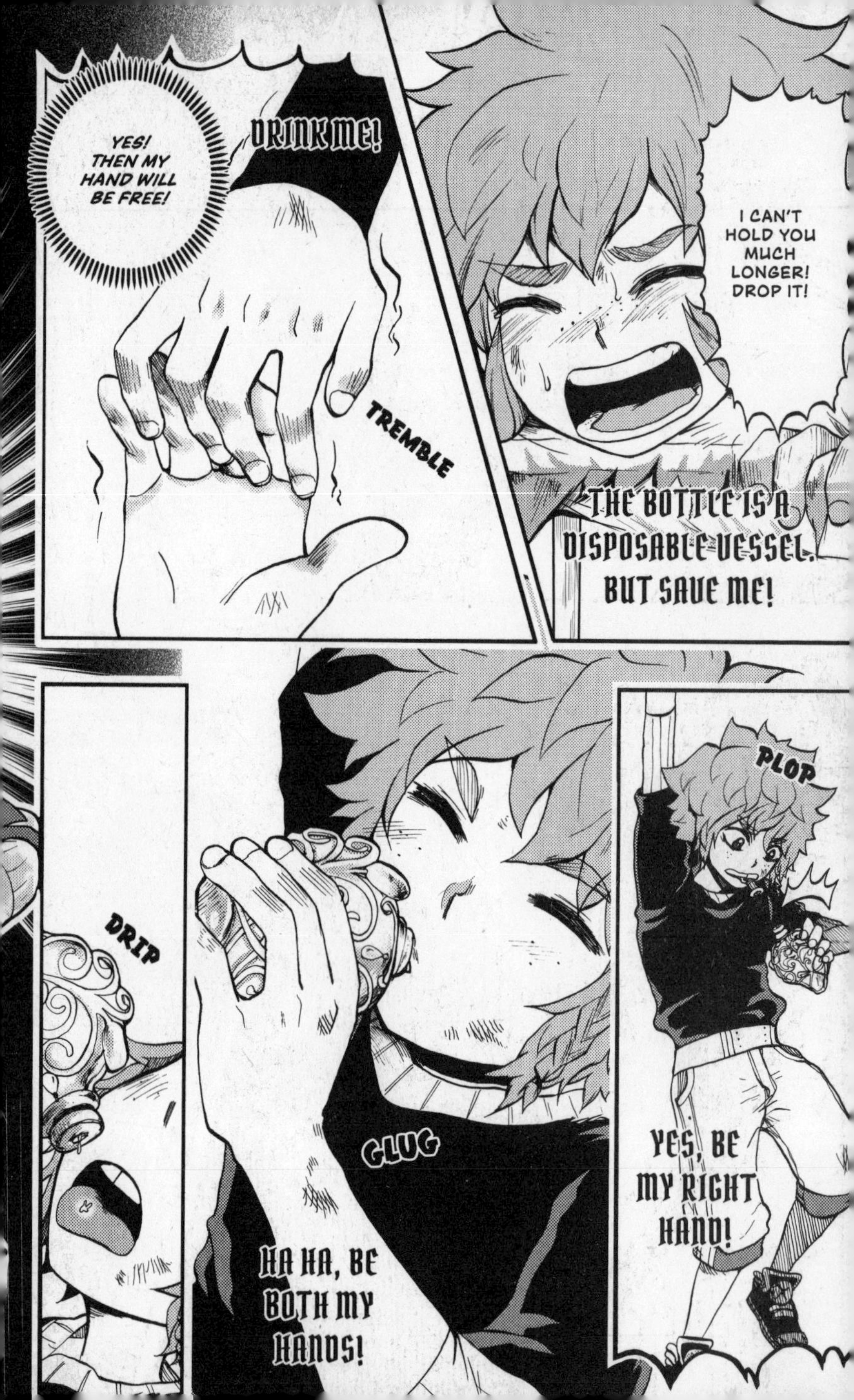
I CAN'T HOLD YOU MUCH LONGER! DROP IT!
THE BOTTLE IS A DISPOSABLE VESSEL. BUT SAVE ME!
DRINK ME!
YES! THEN MY HAND WILL BE FREE!
TREMBLE
PLOP
YES, BE MY RIGHT HAND!
GLUG
HA HA, BE BOTH MY HANDS!
DRIP

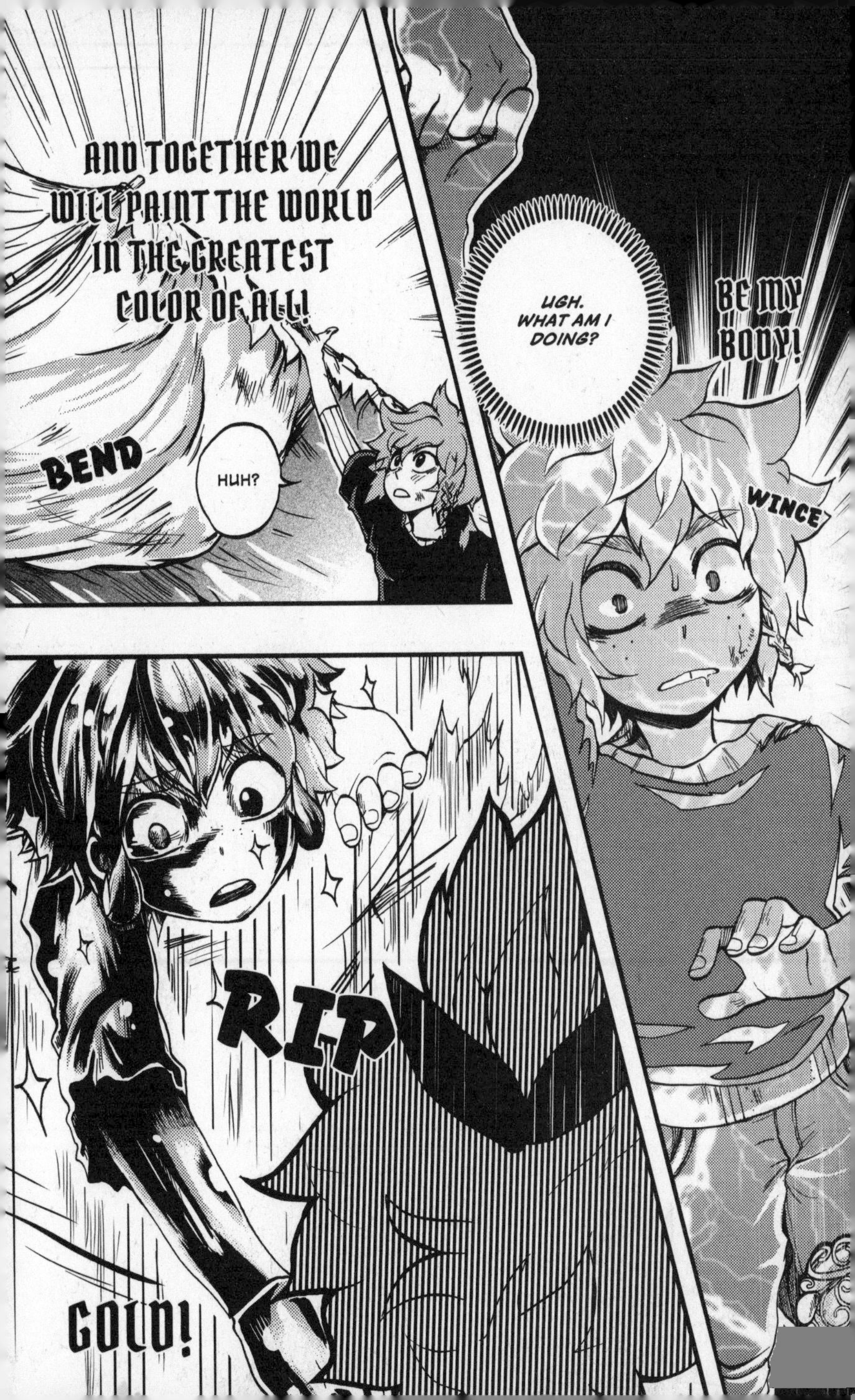
BE MY BODY!
UGH. WHAT AM I DOING?
WINCE
AND TOGETHER WE WILL PAINT THE WORLD IN THE GREATEST COLOR OF ALL!
HUH?
BEND
RIP
GOLD!

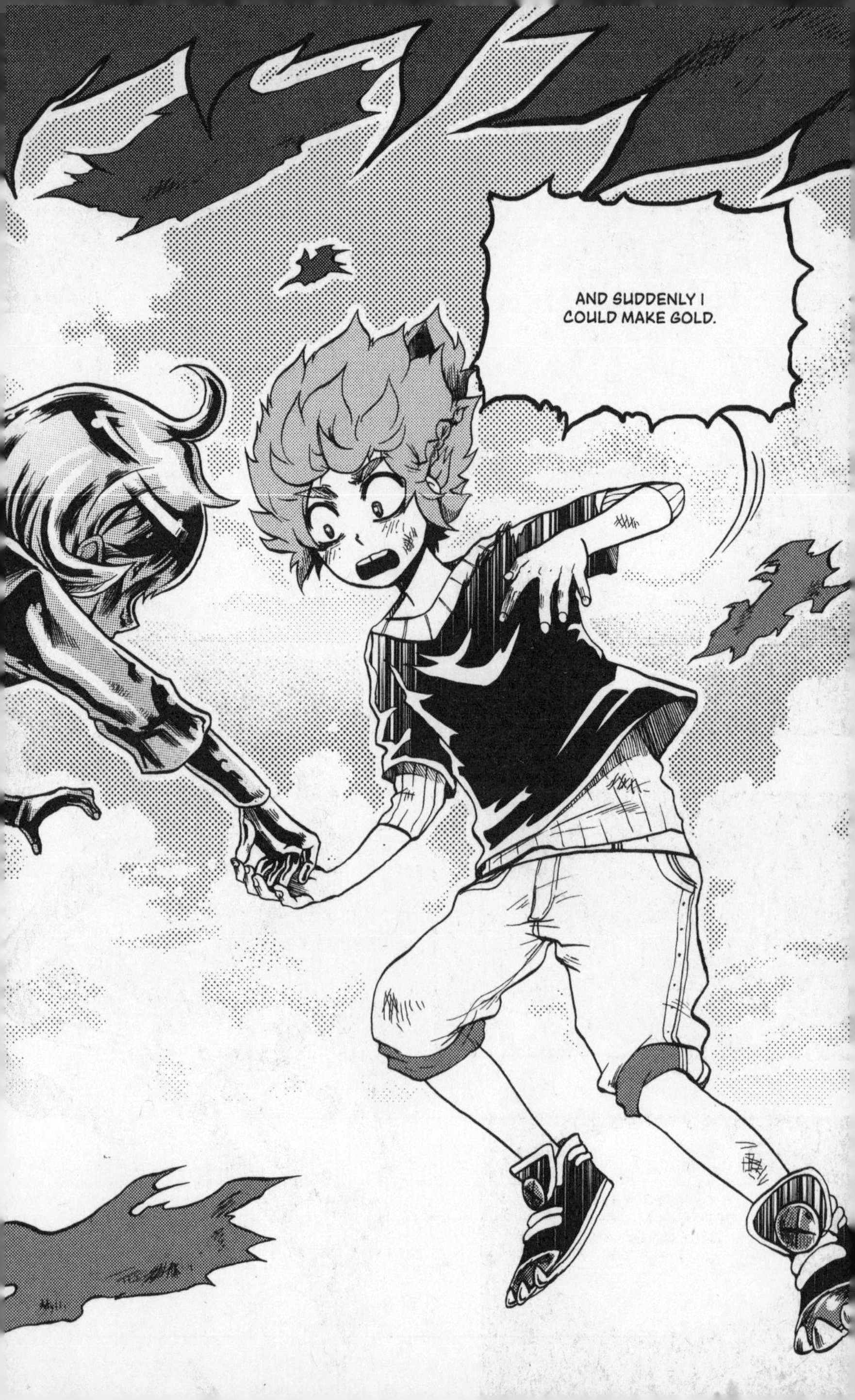
AND SUDDENLY I COULD MAKE GOLD.

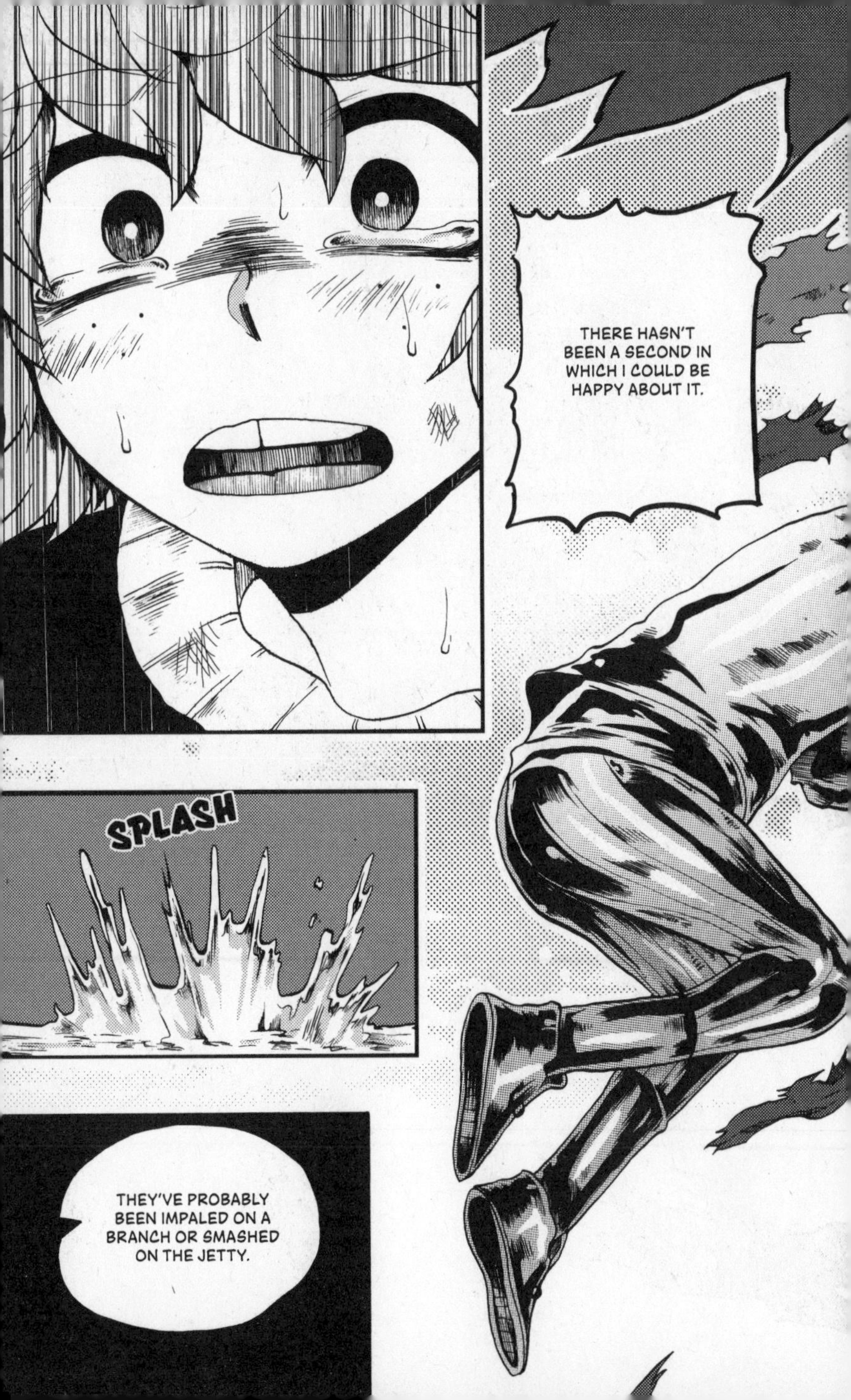
THERE HASN'T BEEN A SECOND IN WHICH I COULD BE HAPPY ABOUT IT.
SPLASH
THEY'VE PROBABLY BEEN IMPALED ON A BRANCH OR SMASHED ON THE JETTY.

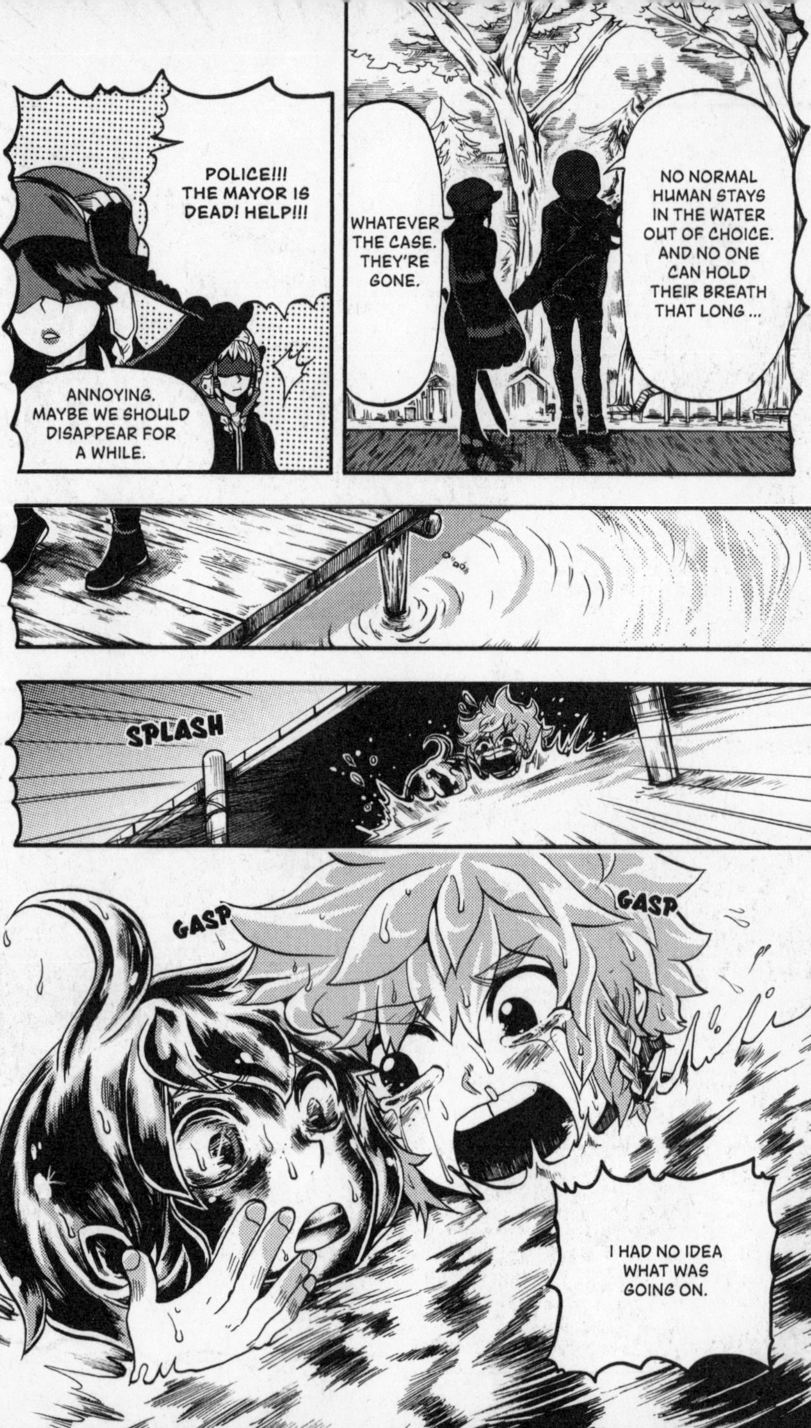
NO NORMAL HUMAN STAYS IN THE WATER OUT OF CHOICE. AND NO ONE CAN HOLD THEIR BREATH THAT LONG ...
WHATEVER THE CASE. THEY'RE GONE.
POLICE!!! THE MAYOR IS DEAD! HELP!!!
ANNOYING. MAYBE WE SHOULD DISAPPEAR FOR A WHILE.
SPLASH
GASP
GASP
I HAD NO IDEA WHAT WAS GOING ON.

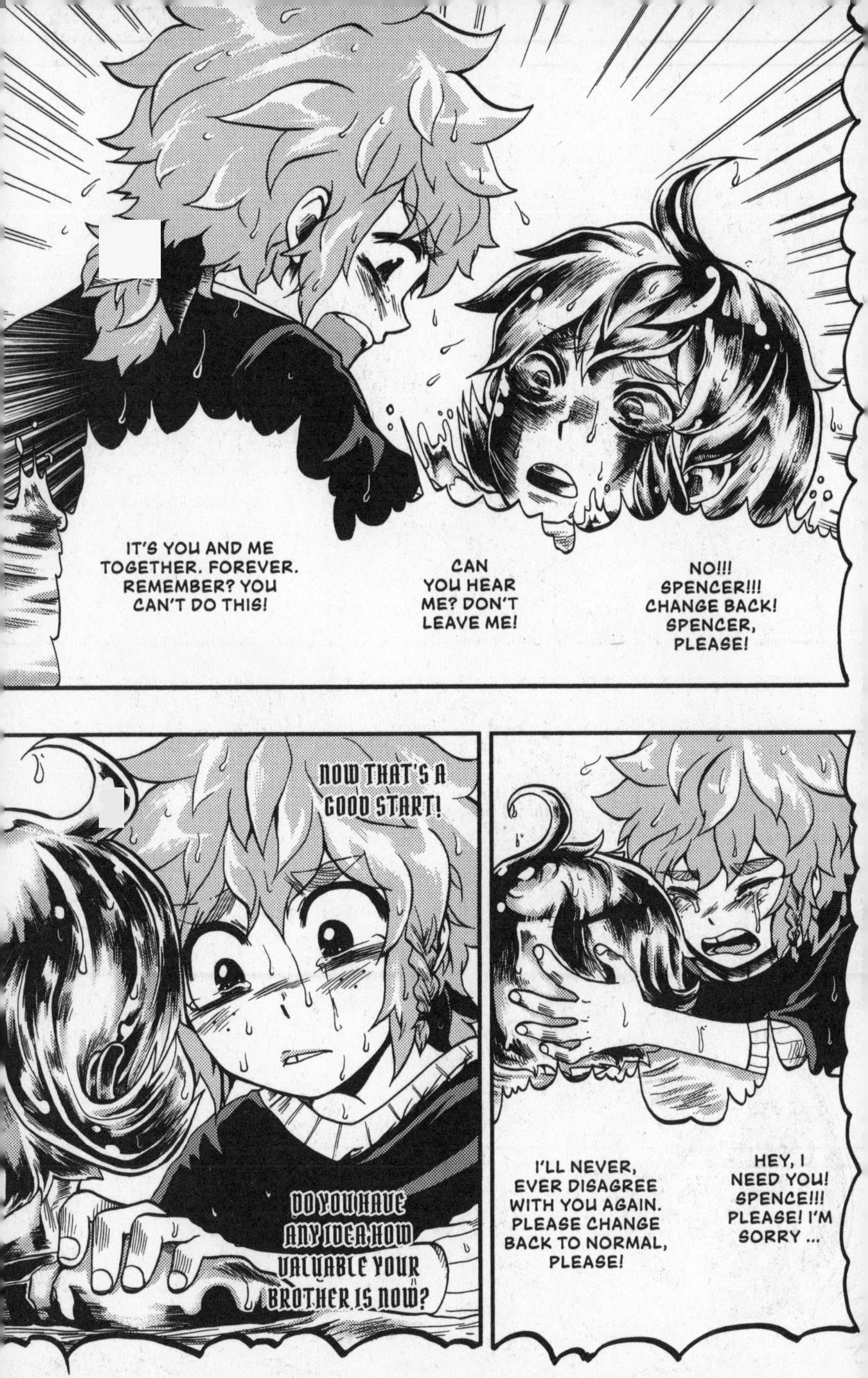
NO!!! SPENCER!!! CHANGE BACK! SPENCER, PLEASE!
CAN YOU HEAR ME? DON'T LEAVE ME!
IT'S YOU AND ME TOGETHER. FOREVER. REMEMBER? YOU CAN'T DO THIS!
HEY, I NEED YOU! SPENCE!!! PLEASE! I'M SORRY ...
I'LL NEVER, EVER DISAGREE WITH YOU AGAIN. PLEASE CHANGE BACK TO NORMAL, PLEASE!
NOW THAT'S A GOOD START!
DO YOU HAVE ANY IDEA HOW VALUABLE YOUR BROTHER IS NOW?

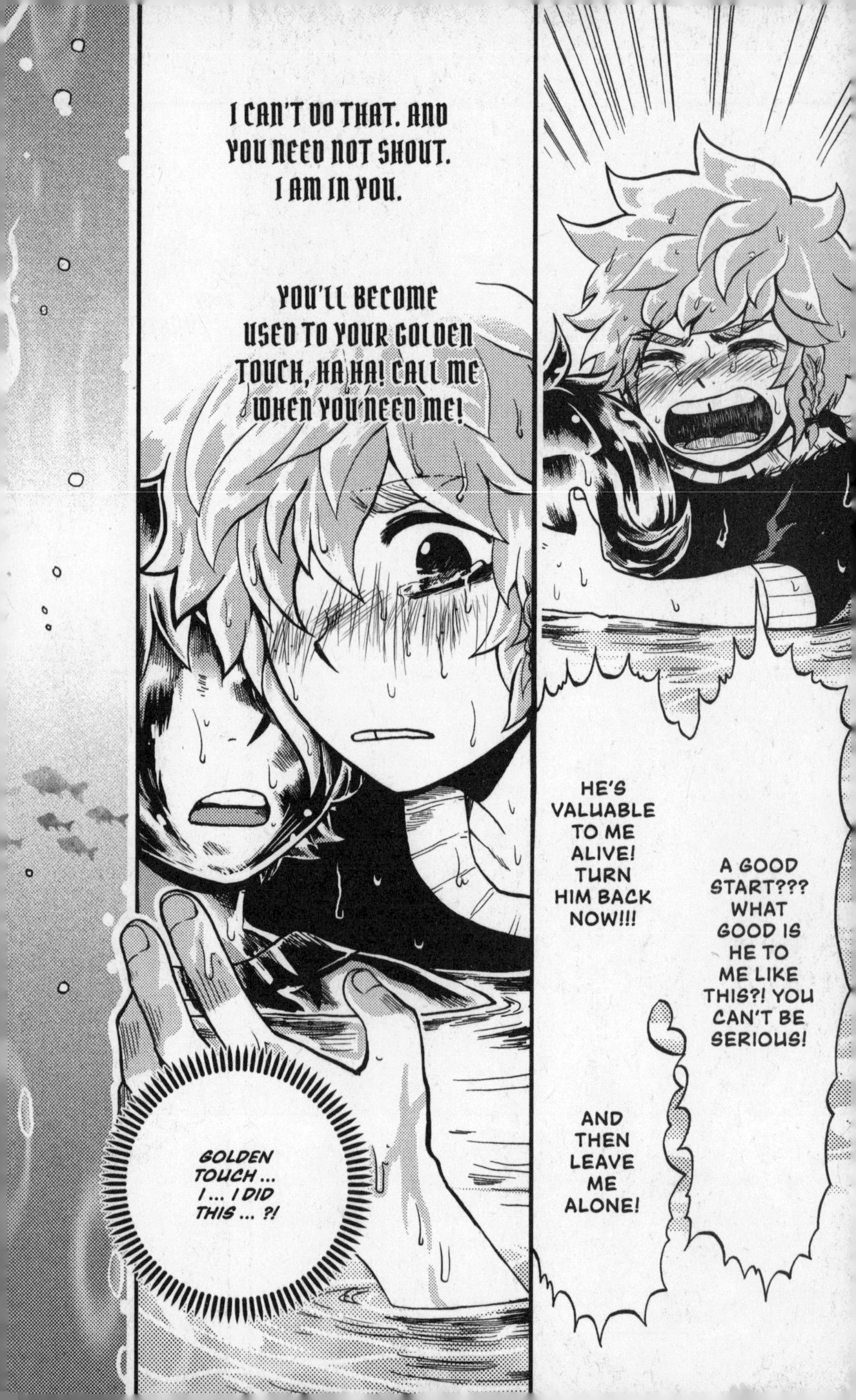
A GOOD START??? WHAT GOOD IS HE TO ME LIKE THIS?! YOU CAN'T BE SERIOUS!
HE'S VALUABLE TO ME ALIVE! TURN HIM BACK NOW!!!
AND THEN LEAVE ME ALONE!
I CAN'T DO THAT. AND YOU NEED NOT SHOUT. I AM IN YOU.
YOU'LL BECOME USED TO YOUR GOLDEN TOUCH, HA HA! CALL ME WHEN YOU NEED ME!
GOLDEN TOUCH ... I ... I DID THIS ... ?!

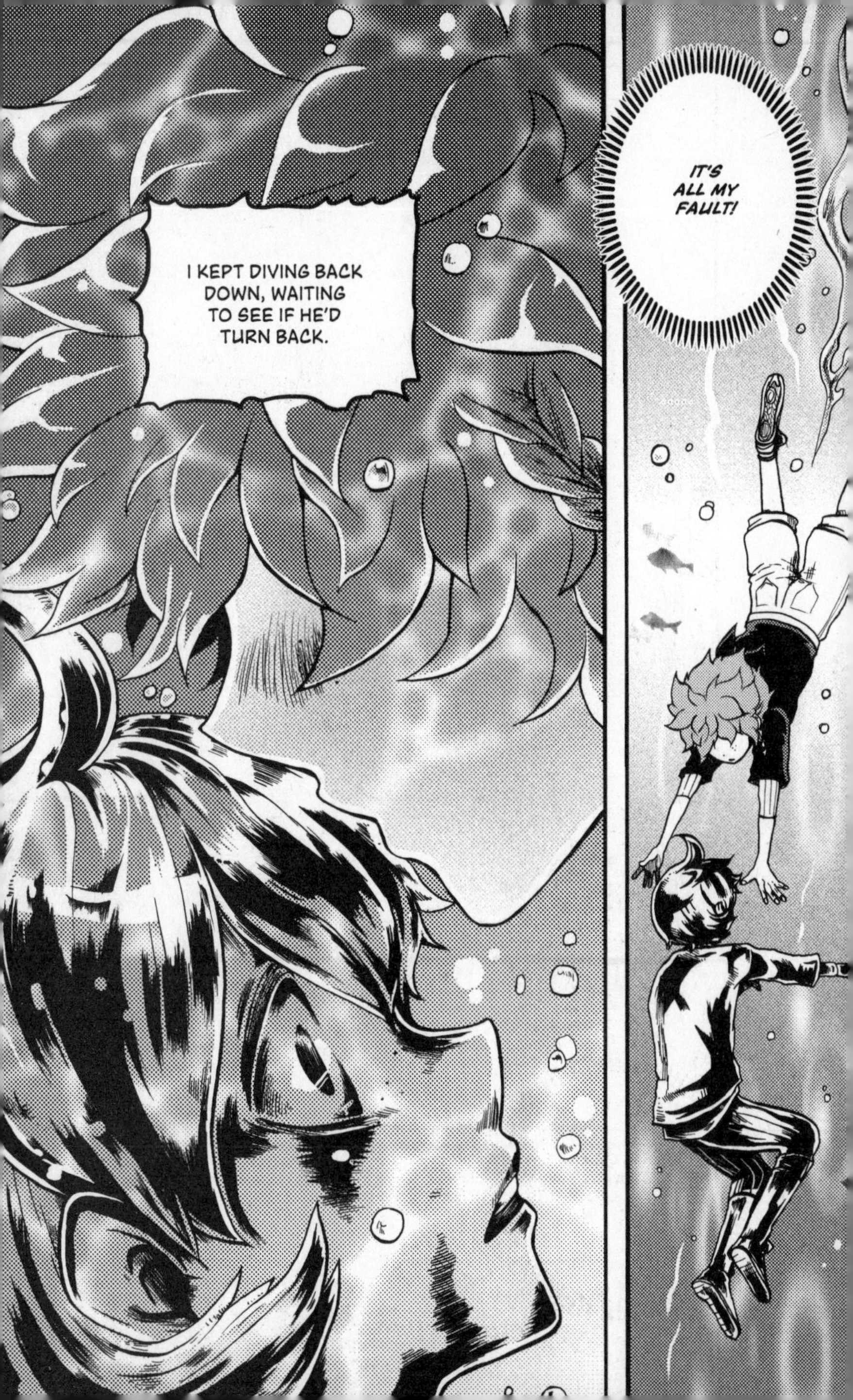
IT'S ALL MY FAULT!
I KEPT DIVING BACK DOWN, WAITING TO SEE IF HE'D TURN BACK.

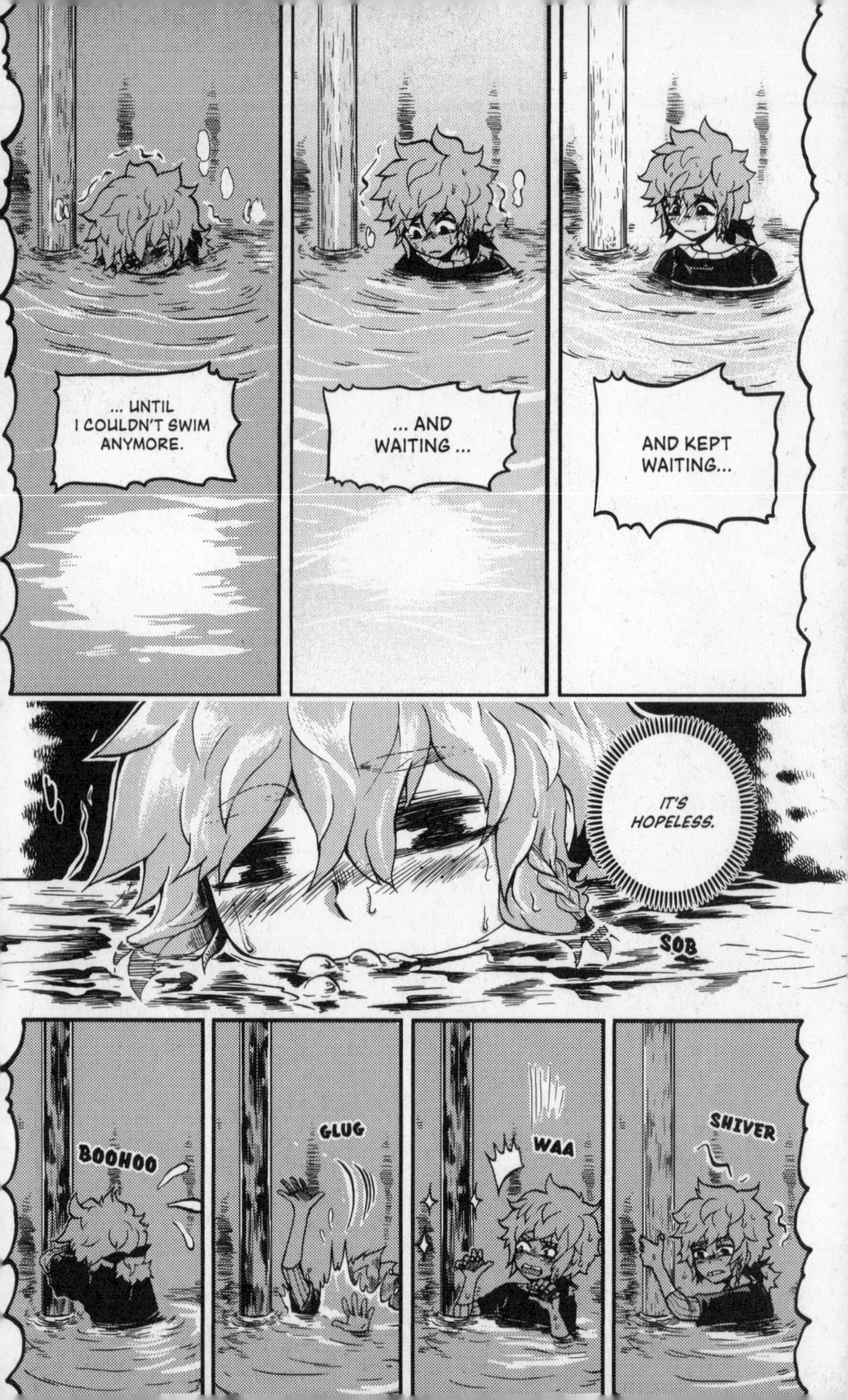
AND KEPT WAITING...
... AND WAITING ...
... UNTIL I COULDN'T SWIM ANYMORE.
IT'S HOPELESS.
SOB
SHIVER
WAA
GLUG
BOOHOO

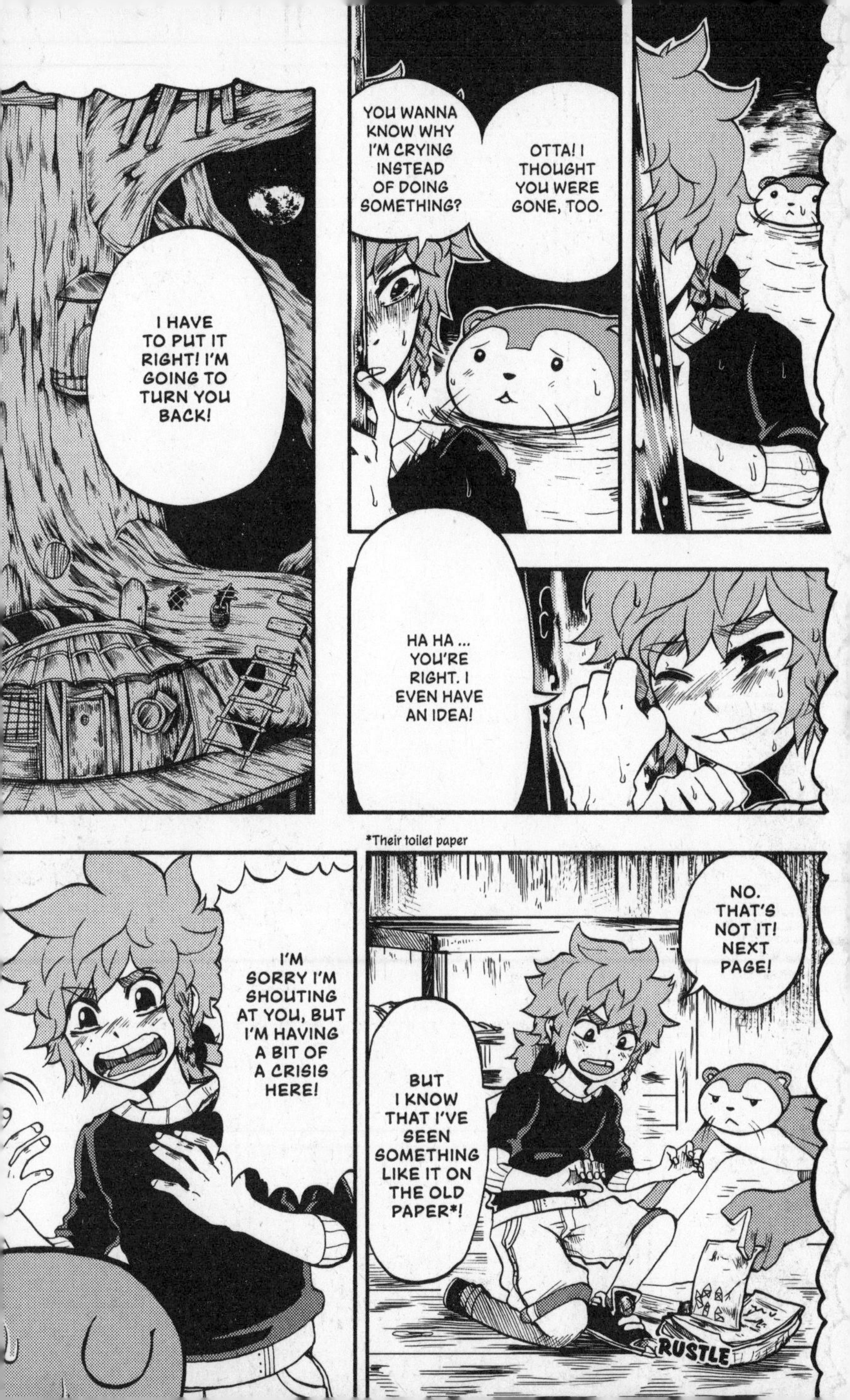
OTTA! I THOUGHT YOU WERE GONE, TOO.
YOU WANNA KNOW WHY I'M CRYING INSTEAD OF DOING SOMETHING?
HA HA ... YOU'RE RIGHT. I EVEN HAVE AN IDEA!
I HAVE TO PUT IT RIGHT! I'M GOING TO TURN YOU BACK!
*Their toilet paper
NO. THAT'S NOT IT! NEXT PAGE!
BUT I KNOW THAT I'VE SEEN SOMETHING LIKE IT ON THE OLD PAPER*!
RUSTLE
I'M SORRY I'M SHOUTING AT YOU, BUT I'M HAVING A BIT OF A CRISIS HERE!

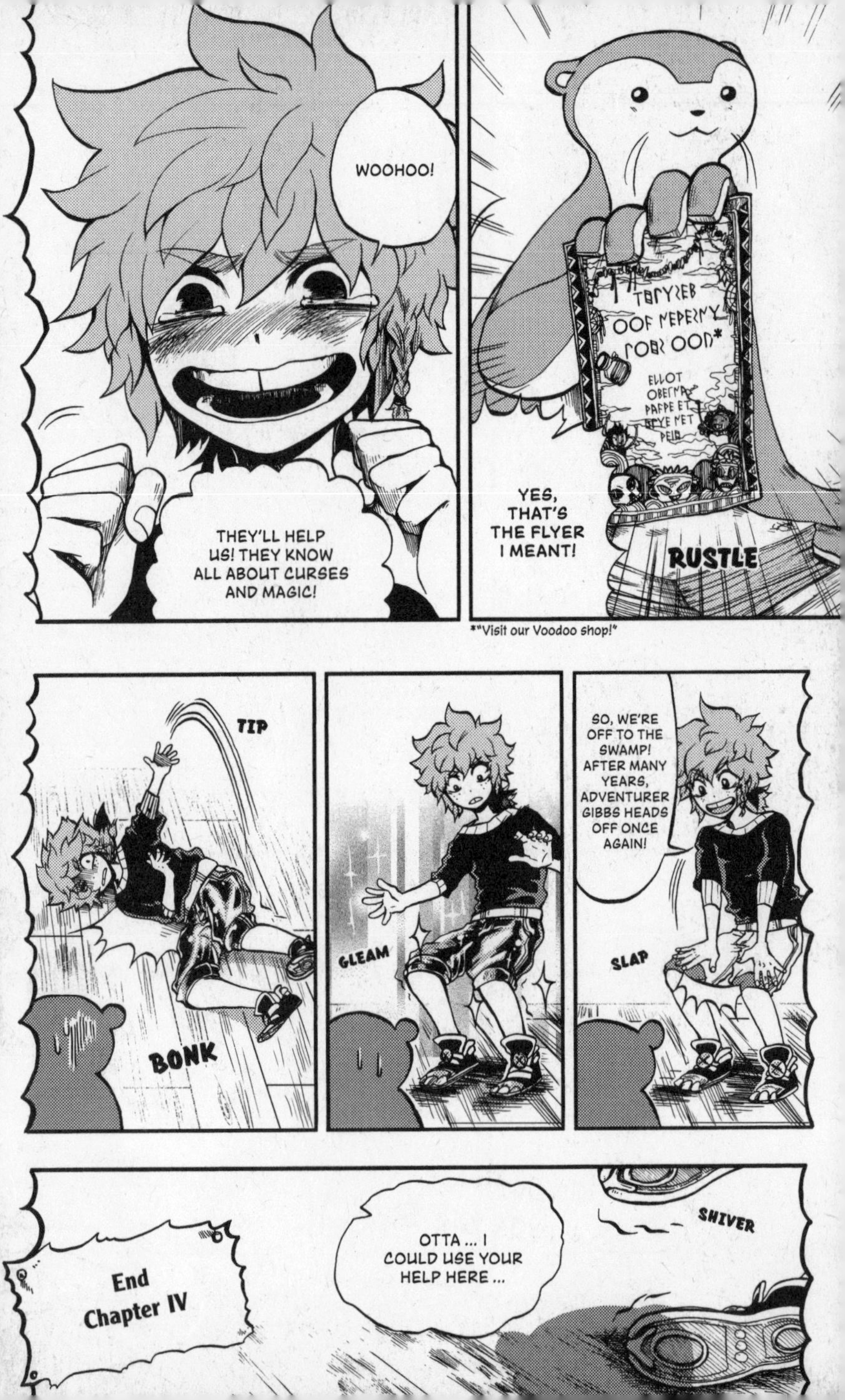
YES, THAT'S THE FLYER I MEANT!
RUSTLE
WOOHOO!
THEY'LL HELP US! THEY KNOW ALL ABOUT CURSES AND MAGIC!
*"Visit our Voodoo shop!"
SO, WE'RE OFF TO THE SWAMP! AFTER MANY YEARS, ADVENTURER GIBBS HEADS OFF ONCE AGAIN!
SLAP
GLEAM
TIP
BONK
SHIVER
OTTA ... I COULD USE YOUR HELP HERE ...
End Chapter IV

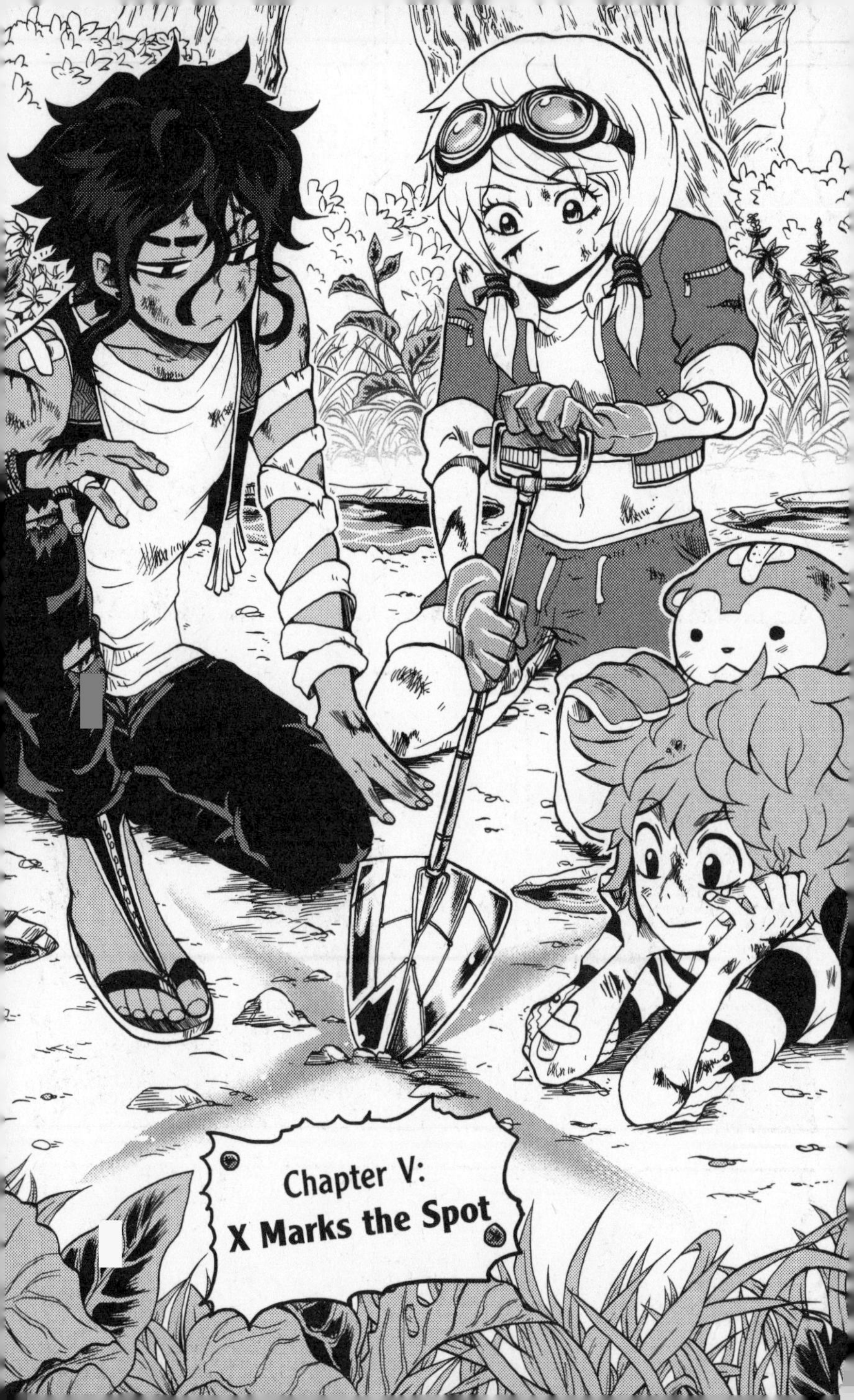
Chapter V:
X Marks the Spot

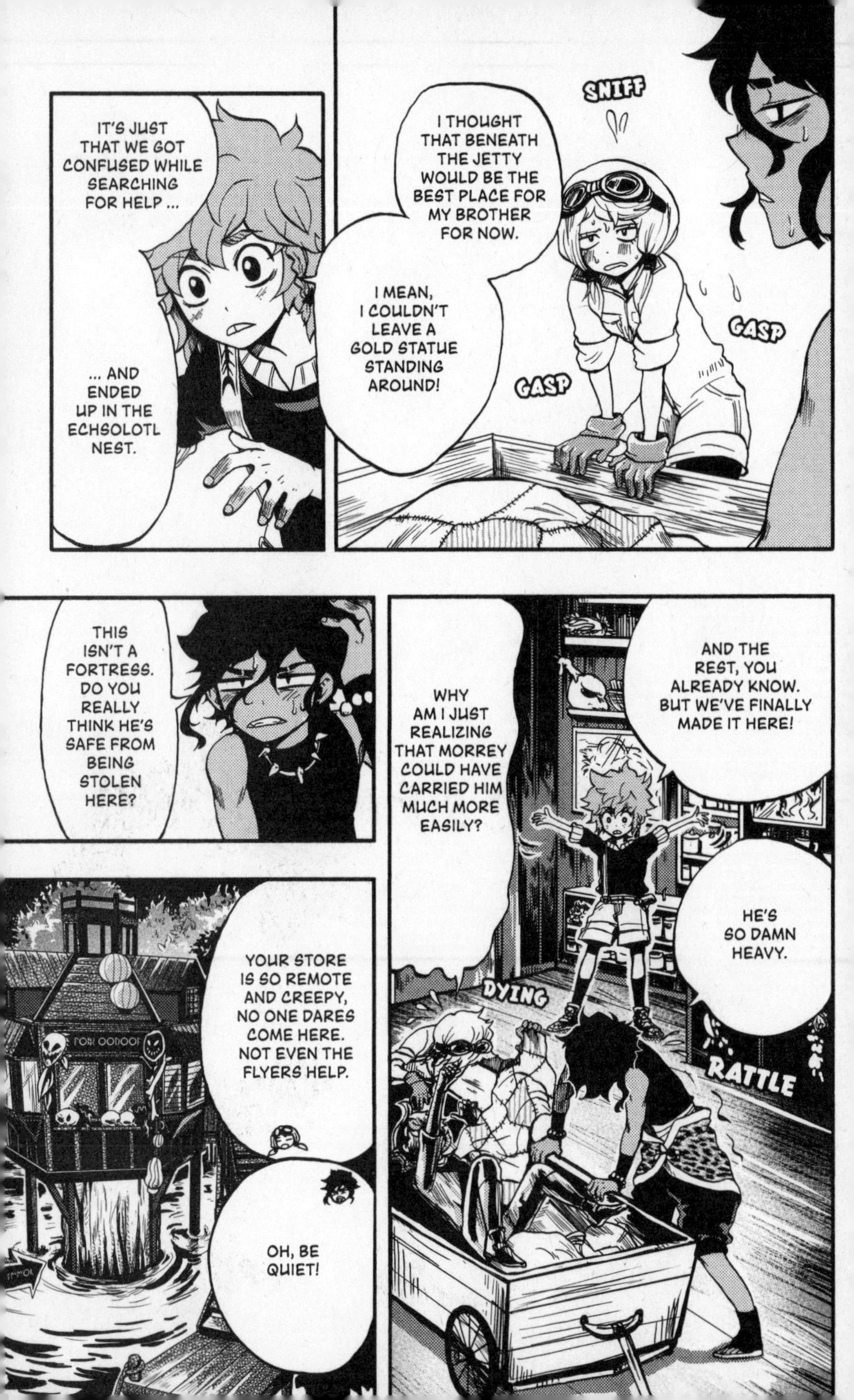
SNIFF
I THOUGHT THAT BENEATH THE JETTY WOULD BE THE BEST PLACE FOR MY BROTHER FOR NOW.
I MEAN, I COULDN'T LEAVE A GOLD STATUE STANDING AROUND!
GASP
GASP
IT'S JUST THAT WE GOT CONFUSED WHILE SEARCHING FOR HELP ...
... AND ENDED UP IN THE ECHSOLOTL NEST.
AND THE REST, YOU ALREADY KNOW. BUT WE'VE FINALLY MADE IT HERE!
WHY AM I JUST REALIZING THAT MORREY COULD HAVE CARRIED HIM MUCH MORE EASILY?
HE'S SO DAMN HEAVY.
DYING
RATTLE
THIS ISN'T A FORTRESS. DO YOU REALLY THINK HE'S SAFE FROM BEING STOLEN HERE?
YOUR STORE IS SO REMOTE AND CREEPY, NO ONE DARES COME HERE. NOT EVEN THE FLYERS HELP.
OH, BE QUIET!

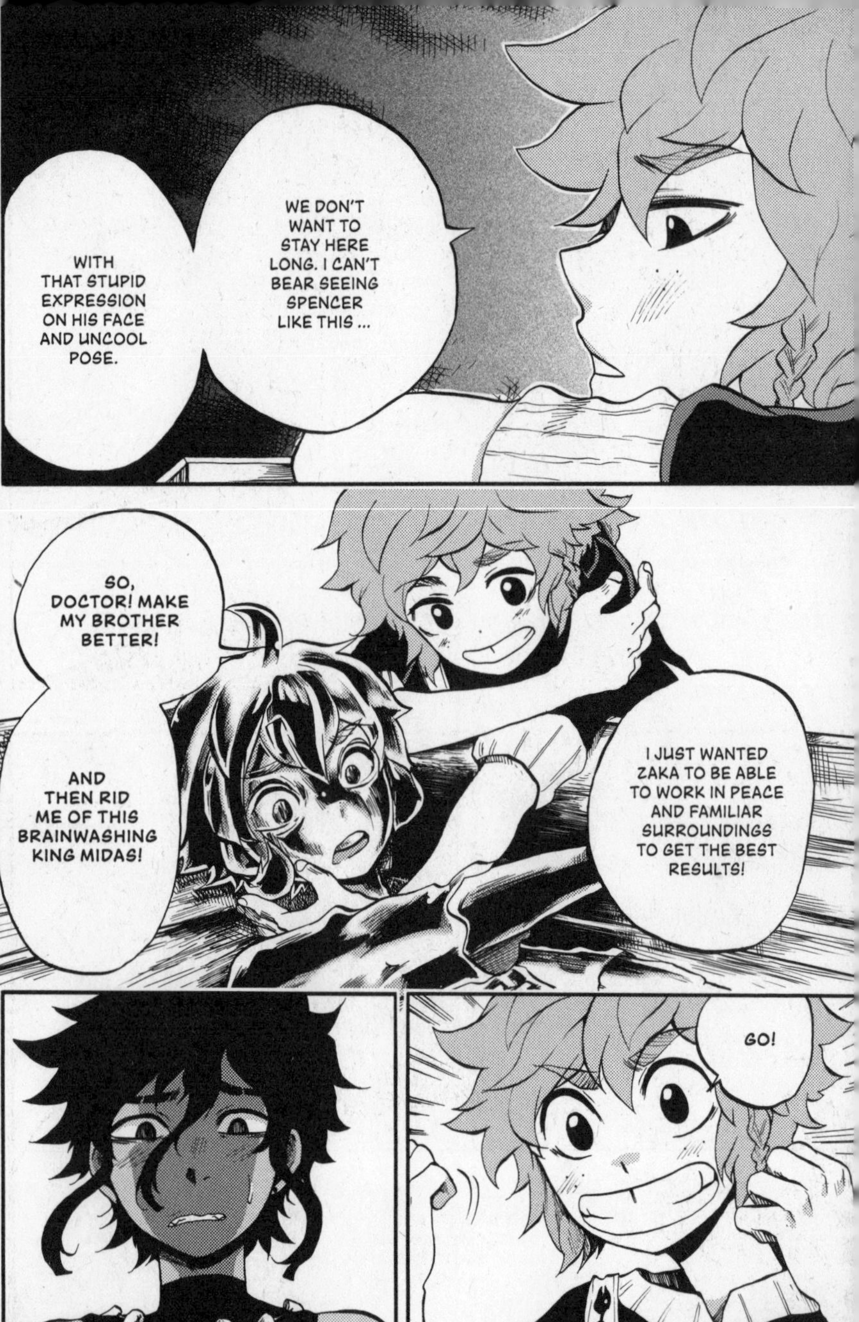
WE DON'T WANT TO STAY HERE LONG. I CAN'T BEAR SEEING SPENCER LIKE THIS ...
WITH THAT STUPID EXPRESSION ON HIS FACE AND UNCOOL POSE.
I JUST WANTED ZAKA TO BE ABLE TO WORK IN PEACE AND FAMILIAR SURROUNDINGS TO GET THE BEST RESULTS!
SO, DOCTOR! MAKE MY BROTHER BETTER!
AND THEN RID ME OF THIS BRAINWASHING KING MIDAS!
GO!

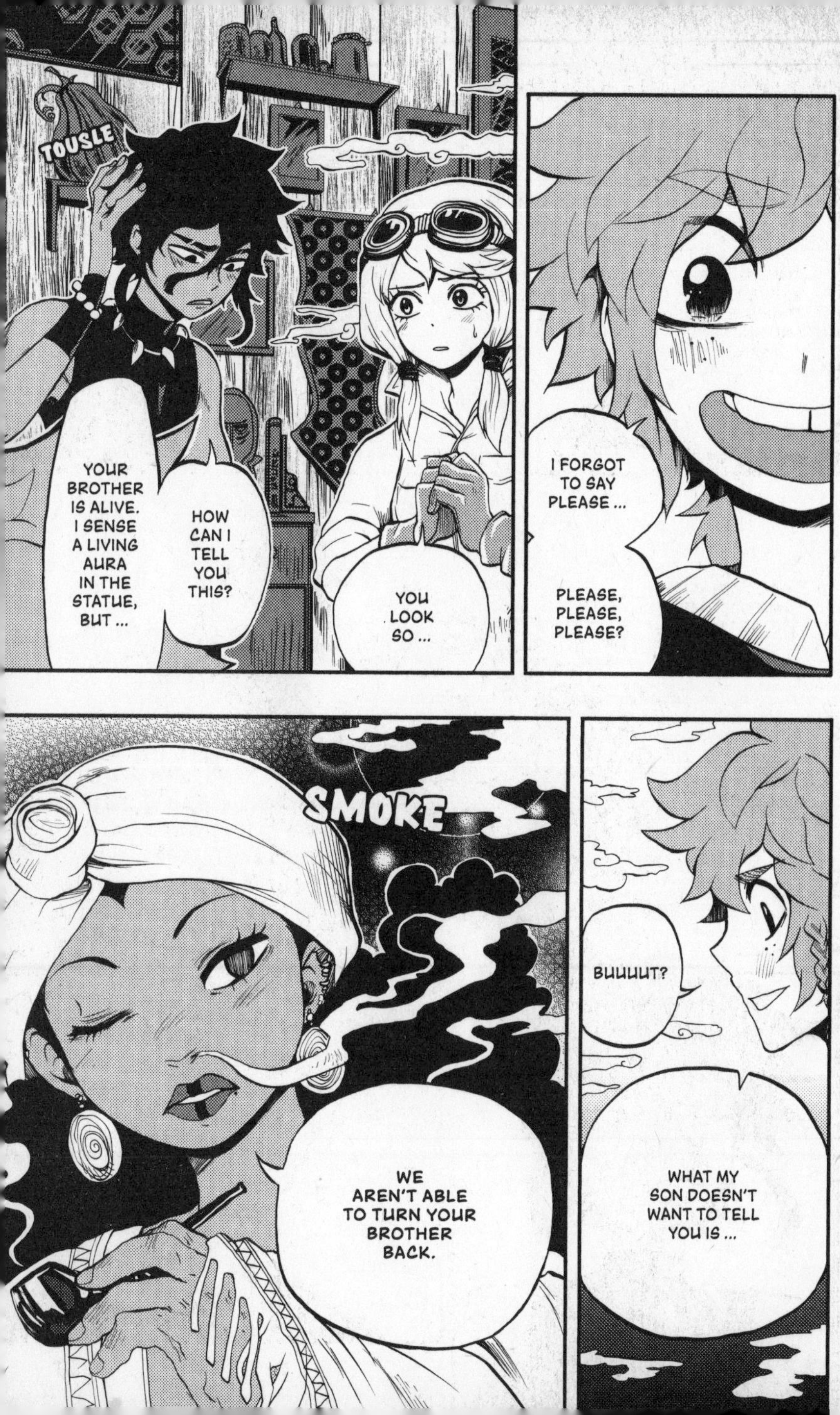
I FORGOT TO SAY PLEASE ...
PLEASE, PLEASE, PLEASE?
TOUSLE
YOU LOOK SO ...
HOW CAN I TELL YOU THIS?
YOUR BROTHER IS ALIVE. I SENSE A LIVING AURA IN THE STATUE, BUT ...
BUUUUT?
WHAT MY SON DOESN'T WANT TO TELL YOU IS ...
SMOKE
WE AREN'T ABLE TO TURN YOUR BROTHER BACK.

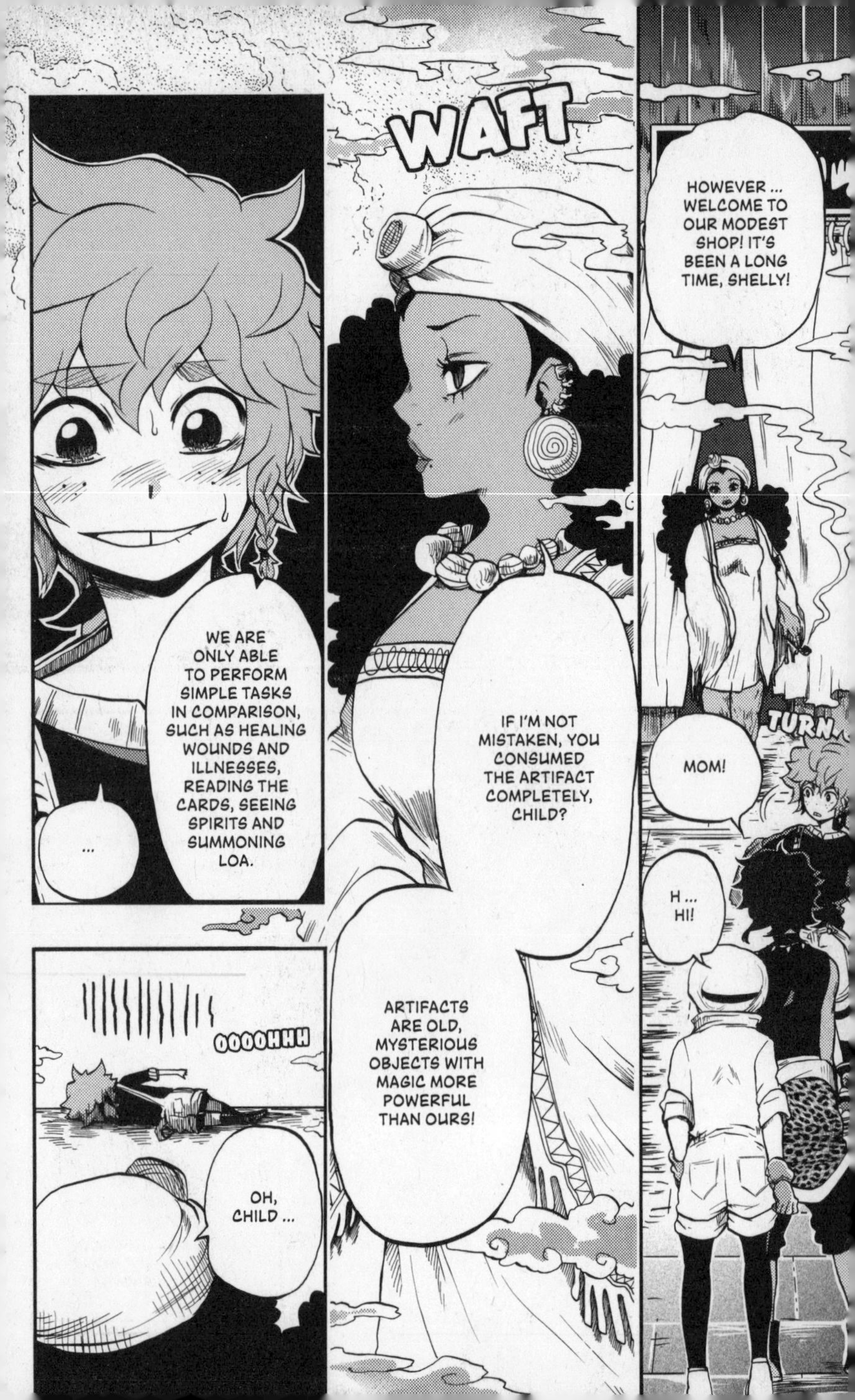
HOWEVER ... WELCOME TO OUR MODEST SHOP! IT'S BEEN A LONG TIME, SHELLY!
TURN
MOM!
H ... HI!
WAFT
IF I'M NOT MISTAKEN, YOU CONSUMED THE ARTIFACT COMPLETELY, CHILD?
ARTIFACTS ARE OLD, MYSTERIOUS OBJECTS WITH MAGIC MORE POWERFUL THAN OURS!
WE ARE ONLY ABLE TO PERFORM SIMPLE TASKS IN COMPARISON, SUCH AS HEALING WOUNDS AND ILLNESSES, READING THE CARDS, SEEING SPIRITS AND SUMMONING LOA.
...
OOOOHHH
OH, CHILD ...

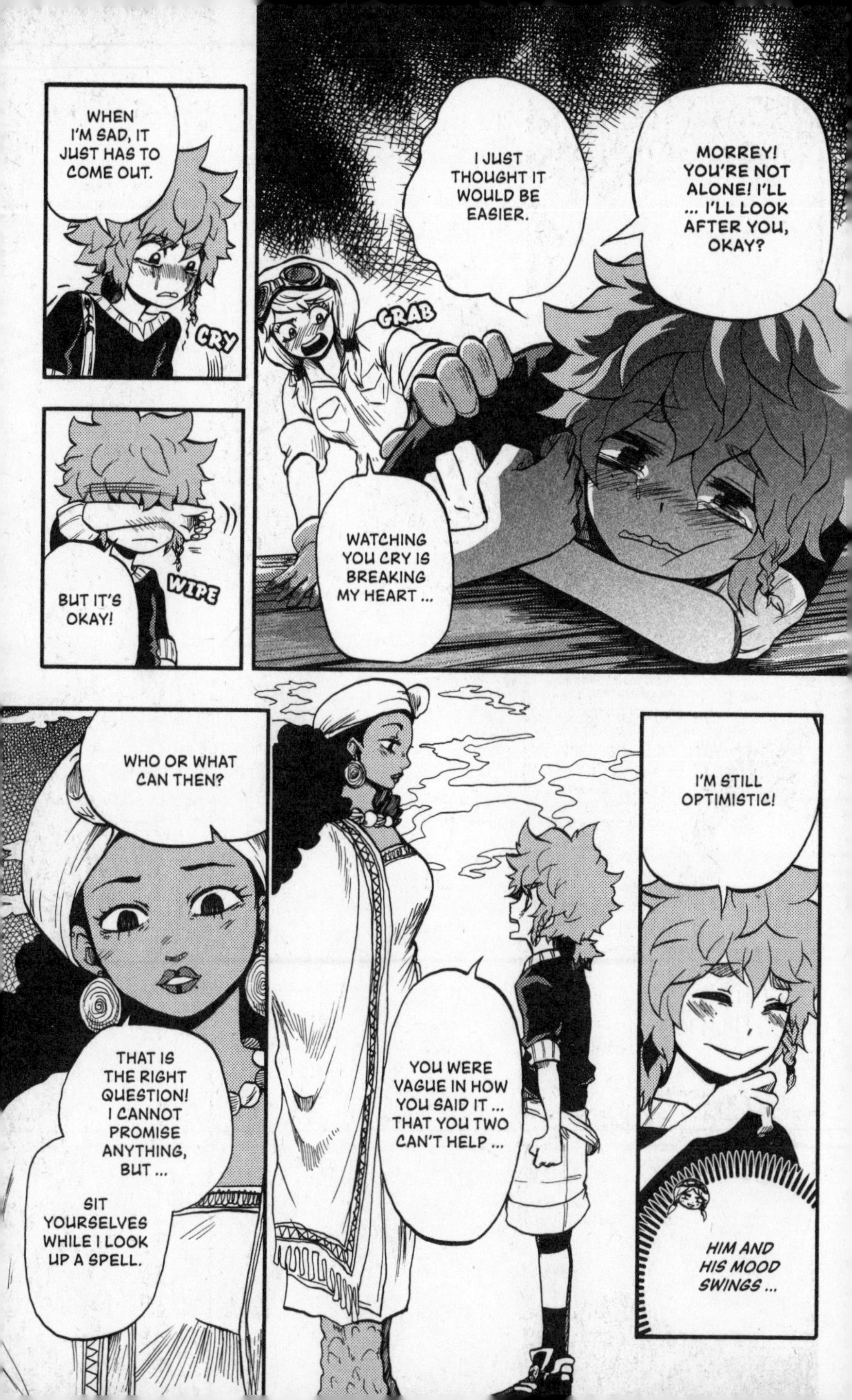
MORREY! YOU'RE NOT ALONE! I'LL ... I'LL LOOK AFTER YOU, OKAY?
I JUST THOUGHT IT WOULD BE EASIER.
GRAB
WATCHING YOU CRY IS BREAKING MY HEART ...
WHEN I'M SAD, IT JUST HAS TO COME OUT.
CRY
WIPE
BUT IT'S OKAY!
I'M STILL OPTIMISTIC!
HIM AND HIS MOOD SWINGS ...
YOU WERE VAGUE IN HOW YOU SAID IT ... THAT YOU TWO CAN'T HELP ...
WHO OR WHAT CAN THEN?
THAT IS THE RIGHT QUESTION! I CANNOT PROMISE ANYTHING, BUT ...
SIT YOURSELVES WHILE I LOOK UP A SPELL.

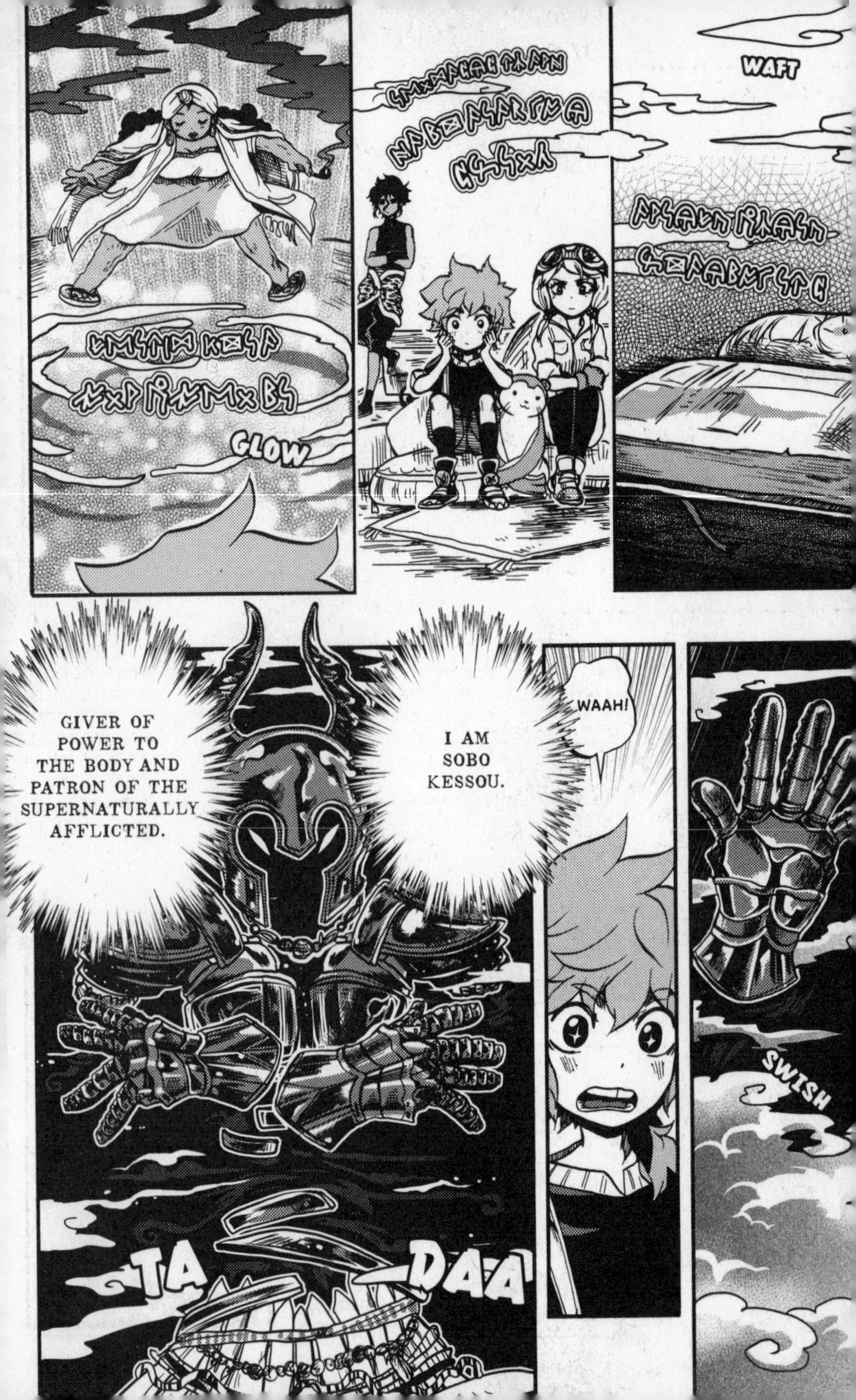
WAFT
GLOW
SWISH
WAAH!
I AM SOBO KESSOU.
GIVER OF POWER TO THE BODY AND PATRON OF THE SUPERNATURALLY AFFLICTED.
TA DAA

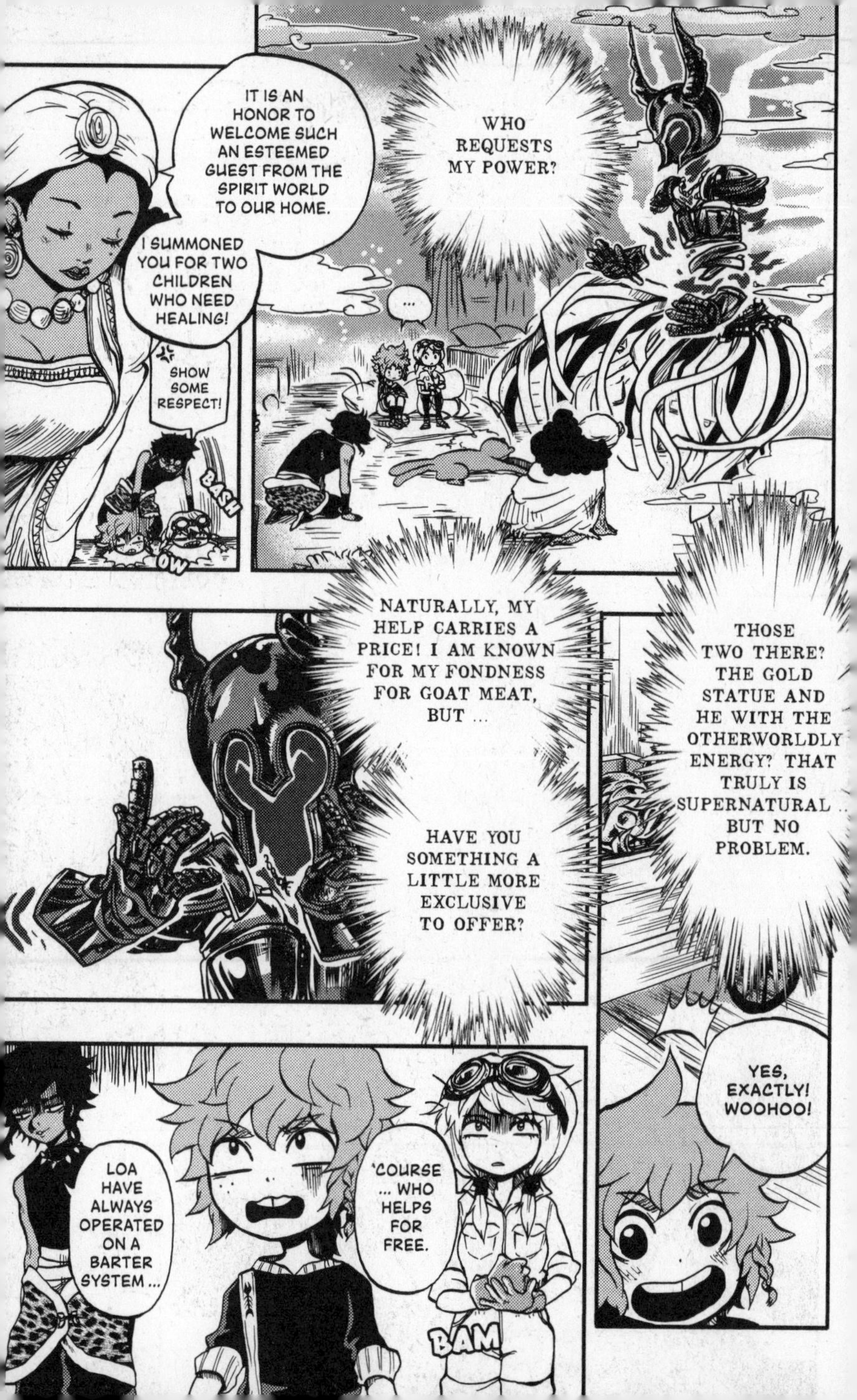
WHO REQUESTS MY POWER?
...
IT IS AN HONOR TO WELCOME SUCH AN ESTEEMED GUEST FROM THE SPIRIT WORLD TO OUR HOME.
I SUMMONED YOU FOR TWO CHILDREN WHO NEED HEALING!
SHOW SOME RESPECT!
BASH
OW
THOSE TWO THERE? THE GOLD STATUE AND HE WITH THE OTHERWORLDLY ENERGY? THAT TRULY IS SUPERNATURAL ... BUT NO PROBLEM.
YES, EXACTLY! WOOHOO!
NATURALLY, MY HELP CARRIES A PRICE! I AM KNOWN FOR MY FONDNESS FOR GOAT MEAT, BUT ...
HAVE YOU SOMETHING A LITTLE MORE EXCLUSIVE TO OFFER?
'COURSE ... WHO HELPS FOR FREE.
LOA HAVE ALWAYS OPERATED ON A BARTER SYSTEM ...
BAM

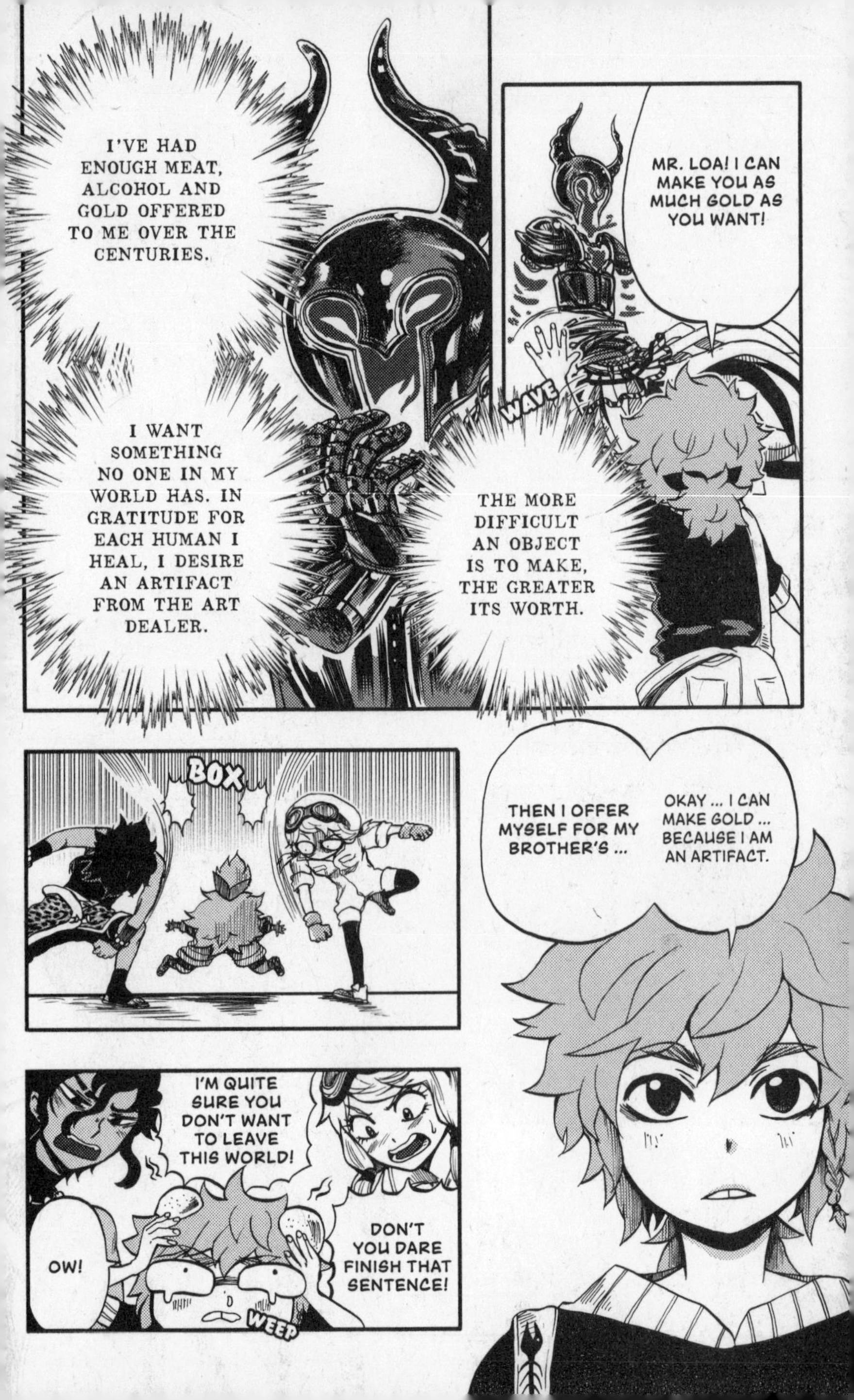
MR. LOA! I CAN MAKE YOU AS MUCH GOLD AS YOU WANT!
WAVE
I'VE HAD ENOUGH MEAT, ALCOHOL AND GOLD OFFERED TO ME OVER THE CENTURIES.
I WANT SOMETHING NO ONE IN MY WORLD HAS. IN GRATITUDE FOR EACH HUMAN I HEAL, I DESIRE AN ARTIFACT FROM THE ART DEALER.
THE MORE DIFFICULT AN OBJECT IS TO MAKE, THE GREATER ITS WORTH.
OKAY ... I CAN MAKE GOLD ... BECAUSE I AM AN ARTIFACT.
THEN I OFFER MYSELF FOR MY BROTHER'S ...
BOX
I'M QUITE SURE YOU DON'T WANT TO LEAVE THIS WORLD!
DON'T YOU DARE FINISH THAT SENTENCE!
OW!
WEEP

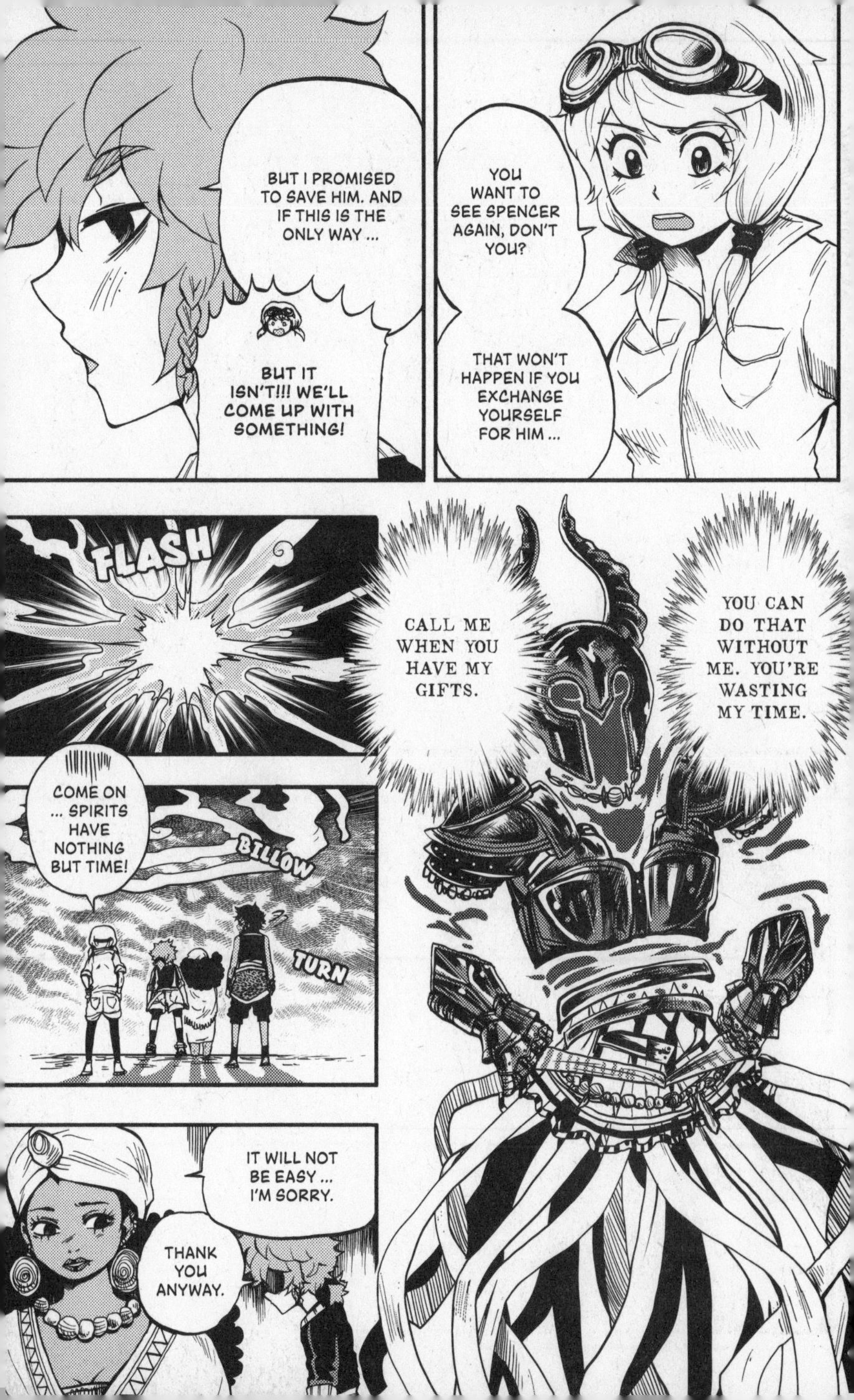
YOU WANT TO SEE SPENCER AGAIN, DON'T YOU?
THAT WON'T HAPPEN IF YOU EXCHANGE YOURSELF FOR HIM ...
BUT I PROMISED TO SAVE HIM. AND IF THIS IS THE ONLY WAY ...
BUT IT ISN'T!!! WE'LL COME UP WITH SOMETHING!
YOU CAN DO THAT WITHOUT ME. YOU'RE WASTING MY TIME.
CALL ME WHEN YOU HAVE MY GIFTS.
FLASH
COME ON ... SPIRITS HAVE NOTHING BUT TIME!
BILLOW
TURN
IT WILL NOT BE EASY ... I'M SORRY.
THANK YOU ANYWAY.

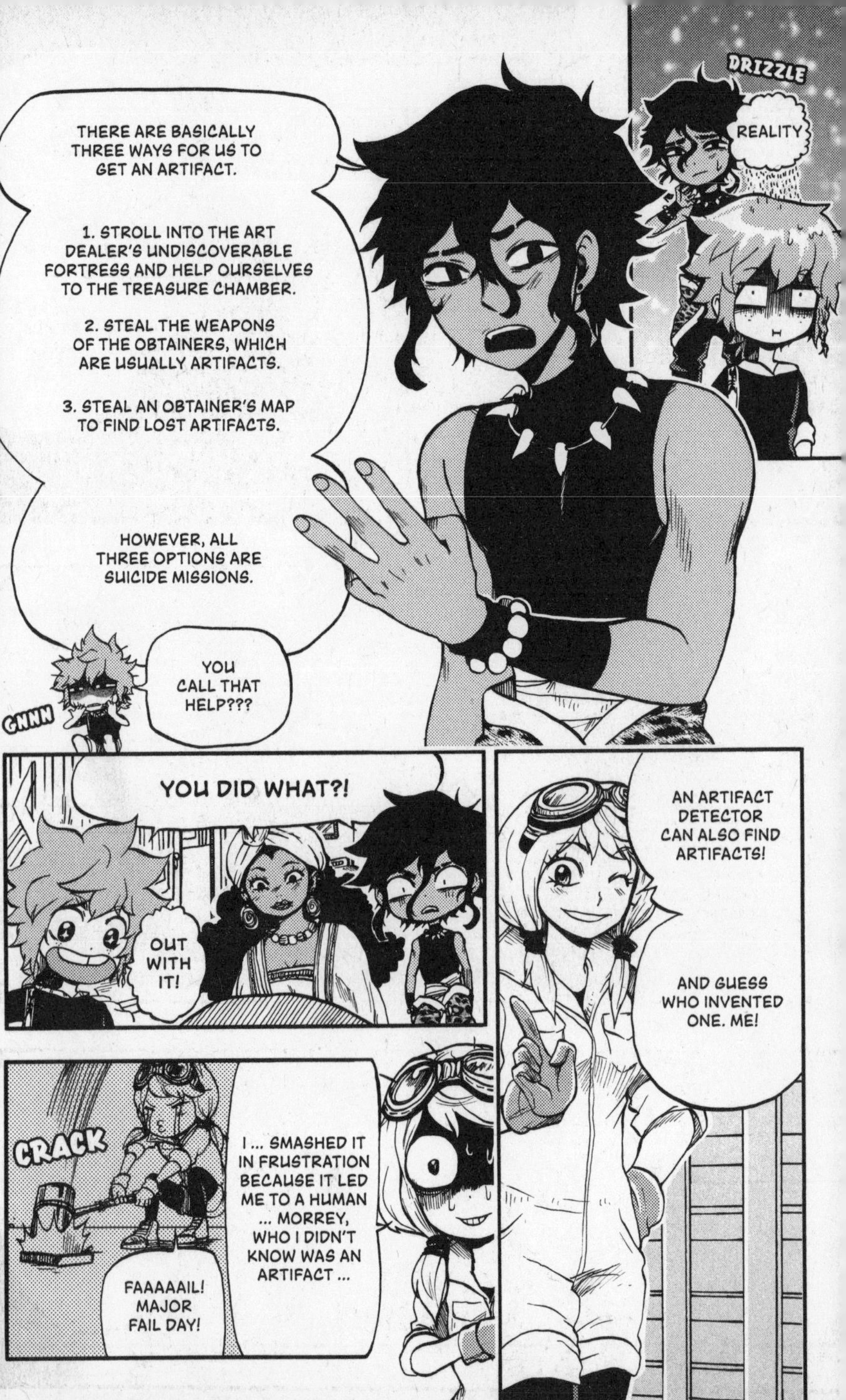
DRIZZLE
REALITY
THERE ARE BASICALLY THREE WAYS FOR US TO GET AN ARTIFACT.
1. STROLL INTO THE ART DEALER'S UNDISCOVERABLE FORTRESS AND HELP OURSELVES TO THE TREASURE CHAMBER.
2. STEAL THE WEAPONS OF THE OBTAINERS, WHICH ARE USUALLY ARTIFACTS.
3. STEAL AN OBTAINER'S MAP TO FIND LOST ARTIFACTS.
HOWEVER, ALL THREE OPTIONS ARE SUICIDE MISSIONS.
YOU CALL THAT HELP???
GNNN
AN ARTIFACT DETECTOR CAN ALSO FIND ARTIFACTS!
AND GUESS WHO INVENTED ONE. ME!
YOU DID WHAT?!
OUT WITH IT!
I ... SMASHED IT IN FRUSTRATION BECAUSE IT LED ME TO A HUMAN ... MORREY, WHO I DIDN'T KNOW WAS AN ARTIFACT ...
CRACK
FAAAAAIL! MAJOR FAIL DAY!

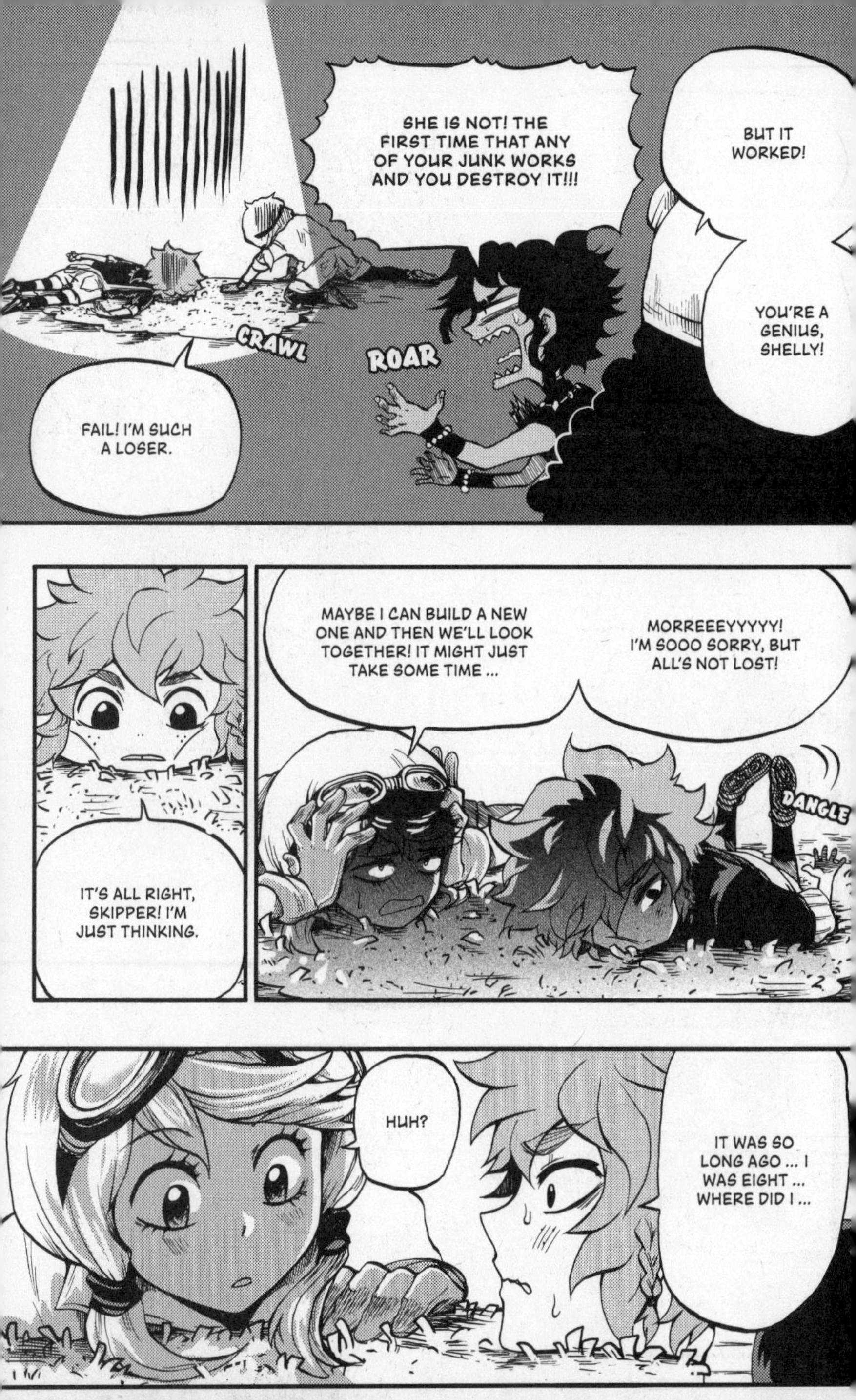
BUT IT WORKED!
YOU'RE A GENIUS, SHELLY!
SHE IS NOT! THE FIRST TIME THAT ANY OF YOUR JUNK WORKS AND YOU DESTROY IT!!!
ROAR
CRAWL
FAIL! I'M SUCH A LOSER.
MORREEEYYYYY! I'M SOOO SORRY, BUT ALL'S NOT LOST!
MAYBE I CAN BUILD A NEW ONE AND THEN WE'LL LOOK TOGETHER! IT MIGHT JUST TAKE SOME TIME ...
DANGLE
IT'S ALL RIGHT, SKIPPER! I'M JUST THINKING.
IT WAS SO LONG AGO ... I WAS EIGHT ... WHERE DID I ...
HUH?

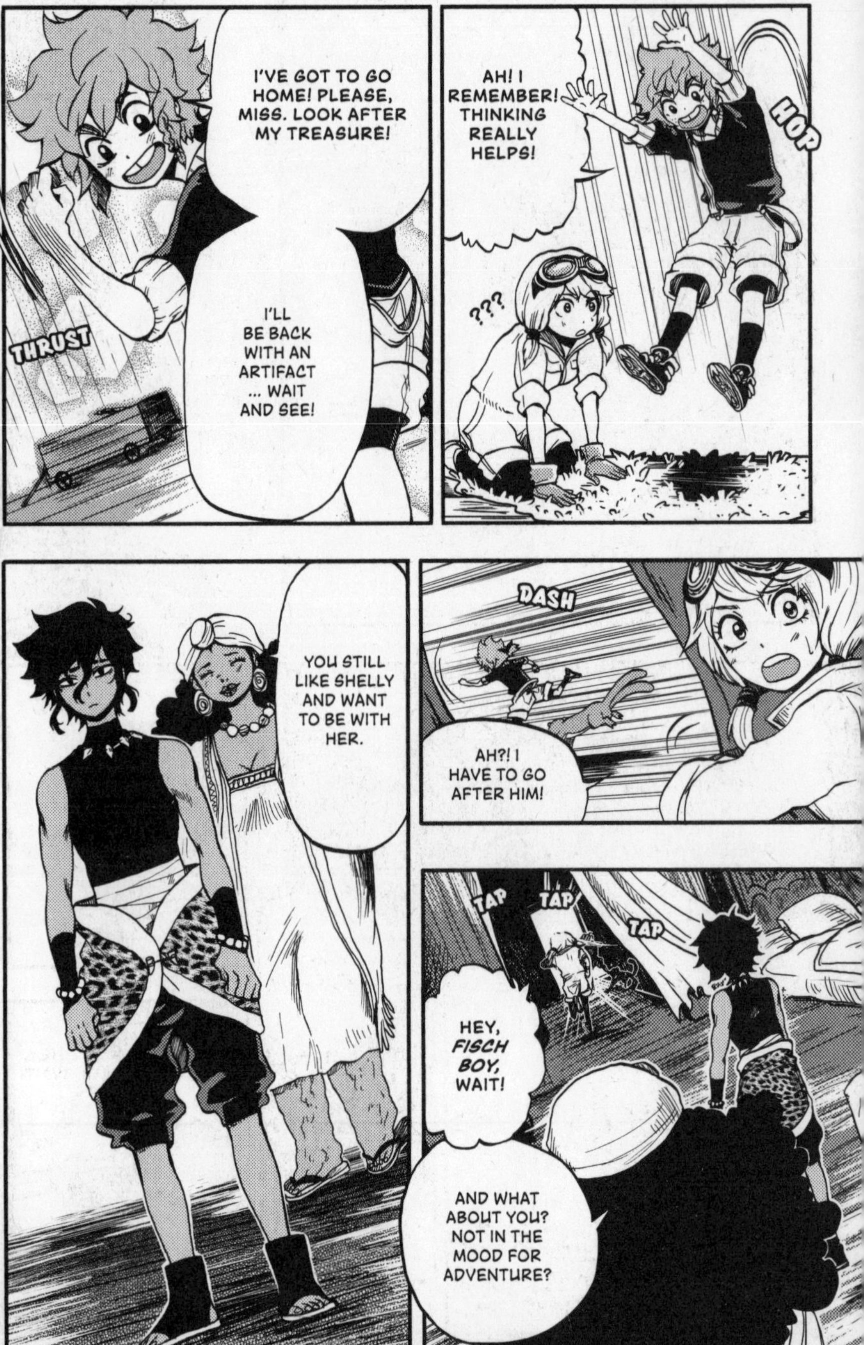
AH! I REMEMBER! THINKING REALLY HELPS!
HOP
???
I'VE GOT TO GO HOME! PLEASE, MISS. LOOK AFTER MY TREASURE!
I'LL BE BACK WITH AN ARTIFACT ... WAIT AND SEE!
THRUST
DASH
AH?! I HAVE TO GO AFTER HIM!
TAP
TAP
TAP
HEY, *FISCH BOY,* WAIT!
AND WHAT ABOUT YOU? NOT IN THE MOOD FOR ADVENTURE?
YOU STILL LIKE SHELLY AND WANT TO BE WITH HER.

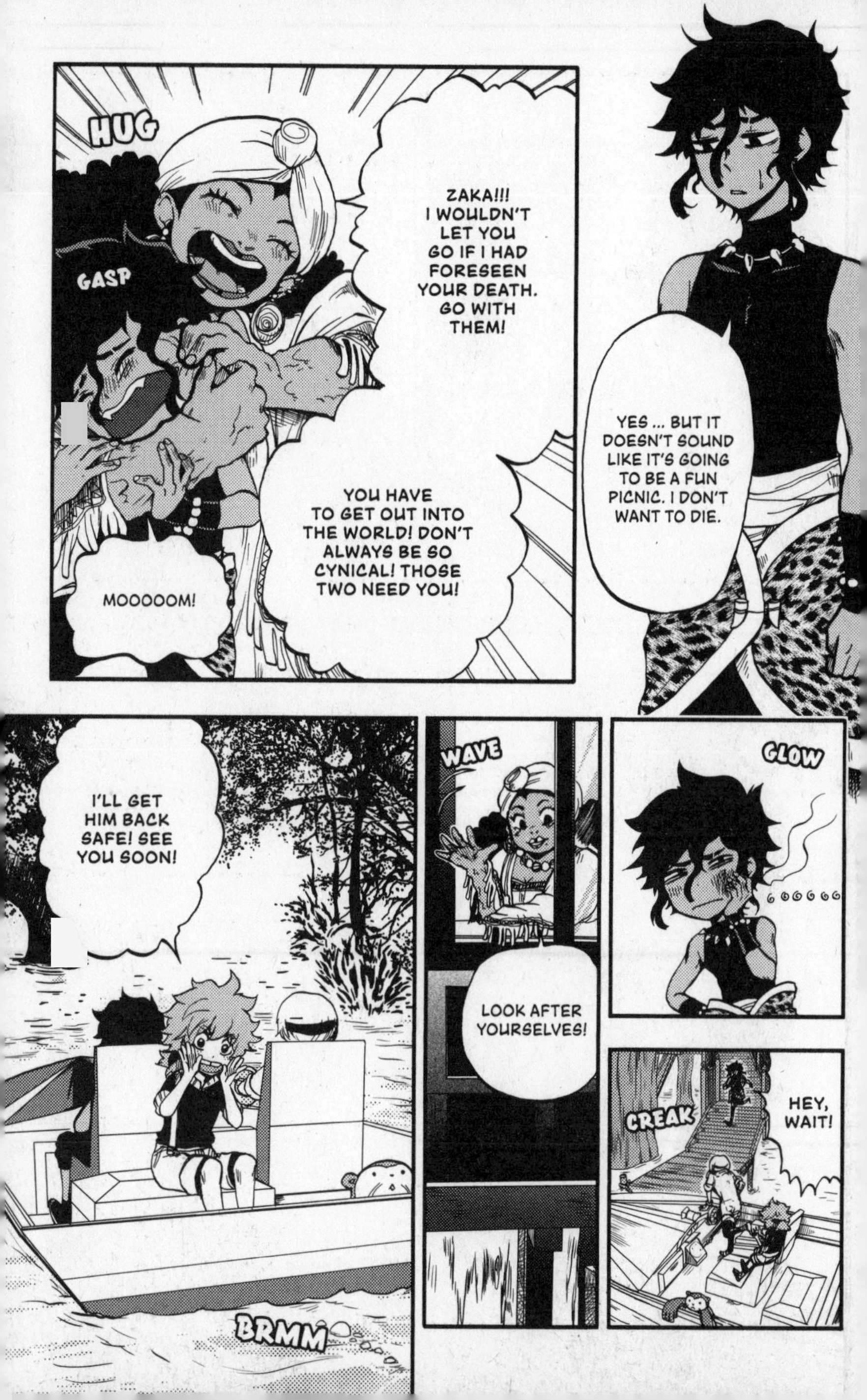
YES ... BUT IT DOESN'T SOUND LIKE IT'S GOING TO BE A FUN PICNIC. I DON'T WANT TO DIE.
HUG
ZAKA!!! I WOULDN'T LET YOU GO IF I HAD FORESEEN YOUR DEATH. GO WITH THEM!
YOU HAVE TO GET OUT INTO THE WORLD! DON'T ALWAYS BE SO CYNICAL! THOSE TWO NEED YOU!
GASP
MOOOOOM!
GLOW
HEY, WAIT!
CREAK
WAVE
LOOK AFTER YOURSELVES!
I'LL GET HIM BACK SAFE! SEE YOU SOON!
BRMM

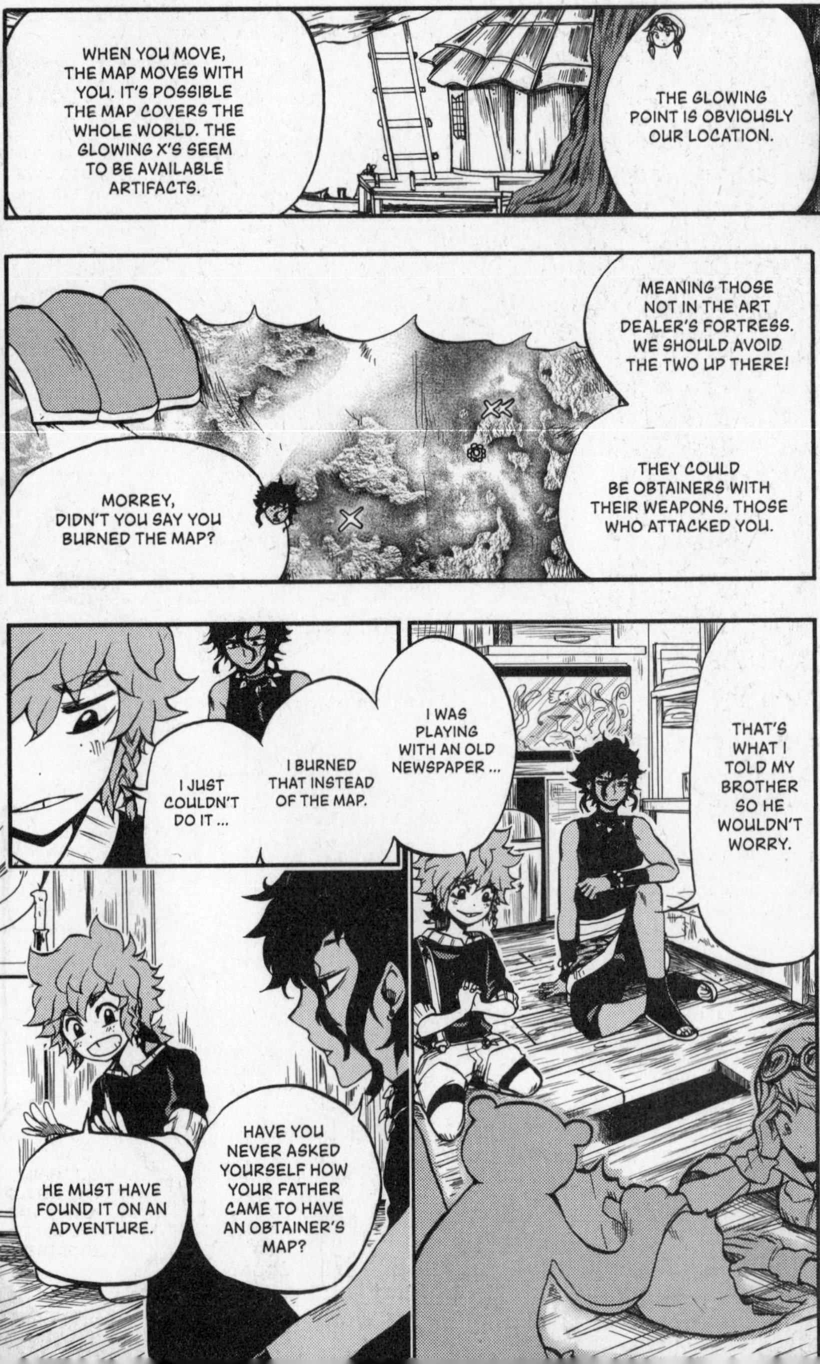
THE GLOWING POINT IS OBVIOUSLY OUR LOCATION.
WHEN YOU MOVE, THE MAP MOVES WITH YOU. IT'S POSSIBLE THE MAP COVERS THE WHOLE WORLD. THE GLOWING X'S SEEM TO BE AVAILABLE ARTIFACTS.
MEANING THOSE NOT IN THE ART DEALER'S FORTRESS. WE SHOULD AVOID THE TWO UP THERE!
THEY COULD BE OBTAINERS WITH THEIR WEAPONS. THOSE WHO ATTACKED YOU.
MORREY, DIDN'T YOU SAY YOU BURNED THE MAP?
THAT'S WHAT I TOLD MY BROTHER SO HE WOULDN'T WORRY.
I WAS PLAYING WITH AN OLD NEWSPAPER ...
I BURNED THAT INSTEAD OF THE MAP.
I JUST COULDN'T DO IT ...
HAVE YOU NEVER ASKED YOURSELF HOW YOUR FATHER CAME TO HAVE AN OBTAINER'S MAP?
HE MUST HAVE FOUND IT ON AN ADVENTURE.

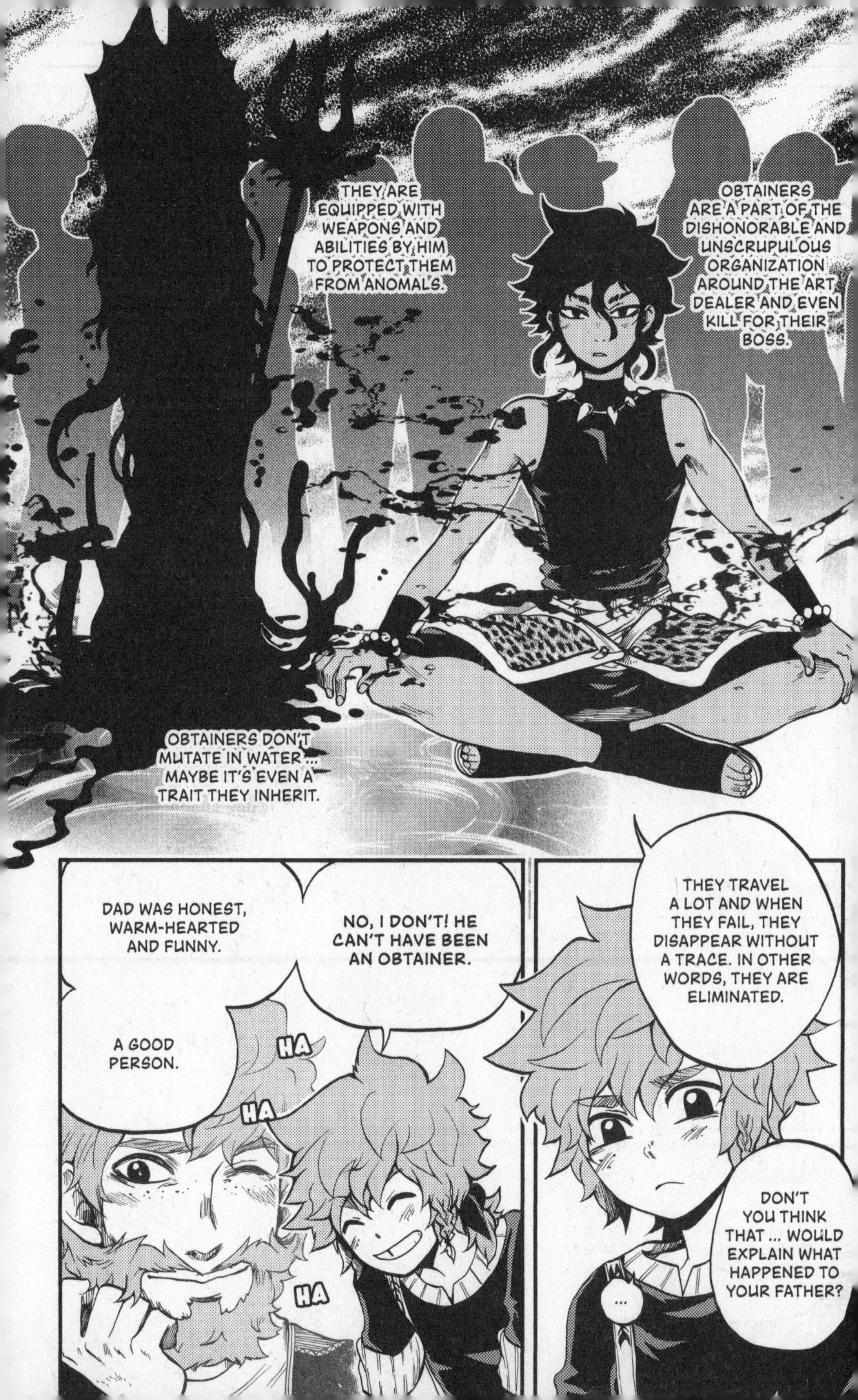
OBTAINERS ARE A PART OF THE DISHONORABLE AND UNSCRUPULOUS ORGANIZATION AROUND THE ART DEALER AND EVEN KILL FOR THEIR BOSS.
THEY ARE EQUIPPED WITH WEAPONS AND ABILITIES BY HIM TO PROTECT THEM FROM ANOMALS.
OBTAINERS DON'T MUTATE IN WATER ... MAYBE IT'S EVEN A TRAIT THEY INHERIT.
THEY TRAVEL A LOT AND WHEN THEY FAIL, THEY DISAPPEAR WITHOUT A TRACE. IN OTHER WORDS, THEY ARE ELIMINATED.
DON'T YOU THINK THAT ... WOULD EXPLAIN WHAT HAPPENED TO YOUR FATHER?
...
NO, I DON'T! HE CAN'T HAVE BEEN AN OBTAINER.
DAD WAS HONEST, WARM-HEARTED AND FUNNY.
A GOOD PERSON.
HA
HA
HA

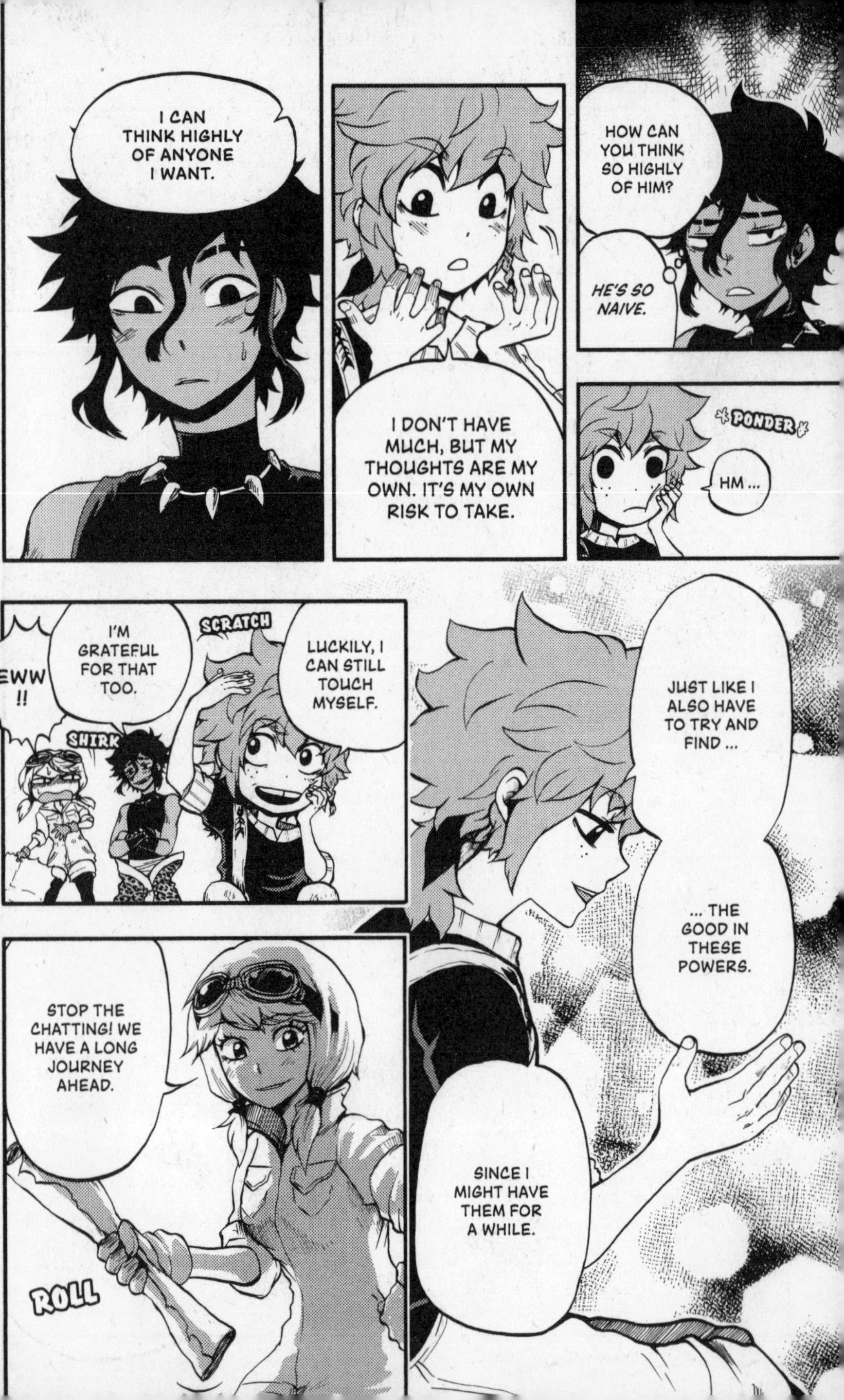
HOW CAN YOU THINK SO HIGHLY OF HIM?
HE'S SO NAIVE.
PONDER
HM ...
I DON'T HAVE MUCH, BUT MY THOUGHTS ARE MY OWN. IT'S MY OWN RISK TO TAKE.
I CAN THINK HIGHLY OF ANYONE I WANT.
JUST LIKE I ALSO HAVE TO TRY AND FIND ...
... THE GOOD IN THESE POWERS.
SINCE I MIGHT HAVE THEM FOR A WHILE.
LUCKILY, I CAN STILL TOUCH MYSELF.
SCRATCH
I'M GRATEFUL FOR THAT TOO.
SHIRK
EWW !!
STOP THE CHATTING! WE HAVE A LONG JOURNEY AHEAD.
ROLL

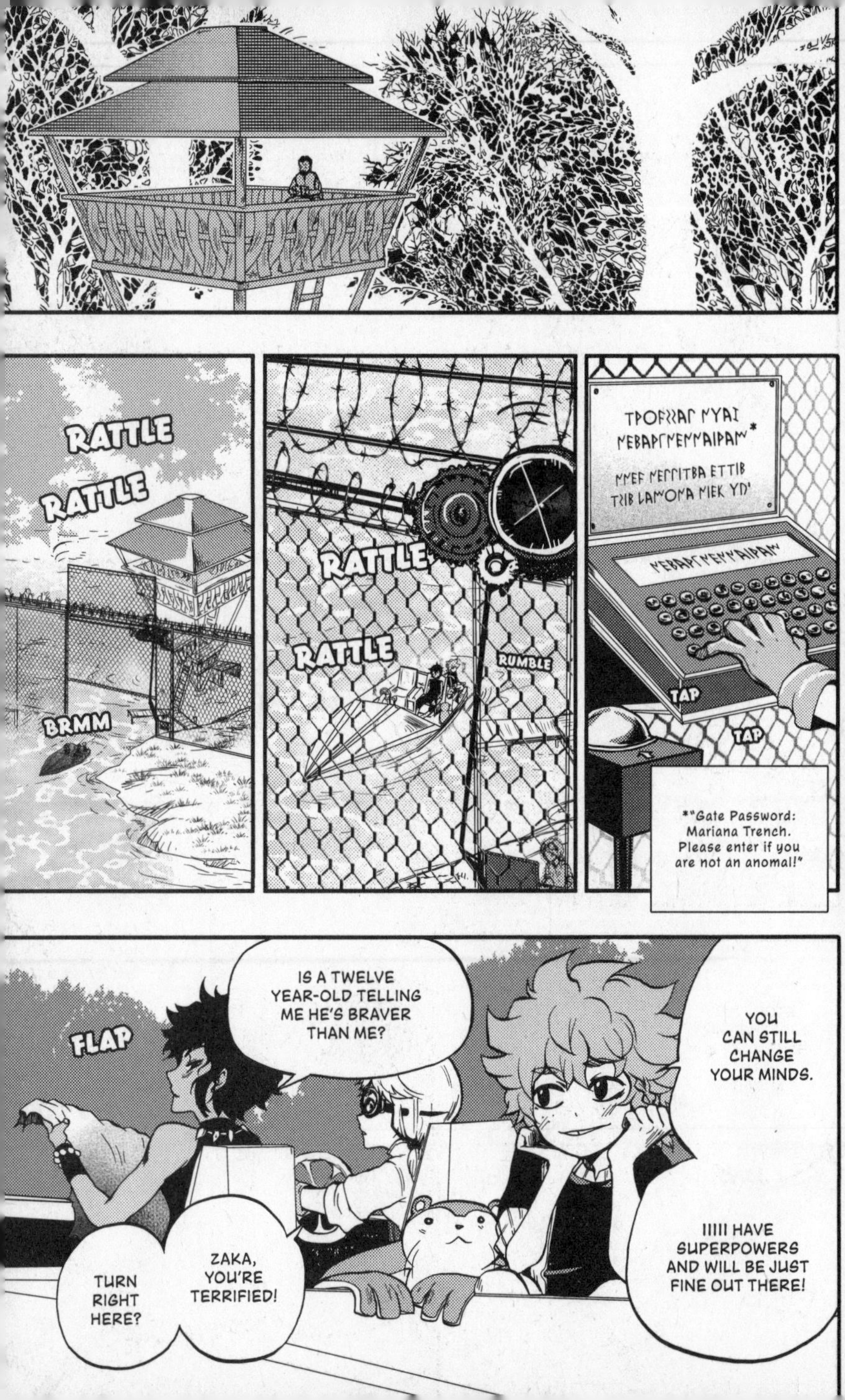
TAP
TAP
*"Gate Password: Mariana Trench. Please enter if you are not an anomal!"
RATTLE
RATTLE
RUMBLE
RATTLE
RATTLE
BRMM
YOU CAN STILL CHANGE YOUR MINDS.
IS A TWELVE YEAR-OLD TELLING ME HE'S BRAVER THAN ME?
FLAP
IIIII HAVE SUPERPOWERS AND WILL BE JUST FINE OUT THERE!
ZAKA, YOU'RE TERRIFIED!
TURN RIGHT HERE?

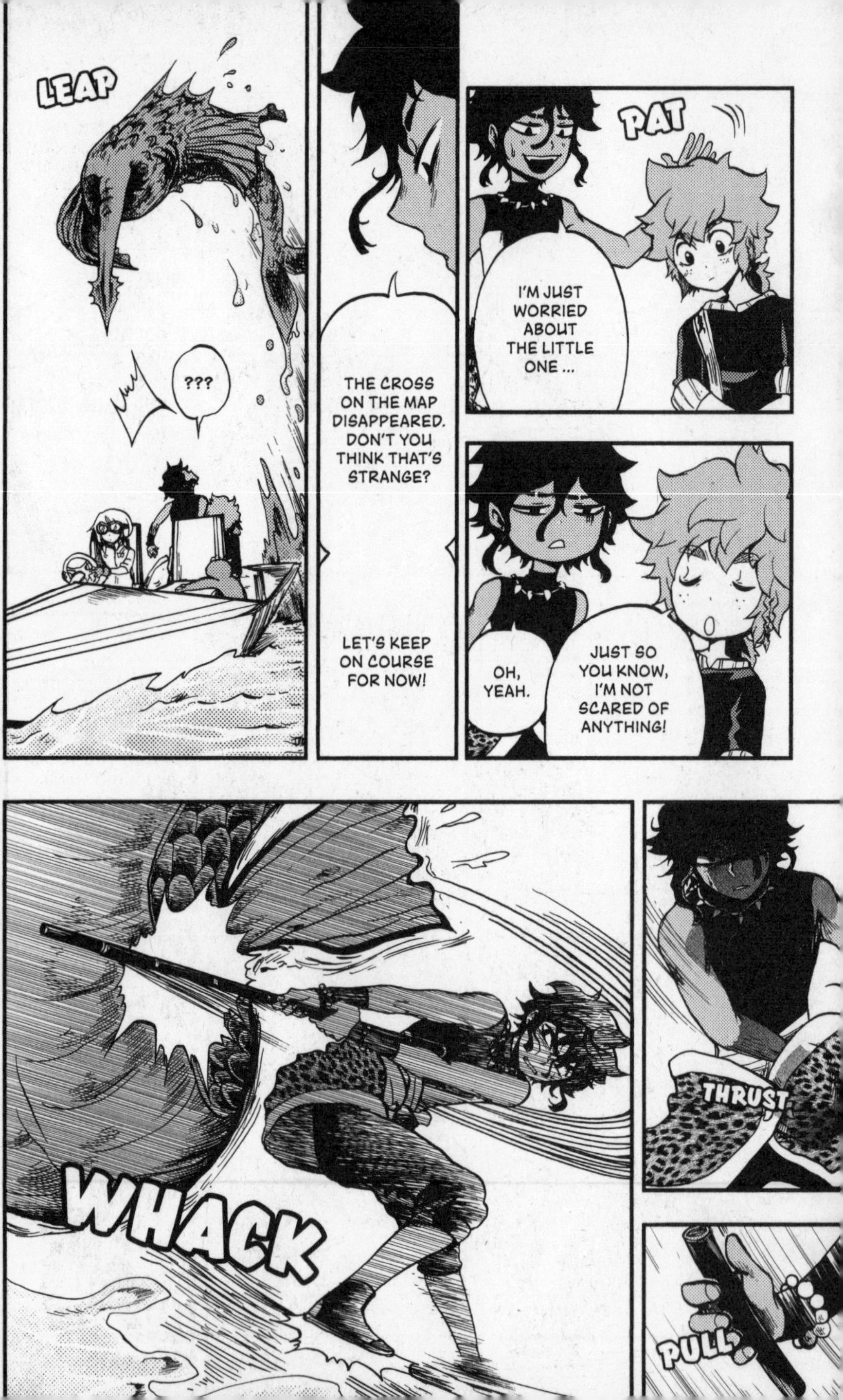
PAT
I'M JUST WORRIED ABOUT THE LITTLE ONE ...
JUST SO YOU KNOW, I'M NOT SCARED OF ANYTHING!
OH, YEAH.
THE CROSS ON THE MAP DISAPPEARED. DON'T YOU THINK THAT'S STRANGE?
LET'S KEEP ON COURSE FOR NOW!
LEAP
???
THRUST
PULL
WHACK

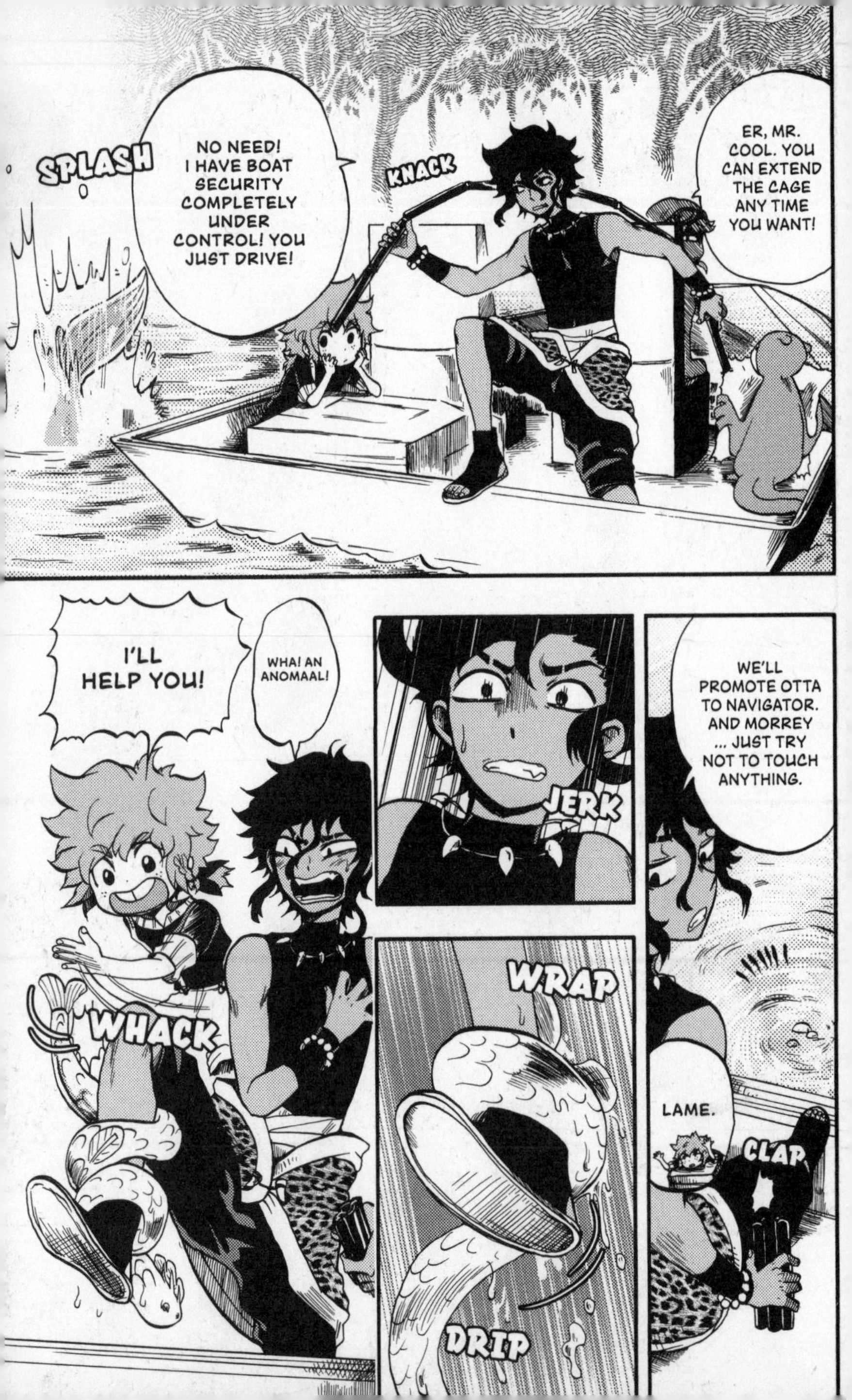
ER, MR. COOL. YOU CAN EXTEND THE CAGE ANY TIME YOU WANT!
KNACK
NO NEED! I HAVE BOAT SECURITY COMPLETELY UNDER CONTROL! YOU JUST DRIVE!
SPLASH
WE'LL PROMOTE OTTA TO NAVIGATOR. AND MORREY ... JUST TRY NOT TO TOUCH ANYTHING.
LAME.
CLAP
JERK
WRAP
DRIP
WHA! AN ANOMAAL!
I'LL HELP YOU!
WHACK

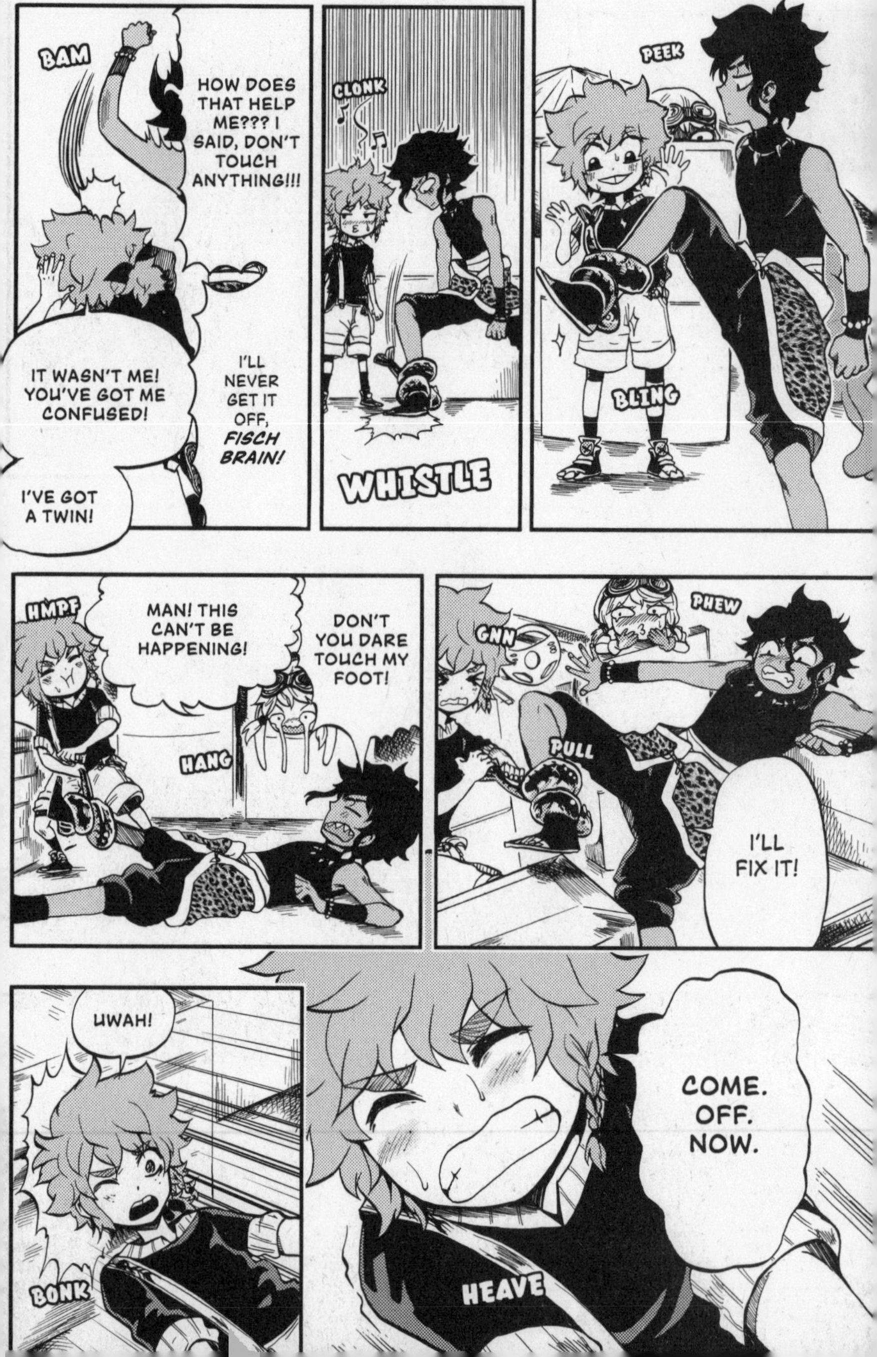
PEEK
BLING
CLONK
WHISTLE
HOW DOES THAT HELP ME??? I SAID, DON'T TOUCH ANYTHING!!!
BAM
I'LL NEVER GET IT OFF, *FISCH BRAIN!*
IT WASN'T ME! YOU'VE GOT ME CONFUSED!
I'VE GOT A TWIN!
PHEW
GNN
PULL
I'LL FIX IT!
DON'T YOU DARE TOUCH MY FOOT!
MAN! THIS CAN'T BE HAPPENING!
HMPF
HANG
COME. OFF. NOW.
HEAVE
UWAH!
BONK

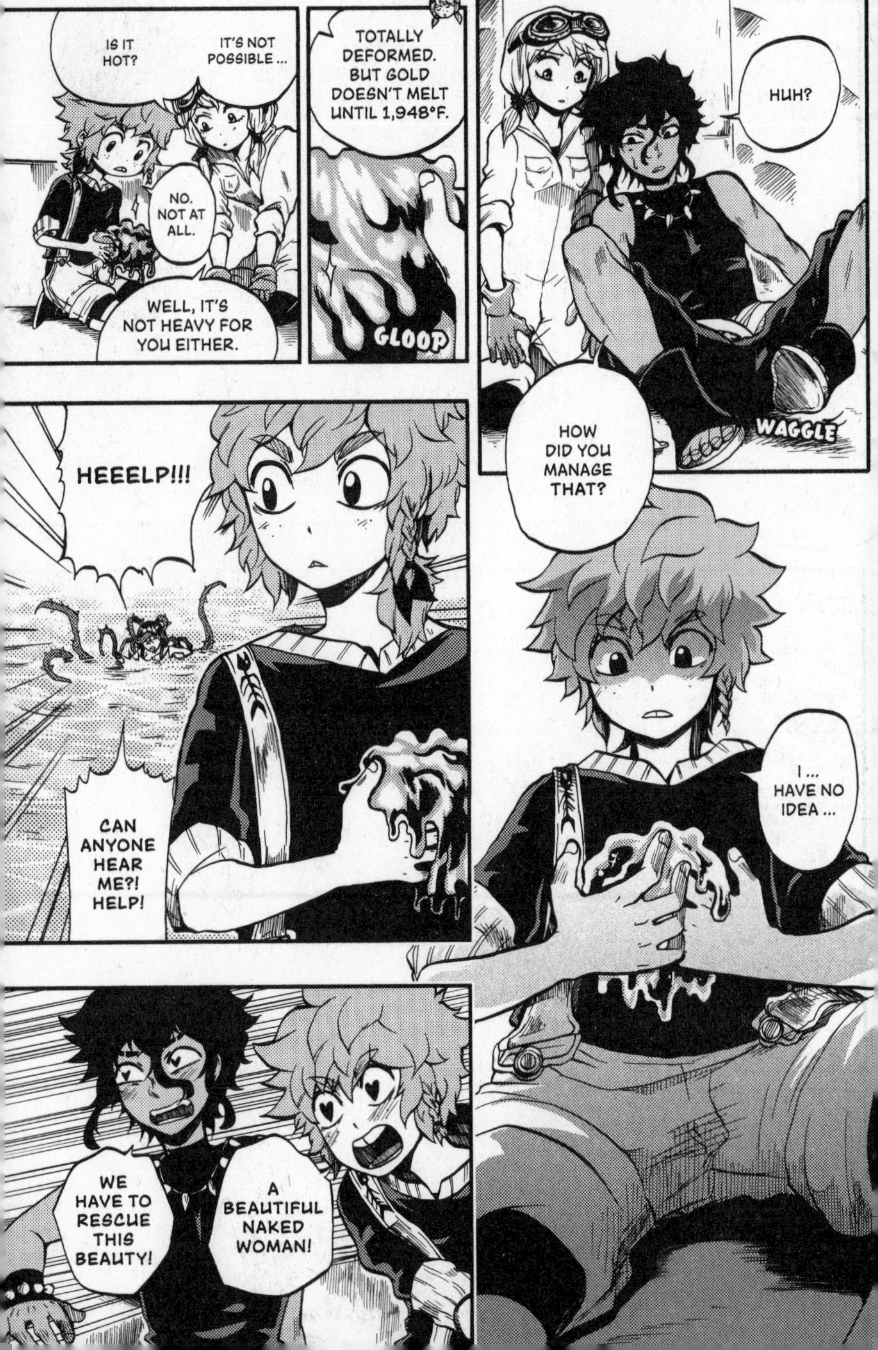
HUH?
WAGGLE
TOTALLY DEFORMED. BUT GOLD DOESN'T MELT UNTIL 1,948°F.
GLOOP
IT'S NOT POSSIBLE ...
IS IT HOT?
NO. NOT AT ALL.
WELL, IT'S NOT HEAVY FOR YOU EITHER.
HOW DID YOU MANAGE THAT?
I ... HAVE NO IDEA ...
HEEELP!!!
CAN ANYONE HEAR ME?! HELP!
A BEAUTIFUL NAKED WOMAN!
WE HAVE TO RESCUE THIS BEAUTY!

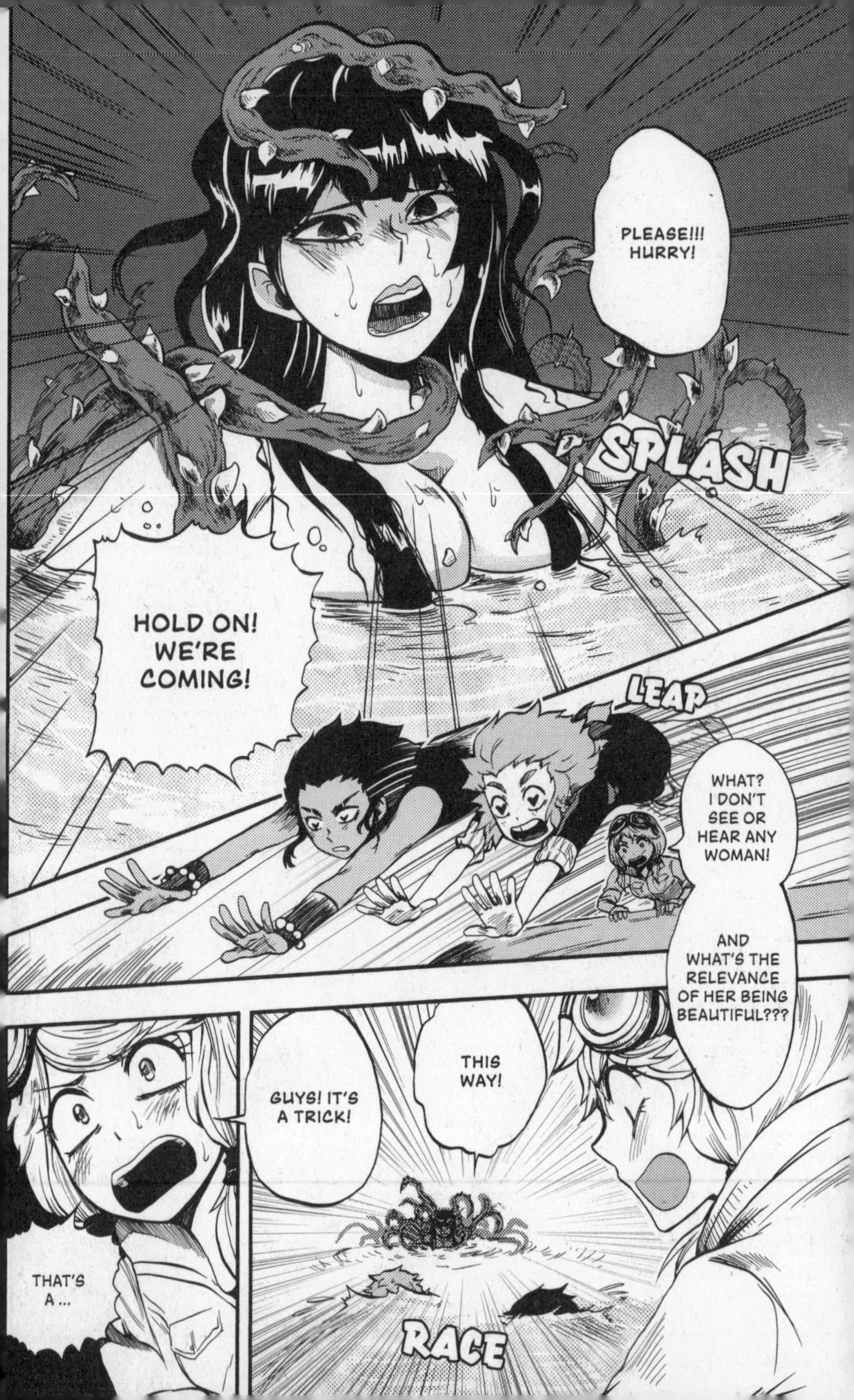
PLEASE!!! HURRY!
SPLASH
HOLD ON! WE'RE COMING!
LEAP
WHAT? I DON'T SEE OR HEAR ANY WOMAN!
AND WHAT'S THE RELEVANCE OF HER BEING BEAUTIFUL???
THIS WAY!
GUYS! IT'S A TRICK!
RACE
THAT'S A ...

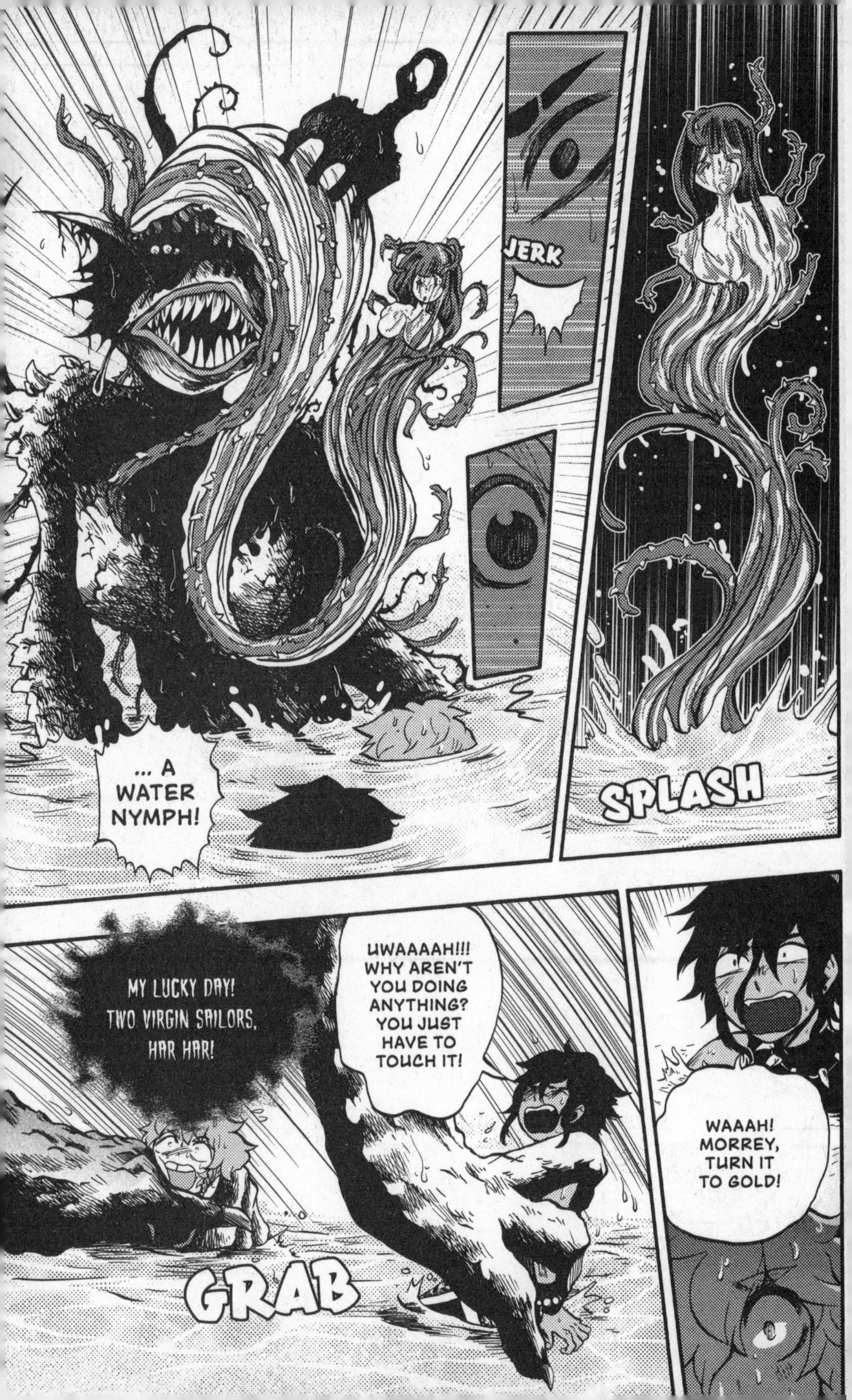
SPLASH
JERK
... A WATER NYMPH!
WAAAH! MORREY, TURN IT TO GOLD!
UWAAAAH!!! WHY AREN'T YOU DOING ANYTHING? YOU JUST HAVE TO TOUCH IT!
MY LUCKY DAY! TWO VIRGIN SAILORS, HAR HAR!
GRAB

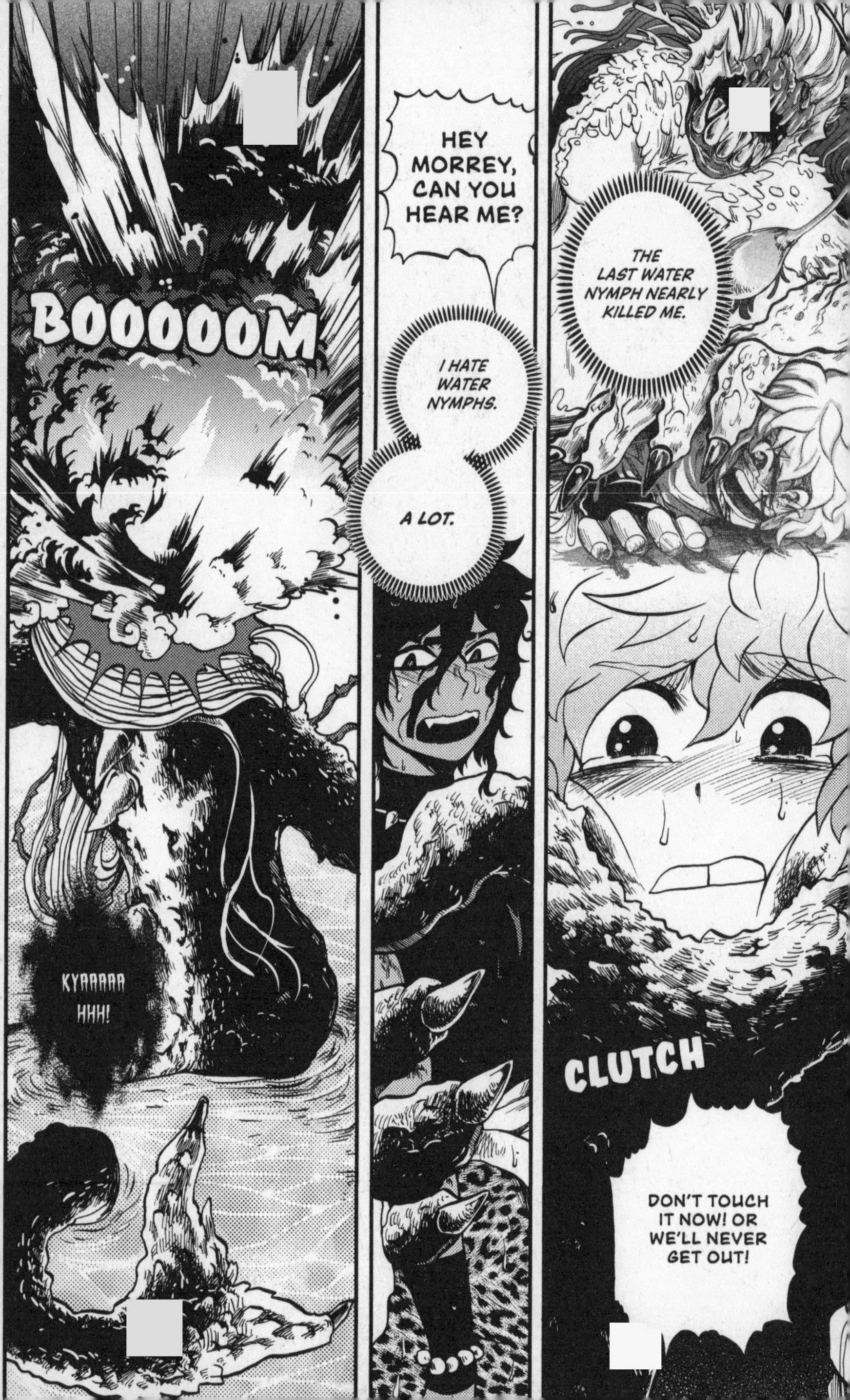
THE LAST WATER NYMPH NEARLY KILLED ME.
CLUTCH
DON'T TOUCH IT NOW! OR WE'LL NEVER GET OUT!
HEY MORREY, CAN YOU HEAR ME?
I HATE WATER NYMPHS.
A LOT.
BOOOOOM
KYAAAAAHHH!

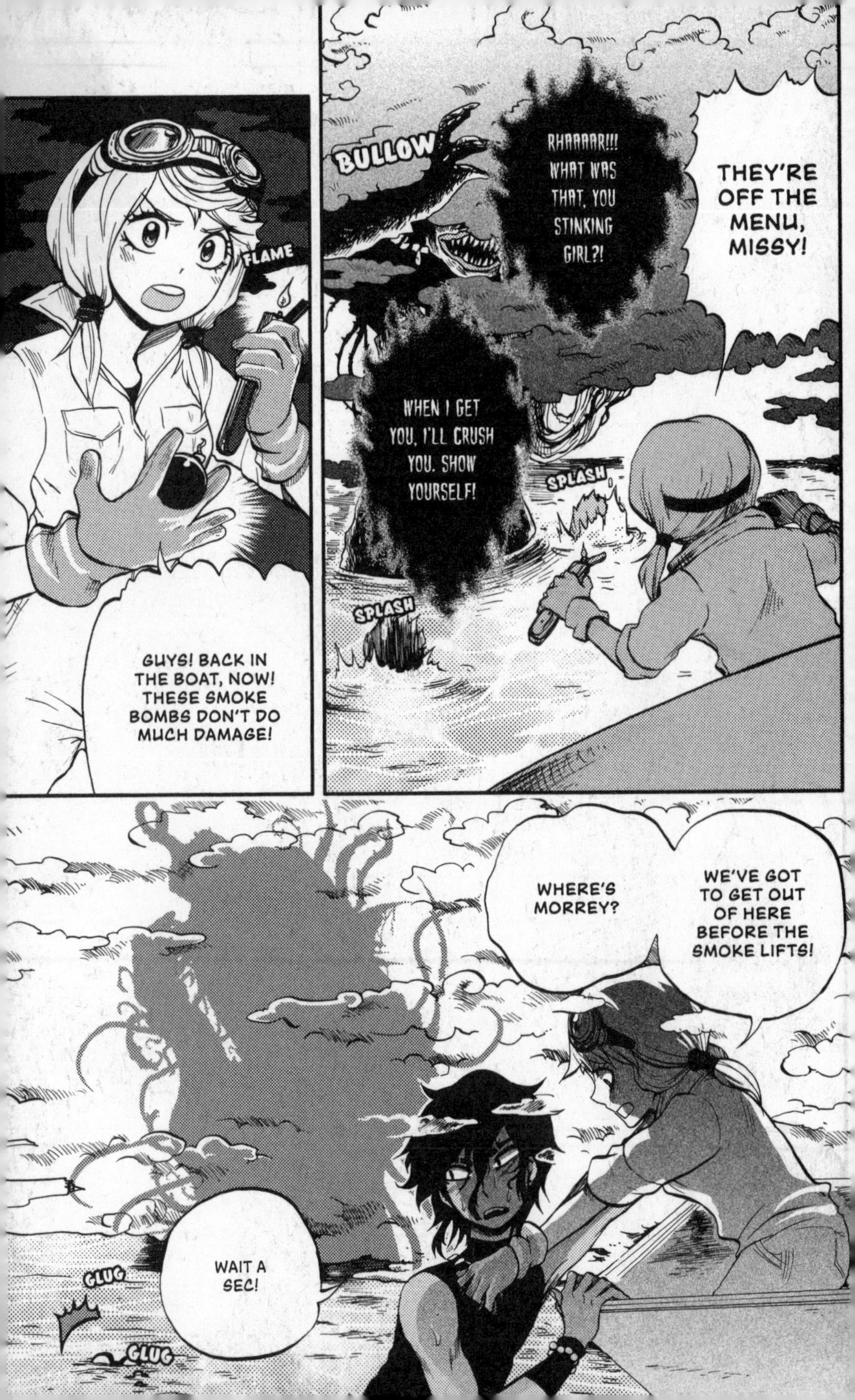
THEY'RE OFF THE MENU, MISSY!
RHAAAAR!!! WHAT WAS THAT, YOU STINKING GIRL?!
BULLOW
WHEN I GET YOU, I'LL CRUSH YOU. SHOW YOURSELF!
SPLASH
SPLASH
FLAME
GUYS! BACK IN THE BOAT, NOW! THESE SMOKE BOMBS DON'T DO MUCH DAMAGE!
WE'VE GOT TO GET OUT OF HERE BEFORE THE SMOKE LIFTS!
WHERE'S MORREY?
WAIT A SEC!
GLUG
GLUG

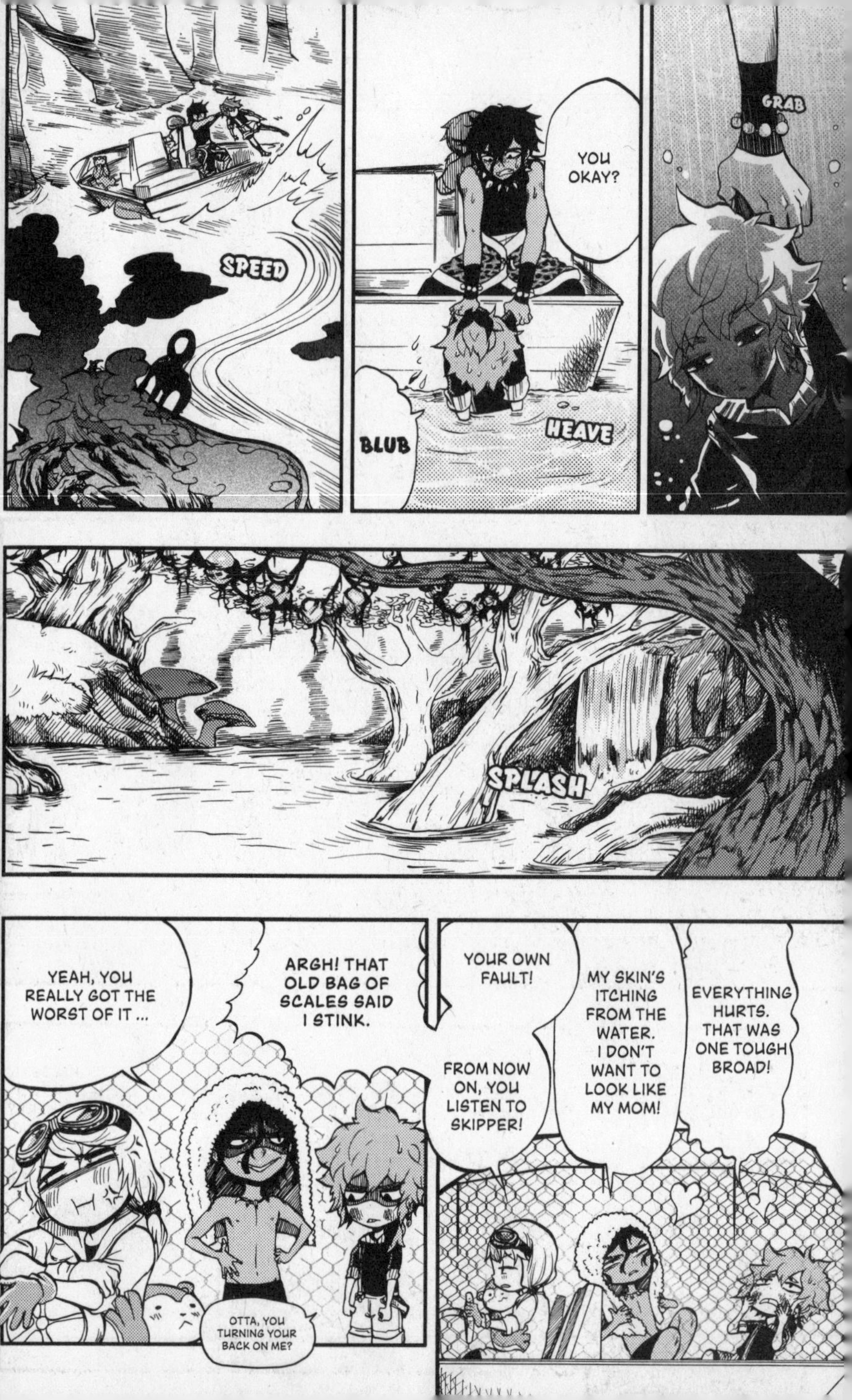
GRAB
YOU OKAY?
HEAVE
BLUB
SPEED
SPLASH
EVERYTHING HURTS. THAT WAS ONE TOUGH BROAD!
MY SKIN'S ITCHING FROM THE WATER. I DON'T WANT TO LOOK LIKE MY MOM!
YOUR OWN FAULT!
FROM NOW ON, YOU LISTEN TO SKIPPER!
ARGH! THAT OLD BAG OF SCALES SAID I STINK.
YEAH, YOU REALLY GOT THE WORST OF IT ...
OTTA, YOU TURNING YOUR BACK ON ME?

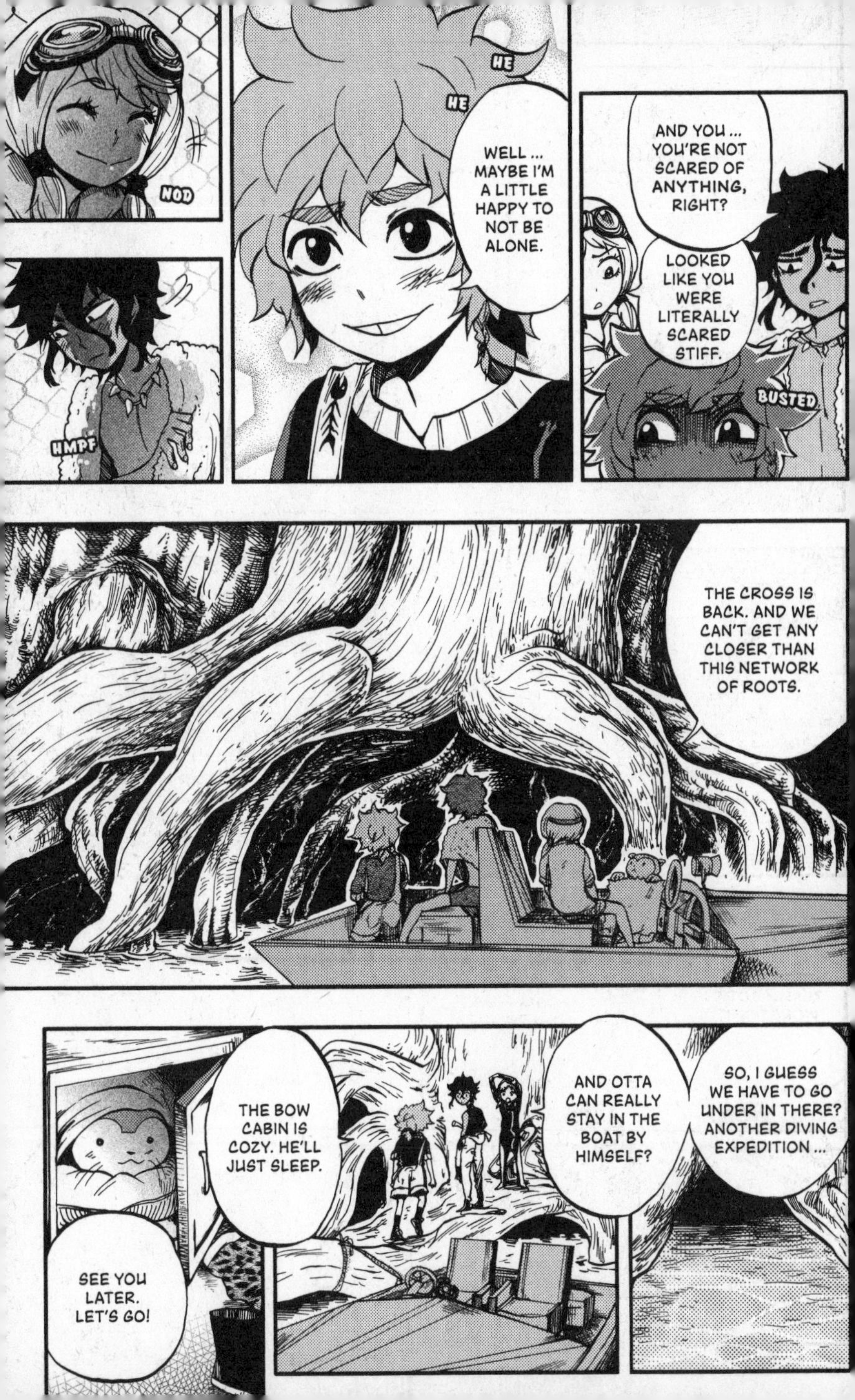
AND YOU ... YOU'RE NOT SCARED OF ANYTHING, RIGHT?
LOOKED LIKE YOU WERE LITERALLY SCARED STIFF.
BUSTED
HE
HE
WELL ... MAYBE I'M A LITTLE HAPPY TO NOT BE ALONE.
NOD
HMPF
THE CROSS IS BACK. AND WE CAN'T GET ANY CLOSER THAN THIS NETWORK OF ROOTS.
SO, I GUESS WE HAVE TO GO UNDER IN THERE? ANOTHER DIVING EXPEDITION ...
AND OTTA CAN REALLY STAY IN THE BOAT BY HIMSELF?
THE BOW CABIN IS COZY. HE'LL JUST SLEEP.
SEE YOU LATER. LET'S GO!

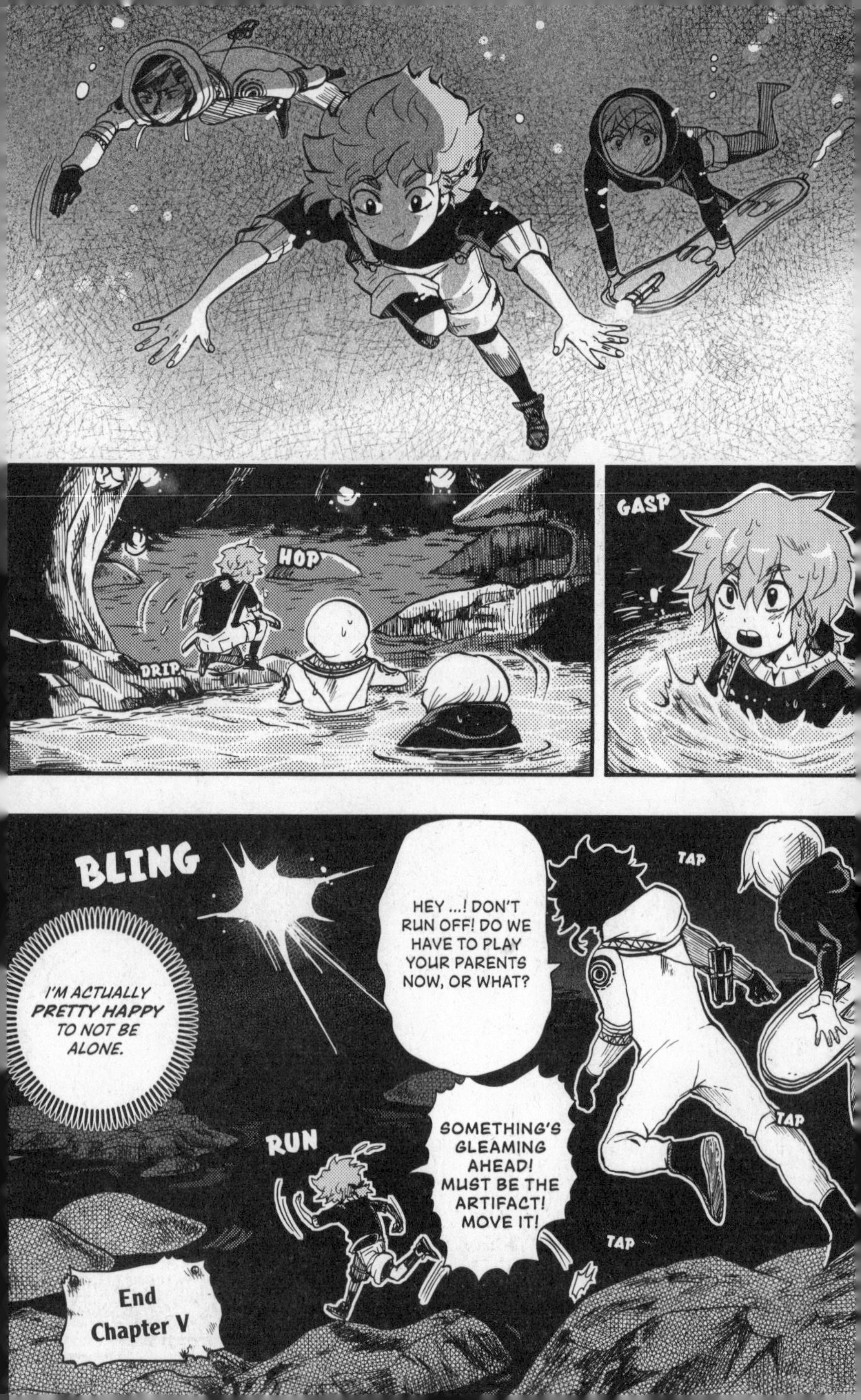
GASP
HOP
DRIP
BLING
SOMETHING'S GLEAMING AHEAD! MUST BE THE ARTIFACT! MOVE IT!
RUN
HEY ...! DON'T RUN OFF! DO WE HAVE TO PLAY YOUR PARENTS NOW, OR WHAT?
TAP
TAP
TAP
I'M ACTUALLY PRETTY HAPPY TO NOT BE ALONE.
End Chapter V

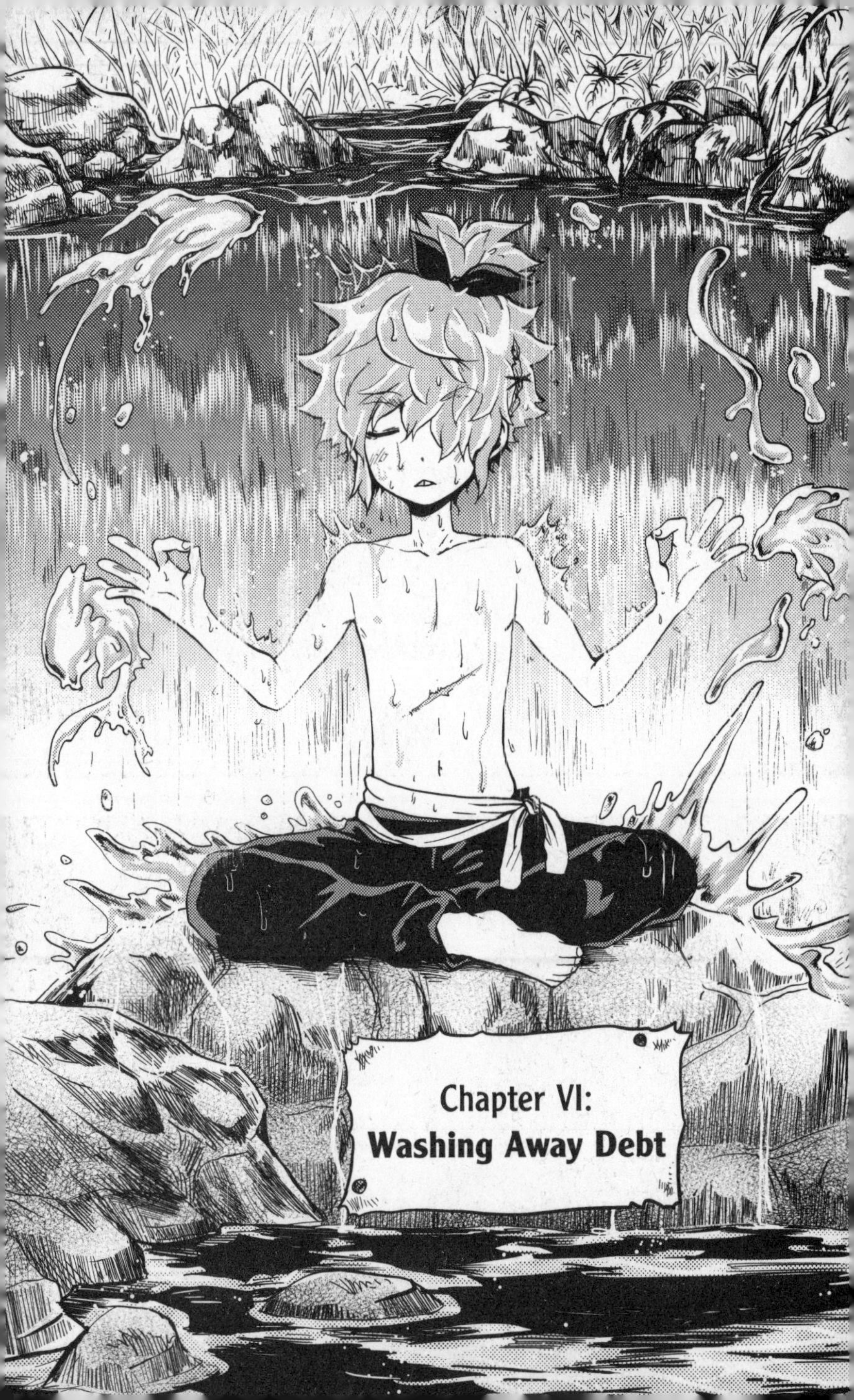
Chapter VI:
Washing Away Debt

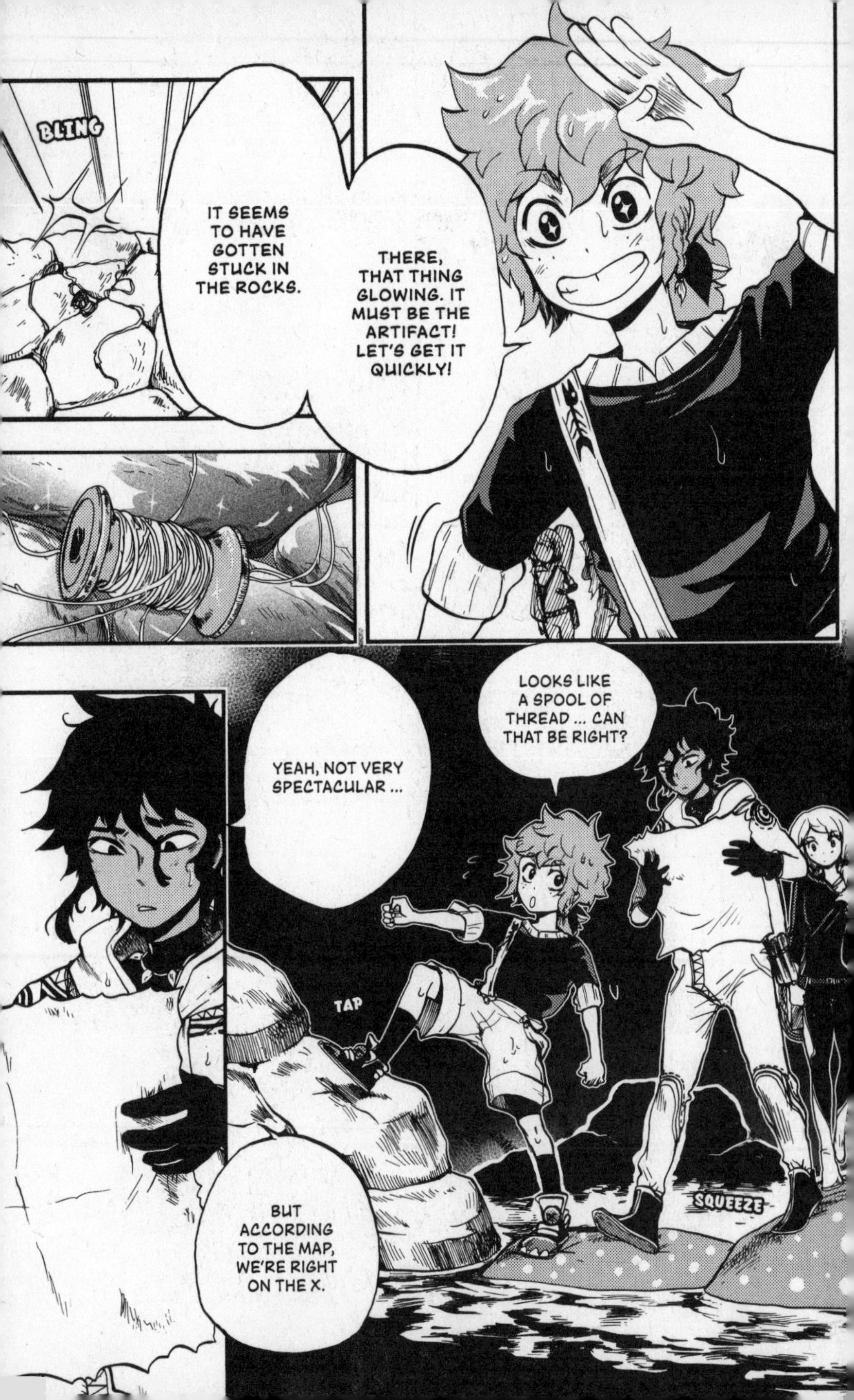
THERE, THAT THING GLOWING. IT MUST BE THE ARTIFACT! LET'S GET IT QUICKLY!
BLING
IT SEEMS TO HAVE GOTTEN STUCK IN THE ROCKS.
LOOKS LIKE A SPOOL OF THREAD ... CAN THAT BE RIGHT?
YEAH, NOT VERY SPECTACULAR ...
TAP
SQUEEZE
BUT ACCORDING TO THE MAP, WE'RE RIGHT ON THE X.

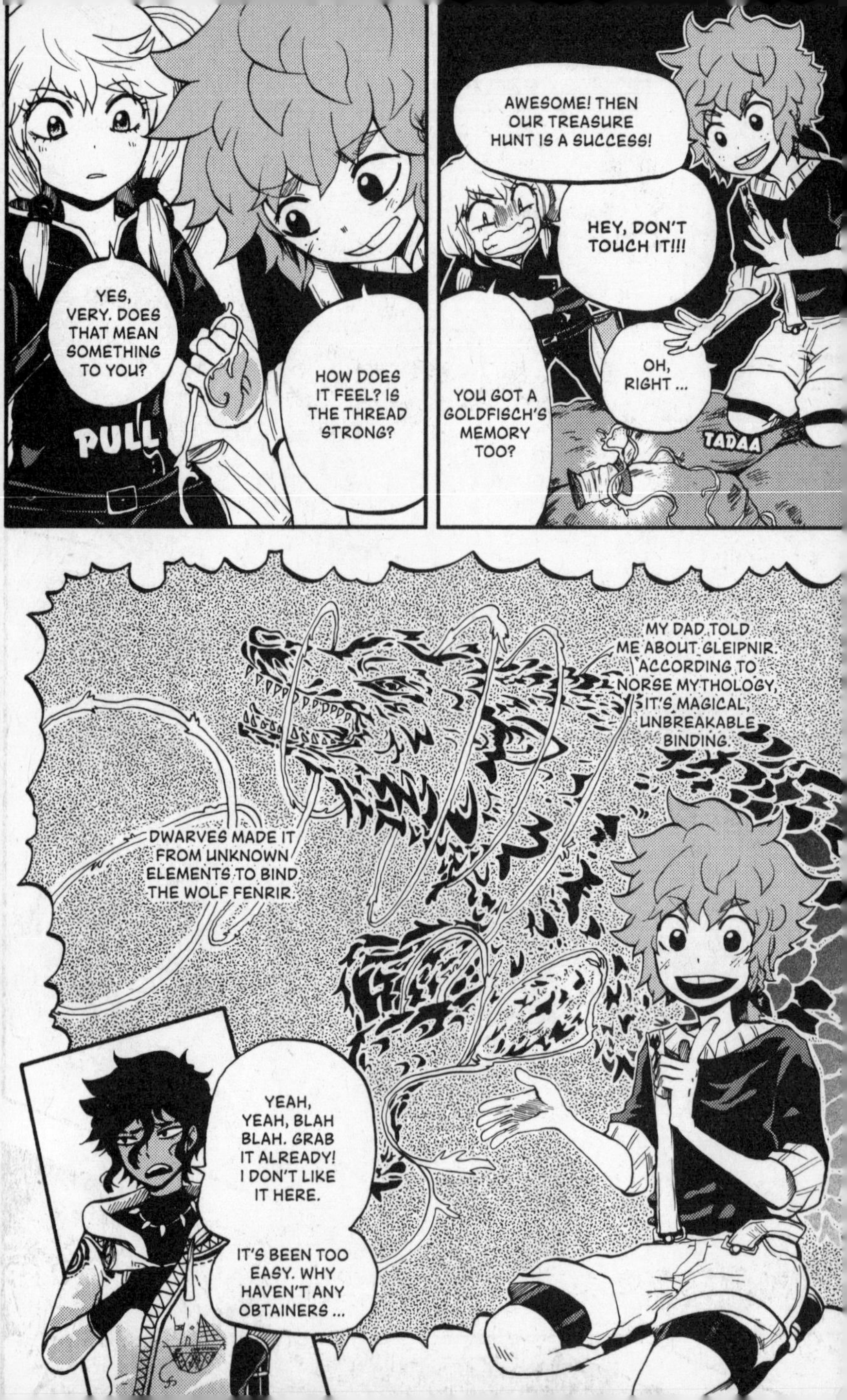
AWESOME! THEN OUR TREASURE HUNT IS A SUCCESS!
HEY, DON'T TOUCH IT!!!
OH, RIGHT ...
TADAA
YOU GOT A GOLDFISCH'S MEMORY TOO?
HOW DOES IT FEEL? IS THE THREAD STRONG?
YES, VERY. DOES THAT MEAN SOMETHING TO YOU?
PULL
MY DAD TOLD ME ABOUT GLEIPNIR. ACCORDING TO NORSE MYTHOLOGY, IT'S MAGICAL, UNBREAKABLE BINDING.
DWARVES MADE IT FROM UNKNOWN ELEMENTS TO BIND THE WOLF FENRIR.
YEAH, YEAH, BLAH BLAH. GRAB IT ALREADY! I DON'T LIKE IT HERE.
IT'S BEEN TOO EASY. WHY HAVEN'T ANY OBTAINERS ...

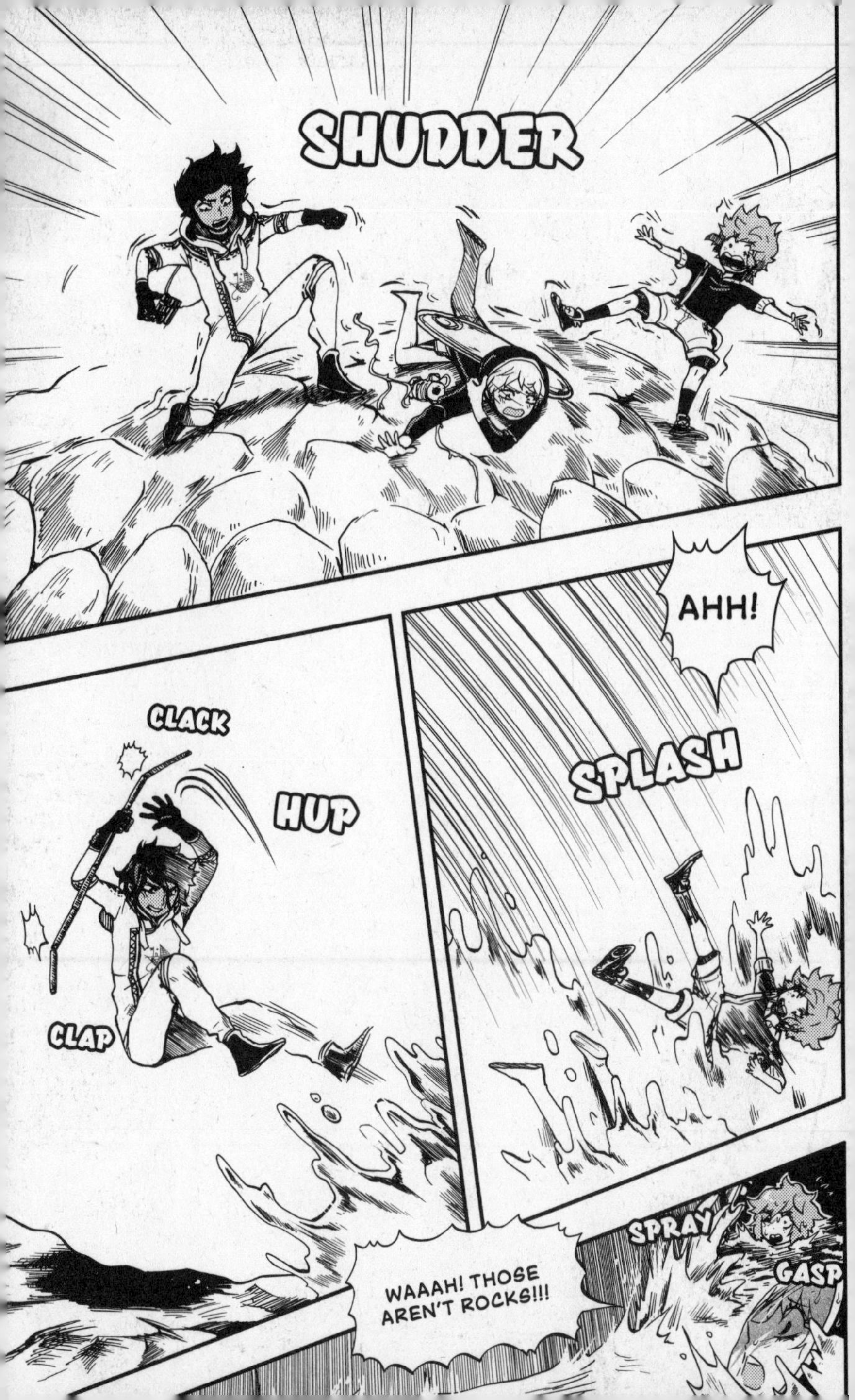
SHUDDER
AHH!
SPLASH
CLACK
HUP
CLAP
SPRAY
GASP
WAAAH! THOSE AREN'T ROCKS!!!

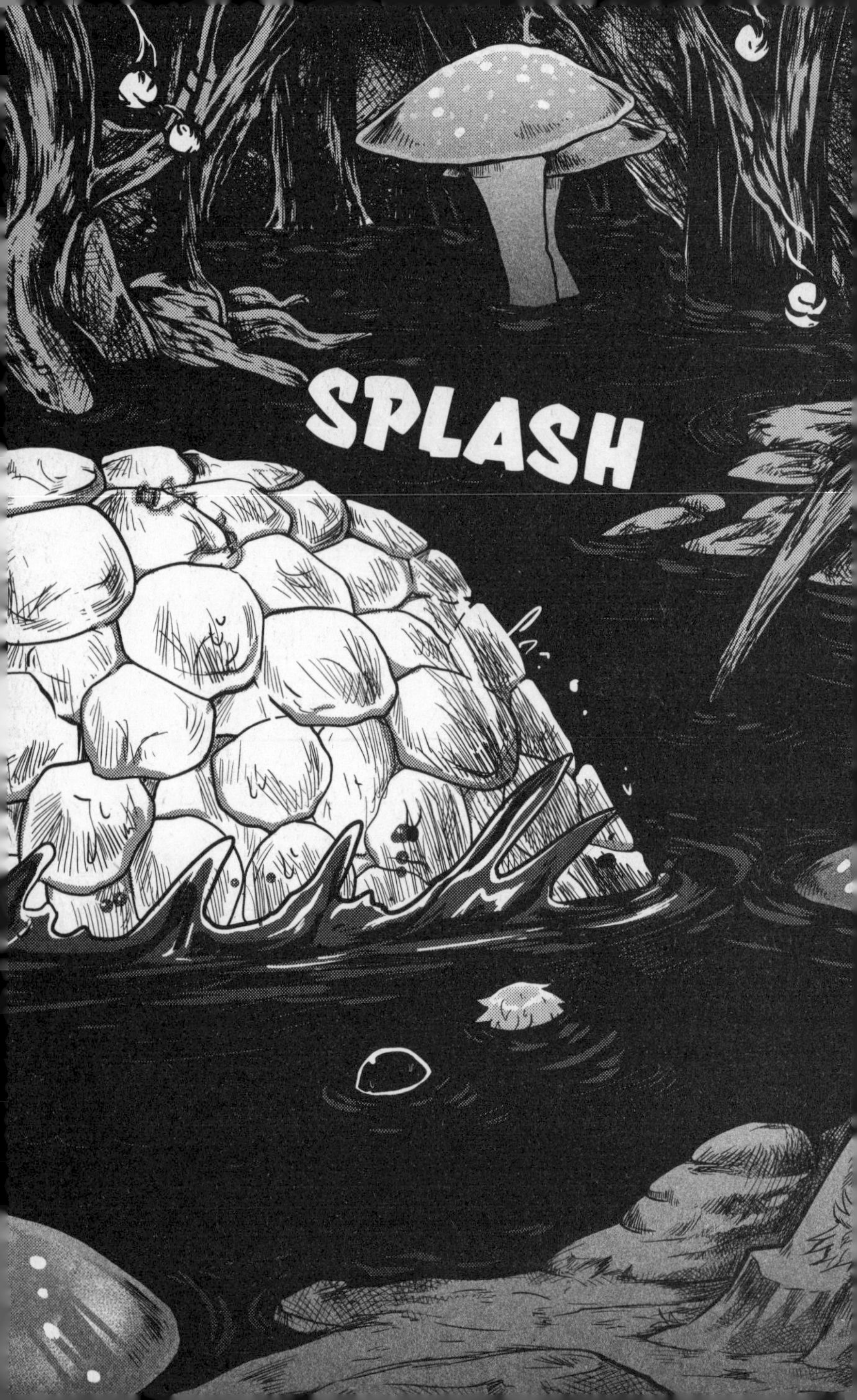
SPLASH

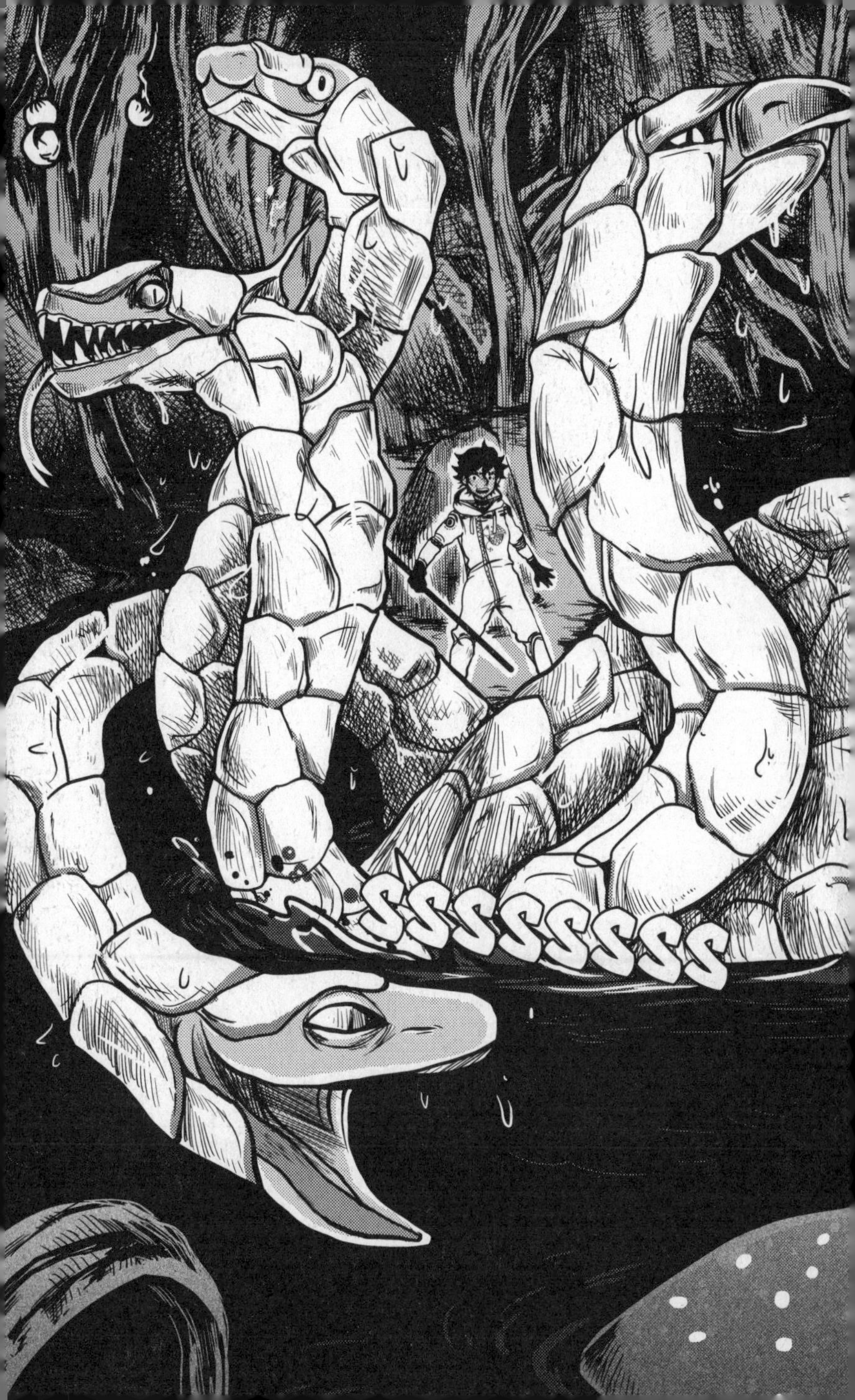
SSSSSSSSS

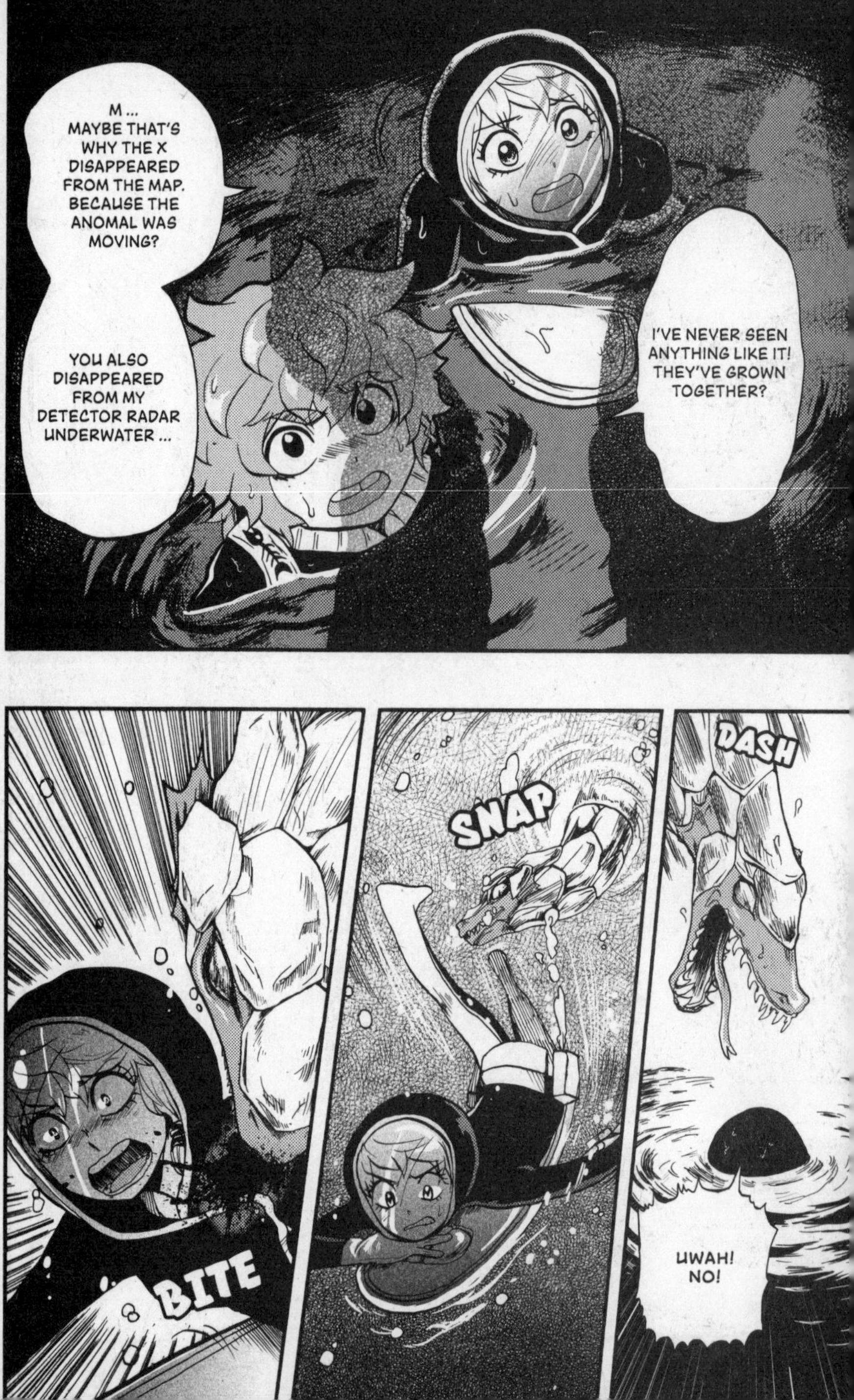
I'VE NEVER SEEN ANYTHING LIKE IT! THEY'VE GROWN TOGETHER?
M ... MAYBE THAT'S WHY THE X DISAPPEARED FROM THE MAP. BECAUSE THE ANOMAL WAS MOVING?
YOU ALSO DISAPPEARED FROM MY DETECTOR RADAR UNDERWATER ...
DASH
UWAH! NO!
SNAP
BITE

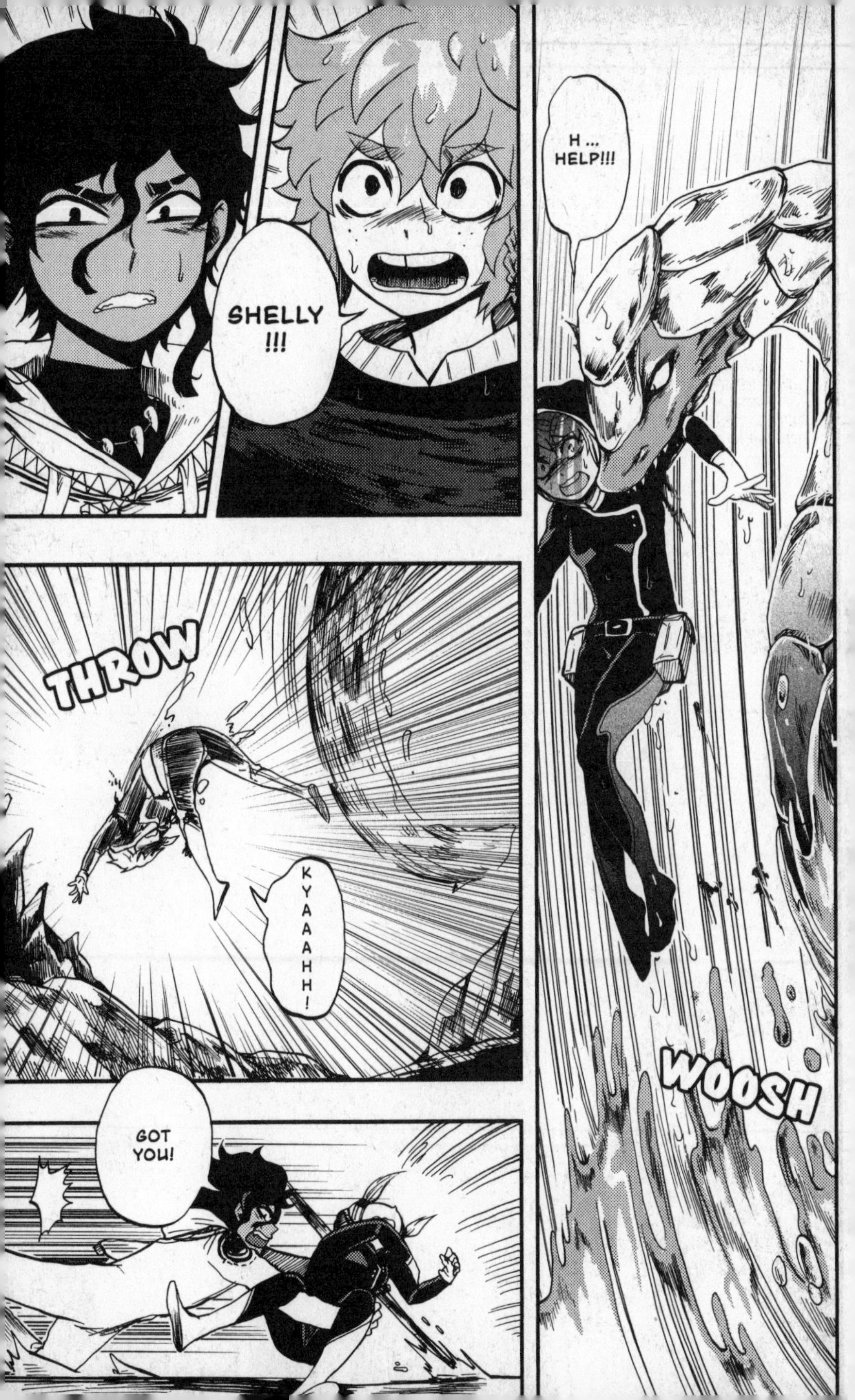
H ... HELP!!!
WOOSH
SHELLY !!!
THROW
KYAAAAHH!
GOT YOU!

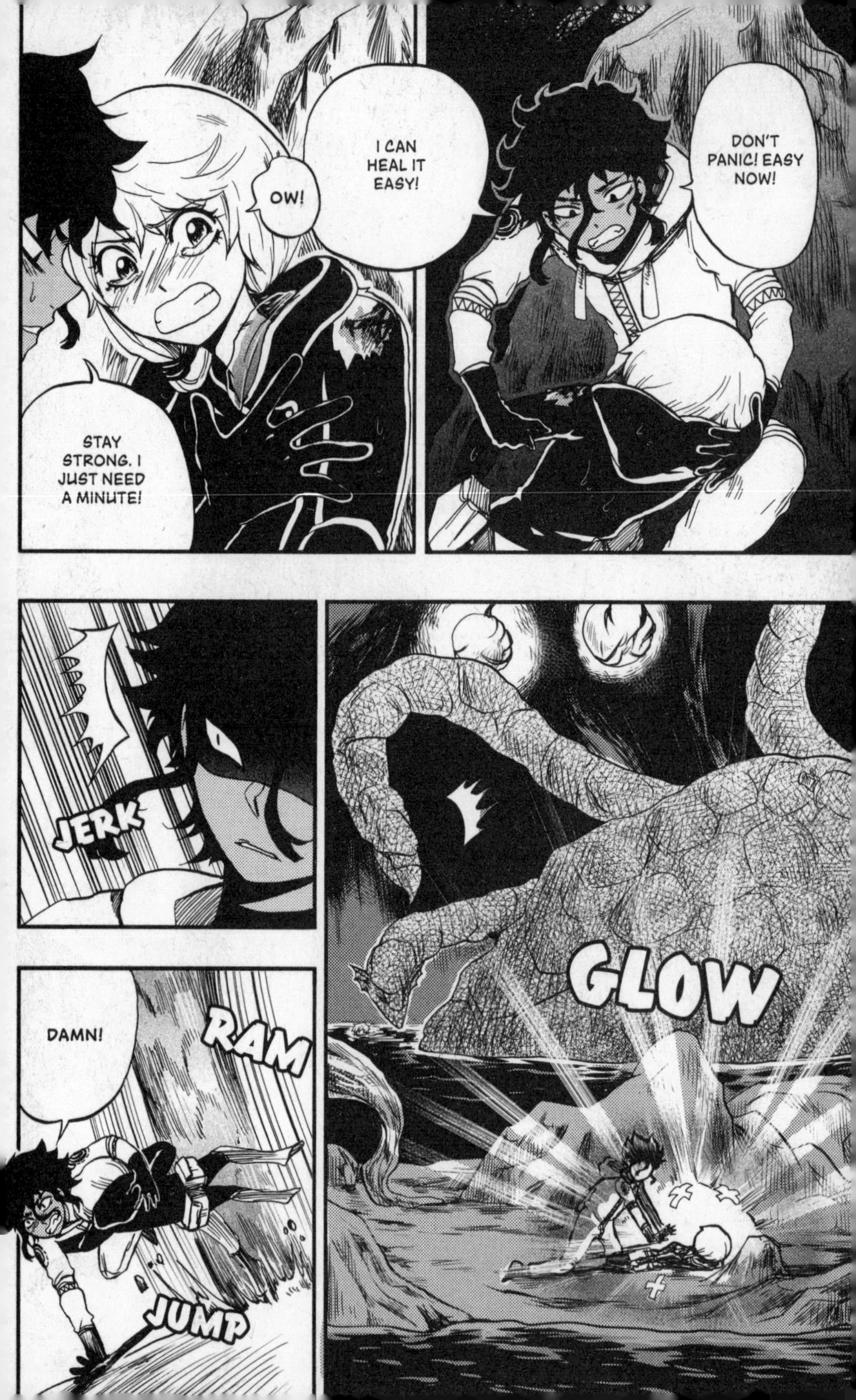
DON'T PANIC! EASY NOW!
I CAN HEAL IT EASY!
OW!
STAY STRONG. I JUST NEED A MINUTE!
GLOW
JERK
DAMN!
RAM
JUMP

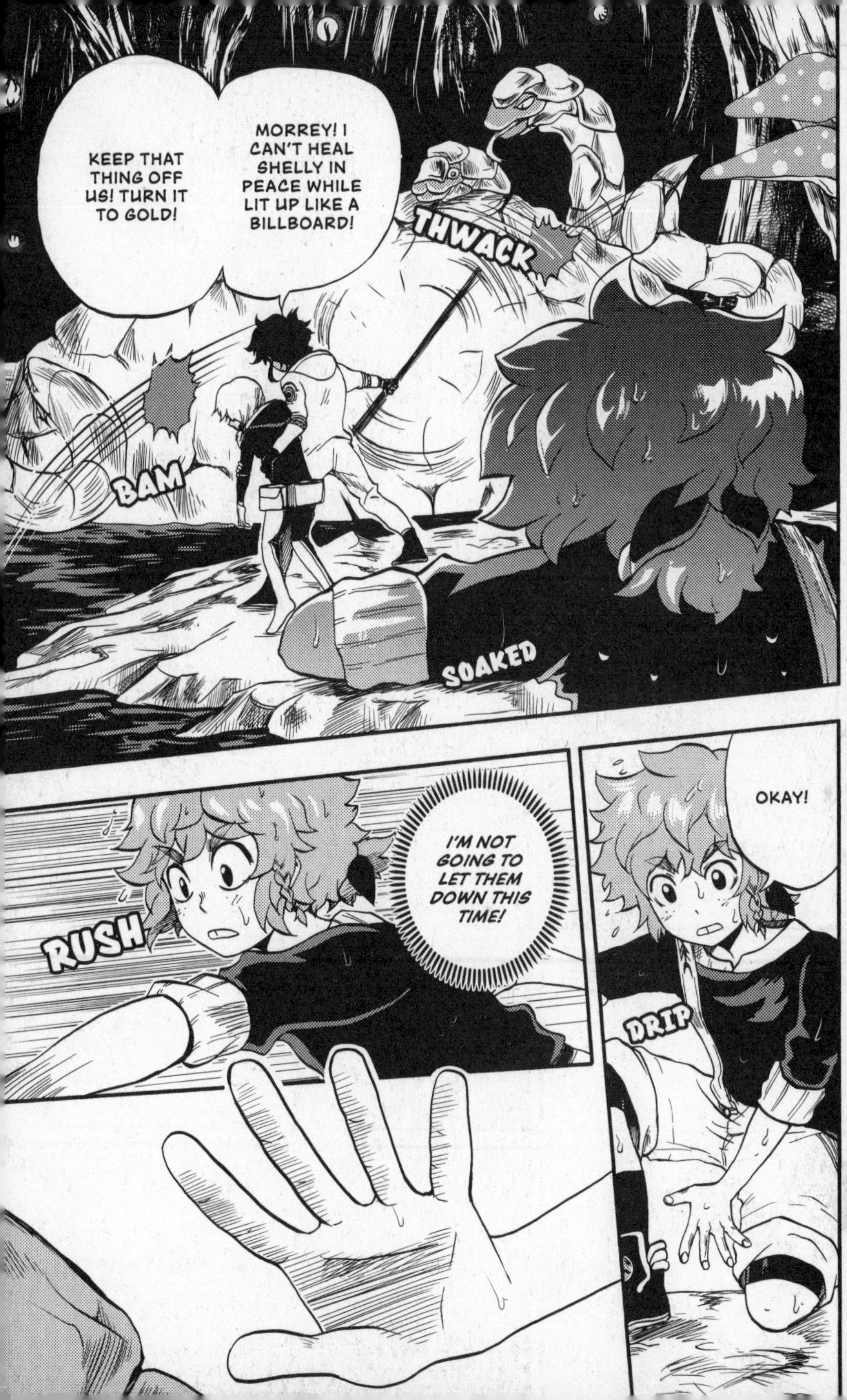
MORREY! I CAN'T HEAL SHELLY IN PEACE WHILE LIT UP LIKE A BILLBOARD!
KEEP THAT THING OFF US! TURN IT TO GOLD!
THWACK
BAM
SOAKED
OKAY!
DRIP
I'M NOT GOING TO LET THEM DOWN THIS TIME!
RUSH

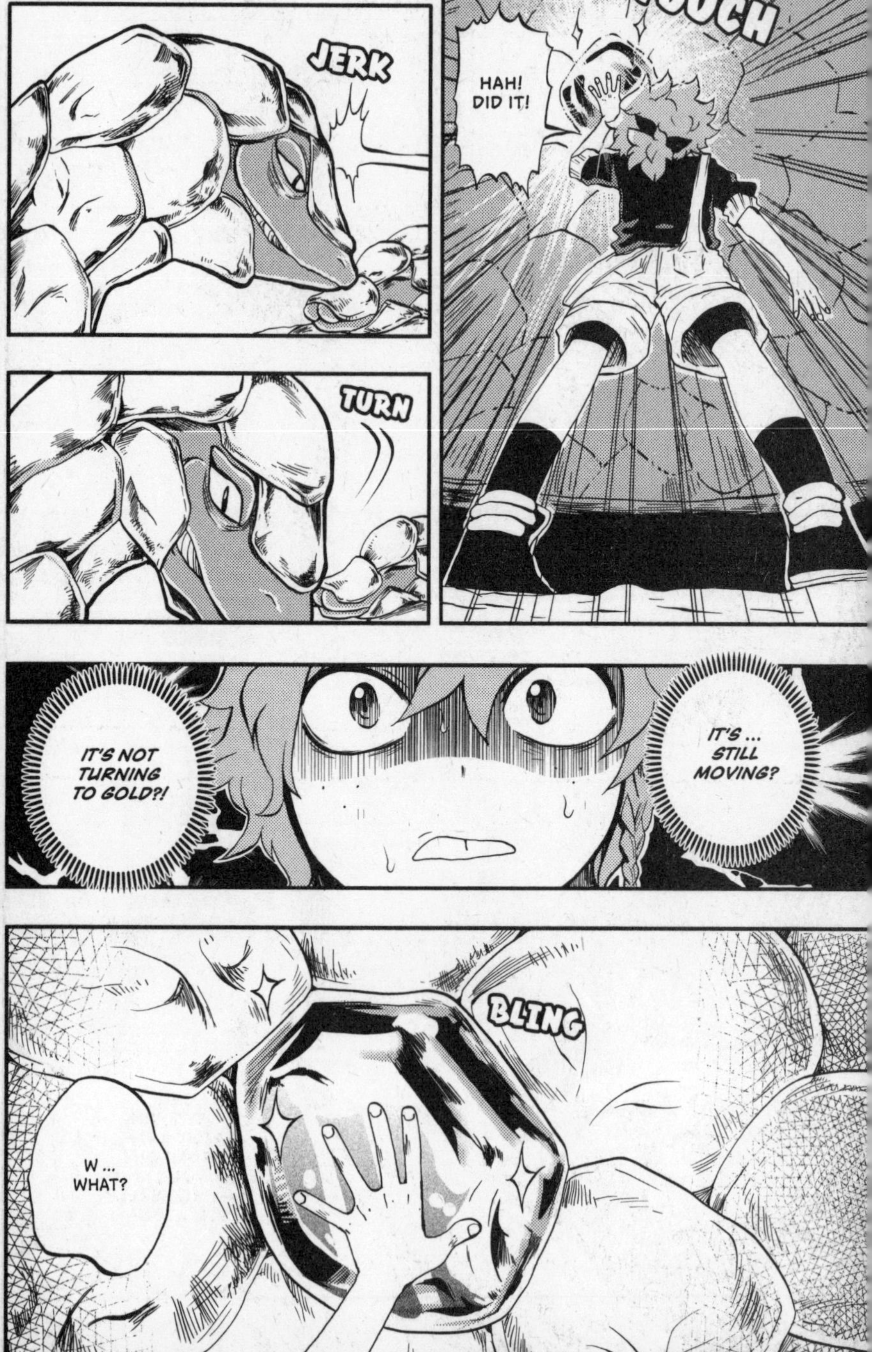
TOUCH
HAH! DID IT!
JERK
TURN
IT'S ... STILL MOVING?
IT'S NOT TURNING TO GOLD?!
BLING
W ... WHAT?

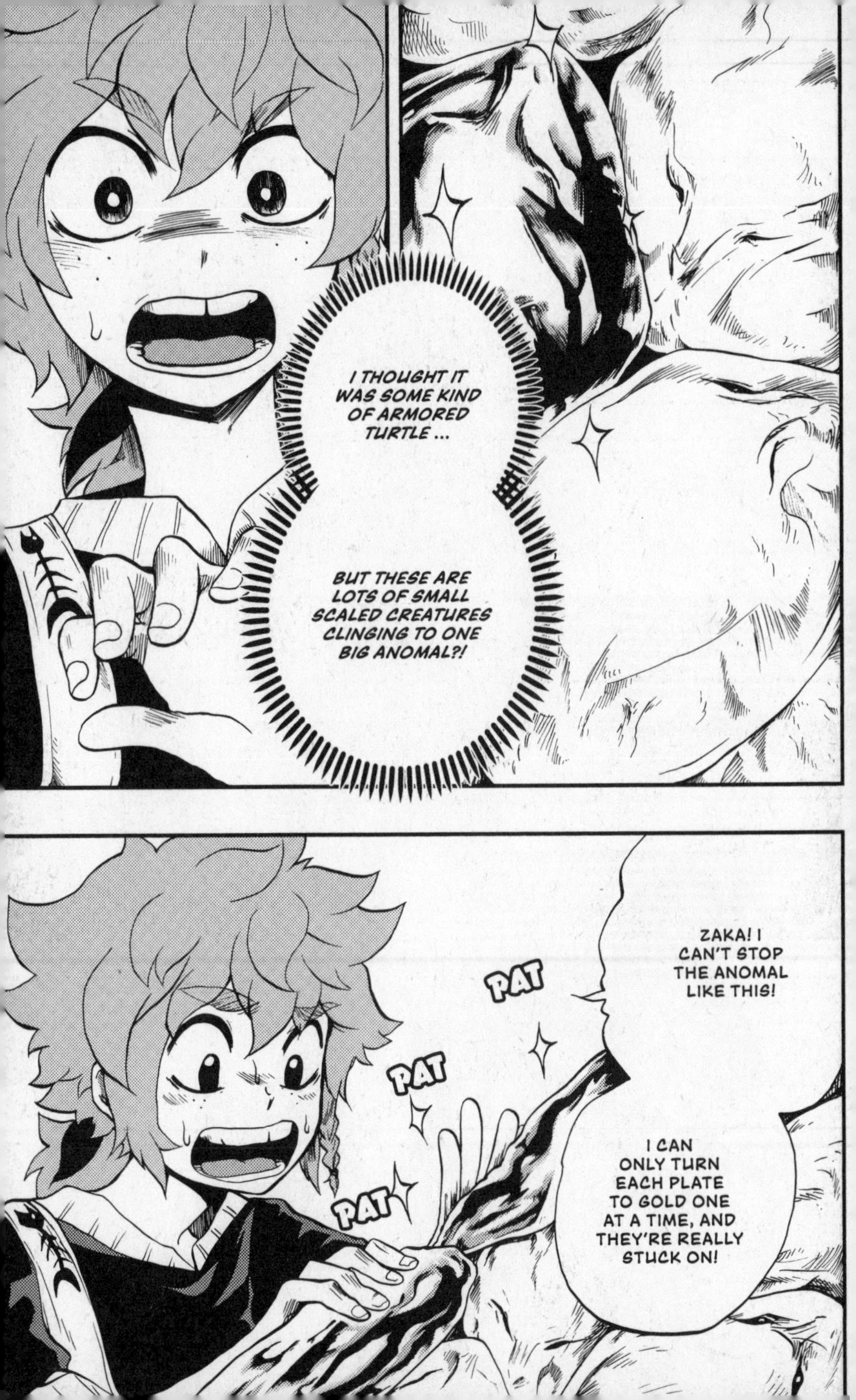
I THOUGHT IT WAS SOME KIND OF ARMORED TURTLE ...
BUT THESE ARE LOTS OF SMALL SCALED CREATURES CLINGING TO ONE BIG ANOMAL?!
ZAKA! I CAN'T STOP THE ANOMAL LIKE THIS!
PAT
PAT
PAT
I CAN ONLY TURN EACH PLATE TO GOLD ONE AT A TIME, AND THEY'RE REALLY STUCK ON!

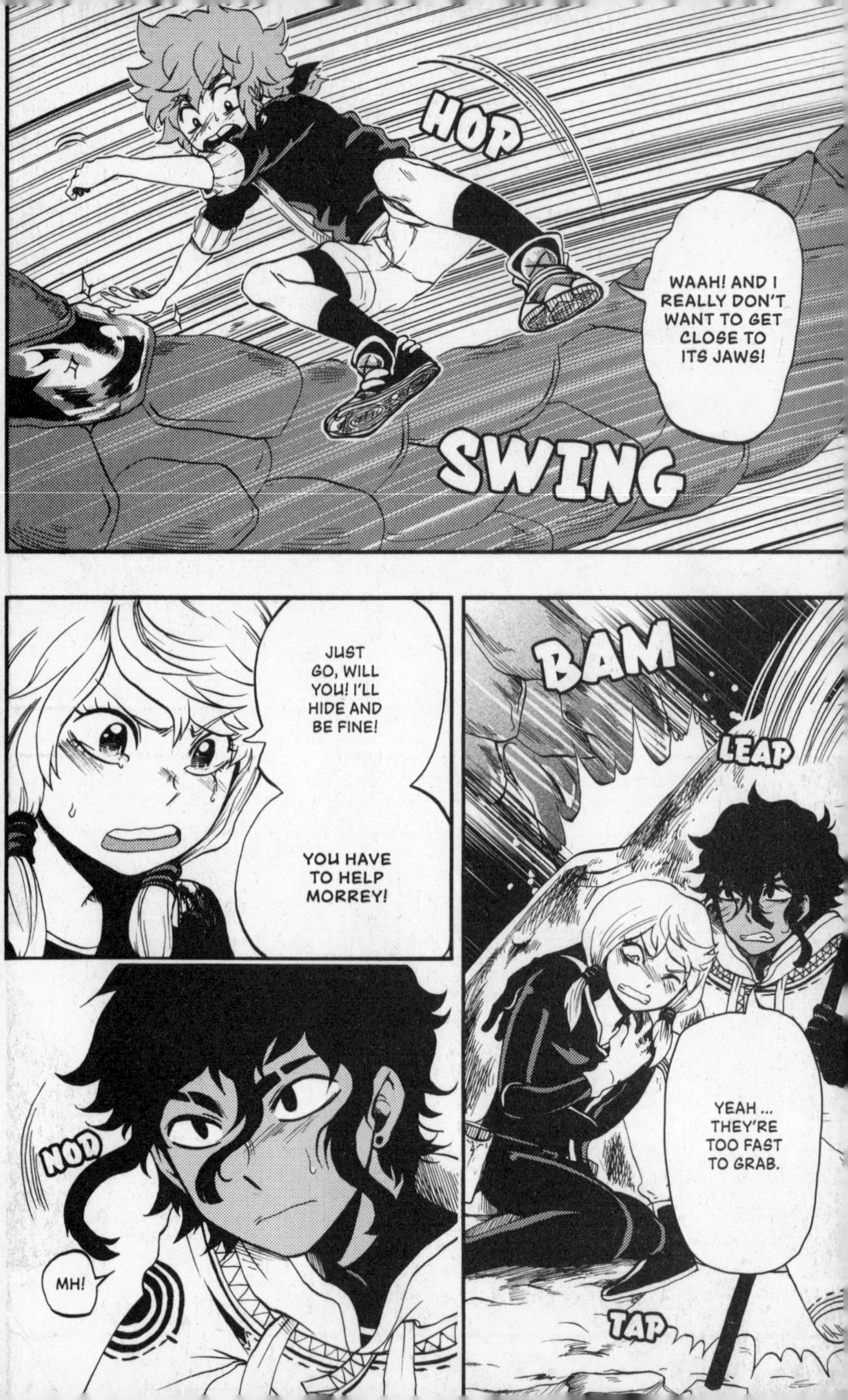
HOP
WAAH! AND I REALLY DON'T WANT TO GET CLOSE TO ITS JAWS!
SWING
BAM
LEAP
YEAH ... THEY'RE TOO FAST TO GRAB.
TAP
JUST GO, WILL YOU! I'LL HIDE AND BE FINE!
YOU HAVE TO HELP MORREY!
NOD
MH!

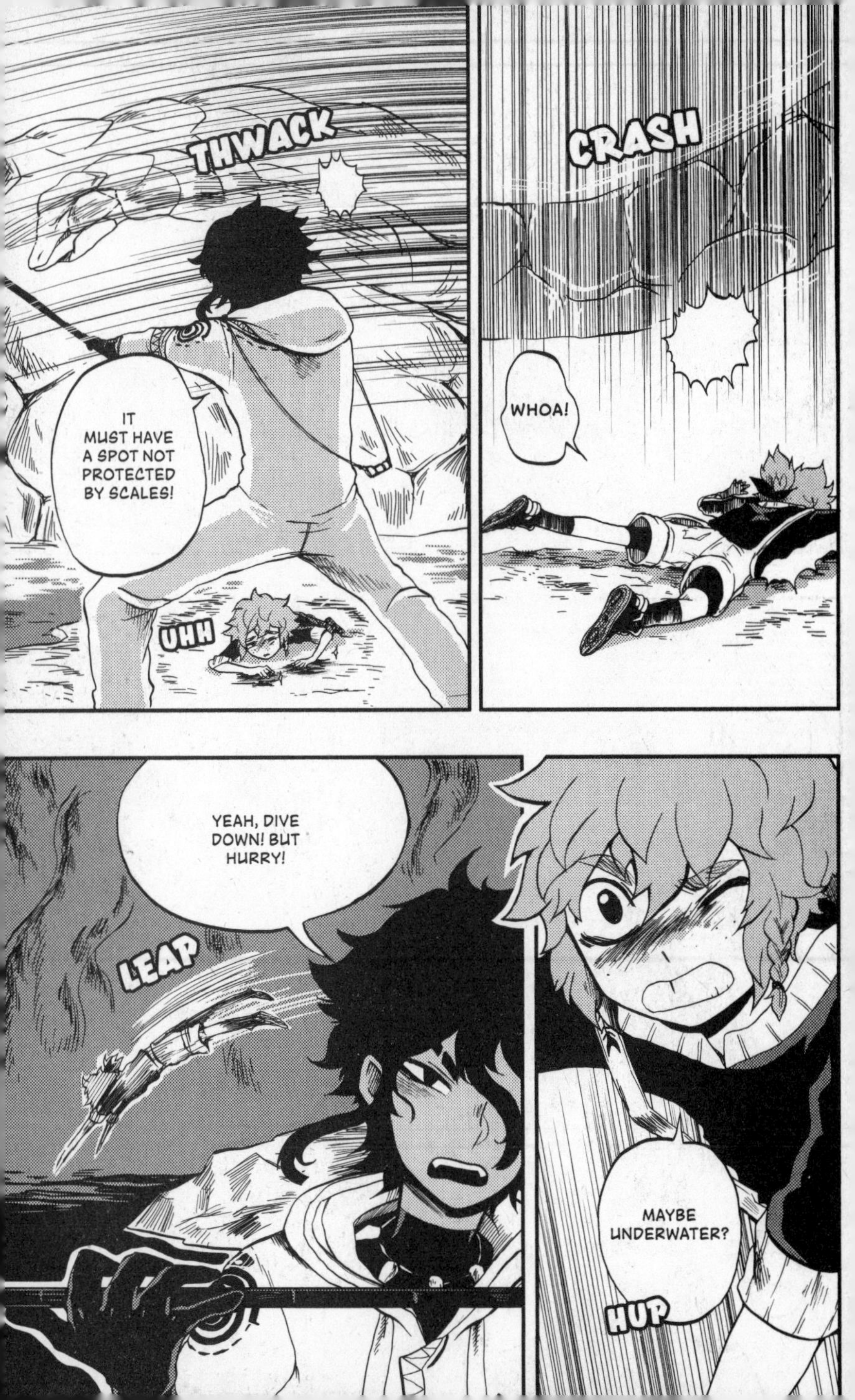
CRASH
WHOA!
THWACK
IT MUST HAVE A SPOT NOT PROTECTED BY SCALES!
UHH
MAYBE UNDERWATER?
HUP
YEAH, DIVE DOWN! BUT HURRY!
LEAP

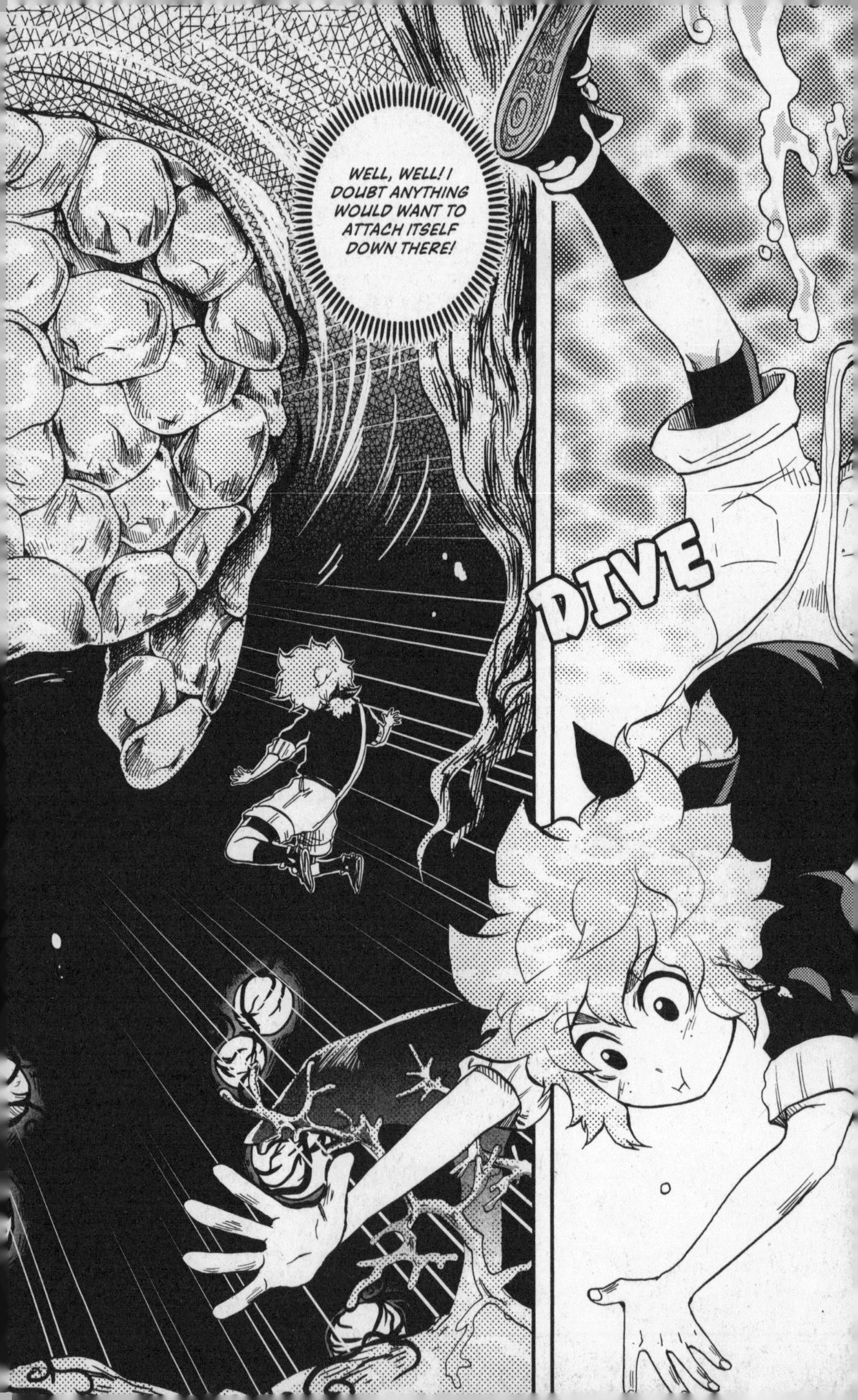
DIVE
WELL, WELL! I DOUBT ANYTHING WOULD WANT TO ATTACH ITSELF DOWN THERE!

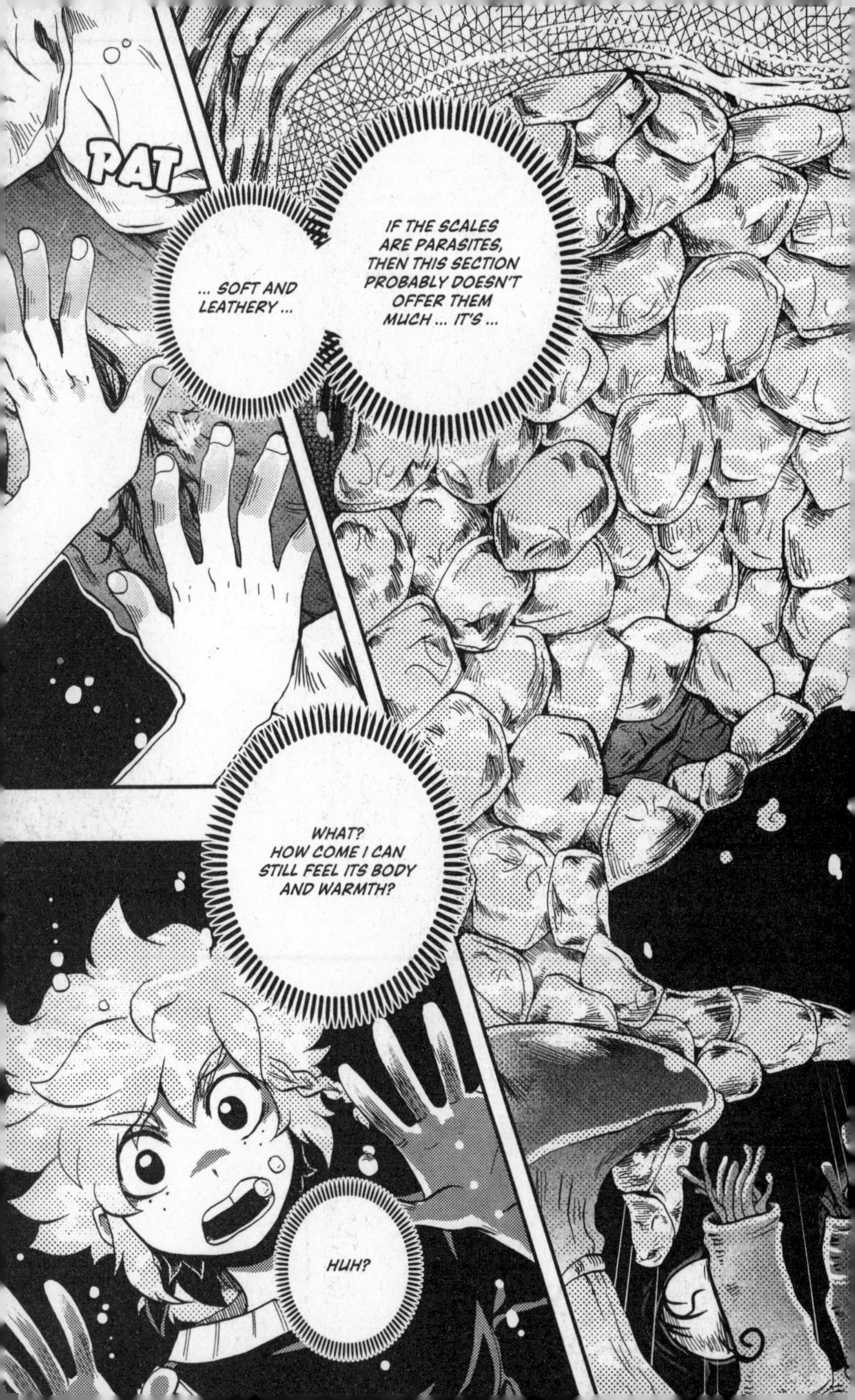
IF THE SCALES ARE PARASITES, THEN THIS SECTION PROBABLY DOESN'T OFFER THEM MUCH ... IT'S ...
PAT
... SOFT AND LEATHERY ...
WHAT? HOW COME I CAN STILL FEEL ITS BODY AND WARMTH?
HUH?

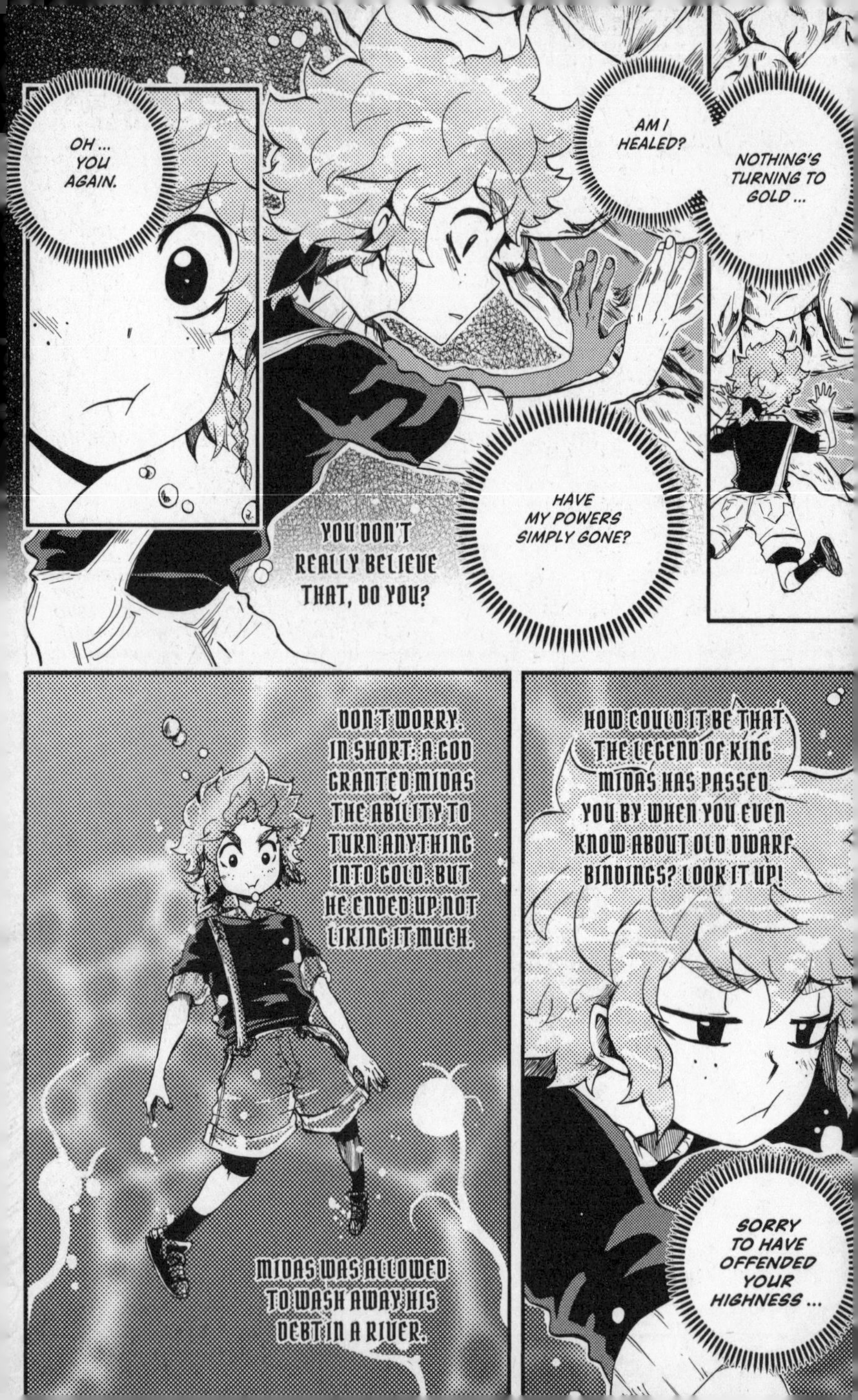
NOTHING'S TURNING TO GOLD ...
AM I HEALED?
HAVE MY POWERS SIMPLY GONE?
YOU DON'T REALLY BELIEVE THAT, DO YOU?
OH ... YOU AGAIN.
HOW COULD IT BE THAT THE LEGEND OF KING MIDAS HAS PASSED YOU BY WHEN YOU EVEN KNOW ABOUT OLD DWARF BINDINGS? LOOK IT UP!
SORRY TO HAVE OFFENDED YOUR HIGHNESS ...
DON'T WORRY. IN SHORT: A GOD GRANTED MIDAS THE ABILITY TO TURN ANYTHING INTO GOLD. BUT HE ENDED UP NOT LIKING IT MUCH.
MIDAS WAS ALLOWED TO WASH AWAY HIS DEBT IN A RIVER.

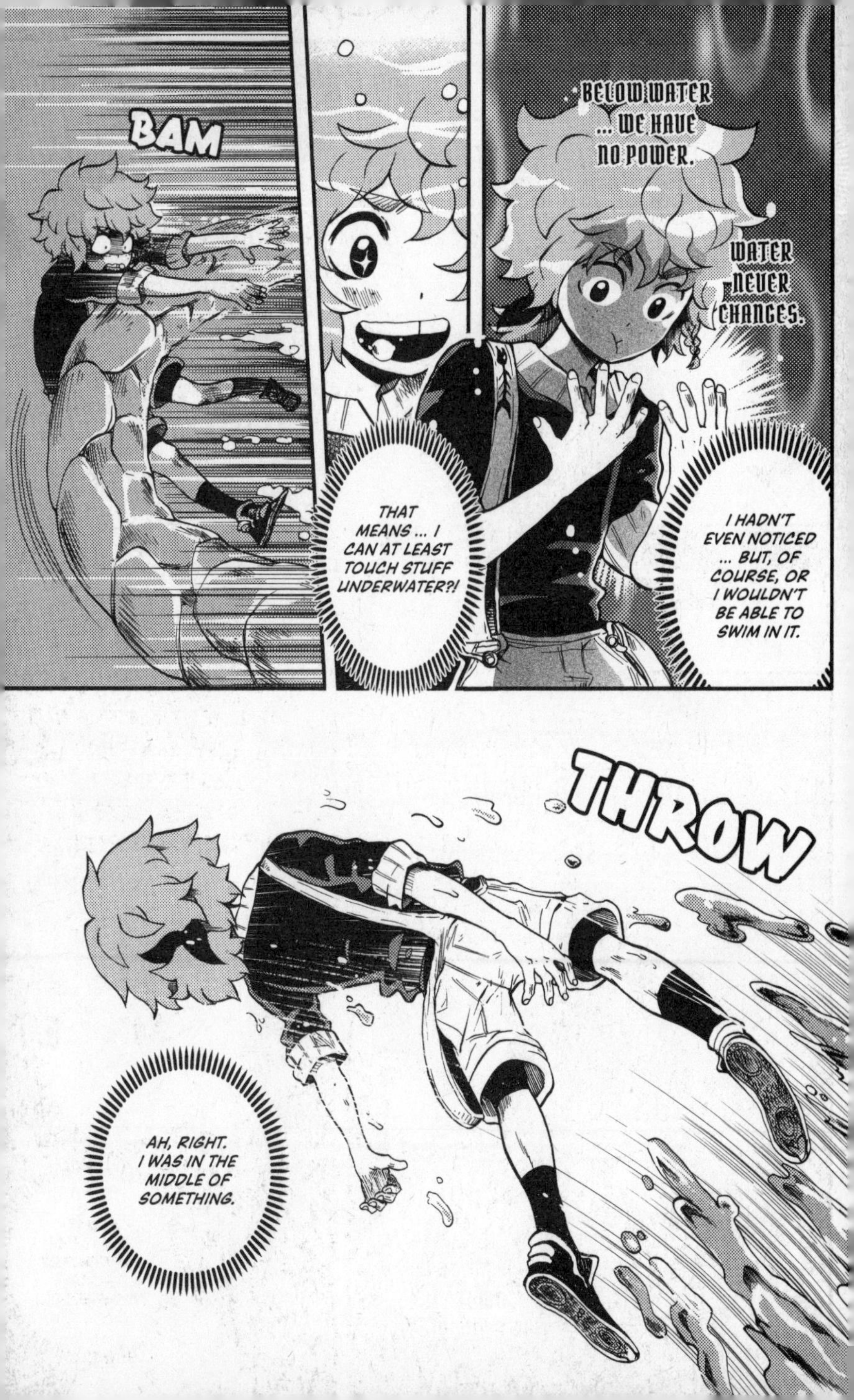
BELOW WATER ... WE HAVE NO POWER.
WATER NEVER CHANGES.
I HADN'T EVEN NOTICED ... BUT, OF COURSE, OR I WOULDN'T BE ABLE TO SWIM IN IT.
THAT MEANS ... I CAN AT LEAST TOUCH STUFF UNDERWATER?!
BAM
THROW
AH, RIGHT. I WAS IN THE MIDDLE OF SOMETHING.

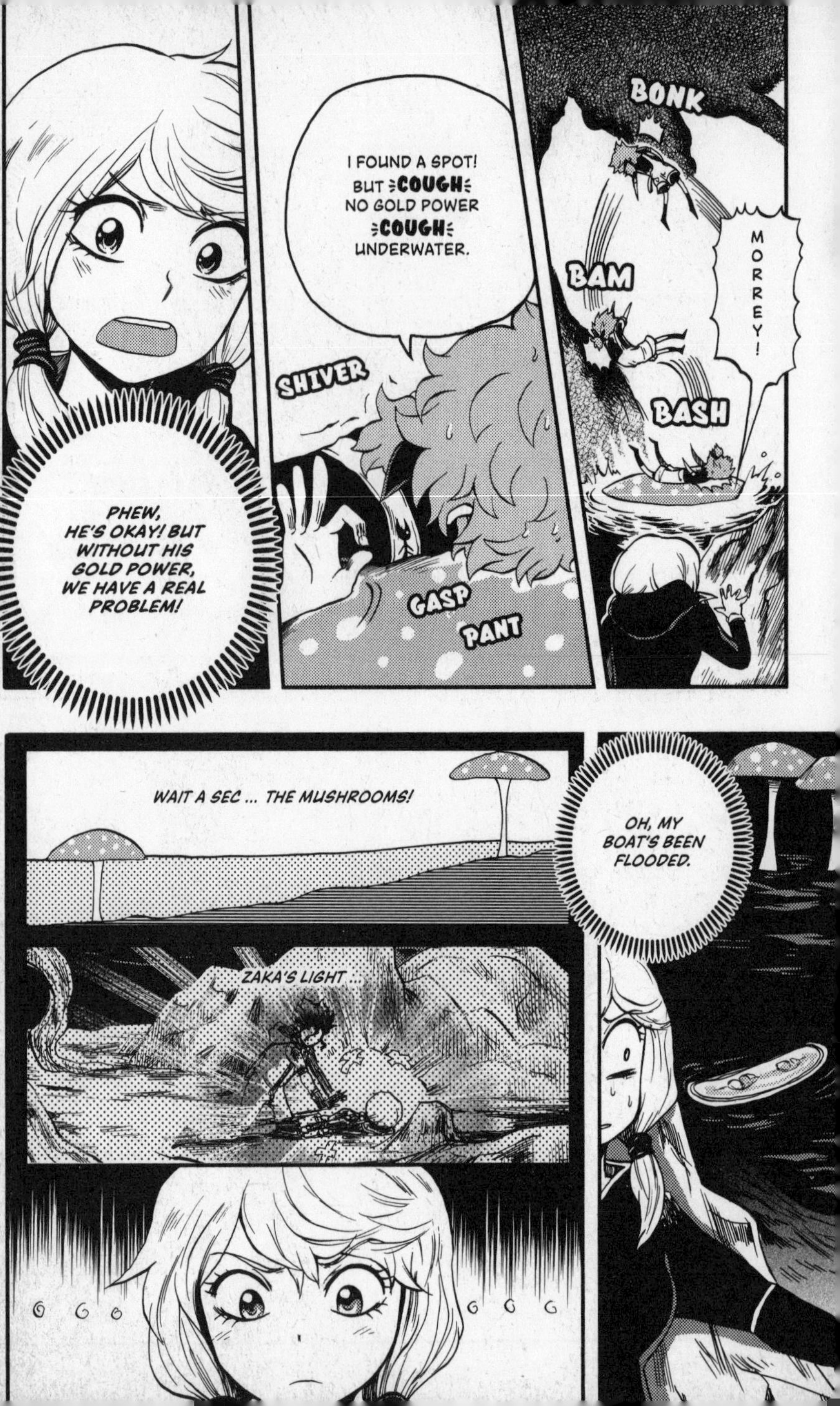
BONK
MORREY!
BAM
BASH
I FOUND A SPOT! BUT COUGH NO GOLD POWER COUGH UNDERWATER.
SHIVER
GASP
PANT
PHEW, HE'S OKAY! BUT WITHOUT HIS GOLD POWER, WE HAVE A REAL PROBLEM!
OH, MY BOAT'S BEEN FLOODED.
WAIT A SEC ... THE MUSHROOMS!
ZAKA'S LIGHT ...

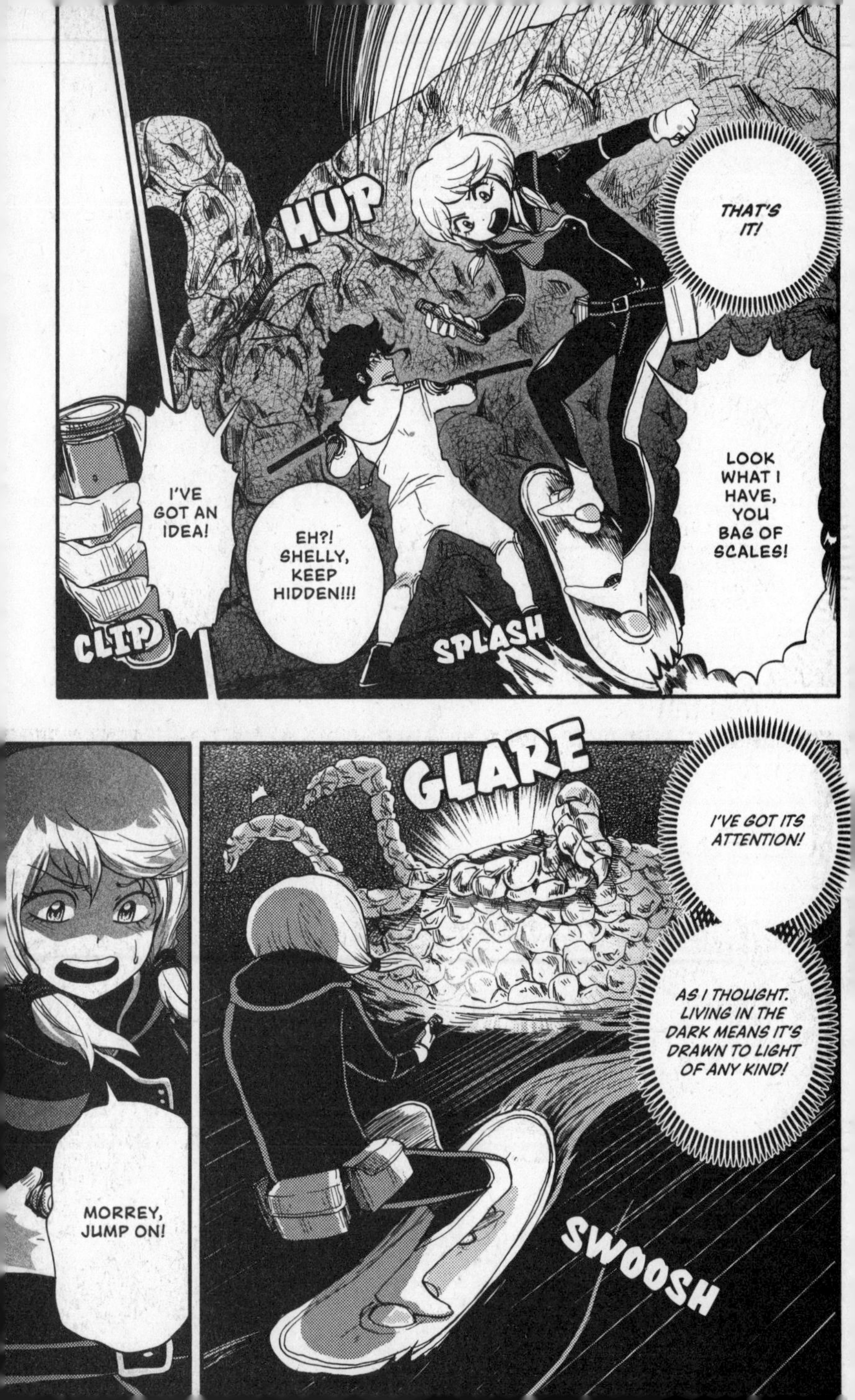
THAT'S IT!
LOOK WHAT I HAVE, YOU BAG OF SCALES!
HUP
SPLASH
EH?! SHELLY, KEEP HIDDEN!!!
I'VE GOT AN IDEA!
CLIP
GLARE
I'VE GOT ITS ATTENTION!
AS I THOUGHT. LIVING IN THE DARK MEANS IT'S DRAWN TO LIGHT OF ANY KIND!
SWOOSH
MORREY, JUMP ON!

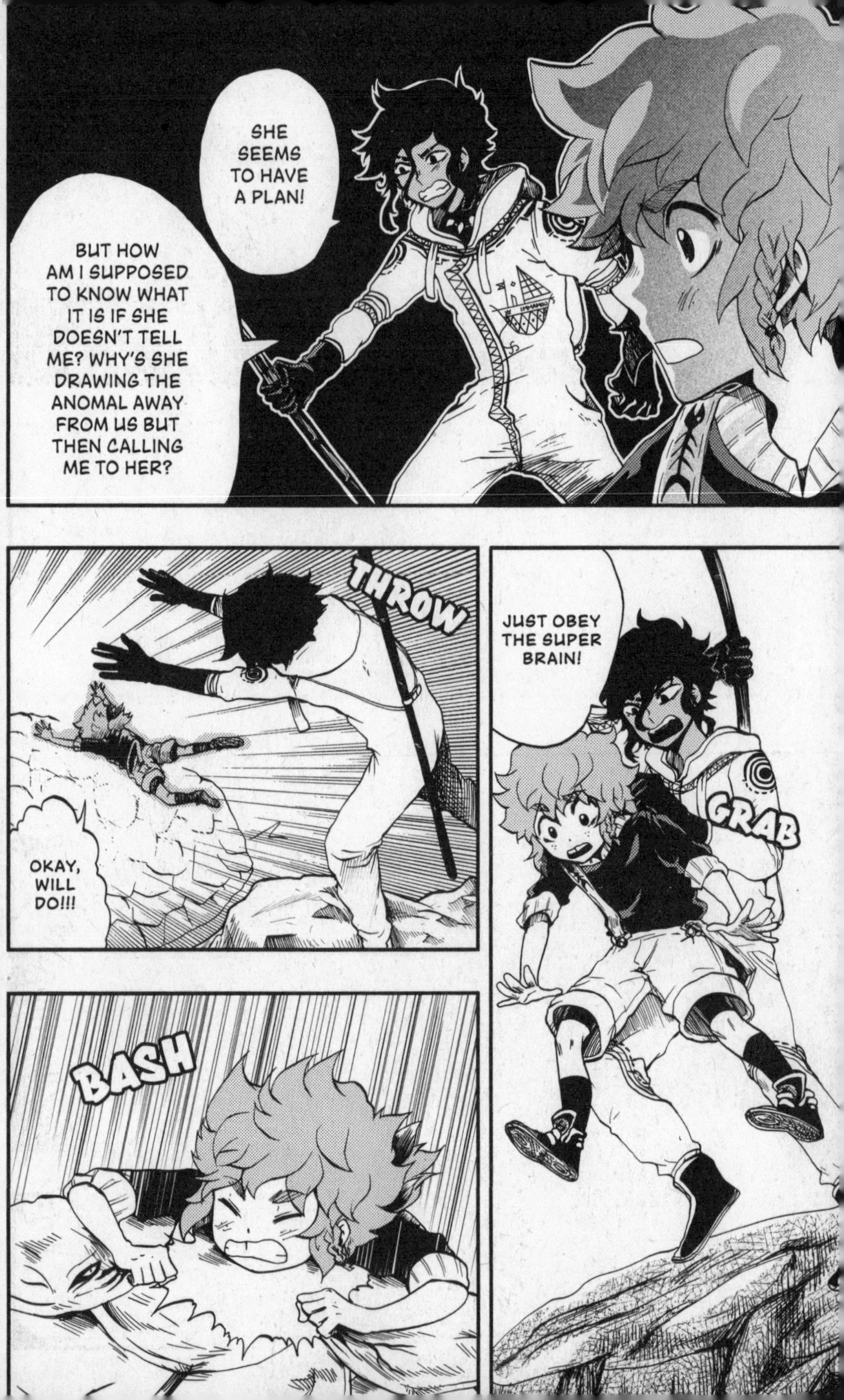
SHE SEEMS TO HAVE A PLAN!
BUT HOW AM I SUPPOSED TO KNOW WHAT IT IS IF SHE DOESN'T TELL ME? WHY'S SHE DRAWING THE ANOMAL AWAY FROM US BUT THEN CALLING ME TO HER?
JUST OBEY THE SUPER BRAIN!
GRAB
THROW
OKAY, WILL DO!!!
BASH

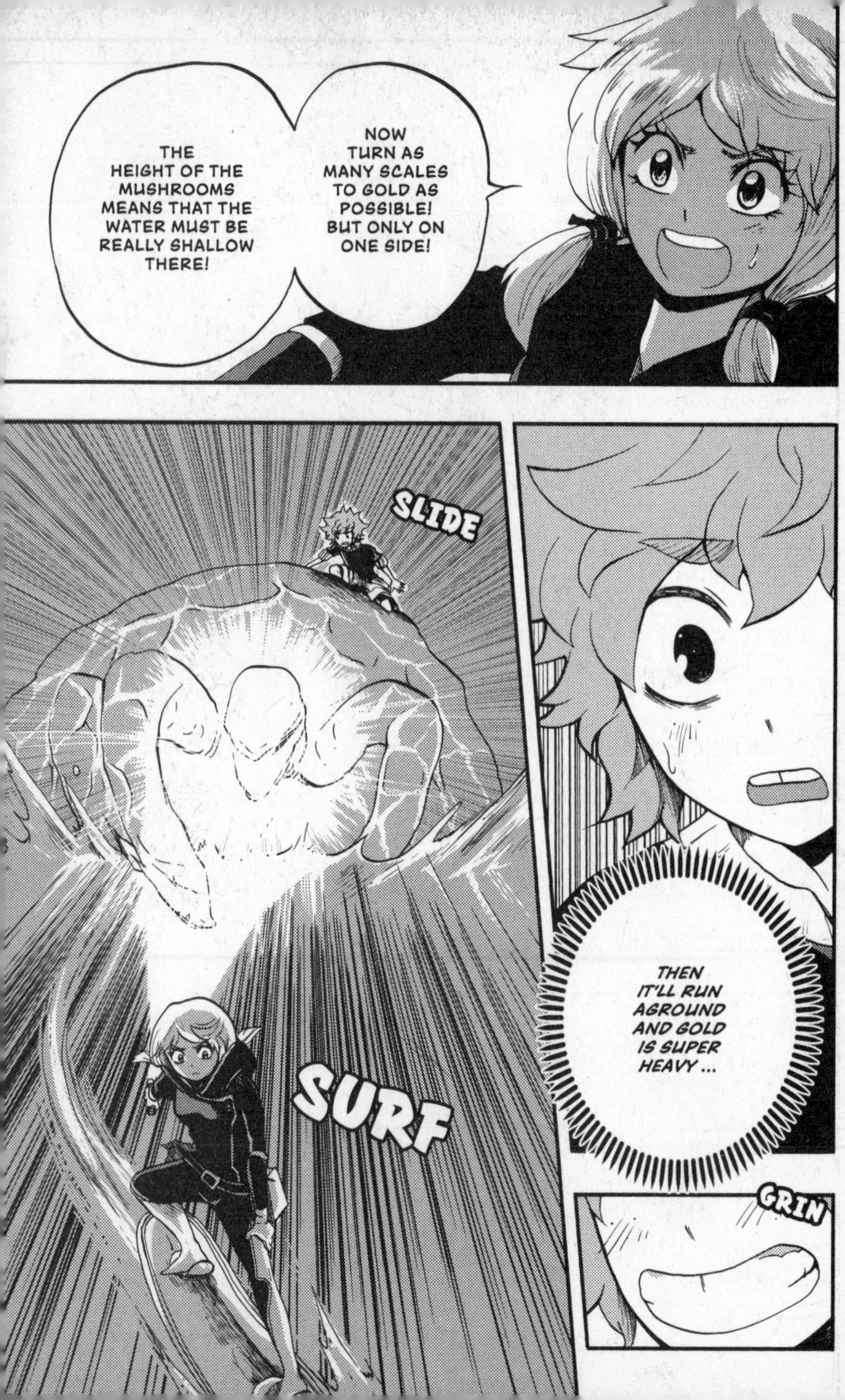
NOW TURN AS MANY SCALES TO GOLD AS POSSIBLE! BUT ONLY ON ONE SIDE!
THE HEIGHT OF THE MUSHROOMS MEANS THAT THE WATER MUST BE REALLY SHALLOW THERE!
THEN IT'LL RUN AGROUND AND GOLD IS SUPER HEAVY ...
GRIN
SLIDE
SURF

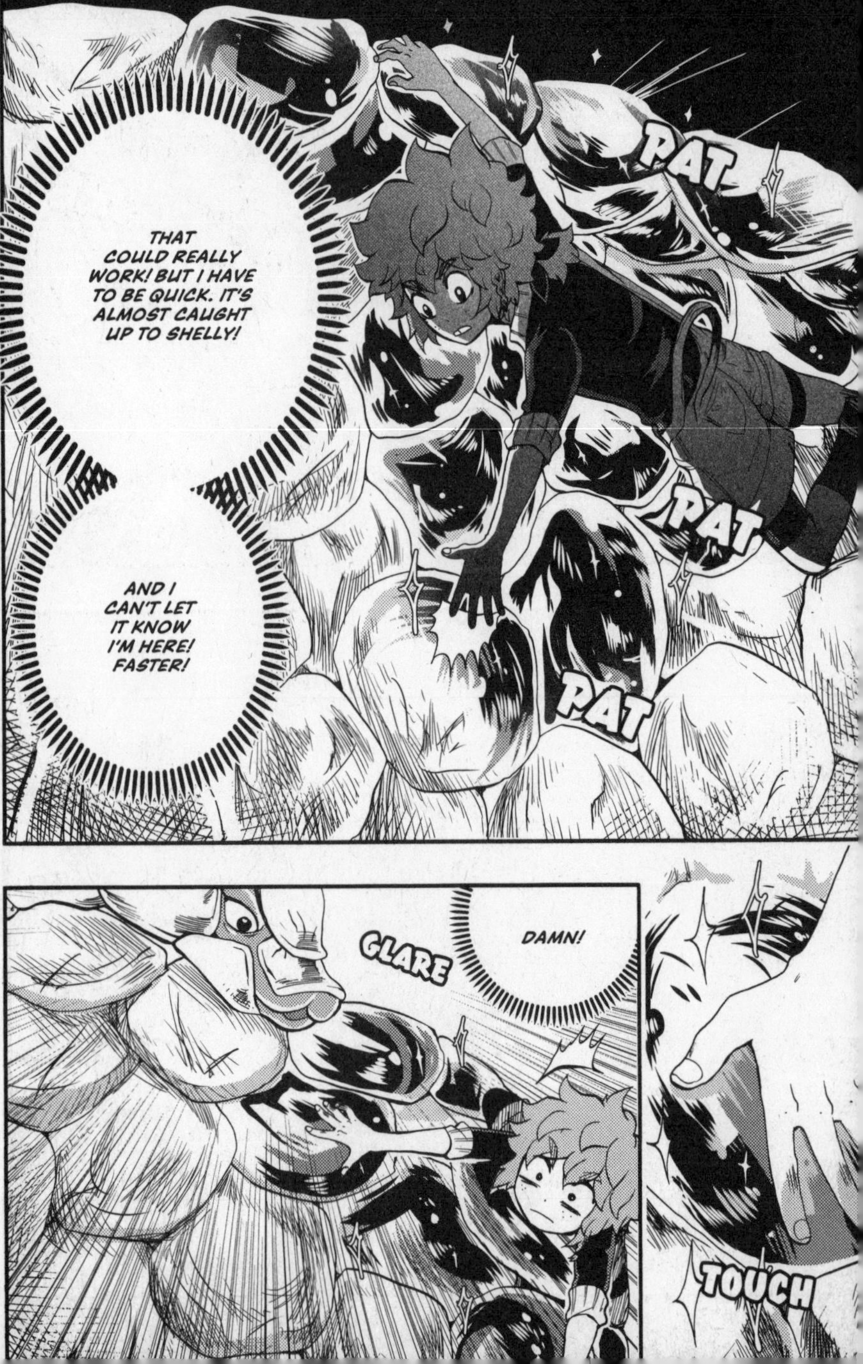
PAT
THAT COULD REALLY WORK! BUT I HAVE TO BE QUICK. IT'S ALMOST CAUGHT UP TO SHELLY!
PAT
AND I CAN'T LET IT KNOW I'M HERE! FASTER!
PAT
TOUCH
DAMN!
GLARE

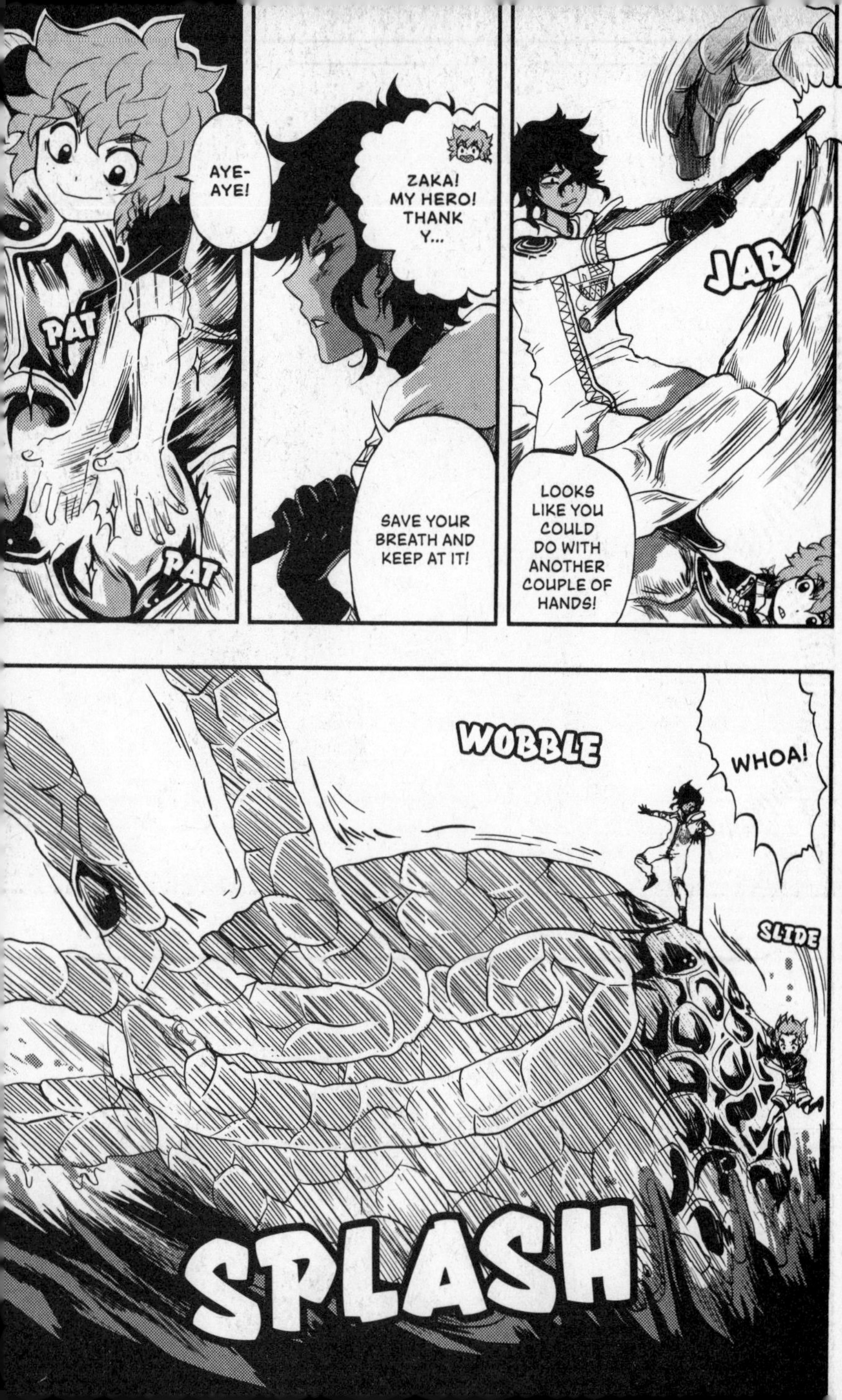
JAB
LOOKS LIKE YOU COULD DO WITH ANOTHER COUPLE OF HANDS!
ZAKA! MY HERO! THANK Y...
SAVE YOUR BREATH AND KEEP AT IT!
AYE-AYE!
PAT
PAT
WHOA!
WOBBLE
SLIDE
SPLASH

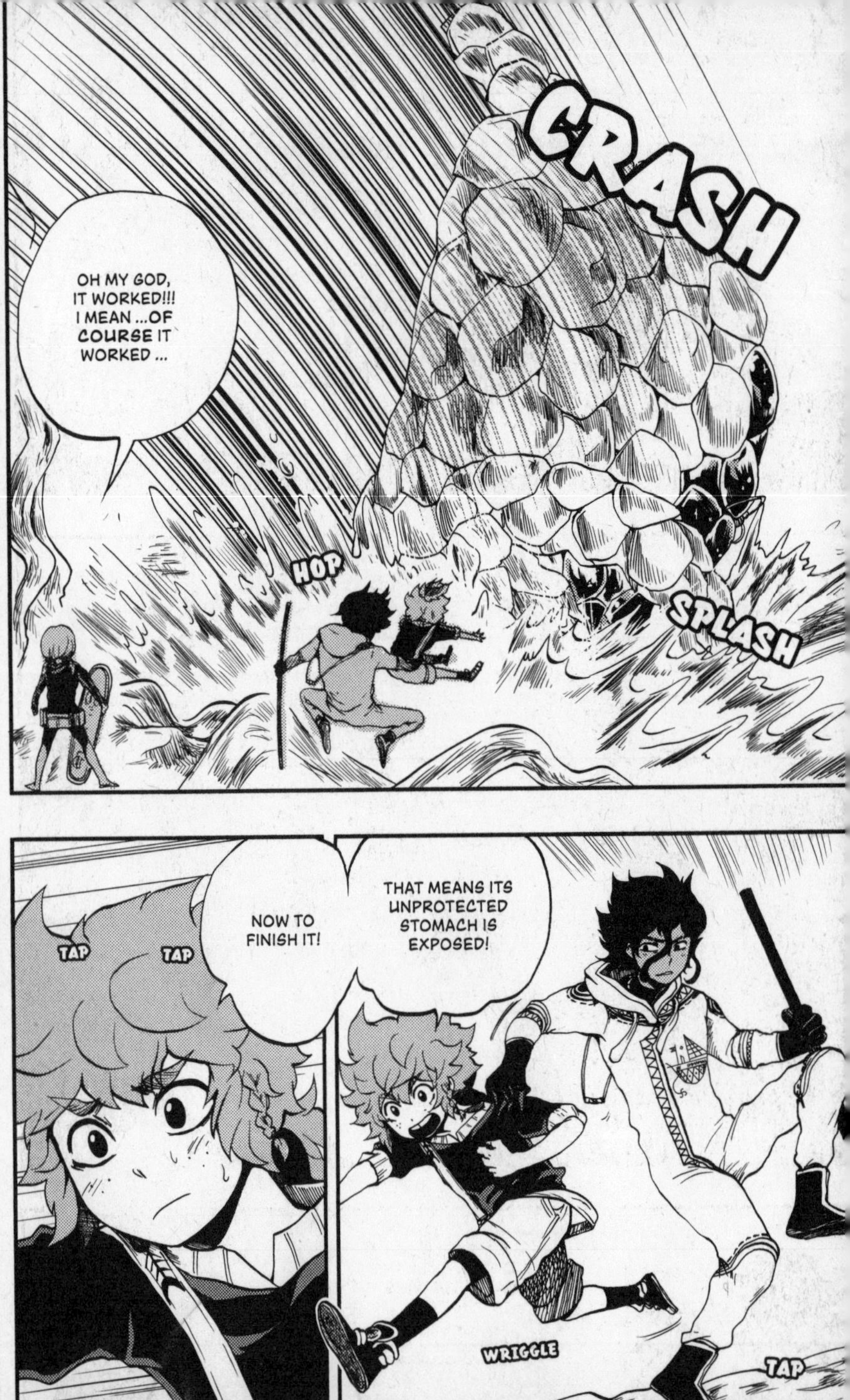
CRASH
OH MY GOD, IT WORKED!!! I MEAN ...OF COURSE IT WORKED ...
HOP
SPLASH
THAT MEANS ITS UNPROTECTED STOMACH IS EXPOSED!
NOW TO FINISH IT!
WRIGGLE
TAP
TAP
TAP

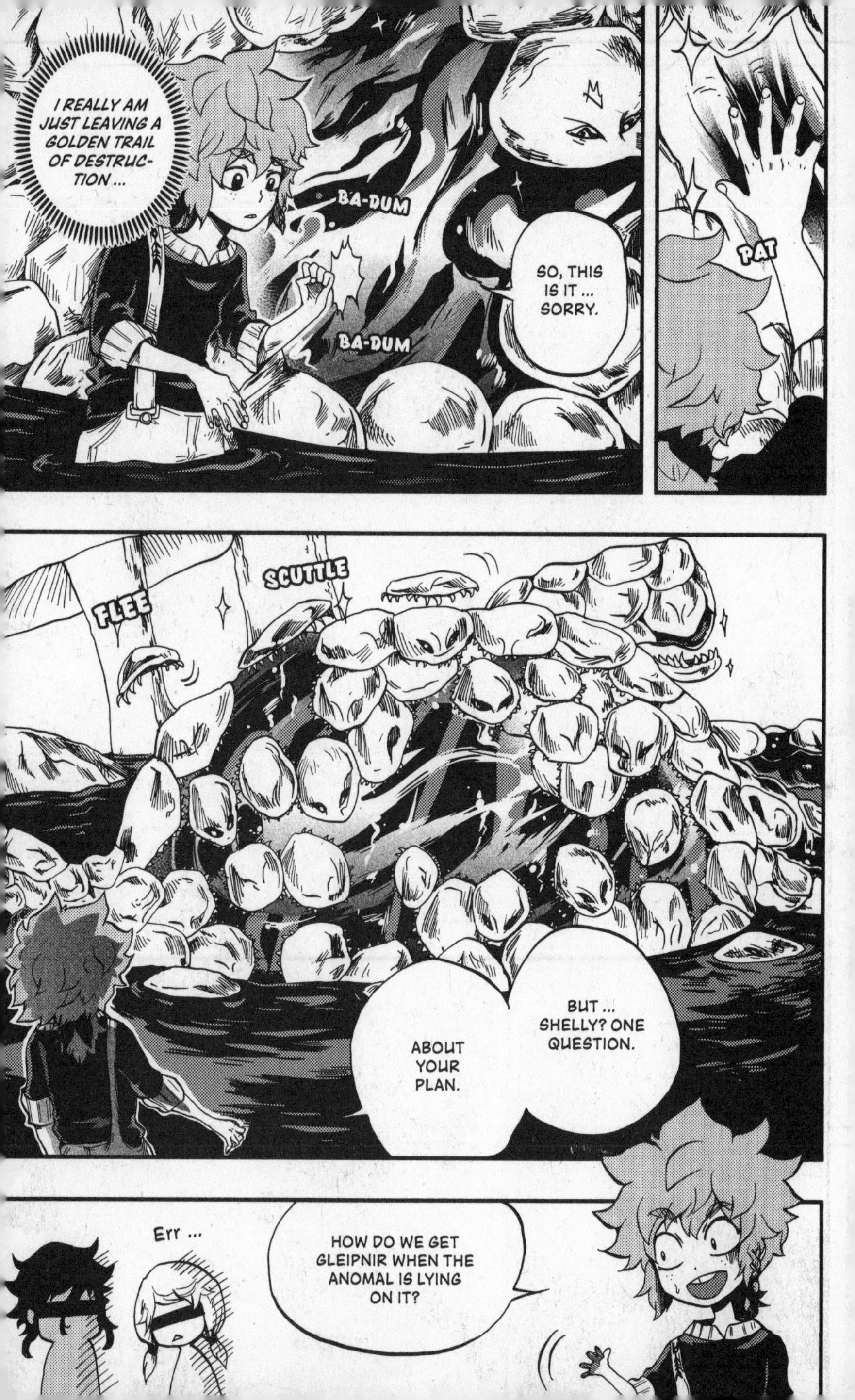
PAT
SO, THIS IS IT ... SORRY.
BA-DUM
BA-DUM
I REALLY AM JUST LEAVING A GOLDEN TRAIL OF DESTRUC-TION ...
SCUTTLE
FLEE
BUT ... SHELLY? ONE QUESTION.
ABOUT YOUR PLAN.
HOW DO WE GET GLEIPNIR WHEN THE ANOMAL IS LYING ON IT?
Err ...

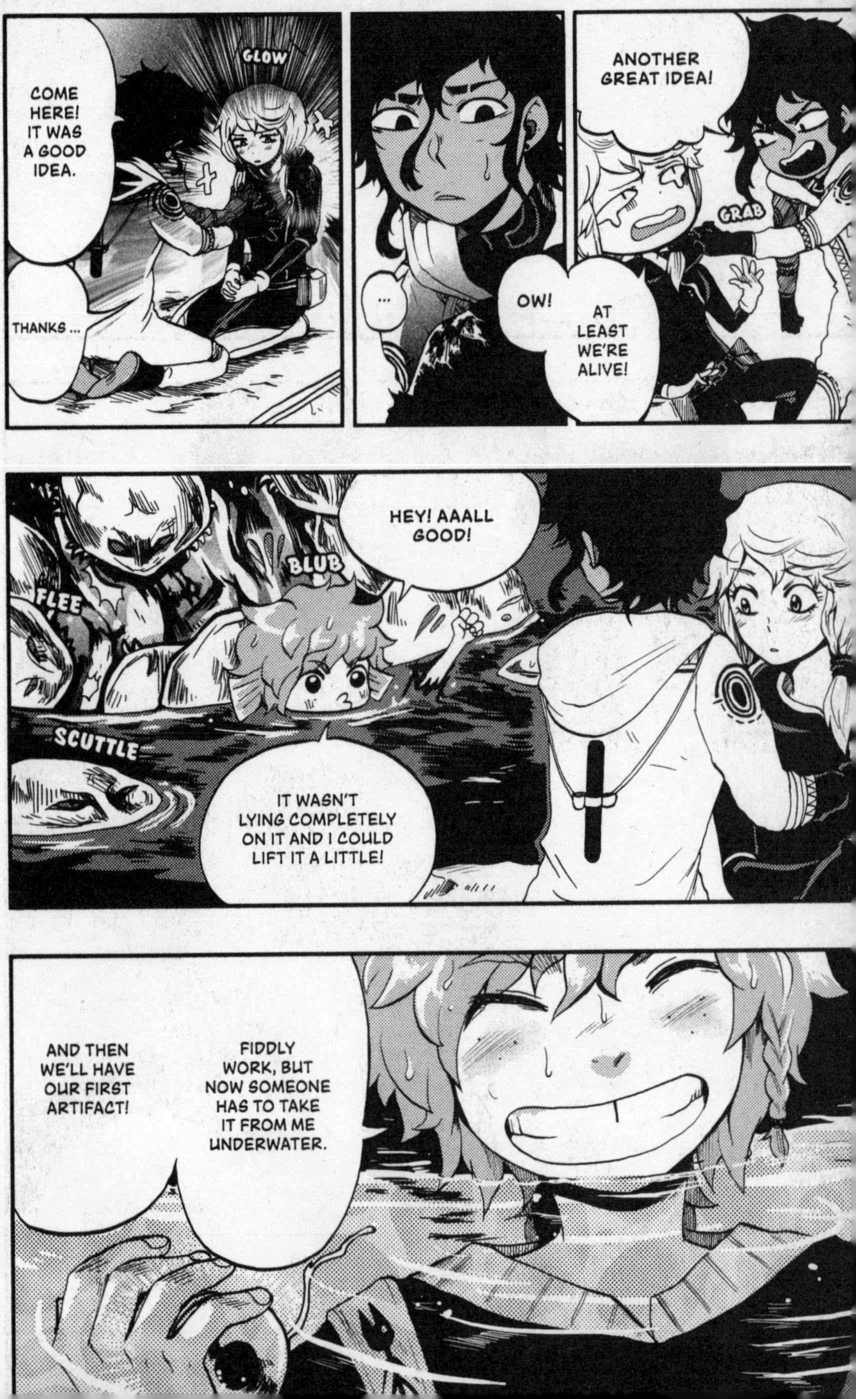
ANOTHER GREAT IDEA!
GRAB
OW!
AT LEAST WE'RE ALIVE!
...
GLOW
COME HERE! IT WAS A GOOD IDEA.
THANKS ...
HEY! AAALL GOOD!
BLUB
FLEE
SCUTTLE
IT WASN'T LYING COMPLETELY ON IT AND I COULD LIFT IT A LITTLE!
FIDDLY WORK, BUT NOW SOMEONE HAS TO TAKE IT FROM ME UNDERWATER.
AND THEN WE'LL HAVE OUR FIRST ARTIFACT!

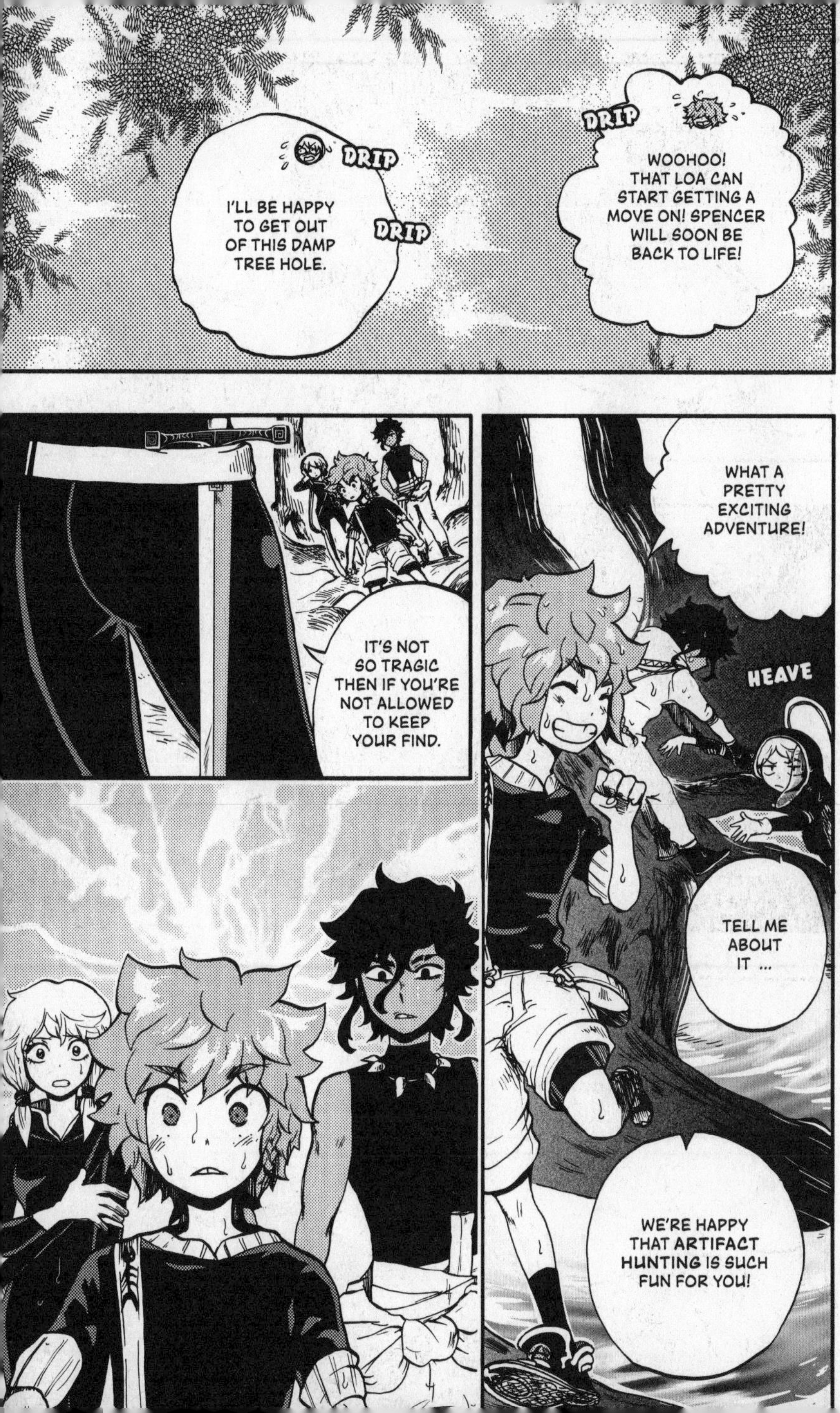
DRIP
WOOHOO! THAT LOA CAN START GETTING A MOVE ON! SPENCER WILL SOON BE BACK TO LIFE!
DRIP
I'LL BE HAPPY TO GET OUT OF THIS DAMP TREE HOLE.
DRIP
WHAT A PRETTY EXCITING ADVENTURE!
HEAVE
TELL ME ABOUT IT ...
WE'RE HAPPY THAT ARTIFACT HUNTING IS SUCH FUN FOR YOU!
IT'S NOT SO TRAGIC THEN IF YOU'RE NOT ALLOWED TO KEEP YOUR FIND.

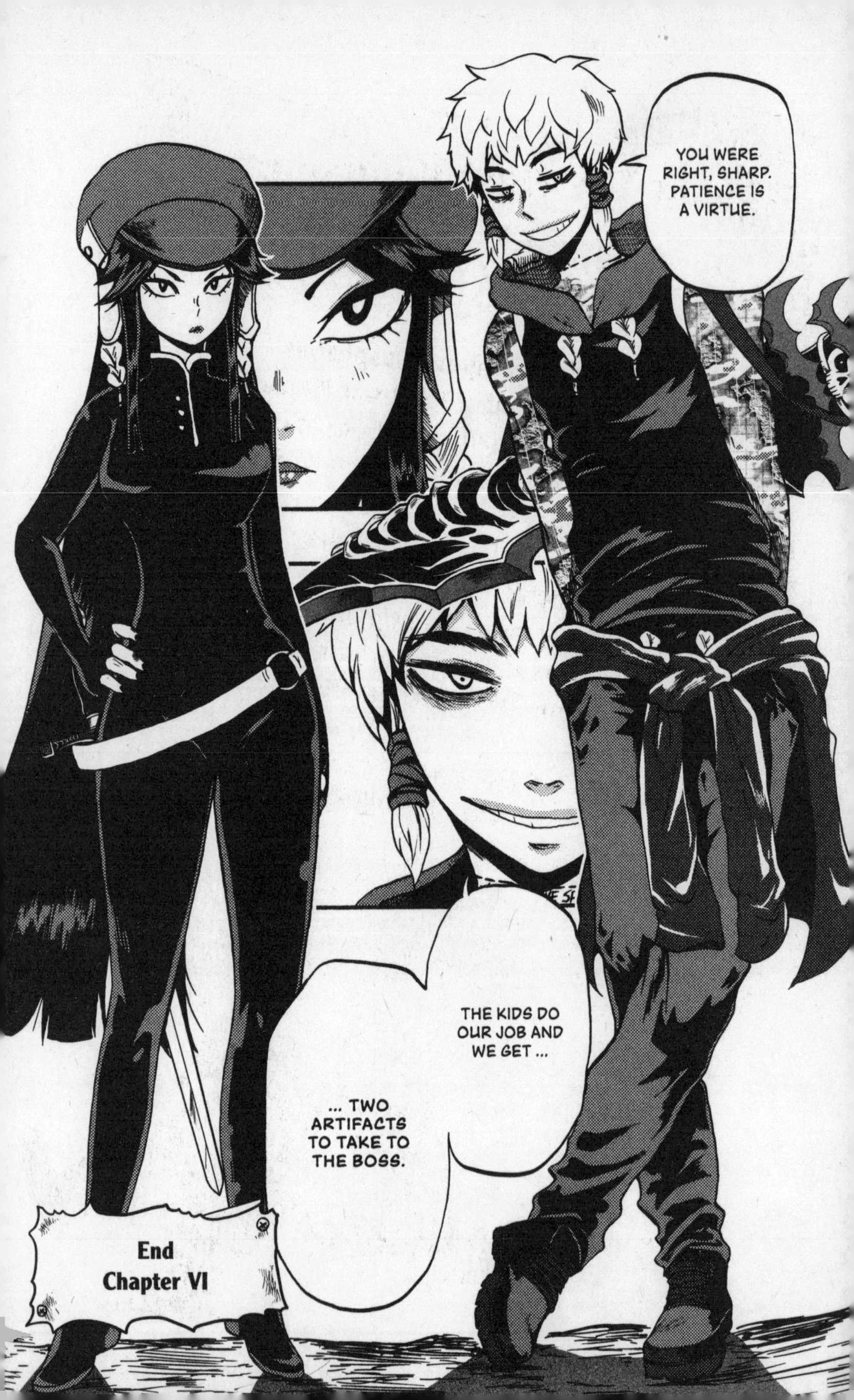
YOU WERE RIGHT, SHARP. PATIENCE IS A VIRTUE.
THE KIDS DO OUR JOB AND WE GET ...
... TWO ARTIFACTS TO TAKE TO THE BOSS.
End Chapter VI

In The Next Volume of GOLDFISCH

Using a totally-not-suspicious treasure map inherited from Morrey's father, Morrey, Shelly and Zaka have been able to track down their first Artifact! But now that they've been cornered by two Obtainers wielding legendary Artifact weapons, there's nowhere left to run. Will Morrey's powers, Shelly's ingenuity and Zaka's magic be enough to keep them safe from the nefarious Obtainers?

Find out more in the next volume of Goldfisch!

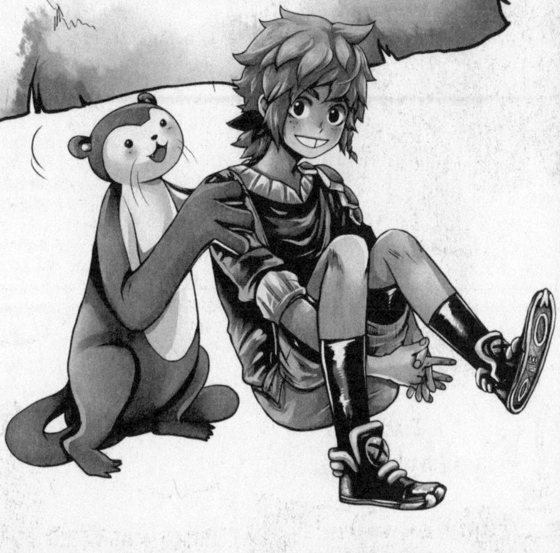

AFTERWORD

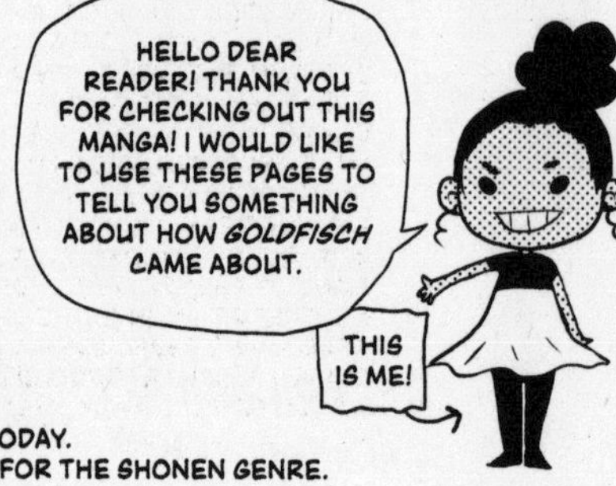
HELLO DEAR READER! THANK YOU FOR CHECKING OUT THIS MANGA! I WOULD LIKE TO USE THESE PAGES TO TELL YOU SOMETHING ABOUT HOW *GOLDFISCH* CAME ABOUT.
THIS IS ME!

LET'S START AT THE BEGINNING.
THE IDEA FOR MORREY AND HIS MIDAS TOUCH IS VERY OLD AND ORIGINALLY CAME ABOUT FOR A COMPETITION. IN 2012, I WANTED TO APPLY TO EVERY GERMAN PUBLISHER WITH IT. I DIDN'T HAVE MUCH CONFIDENCE AT THE TIME AND WAS QUITE UNSURE. DURING THE FIRST PORTFOLIO VIEWING IT BECAME CLEAR HOW CONFUSED AND UNSTRUCTURED MY STORY WAS. I HAD NO IDEA WHAT IT WAS I WANTED TO SAY AND, NATURALLY, I WAS REJECTED. MY DRAWINGS WERE ALSO MUCH WORSE THAN THEY ARE TODAY.
IT SEEMS THAT THEY WERE FAR TOO STATIC FOR THE SHONEN GENRE.

AFTER THAT, I THOUGHT THAT THE IDEA ITSELF WAS STUPID. FRUSTRATED, I PUT IT IN A DRAWER AND TURNED TO OTHER THINGS.

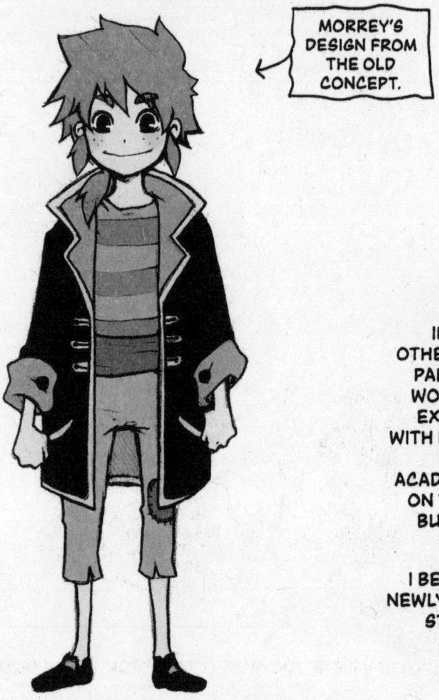
MORREY'S DESIGN FROM THE OLD CONCEPT.

IN MID-2014 TOKYOPOP INVITED ME AND SOME OTHER ARTISTS TO *TOKYOPOP ACADEMY*. WE TOOK PART IN STORYTELLING AND CHARACTER DESIGN WORKSHOPS AND RECEIVED FEEDBACK FROM AN EXPERIENCED EDITOR. I WAS ALREADY FAMILIAR WITH DRAMATIC THEORY AND THE RULES OF STORY CONSTRUCTION, BUT IT WAS ONLY AFTER THE ACADEMY THAT I RESOLVED TO WORK INTENSIVELY ON THE SUBJECT OF STORYTELLING. I SET ABOUT BUILDING A STORY NOT SO MUCH FROM THE GUT BUT BY STICKING TO A FEW RULES INSTEAD.

I BEGAN LOOKING FOR AN IDEA I COULD APPLY MY NEWLY ACQUIRED KNOWLEDGE TO AND ONCE AGAIN STUMBLED ACROSS MY OLD *GOLDFISCH* STORY.

I WANTED TO USE IT TO MAKE A CONCEPT FOR A ONE-SHOT AND SUBMIT THAT FOR APPLICATION. I THOUGHT THAT THE CHANCES OF A NEWCOMER GETTING A SERIES WERE FAR TOO SLIM. BUT IT'S TERRIBLY DIFFICULT TO CREATE SHORT SHONEN STORIES WITHOUT THE DRAMA AND ACTION SUFFERING. I ALSO ALWAYS MAKE EVERYTHING TOO LONG, SO I DESPAIRED SOMEWHAT TRYING TO FIT EVERYTHING INTO SIX CHAPTERS. I ALSO PUT A LOT OF WORK INTO THE DESIGN OF MY APPLICATION: INKING MANY OF THE BACKGROUNDS AND PUTTING A LOT OF DETAIL INTO THE CHARACTERS. AFTER MANY REJECTIONS AND YEARS DURING WHICH I PRODUCED STORIES THAT WOULD BE FILED AWAY, I REALIZED ...

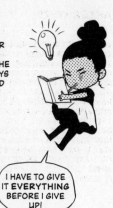

I HAVE TO GIVE IT **EVERYTHING** BEFORE I GIVE UP!

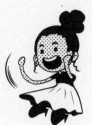

I FRETTED AND FEARED AND AFTER A FEW WEEKS THE ANSWER CAME. I REALLY HAD DONE IT! TOKYOPOP HAD WRITTEN TO TELL ME THAT THEY WANTED TO MAKE *GOLDFISCH* AND I WOULD HAVE YANNICK AS MY EDITOR (THANK YOU TO HIM FOR THE TEAMWORK!). BUT TOKYOPOP ALSO SAID THAT THEY WANTED TO PUBLISH IT AS A SERIES AND THAT I SHOULD THINK ABOUT HOW TO TURN MY ONE-SHOT INTO ONE.

I WAS THRILLED THAT MY DREAM OF A SERIES WOULD BE GRANTED WITH MY FIRST PROJECT, BUT THEN I THOUGHT ...

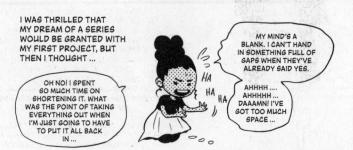

MY MIND'S A BLANK. I CAN'T HAND IN SOMETHING FULL OF GAPS WHEN THEY'VE ALREADY SAID YES.
HA HA HA
AHHHH .... AHHHHH ... DAAAMN! I'VE GOT TOO MUCH SPACE ...
OH NO! I SPENT SO MUCH TIME ON SHORTENING IT. WHAT WAS THE POINT OF TAKING EVERYTHING OUT WHEN I'M JUST GOING TO HAVE TO PUT IT ALL BACK IN ...

AND NATURALLY NOW I HAVE FAR TOO MUCH STORY FOR THREE BOOKS.

UNTIL NEXT TIME OR WHENEVER!
YOURS, NANA YAA!

I WOULD LIKE TO USE THIS SPACE TO THANK NIGHTY, MARIA AND ANNE, WHO HELPED ME A LOT WITH STRUCTURING MY APPLICATION! HOPEFULLY, I'LL GET TO THE DRAWING PROCESS IN THE NEXT AFTERWORD (BOOK 2)! BUT HERE I WOULD NATURALLY LIKE TO SAY A BIG FAT THANK-YOU TO JOLLY, WHO DID A LOT OF THE RASTERIZING FOR ME!

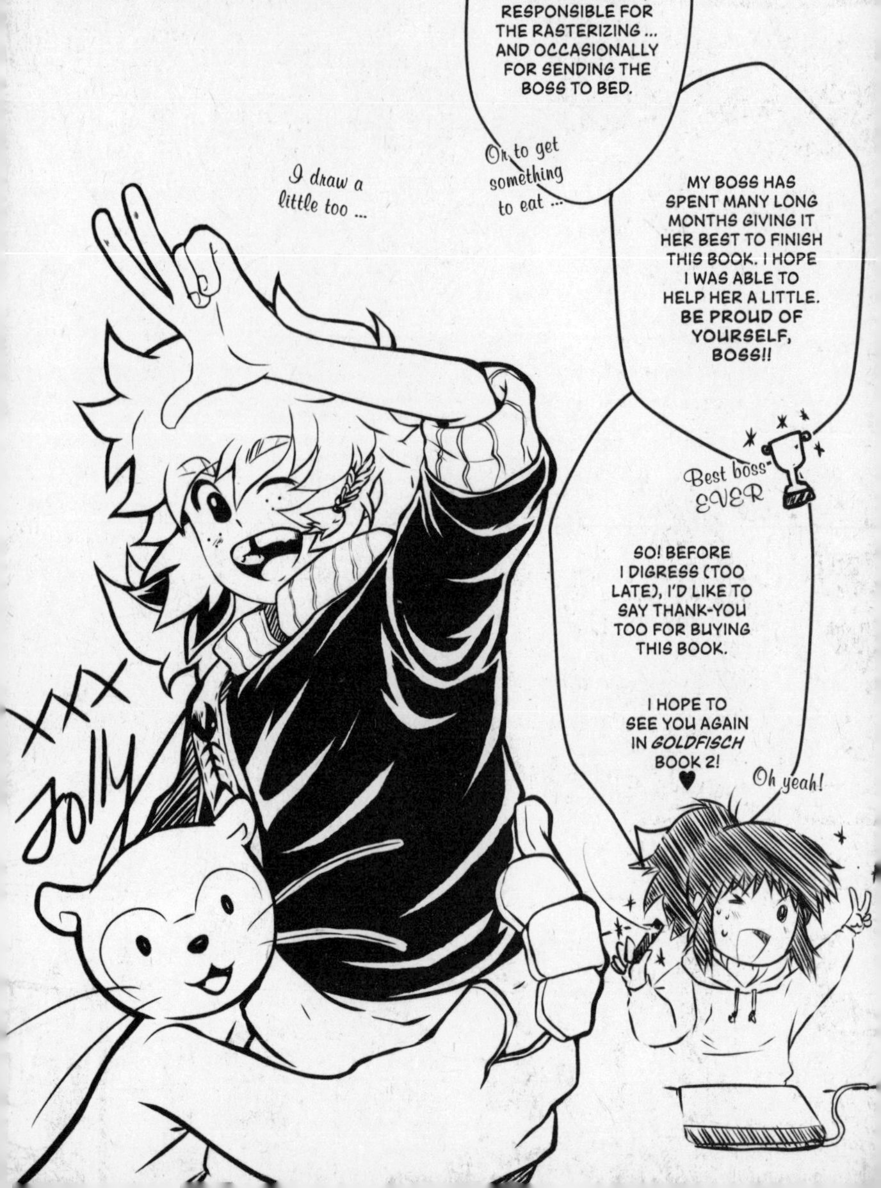
HELLO DEAR READER! I HOPE YOU ENJOYED IT! I'M JOLLY, NANA YAA'S ASSISTANT, RESPONSIBLE FOR THE RASTERIZING ... AND OCCASIONALLY FOR SENDING THE BOSS TO BED.
MY BOSS HAS SPENT MANY LONG MONTHS GIVING IT HER BEST TO FINISH THIS BOOK. I HOPE I WAS ABLE TO HELP HER A LITTLE. BE PROUD OF YOURSELF, BOSS!!
Best boss EVER
SO! BEFORE I DIGRESS (TOO LATE), I'D LIKE TO SAY THANK-YOU TOO FOR BUYING THIS BOOK.
I HOPE TO SEE YOU AGAIN IN *GOLDFISCH* BOOK 2! ♥
Oh yeah!
Or, to get something to eat ...
I draw a little too ...
Jolly

Setting designs / discards (got a little carried away and had fun)

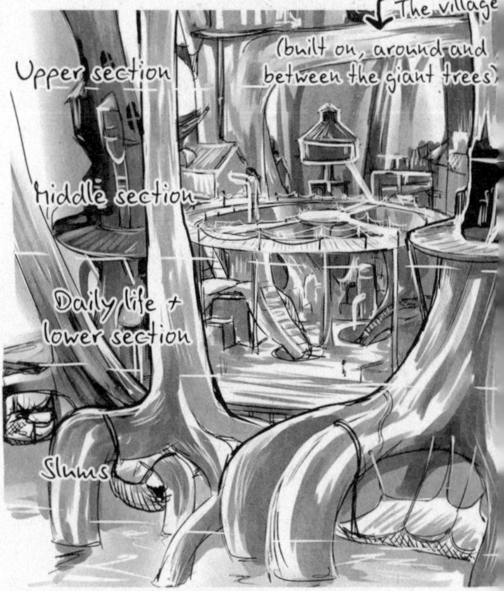
The village
(built on, around and between the giant trees)
Upper section
Middle section
Daily life + lower section
Slums

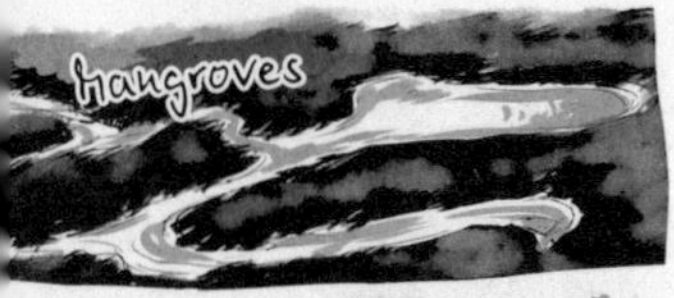
Mangroves

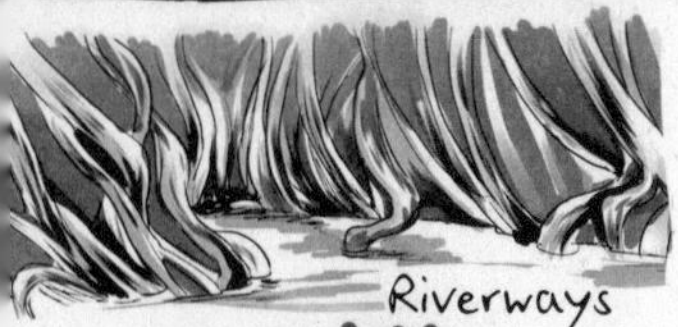
Riverways

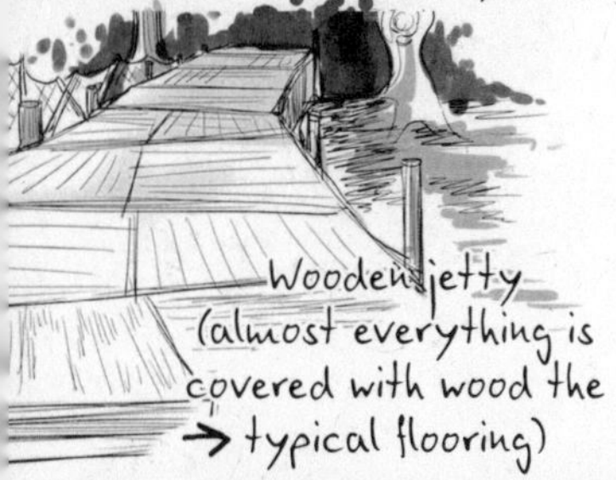
Wooden jetty
(almost everything is covered with wood the → typical flooring)

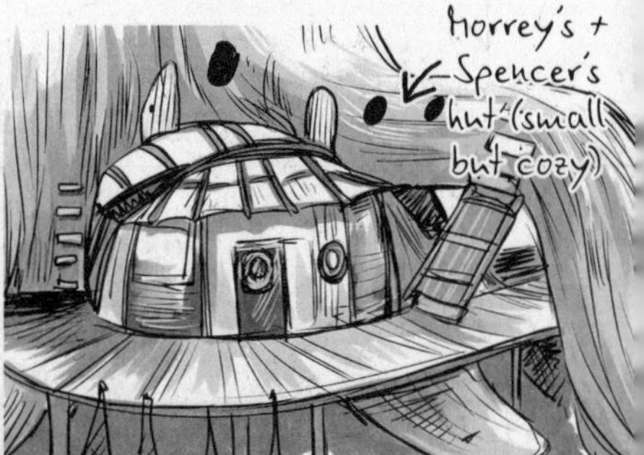
Morrey's + Spencer's hut (small but cozy)

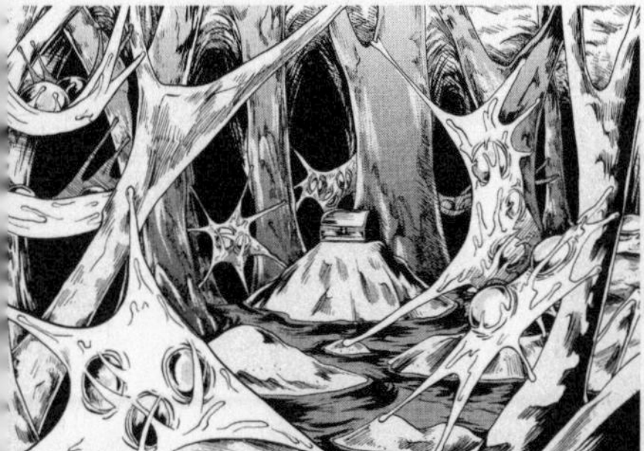

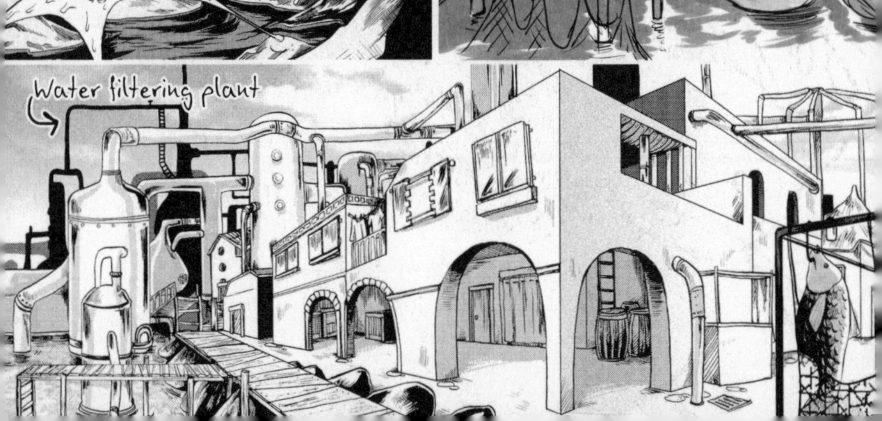
Water filtering plant

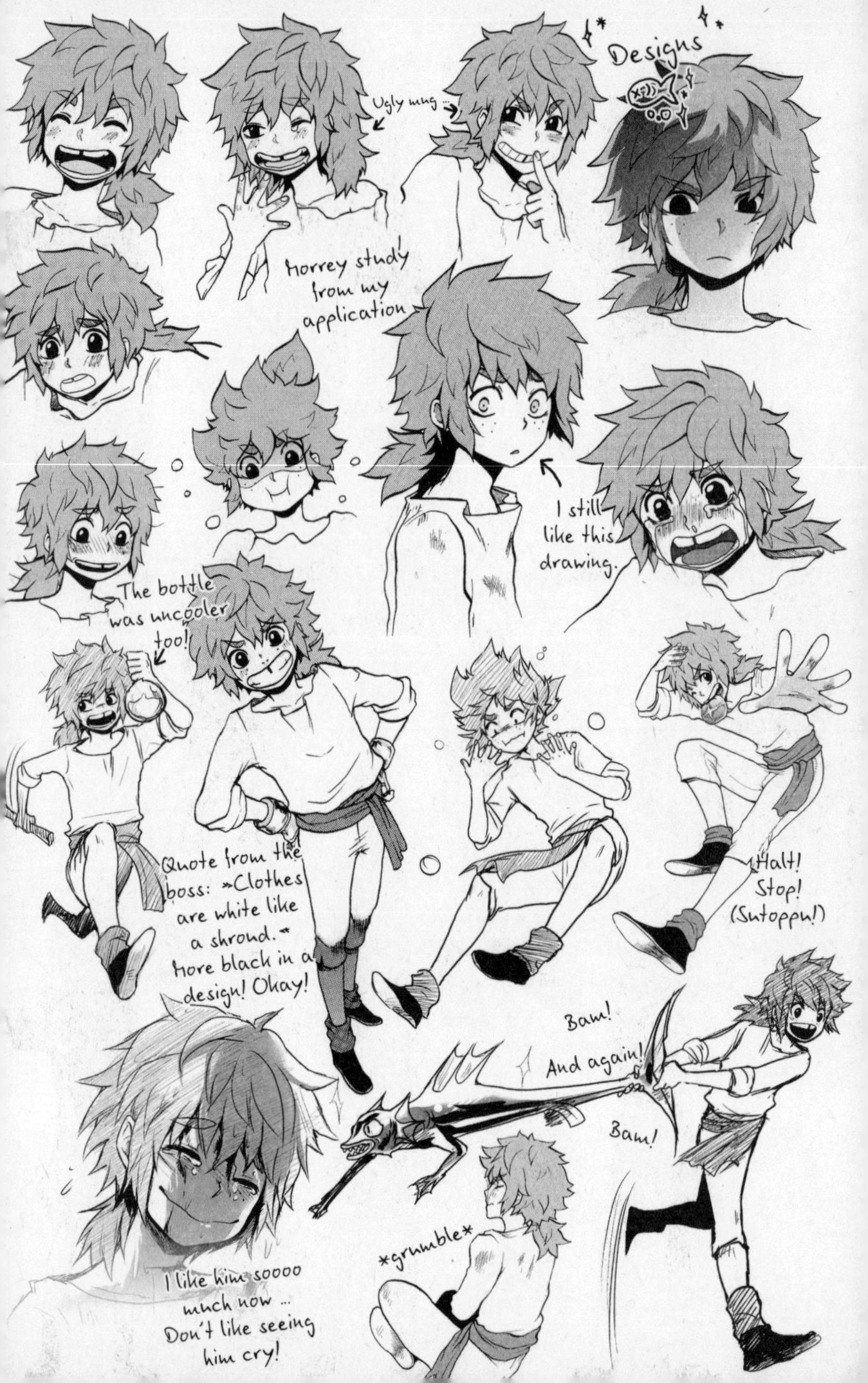
Designs
Ugly mug ...
Morrey study from my application
I still like this drawing.
The bottle was uncooler too!
Halt! Stop! (Sutoppu!)
Quote from the boss: »Clothes are white like a shroud.« More black in a design! Okay!
Bam!
And again!
Bam!
grumble
I like him soooo much now ... Don't like seeing him cry!

Clothes designs, which were later recombined new!

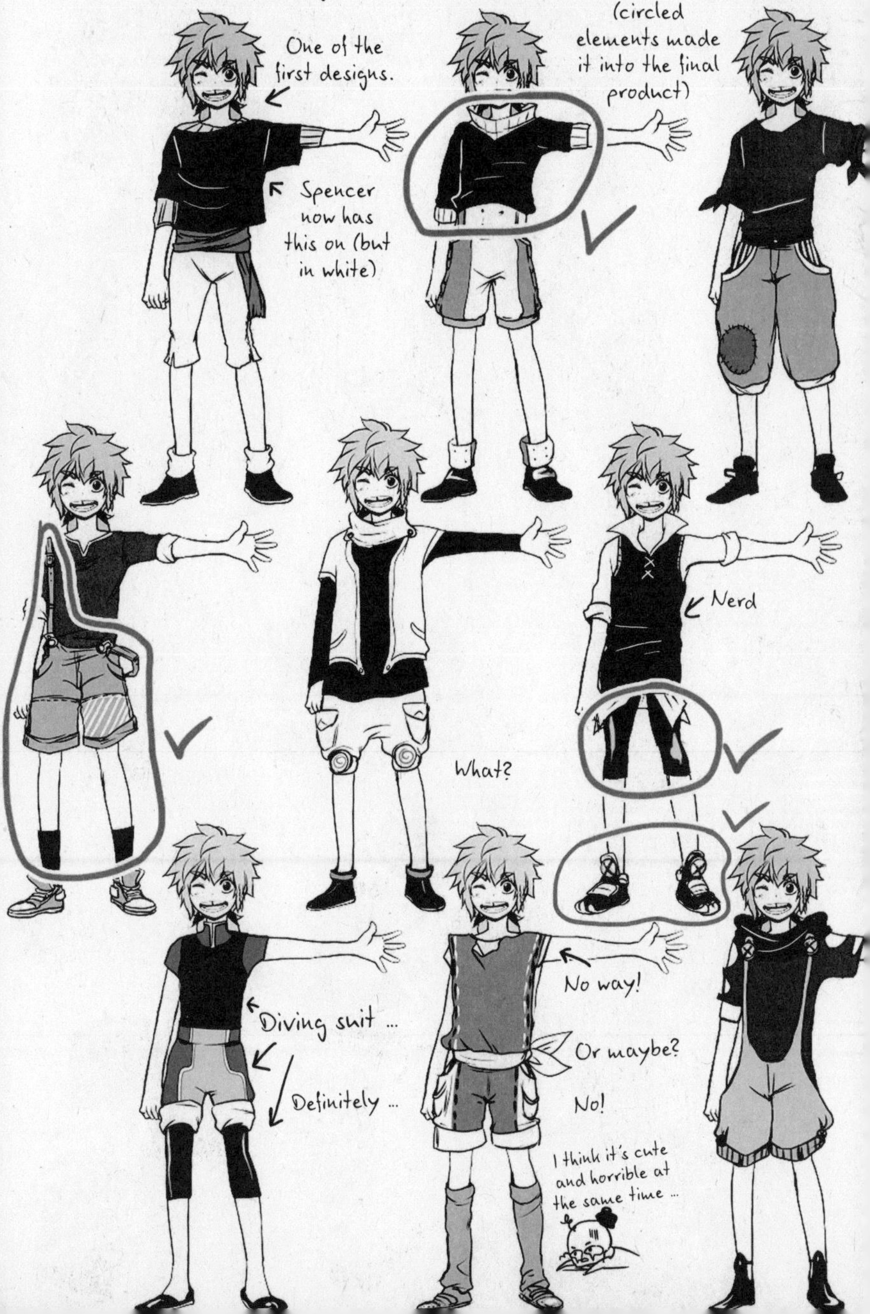
(circled elements made it into the final product)
One of the first designs.
Spencer now has this on (but in white)
Nerd
What?
No way!
Or maybe?
No!
Diving suit ...
Definitely ...
I think it's cute and horrible at the same time ...

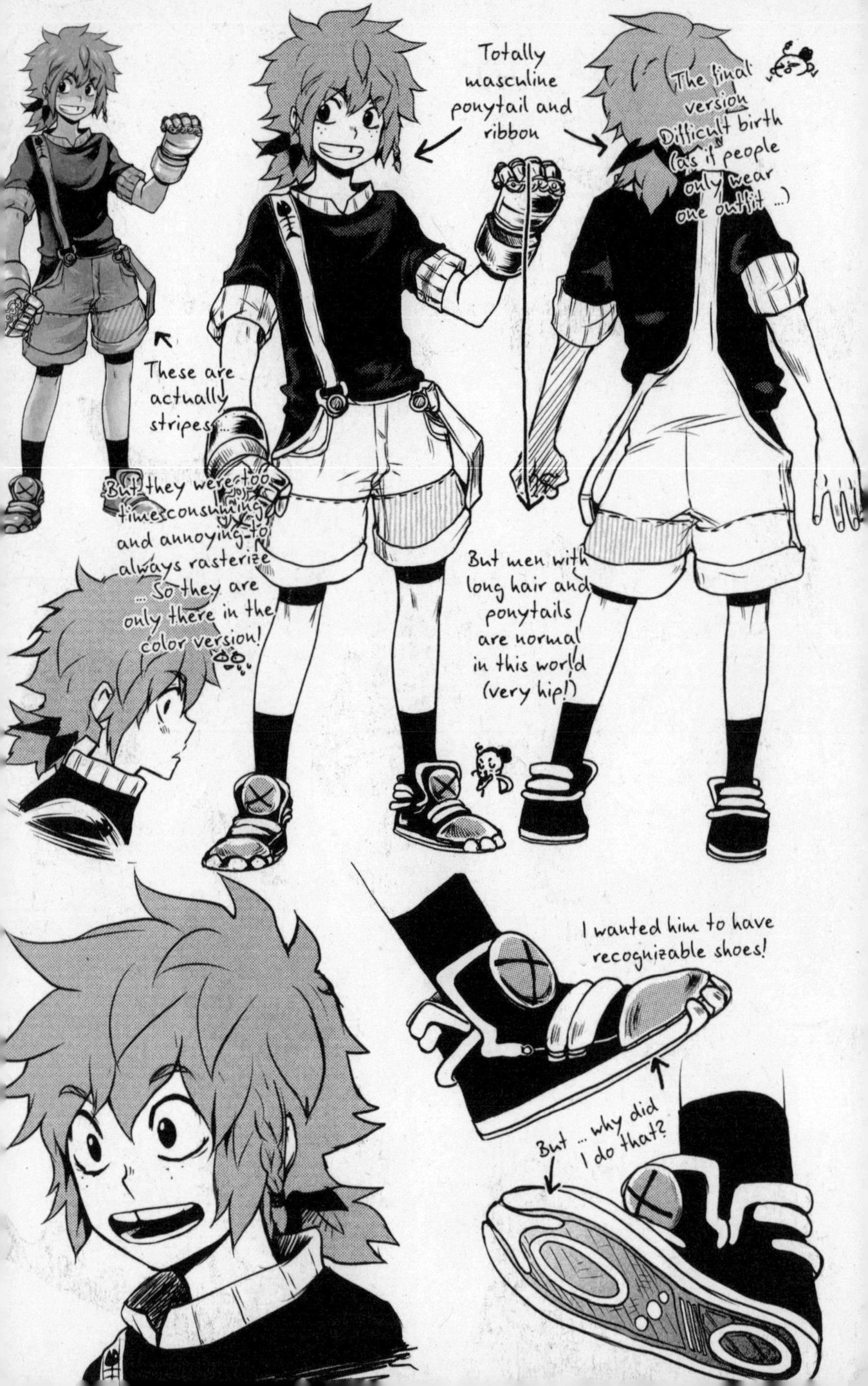
The final version
Difficult birth
(as if people only wear one outfit ...)
Totally masculine ponytail and ribbon
These are actually stripes...
But they were too time consuming and annoying to always rasterize
... So they are only there in the color version!
But men with long hair and ponytails are normal in this world (very hip!)
I wanted him to have recognizable shoes!
But ... why did I do that?

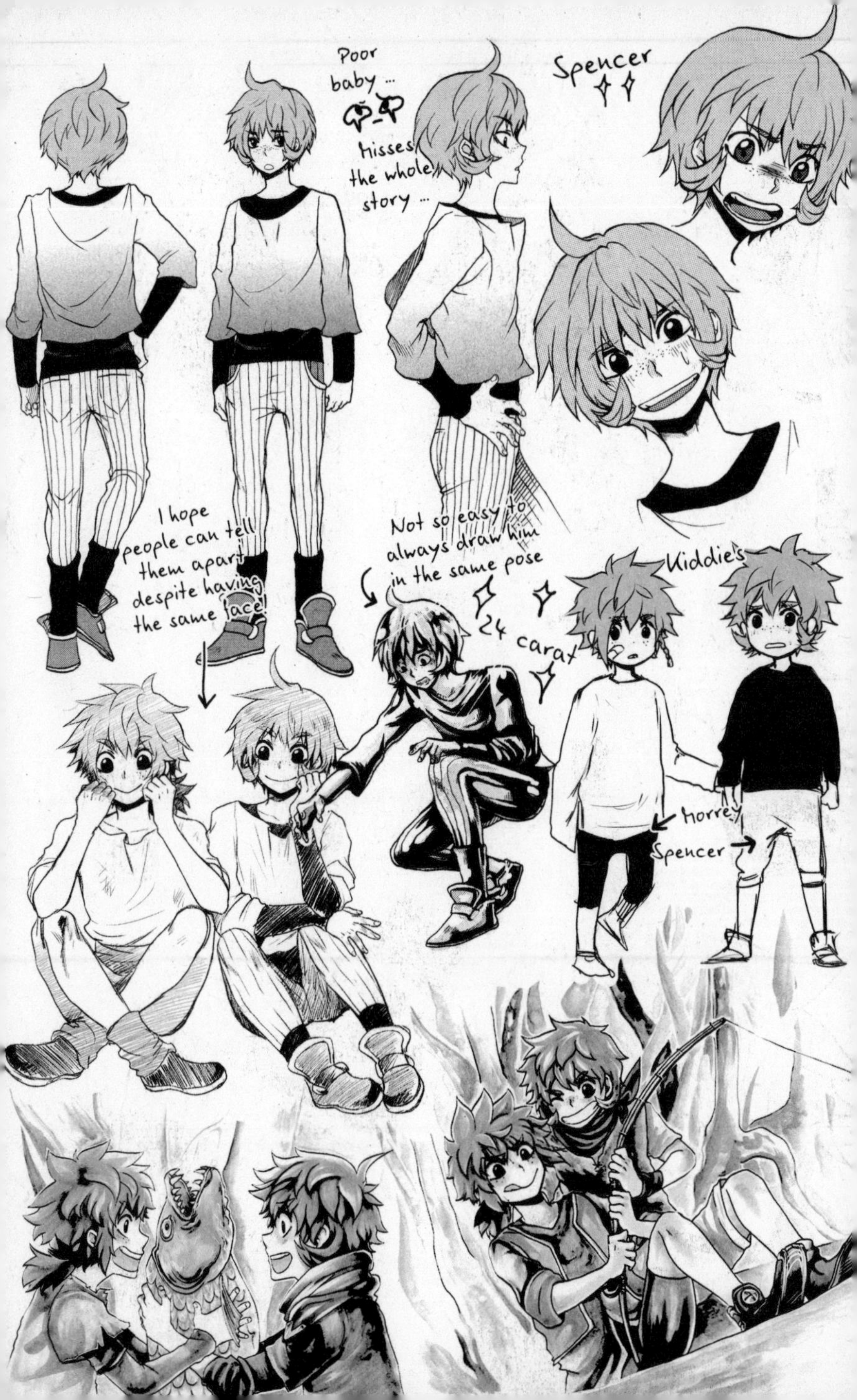
Poor baby ...
Misses the whole story ...
Spencer
I hope people can tell them apart despite having the same face!
Not so easy to always draw him in the same pose
24 carat
Kiddie's
Morrey
Spencer

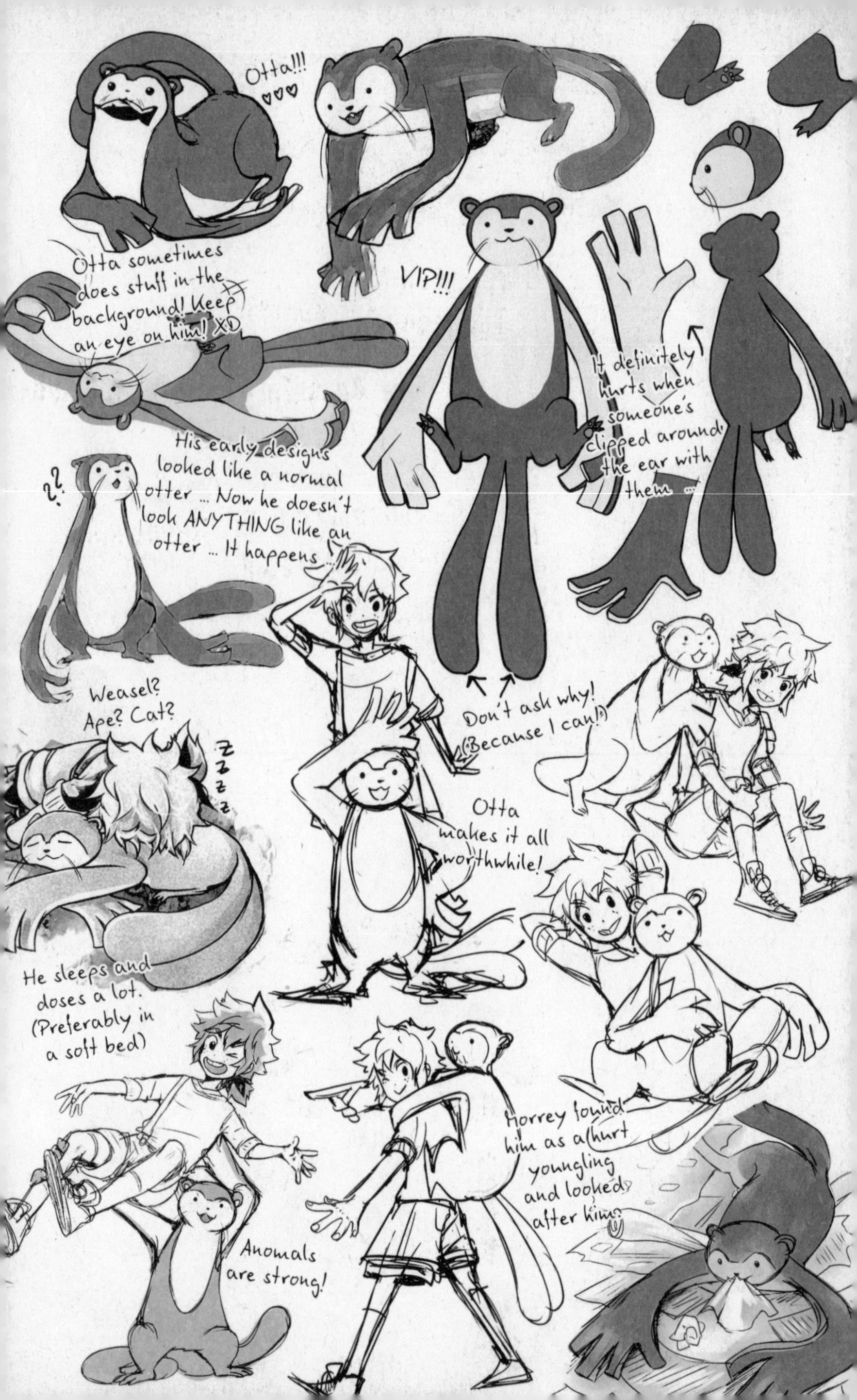
Otta!!! ♡♡♡
VIP!!!
It definitely hurts when someone's clipped around the ear with them ...
Otta sometimes does stuff in the background! Keep an eye on him! XD
His early designs looked like a normal otter ... Now he doesn't look ANYTHING like an otter ... It happens ...
Don't ask why! (Because I can!)
Otta makes it all worthwhile!
Weasel? Ape? Cat?
Z Z Z Z
He sleeps and doses a lot. (Preferably in a soft bed)
Horrey found him as a hurt youngling and looked after him.
Anomals are strong!

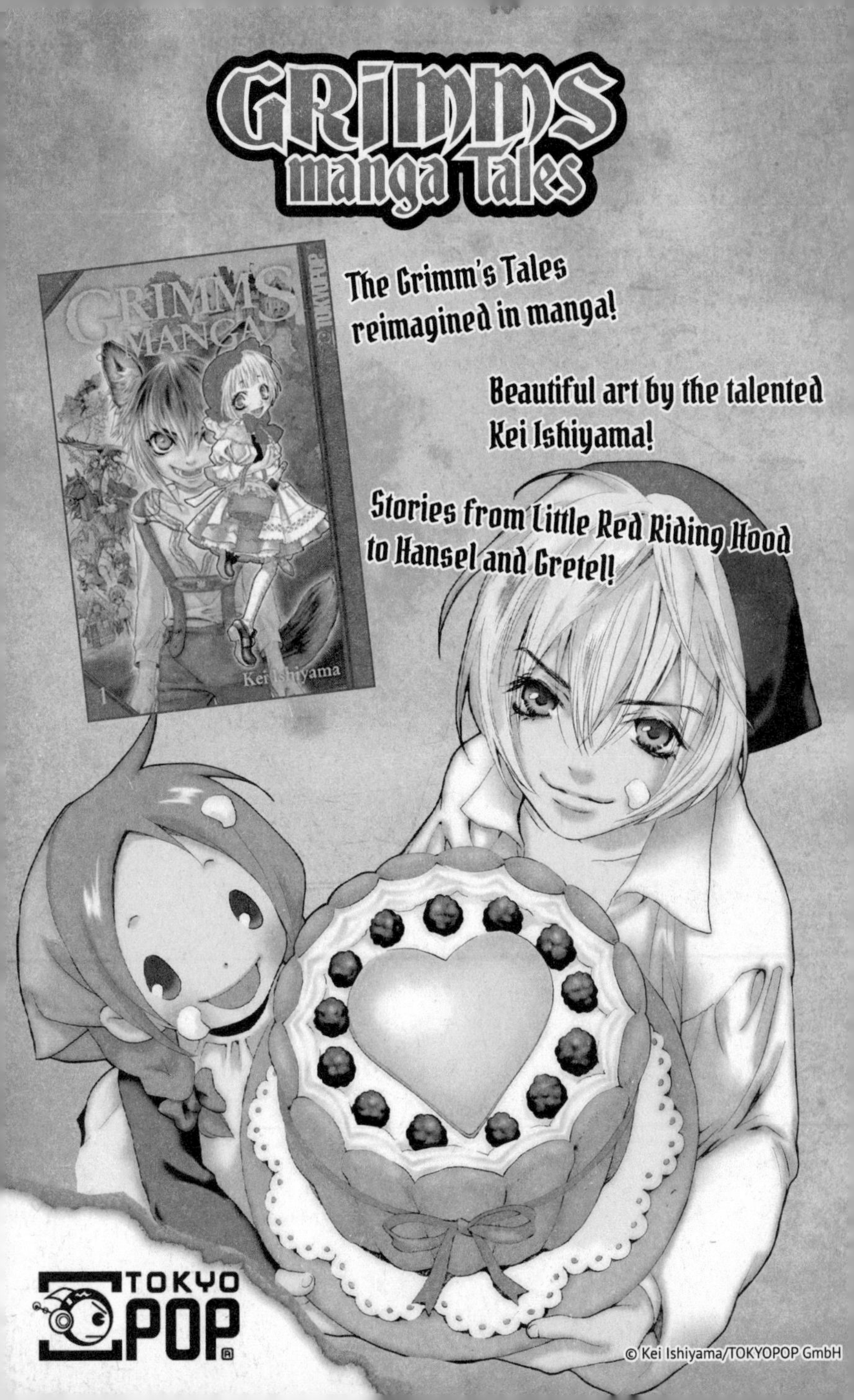
GRIMMS manga Tales
GRIMM'S MANGA
TOKYOPOP
Kei Ishiyama
1
The Grimm's Tales reimagined in manga!
Beautiful art by the talented Kei Ishiyama!
Stories from Little Red Riding Hood to Hansel and Gretel!
TOKYO POP
© Kei Ishiyama/TOKYOPOP GmbH

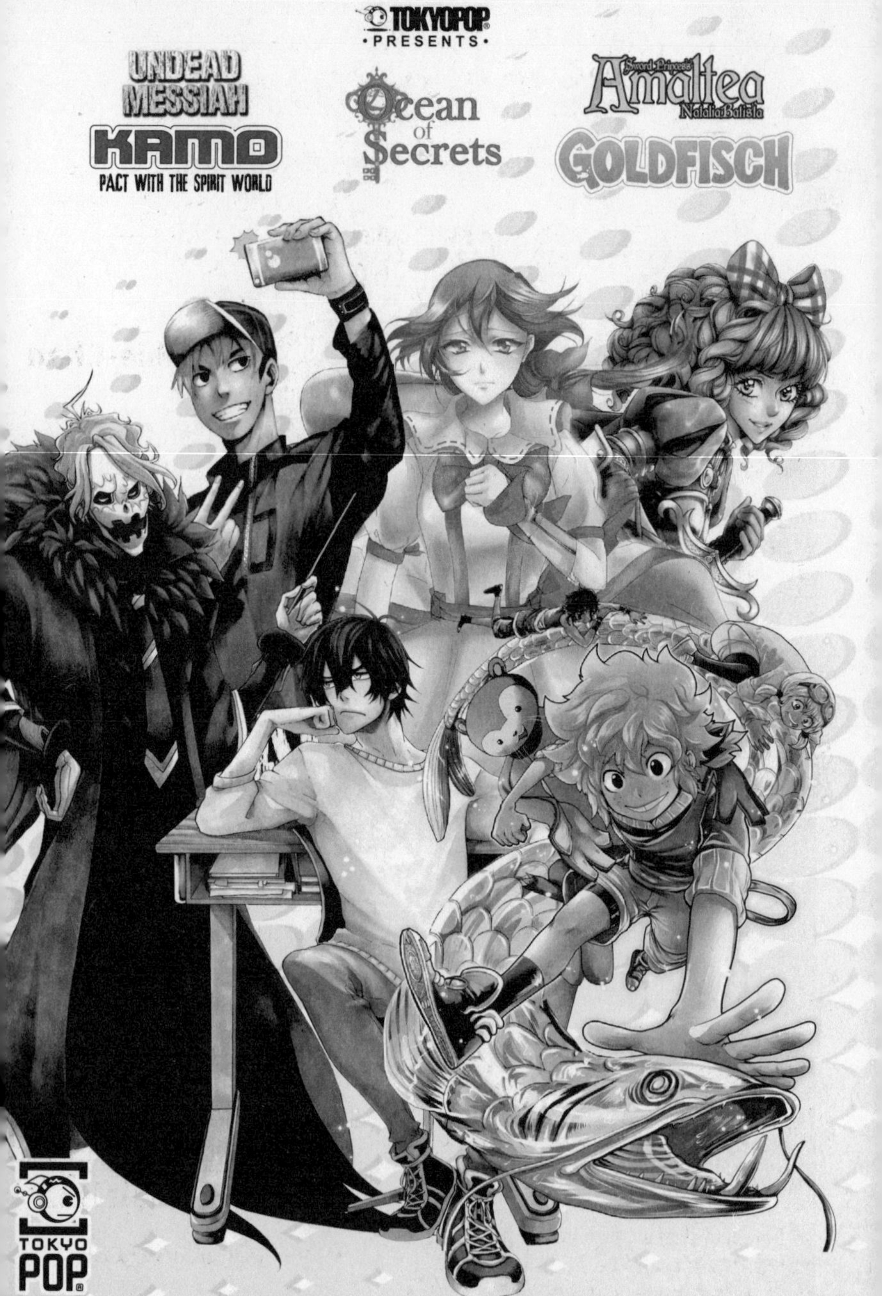
TOKYOPOP
• PRESENTS •
UNDEAD MESSIAH
KAMO
PACT WITH THE SPIRIT WORLD
Ocean of Secrets
Sword Princess Amaltea
Natalia Batista
GOLDFISCH
TOKYO POP

INTERNATIONAL WOMEN of MANGA

 NANA YAA

An award-winning German manga artist with a large following for her free webcomic, *CRUSHED!*!

Sophie-Chan

A self-taught manga artist from the Middle East, with a huge YouTube following!

 Ban Zarbo

A lifelong manga fan from Germany, she and her twin sister take inspiration from their Dominican roots!

Gin Zarbo

An aspiring manga artist since she was a child, along with her twin sister she's releasing her debut title!

Natalia Batista

A Swedish creator whose popular manga has already been published in Sweden, Italy and the Czech Republic!

www.TOKYOPOP.com

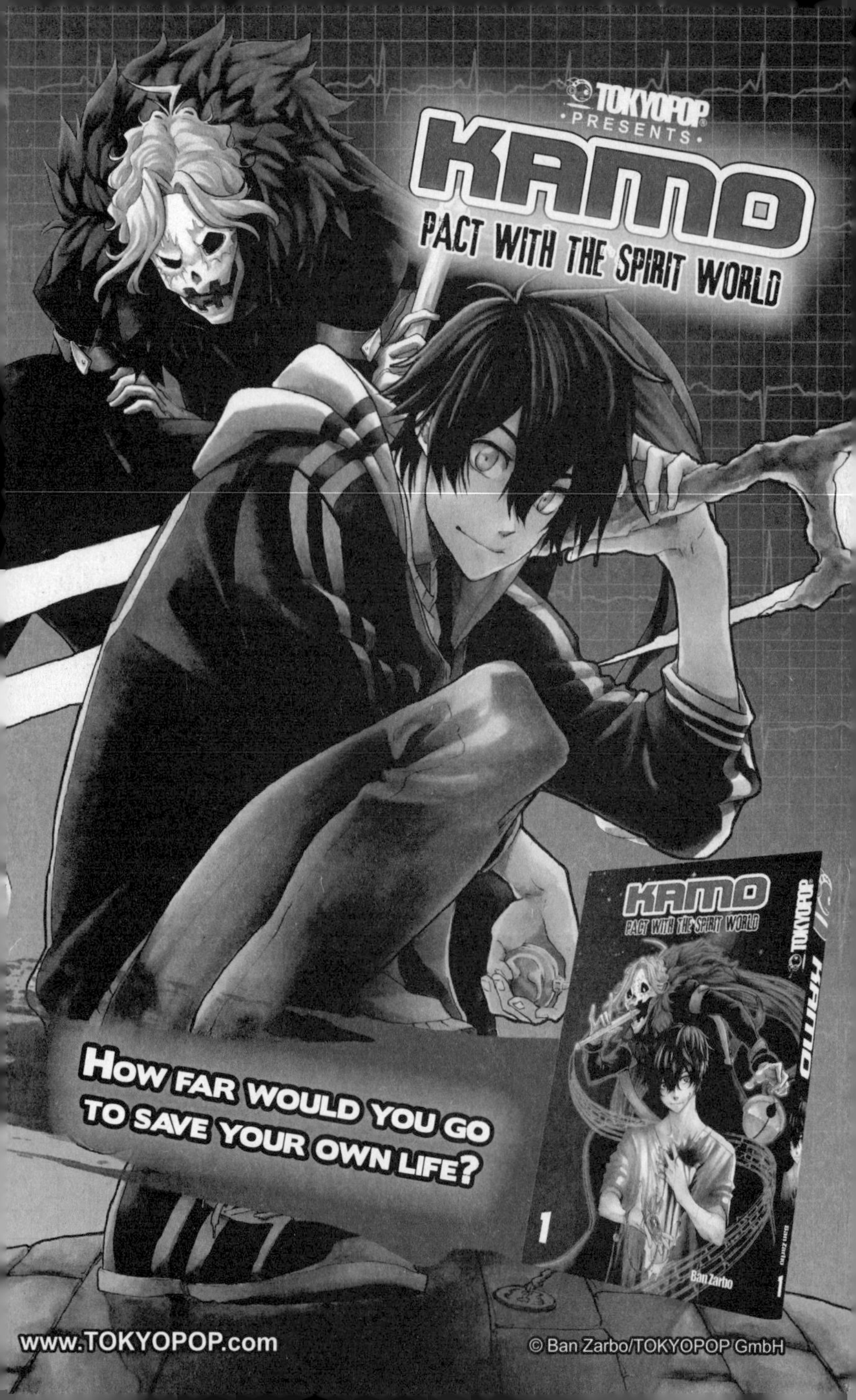
TOKYOPOP PRESENTS
KAMO
PACT WITH THE SPIRIT WORLD
KAMO
PACT WITH THE SPIRIT WORLD
TOKYOPOP
1
Ban Zarbo
HOW FAR WOULD YOU GO TO SAVE YOUR OWN LIFE?
www.TOKYOPOP.com
© Ban Zarbo/TOKYOPOP GmbH

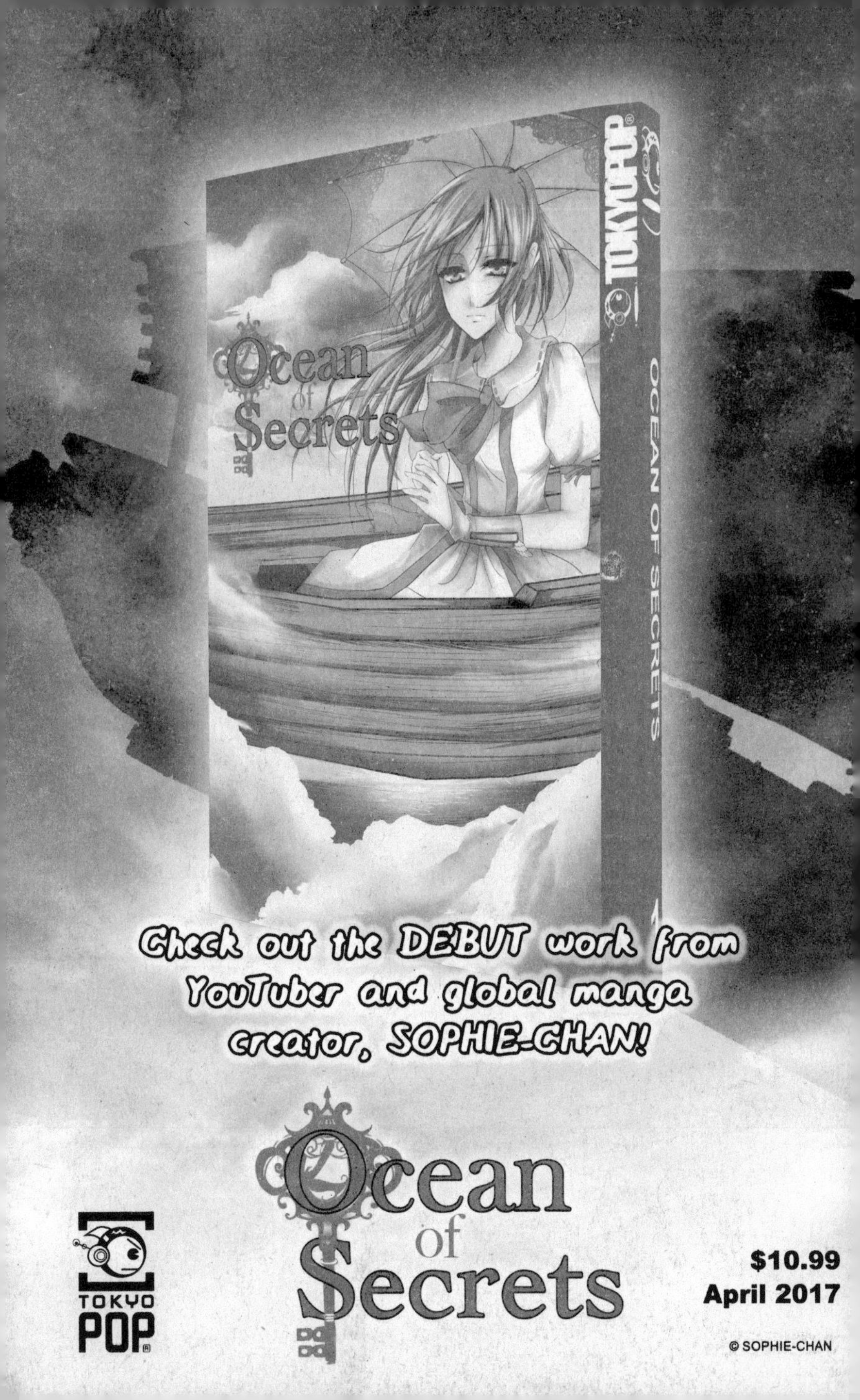
OCEAN OF SECRETS
TOKYOPOP
Check out the DEBUT work from YouTuber and global manga creator, SOPHIE-CHAN!
Ocean of Secrets
TOKYO POP
$10.99
April 2017
© SOPHIE-CHAN

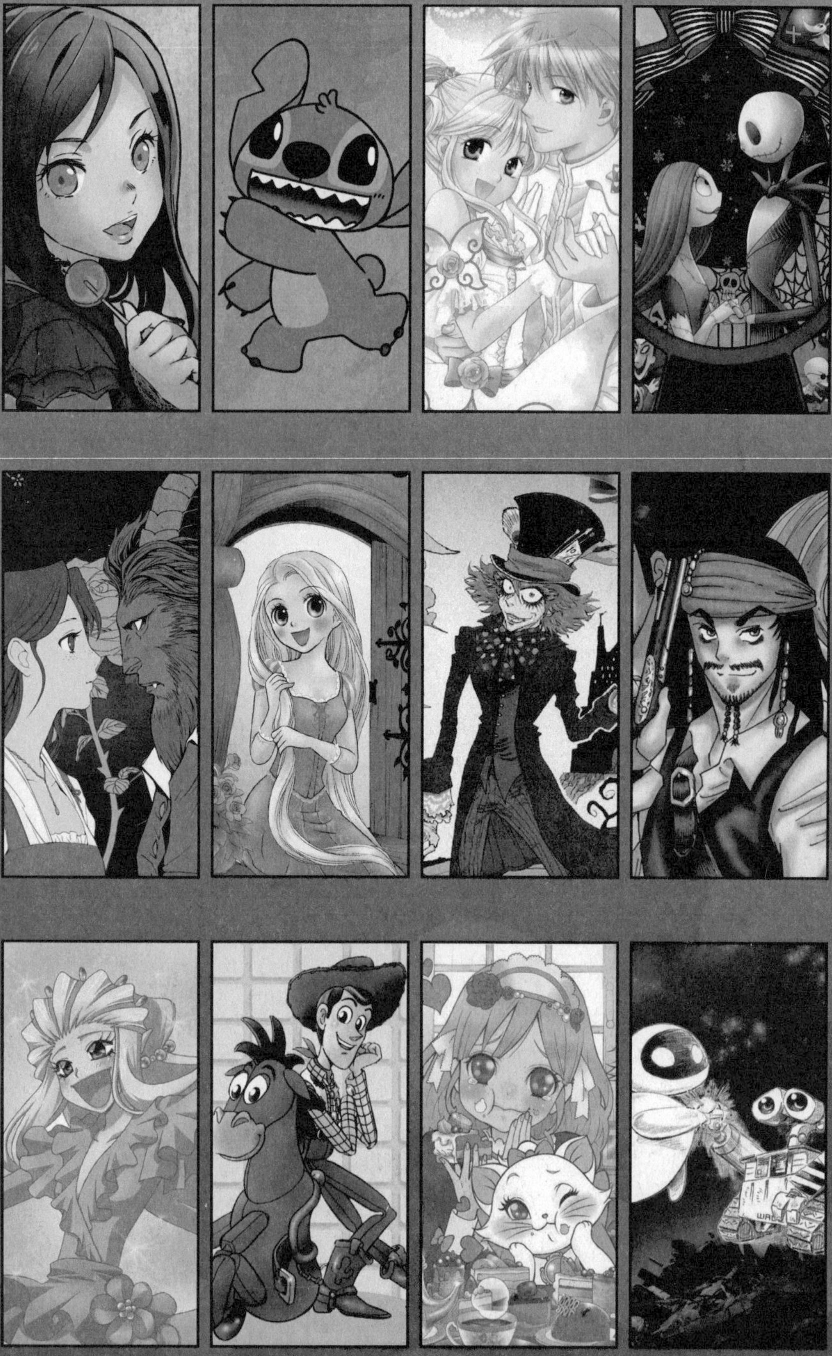

Add These Disney Manga to Your Collection Today!

SHOJO
- ☐ DISNEY BEAUTY AND THE BEAST
- ☐ DISNEY KILALA PRINCESS SERIES

KAWAII
- ☐ MAGICAL DANCE
- ☐ DISNEY STITCH! SERIES

FANTASY
- ☐ DISNEY DESCENDANTS SERIES
- ☐ DISNEY TANGLED
- ☐ DISNEY PRINCESS AND THE FROG
- ☐ DISNEY FAIRIES SERIES
- ☐ MIRIYA AND MARIE

PIXAR
- ☐ DISNEY•PIXAR TOY STORY
- ☐ DISNEY•PIXAR MONSTERS, INC.
- ☐ DISNEY•PIXAR WALL-E
- ☐ DISNEY•PIXAR FINDING NEMO

ADVENTURE
- ☐ DISNEY TIM BURTON'S THE NIGHTMARE BEFORE CHRISTMAS
- ☐ DISNEY ALICE IN WONDERLAND
- ☐ DISNEY PIRATES OF THE CARIBBEAN SERIES

THE AUTHOR

Nana Yaa won her first manga competition at the young age of 17, which lead her to an appearance on Germany's late night talk show, TV Total. Most recently she was awarded the *2017 AnimaniA Award for Best National Manga*, and charted in the top 10 in Germany's manga charts with her new series, *Goldfisch*.

Now 26, Nana Yaa is one of the most prolific creators of the German manga scene, having self-published numerous volumes and short stories, as well as contributing to multiple anthologies through the independent publisher Shwarzer Turm. She's well known in Germany for her yaoi webcomic, *CRUSHED!!*

Facebook: Yaatelier
Twitter: Himalayaa

STOP

THIS IS THE BACK OF THE BOOK!

How do you read manga-style? It's simple! To learn, just start in the top right panel and follow the numbers:

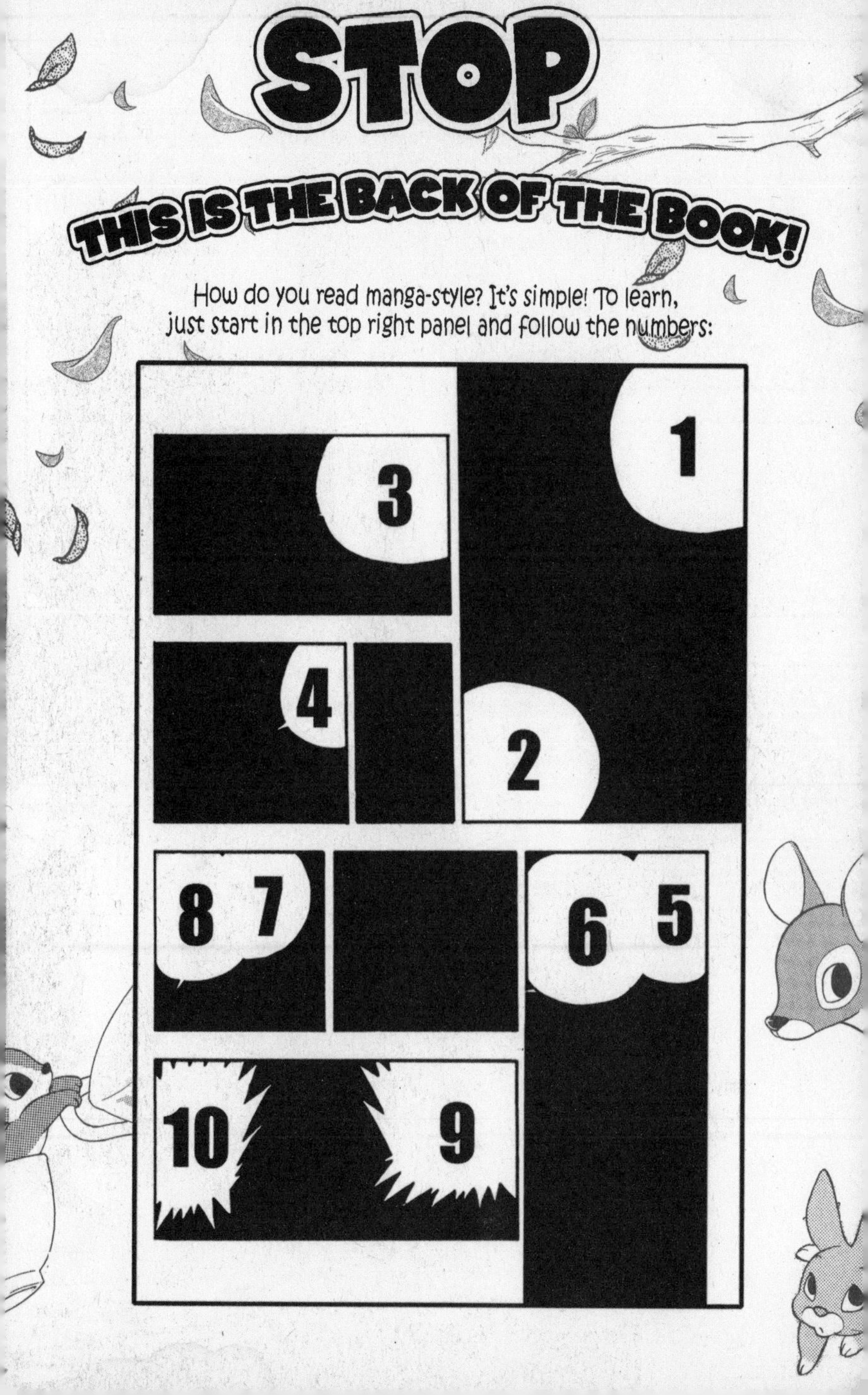
1
2
3
4
5
6
7
8
9
10

Goldfisch Volume 1
Manga by Nana Yaa

Publishing Assistant - Janae Young
Marketing Assistant - Kae Winters
Technology and Digital Media Assistant - Phillip Hong
Translator - Michael Waaler
Editor - M. Cara Carper
Graphic Designer - Phillip Hong
Retouching and Lettering - Vibrraant Publishing Studio
Editor-in-Chief & Publisher - Stu Levy

A  Manga

TOKYOPOP and ⟁ are trademarks or registered trademarks of TOKYOPOP Inc.

TOKYOPOP Inc.
5200 W. Century Blvd. Suite 705
Los Angeles, 90045

E-mail: info@TOKYOPOP.com
Come visit us online at www.TOKYOPOP.com

f www.facebook.com/TOKYOPOP
y www.twitter.com/TOKYOPOP
▶ www.youtube.com/TOKYOPOPTV
P www.pinterest.com/TOKYOPOP
◉ www.instagram.com/TOKYOPOP
t. TOKYOPOP.tumblr.com

Copyright © 2018 Nana Yaa / TOKYOPOP GmbH All Rights Reserved

All rights reserved. No portion of this book may be reproduced or transmitted in any form or by any means without written permission from the copyright holders. This manga is a work of fiction. Any resemblance to actual events or locales or persons, living or dead, is entirely coincidental.

ISBN: 978-1-4278-5767-5
First TOKYOPOP Printing: November 2017
10 9 8 7 6 5 4 3 2 1
Printed in CANADA